NO LIFE FORSAKEN

www.penguin.co.uk

NO LIFE
FORSAKEN

The Second Tale of Witness

Steven Erikson

bantam

TRANSWORLD PUBLISHERS

UK | USA | Canada | Ireland | Australia
India | New Zealand | South Africa

Transworld is part of the Penguin Random House group of companies whose
addresses can be found at global.penguinrandomhouse.com.

Penguin Random House UK, One Embassy Gardens, 8 Viaduct Gardens, London SW11 7BW

penguin.co.uk

Penguin
Random House
UK

First published in Great Britain in 2025 by Bantam
an imprint of Transworld Publishers

001

Typeset in 11.5/14 pt Goudy by Falcon Oast Graphic Art Ltd
Printed and bound in Great Britain by Clays Ltd, Elcograf S.p.A.

The authorized representative in the EEA is Penguin Random House Ireland,
Morrison Chambers, 32 Nassau Street, Dublin D02 YH68

A CIP catalogue record for this book is available from the British Library

ISBNs:
9781787632882 (cased)
9781787632899 (tpb)

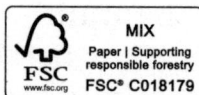

This novel is dedicated to Jeff and Lana of DLC Bookclub,
and all the other BookTubers who've plunged into the Malazan world.

Contents

SEVEN CITIES

— The Malazan Empire —

ca. 1160 Burn's Sleep

BANDIKO SEA

SEA of GALLADA

KARAKARANG

Galladi

TALGAI SEA

Rutu Jelba

SEA of KALTEPE KADESH

BANDIKO DESERT

OTATARAL DESERT

OLEN BRAE

SKARA BRAE

OLONE BRAE

OTATARAL SEA

ARATH FOREST

Ahol Tapur

EHRLITAN

Dosin Pali

ODHAN

Hissar

SIALK

Sialk

Caron Tepasi

Guran

N'KARA MTNS

Pan'potsun ODHAN

PATH'APUR MTNS

Kanfid

Arifr

G'danisban

KARAKU

RARAKU

Lato Revae

KARASHIMESH

Mersin

EB'ARA MTNS

Asmar

Cabus

Teppes

BAKIN MTNS

Bakin

Jamdat

Dhebel

DOJAL ODHAN

HADING SEA

SAHEBA

UBARYD

Omari UBARYD

Halaf

Kayhum

UGARAT ODHAN

VATHAR FOREST

Bylan

Dobre

Geleen

Tarxian

Sarsa

AREN

To Quon Tali

Canhasan

Kaliban

Rang

Belbasi

Karokitch

MAADIL SEA

Taxila

Ashok

Koral Ghul

Ghal'roseh

N'nor

Y'Tur

Longshan

Hatra

Ehjo

G'NATH MTNS

Lothal

Y'Ghatan

A'THALS

Ganath MTNS

ALBAN

B'YATH

N'Sotka

KOKAKAL SEA

MORN MOUNTAINS

MOUNTAINS

DRYJHNA OCEAN

Monkan

Sepik

SEPIK SEA

PERISH

NEMILL

JHENA MTNS

Nahal

Sarpachiya

UGARAT ODHAN

OLPHARA FOREST

JHAG ODHAN

CLATAR SEA

SEVEN DEEPS

N

G'danisban
at the time of
Emperor
Mallick
Rel

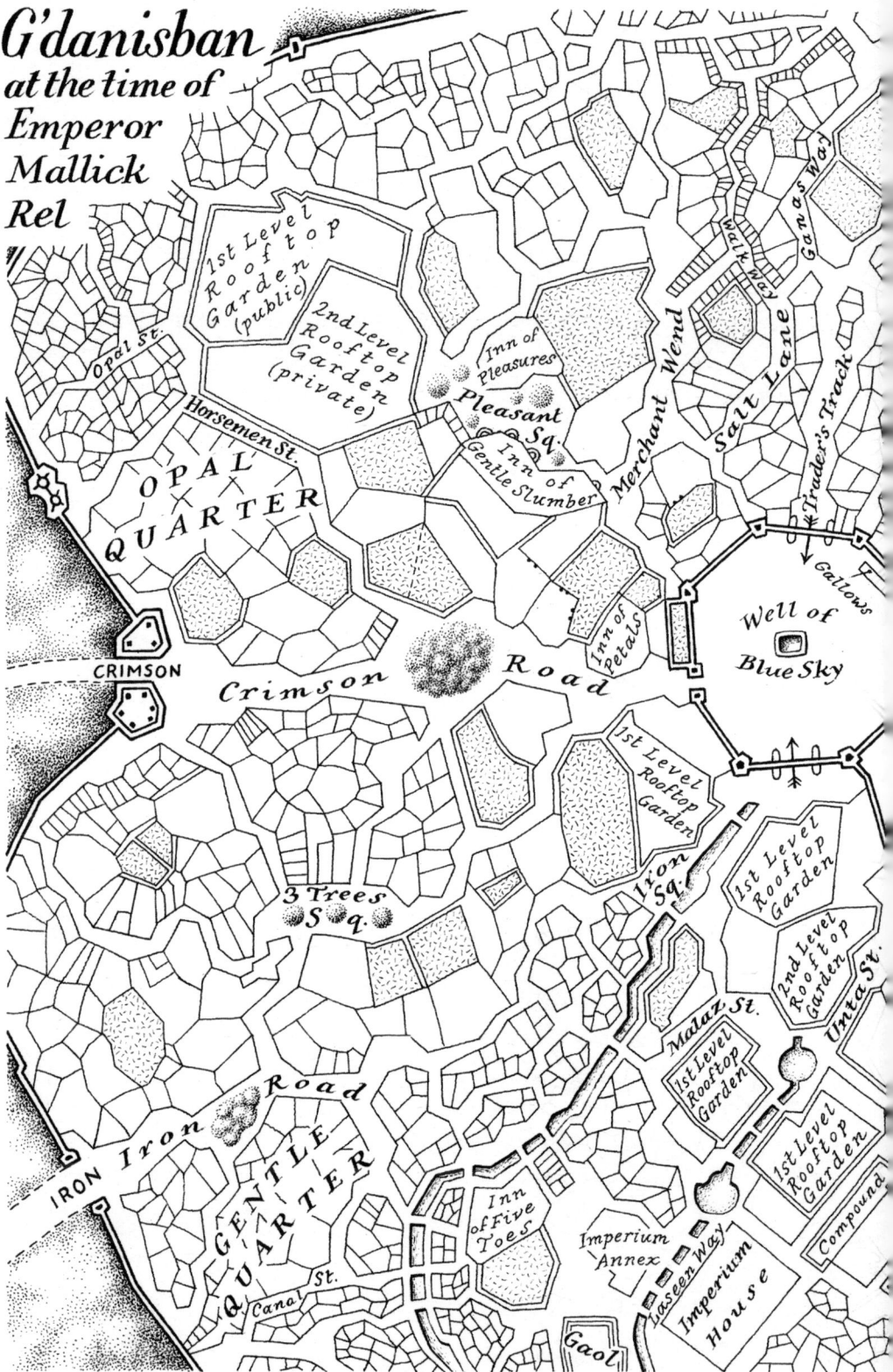

1st Level Rooftop Garden (public)

2nd Level Rooftop Garden (private)

Opal St.

Horsemen St.

OPAL QUARTER

Inn of Pleasures

Pleasant Sq.

Inn of Gentle Slumber

Inn of Petals

Merchant Wend

Salt Lane

Ganas Way

Walkway

Trader's Track

Gallows

Well of Blue Sky

CRIMSON

Crimson Road

3 Trees Sq.

1st Level Rooftop Garden

Iron Sq.

1st Level Rooftop Garden

2nd Level Rooftop Garden

Unta St.

Malaz St.

1st Level Rooftop Garden

IRON Iron Road

GENTLE QUARTER

Inn of Five Toes

Canal St.

Imperium Annex

Laseen Way

Imperium House

Compound

1st Level Rooftop Garden

Gaol

CartWay

Green Wend

Silk Lane

NEW
MARKET
QUARTER

Blood Wall St.

Colonnade

Old
Temple
(Barracks)

Old
Garden
(Training
Ground)

Annex

High Wall St.

Malazan Company H.Q.

Compound

Estate

Fist Wend

2nd Level Rooftop Garden

Commander's Residence

Masso Alley

Sorm
House

Wide Round

Temple
of
Hood
(Abandoned)

Temple Garden

Temple of Da'Sha'ik

Temple of D'rios

Choke St.

BASTRAN
QUARTER

Bastran
Hill

Bastran Road

Tuber Sq.

Old Market St.

Old Wall

Guard Sq.

Cedar
Square

Seven
Gates

Gate Market Way

HILL
QUARTER

Alley Sq.

Soul Wend

Will Sq.

HILL

Gower

BARGE

Fish Alley

OLD
MARKET
QUARTER

DRAMATIS PERSONAE

THE MALAZANS

Jalan Arenfall, High Fist, Seven Cities
Inkaras Sollit, Adjunct to the Emperor
Hadalin Bhilad, Bodyguard to the Adjunct
Gilakas, Claw Agent
Satala, Talon
Brindala, Talon
Aliksos, Claw
Bulk, Claw
Ibinish, Claw
Formult, Claw

XXXIst LEGION, 14th COMPANY, MARINES

Captain Dunsparrow, 5th/6th Squads
Corporal Hasten Thenu, 5th/6th Squads

Captain Hung, 12th Squad
Lieutenant Ormo Foamy, 12th Squad
Corporal Scrapes, 12th Squad
Sergeant Breech, 12th Squad
Sapper Fedilap, 12th Squad
Sapper Pulcrude, 12th Squad
Healer Gains, 12th Squad
Heavy Flutter, 12th Squad
Heavy Scatter, 12th Squad

Captain Veroosh, 8th Squad
Sergeant Buckpug, 8th Squad
Corporal Hackles, 8th Squad
Sapper Hazy Drip, 8th Squad

Healer Puler, 8th Squad
Scout Strip Ankles, 8th Squad
Heavy Torbo, 8th Squad
Heavy Gripcocker, 8th Squad

SEVEN CITIES NATIVES

Shamalle, High Priestess of Va'Shaik, G'danisban
Ban Ryk, Invigil in Temple of Va'Shaik, G'danisban
Pash, handmaiden to Shamalle
Orotol, adherent of Va'Shaik
Baek, adherent of Va'Shaik
Wrest, adherent of Va'Shaik
Harapa Le'en, High Priest of Va'Shaik
Vest Dyan, Inquisitor of Va'Shaik, Defender of the Faith
Bornu Blatt, Inquisitor of Va'Shaik, Master Librarian in Hanar Ara
Salabi, Bornu's assistant
Gracer, a pilgrim
Stult, a pilgrim
Melok, a cultist
Mute, a child
Futhar, Mercenary Company Commander
Arat, a mage in Futhar's Company
Obly the Boy, a barkeep
Sug, gangleader, Under Quarter of G'danisban
Hench, henchman
Stipple, henchman

OTHERS

Iskaral Pust, Magus of High House Shadow
Mule, his mule
Nub, a bhokaral
Aravath, First Witness of Toblakai, Cullar

Mael, an Elder God
Va'Shaik, a goddess
Queen of Dreams, an Elder Goddess

PROLOGUE

'Woe betide the invisible tyranny of belief!'

Purported lament of Destriant Heboric
at his divestiture

None of the hills rising from the plains of the Imperial Warren were natural. The gathering into mounds of shattered bone was a singular deed of . . . something. Was it respect, or obsession? A bit of both?

From where Hasten Thenu stood, such hills rumpled every horizon in an otherwise featureless, level landscape. A dozen perhaps, with more distant hazes suggesting an unending procession.

Although that, of course, was not true. Not an infinity of hills, just as this scoured continent was not without end. Yet, for all the known travels of this place, no shoreline was ever found. And these places, where the hills gathered like archipelagos in a dead sea, why, walk in any direction long enough, and another would come into view. Few things about this realm made sense, beyond the grim observation that the death of a civilization at its height left something of a mess.

As he stood, waiting, Hasten Thenu considered stirring awake a long-lost warren. Or, if not lost, then fallen into disuse. Why, then, was it on his mind? A distant ripple, perhaps, a brief convulsion of time's illimitable laws. Something undone, then done again.

Another moment of indecision, then he gestured with one long-fingered hand, and the scene before him transformed.

The sky the hue of lead was gone. In its place were twisting columns of grey and black smoke spiralling upward, and churning clouds limned in red, from which ash came down like flakes of snow. Upon the land, remnants of buildings made geometric patterns, but even these lingering foundation stones were

1

visibly sagging, baked white by terrible heat and brittle enough to crumble to the whispering wind.

Three Elder Gods had come and gone. A lone figure remained, tall and gaunt, his steps trailing a wake of suspended dust. Burdened beneath the weight of a heavy burlap sack, he walked bent over, his attention fixed upon the ground before him.

When at last he reached the small heap of human bones at the trail's end, he set down the sack, tugging at the neck-ropes to enlarge its ragged mouth. Then he began withdrawing more bones.

Hasten Thenu set out, pulling his half-cloak about his shoulders as the dust spun awake beneath his feet.

It took twenty-three paces to reach the man.

Proximity added details to the figure. He was coated in the dust and crusted fragments of burnt bones, giving him a spectral hue from his long, grey hair down to his battered grey boots.

'I was wondering,' said Hasten.

The figure glanced over. The lined, haggard face twisted in irritation. 'You shouldn't be here, spectre.'

'You're always saying that.'

'How far ahead?'

'More centuries than I care to count, and before you ask, you wear well the millennia. Or if not "well", then passably.'

'The curse holds, then.'

'Whose is now the question,' Hasten said. 'Yours or theirs? Though I'm not sure it makes a difference.'

The man grunted. 'No, I suppose not. What do you want?'

Hasten shrugged. 'My latest visit had me mulling on this particular moment. I wondered at the impulse–'

The man's snort interrupted him. 'You call this an impulse?'

'Considering that you're just starting,' Hasten said, 'then yes, this may well have begun as an impulse. For what it's worth, you continued with this. Until you were done.' He paused, but the man before him did not react to that. 'I guess I'd like to know. Respect? Honouring – and wearing – what's left of your subjects? Or is it guilt? Even remorse? Tell me, High King Kallor, what impels you to gather every last bone of your empire's slaughtered subjects, to build upon this dead land hundreds, if not thousands of barrows? To inter with the dead every damned one of them?'

The High King had drawn out a few more bones from the sack, which he tossed onto the pile before him, raising small puffs of dust and ash. 'Every barrow an island,' he muttered. 'Every island a world of past lives, past loves.' He faced Hasten. 'I do not answer to you; nor you in your myriad forms, your endless iterations. Something has surely cursed you as well, to see you endlessly repeating the madness of life.'

Hasten smiled, offering a faint nod to acknowledge the observation. 'We are more of a kind than either of us would care to think.'

Kallor picked up the sack and upended it, shaking out the last fragments of bone. Tucking it under one arm, he turned to retrace his route. 'Here and there,' he said, 'they ran, huddled against walls or some such. Nobody, it seems, likes to die alone.' He was silent for a moment, then he said, 'Makes collecting up the bones easier.'

'Penance, High King?' Hasten asked, as the man set out back along his trail.

At that Kallor halted and spun round. 'You think the guilt is mine?' Without awaiting a reply, he resumed his walk.

Hasten felt the warren's hold slipping away. Before him, the scene blurred, melting into time's interminable passage since that moment in the company of the High King. Once more the leaden sky, almost all the dust long since settled, and every barrow in sight reduced now to mere mounds of gritty soil clothed in yellow grasses.

Another man stood before him, a quizzical expression on his face. 'You're back?'

Hasten frowned. 'I haven't gone anywhere. I've been waiting for you, Cotillion.'

'Maybe not anywhere,' the Patron of Assassins said, eyes narrowing. 'Perhaps more like anywhen. Though I'm not sure what you'd call that.'

Hasten smiled. 'How about "killing time"? Now, be honest with me, is Shadowthrone really interested in the tale I have to tell?'

'Surprisingly, he is, Hasten.'

'Why?'

'Karsa Orlong.'

'What about him?'

'Well, that's kind of the point,' said Cotillion, 'isn't it? What about him?'

'Most of what I have to tell took place in Seven Cities.'

'You're saying it's unrelated?'

'Of course not,' Hasten snapped. 'It couldn't be more . . . related, if you tried.' Then he shook his head, exasperated. 'No, listen, I admit to being . . . disjointed. Stories piled together, here and there, like islands, with maybe nothing between them. Islands of lives, loves lost. Yet, no matter how I try, I can't think of any other way to tell this tale. Fragments, and no, I wasn't everywhere. A lot of it I've

3

had to piece together, perhaps even invent – I don't know, it's not my particular talent, you know. I'm too focused on the immediate, the stuff within reach–'

'Gods below,' Cotillion cut in, 'just how many qualifiers do you need for this? We want to know what dragged an Elder God into this mess, to begin with–'

'Not directly related to Karsa, that one,' said Hasten. 'Anyway, that was all Shadowthrone's doing, so why does he even need to ask me about it?'

Cotillion glanced away. 'That part of things is a bit delicate.'

'Fine. Here's my chaotic tale, then, Cotillion. And don't think my motivations have anything to do with remorse, regret or even guilt. Not even to honour the fallen, though that's always part of it. No, I'll tell it for the same reason someone once built barrows in this wretched wasteland.'

'And that is?'

'Sometimes you'll find grief in the least expected places.'

Cotillion tilted his head but said nothing as Hasten Thenu then began telling his tale. 'This is about beginnings. In fact, the whole thing is about beginnings. Oh, I won't leave them all hanging, Cotillion. I'm not quite that cruel, despite opinions to the contrary. A few proper endings, I promise. Enough to satisfy? Well, not everyone. No matter. The longer you live, the more faded this thing we call optimism.

'In any case, enough preambling . . .'

On the shores of Raraku Sea, near Imiskmon, Malazan Empire, Seven Cities Continent

Three pots that were more tempered grit than clay sat in the dust on the side of the track, narrow upthrust necks above squat bellies, elongated ears high on one side's shoulder. Banded red alternating with yellow glaze encircled the necks just beneath the flared rims. Upon the shoulder of each pot, opposite the ear, was stamped an impression, a rough circle with two faces in profile facing away from one another, both women, seemingly identical. A painted vine ran round the pots at the base, somewhat obscured by windblown sand and orange dust.

The mule, lathered in sweat and swarmed by desert flies, stood staring down at these pots with a disconsolate air, hide rippling and twitching and tail whipping back and forth amidst all the buzzing. A few moments later, both ears flicked towards the grunting, gasping figure at the top of the rise a little way off the track, taking note of but not heeding the small man's incessant swearing.

4

Was there wine in the pots? They were sealed tight in resin-soaked muslin over which wax had been generously smeared. The mule, in its vague equine fashion, dreamed of wine in the way of all drunks standing parched and possibly hungover in the ferocious heat, cursing the blunt clumsiness of hoofs and bristled nose, the god-cursed absence of hands or nimble tongue, the sheer injustice of the universe.

The man at the cliff edge left off his swearing tirade against the same universe to replace it with a succession of grunts as he pushed the huge, heavy iron hook into the bloated flesh of a horse even the mule knew was dead. High-pitched whistling filled the air with a staggering stench as the gases of decomposition suddenly rushed out to engulf the man.

Gagging, he fell back onto his backside, knobbly knees wavering as nausea rolled through him in shuddering waves. 'Madness!' he gasped, wiping the tears from his eyes. 'What dark, twisted mind conceived of this? Aaagh! Now even my hands stink! My hair – have I any hair? – here, twin handfuls above the ears, aye, this hair I now grip, it too stinks! My nose, which I now pull – stinks! My grizzled chin, my cheeks, all stinks! Horrid horse, what have you done?'

Alas, the language of decay lacked the nuance for a proper answer. Groaning, the man righted himself and began working the hook's buried point back up under the ribs, making the hide bulge, and then split as the point emerged, gory and glistening and crawling with maggots. 'Hah! Genius!' He scrambled to his feet. 'Mule! Where's the rope?'

At that, the mule brayed in alarm and stepped back, since one end of the rope was affixed to its harness.

'Foolish beast! If I kill you, who will I ride? Do you have any idea how far we have to go? My sweetness – no, not that sweetness, the other sweetness – my sweetness awaits, pining and longing and longing and pining, the longest of long pines – and yes I will need a bath first. A deep, sultry, sumptuous, indolent, languid bath! Stand still, damn you, whilst I untie this.'

Which he did, to the mule's begrudging relief, upon which it returned its attention to the three clay pots, while the man scrabbled back up the slope to the cliff's edge and tied one end of the rope to the eye of the hook and then stood, holding the other end and looking around.

No hands, no nimble tongue to manage a quick hidden loop of that rope about one bony ankle. The mule nearly wept, one eye now watching the man tying the rope around a massive boulder perched precariously on the cliff's edge a few paces off to one side of the dead horse. Opportunities lost could be crushing, even for a mule.

'Aha! See the brilliance, you bumbling fool of a beast?' Not awaiting an answer, the man crept to the edge and looked down. Below, at a drop of six or seven man-heights, the turquoise waters of the Raraku Sea sparkled to the gentle breeze tickling the slow rise and ebb of the surface, as the waves crept and slipped into the cracks and folds in the bleached limestone rock-face. Depths were hinted at by the darkening hue plunging ever deeper beneath the placid surface.

Did he not recall this very cliff, after all? In the days before the sea's birth? Thrice more the man-heights reached down to the eventual sandy, silty, pebble-scattered bottom. Was this not perfect?

Why, it was.

He turned to glare at the mule. 'Fishing, you hopeless fool, is an art. Your complaints were obscene, by the way. I've seen you drag worse than a dead horse and never mind where I found the dead horse. The world is full of them! Poor, benighted beasts of unreasoning servitude to witless masters blithely disregarding the misery of their many needs, delivered upon hapless, undeserving beasts of burden.' He paused his tirade, small eyes narrowing upon the mule.

'Those pots are offerings, wretched creature. That wine's not for you! Do you hear?' He lifted his face and squinted sunward. 'Oh Lord of Mules, Donkeys and Other Wastes of Flesh and Bone, why oh why did you send me *this* one? A drunk mule! What did I do to you to earn such opprobrium? Such vicious spite?'

He paused, waiting for an answer.

When none seemed forthcoming, he turned once again to the horse carcass on the cliff's edge. 'Now, one minor task remains.' He set both hands upon the flank of the horse and began pushing. Feet scraped through gravel, scrabbling, the scrabbling getting faster, clouds of dust rising, pebbles spraying in scattershot, legs pumping faster, ever faster. Managing not even a nudge.

Eventually, he collapsed to the ground, gasping, sweat-lathered. 'So near,' he moaned, 'and yet so far!'

What sudden, reeling spasm of consideration impelled the mule then, as it clambered up the slope, swung round and hammered a back-kick into the horse, sending it lurching over the edge, the rope whipping wildly as the carcass plunged to slap heavily upon the waves below?

Squealing in alarm, the man rolled away from the frenzied coil of rope as it played out, and out, then sprang taut as the sinking horse reached its greatest depth, the huge boulder seeming to grunt under the strain.

Leaping to his feet, the man danced a circle, hands in the air. 'My genius prevails!' he sang, more than once, while the mule eyed him with an unreadable expression.

The rope's new thrumming sound finally caught the man's attention, and he ceased his dance, staggering slightly in dizzy consequence. He squinted at the rope, and only now did other sounds reach him, coming from below, from the sea's surface. Hurrying to the edge, he looked down.

To see the water foaming and churning, red froth gathering, the rope vibrating like a fiddle string.

'Aaagh! What are they? Sharks? Pike? Perch? Voracious minnows?' He clutched his tufts of wiry hair. 'Impossible! All the fish I put into this sea were friendly fish! Buckets and buckets of friendly, happy, cheery fish! Who has done this to me? Who has— gods, horrid wife! Now at last I understand her crooked smile as she set the plate down in front of me, fish after fish, endless meals of fish! Nerve-racking smile! Uncanny smile, eyes aglint! Miserable, pultrudinous perfidy! She'll pay, this I swear!'

The rope went limp.

'Gods!' he cried in horror and disbelief. 'My beautiful sea! My bright pellucid pearl of Lady Raraku, my dream world of azure blue and emerald, my sweet nectar of life-giving glory, she who dances with the wind, the sultry breeze, the faint whisper and honeyed murmur! Warm embracer of withered member! Evil wife, what have you done to me?'

The rope snapped tight, thrumming again, biting deep into the soft limestone of the cliff edge.

Spinning round, the man froze in place, breath held.

He saw gripping the rope a wide, ugly hand, and then another. A water-beaded bald pate rose into view, and then broad shoulders with the huge hook slung over one of them. Sun-bronzed body streaming with crooked rivulets that dazzled in the sunlight, the god Mael arrived to stand on the precipice, sea-green eyes fixing upon the man.

The god then lifted the hook and held it out. 'Are you fucking kidding me?'

'Blame my wife!' the man shrieked. Then he ducked and looked to one side, a secretive smile stretching his wide mouth. 'Now I've got him!

7

He thinks me a worshipper, a Jhistal even! Hah! Idiot god of cesspools, puddles and potholes! Senseless seas and orificial oceans!'

Mael crossed his arms. 'What does Shadowthrone want now?'

The man cackled. 'Who? Never heard of him! Shadow-what?' He swung round to smile beatifically at the ancient god. 'Throne-hoarder, shadow-spitter, neither here nor there! I know of no such god of shadows, no god of Meanas and friend to Hounds – did I say friend? Hah hah, how he runs from them and who wouldn't? Horrible beasts!' Then he held out his hands, palms exposed. 'I am but a humble fisher – fisher of gods, hah! – with offerings made, oh blessed barnacled master of molluscs and wimples, salty bubbler in the mudflats, inconstant of tides, forever coming or going or halfway between the two, which is to say, here you are.' He stretched out his arms as would any reasonable supplicant before said supplicant's immortal lord. 'Glorious Mael, Elder God of the Seas! Father of Nerruse – uh, you are her father, right? If wife, gods, that's sick! Or are you one of those? You know, gods marrying their daughter and sister and mother and all of them one person! Insanity! Where's my knife—'

'Stop your babbling!' Mael bellowed.

Staggering back, hands dropping, the man gaped. 'Well,' he said quietly, 'fine, then. Have it your way.' Although the snort that followed did much to undermine his sincerity.

Nonetheless, Iskaral Pust then explained what his god wanted of Mael. In very nearly accurate fashion, but not quite, while the mule listened half-heartedly and continued eyeing the jugs of wine, left by persons unknown in offering to Va'Shaik here on the desolate shore of Raraku Sea.

A single sudden kick neatly clipped off the first of the pots just below the neck, a bit of red wine spilling before settling. The new hole above the pot's belly was perfectly sized, it turned out, to accommodate the mule's greedy muzzle. Fortuitous happenstance, one can be sure.

And thus was promised to Iskaral Pust a wobbling, weaving journey home.

BOOK ONE

THE UNEASY HEARTS OF LAND AND SELF

Faith is not the problem. Imagine it standing alone, a coalesced essence of belief to which nothing beyond itself is attached. No names, no faces, no sermons, no rules. Imagine faith as pure recognition. That which lies between the self and all else. This recognition asserts no specific path among many, no narrow trail skirted by prohibitions, blasphemies, proprieties.

What lies at the heart of such recognition? Perhaps, if distilled down, it is humility. The self is found to be dwelling within something greater, something more profound, something mysterious in its grand design. And from humility is born trust.

Together, humility and trust beget faith. If this is held to be sacred, then all need for rules and prohibitions ceases to be relevant. There is but one path, and to traverse it is an exercise in comportment.

We build religions to divide the indivisible.

That is the problem.

Ponderings
Nessen-Drai

CHAPTER ONE

'Even a god has regrets.'

A quote attributed to Shadowthrone (denied)

*T*he walnut tree surmounting Bastran Hill in the city of G'danisban was closing in on two thousand years since it first cracked its shell. If the mound beneath it had once been a barrow, the tree's massive roots had long since ruptured its stone-lined chambers and passageways, devouring all it might have contained. Surrounding this was the rumpled hilltop of an abandoned cemetery, its stone-pillar grave-markers resembling a skewed, squat forest of dusty stumps spreading out from the living tree at the centre, the pillars mostly broken off below the plinths, leaving little more than the clawed feet of the statuary that had once adorned each grave-marker.

None of this was of any interest to the hulking, slope-shouldered bhokaral crouching high in the tree's leafy canopy, black-marble eyes scanning the sprawl of rooftops and gloom-swallowed alleys and streets of the city as the day's light slowly faded.

It had been years since the last upstart had dared challenge Nub's supremacy among G'danisban's feral bhokarala. Still, vigilance was power's ulcerous companion. Among bhokarala, the absence of stress indicated a high likelihood that the blissful individual was, in fact, dead. Although some prodding was often required to confirm the detail. For Nub's kind, society was fraught, a melange of silent rules and tottering, volatile hierarchies.

So Nub watched, as he did most evenings, from his high perch on a thick, twisting branch of the walnut tree, his every available sense fiercely attuned to paranoia. While language was a confused mystery drifting along the very edges of comprehension, if asked, Nub would pronounce his life as very nearly perfect, despite the bleeding ulcers. If not in actual words, then at least a fang-baring yawn.

11

Was Nub the king of the bhokarala? Not in any royal sense, since bloodlines were not relevant. Brutal violence, the occasional bout of berserk rage and the generous sowing of fear, constituted the only royal charter required.

As for the infestation of humans in his demesne, well, one pretty much looked like the other. Sources of constant irritation, subjects of suspicion, and the repository of all kinds of free food, shiny baubles, and hilarious antics. They also made, Nub grudgingly acknowledged, good servants.

Now, as the sun's heartless eye began to slip down beneath the horizon's red lid, Nub watched, with guarded satisfaction, as his vast clan of subjects began emerging from the crevices, cracks and holes of Bastran Hill's pocked, unruly surface. There had been a time, deep in Nub's dim memory, when the humans had been dangerous to the bhokarala in the city. An age when the humans and his kind had engaged in a protracted war of attrition. The sudden cessation of hostilities was more or less inexplicable as far as Nub was concerned, though he suspected that he was, perhaps, responsible. But such memory was in the long-ago time, a bit murky beneath the usual ricocheting cascade of surface thoughts. In any case, now, at last, the domestication of humans was complete.

In a swarm of dark, wraith-like motion, the bhokarala of G'danisban emerged from the Under Quarter of Bastran Hill, slipping out into the city to begin yet another night of foraging, hunting, gathering, and looting.

A certain agitation began in Nub's mind, and he huffed in annoyance. Too often, these nights, a strange urge took hold, a compelling restlessness tugging him away from his high wooden throne. He fought against it, employing his most formidable mental weapons. Namely, his short attention span and flashes of unreasoning rage. But nothing scratched this particular itch. Growling deep in his chest, he thrashed his branch for a few moments, bouncing up and down until it creaked, and then began a rapid descent that looked out of control until the very last moment, when, with a lithe twist and dip, he landed evenly on all four hands at the base of the tree.

This base was a jumble of broken stone from the uprooted crypt below, as well as innumerable shattered fragments of the small statues that had once adorned every pillar. Alas, it was not one of Nub's many talents to take note of the peculiar similarity between the statues and the bhokarala themselves, hinting at a most unlikely assignation.

After all, the dubious attribution of a cemetery with graves, carved pillars of stone and statuary being the creation of small-brained, squat, bandy-legged, pointy-eared simians honouring their dead, was simply absurd.

Such assessments were beyond Nub, thus avoiding any additional source of anxiety. Once on the ground, he straightened as much as physiology allowed – knees angled outward, hips flared and long arms held out almost horizontal – and quickly set off northward. Pulled, lightly, but so insistingly pulled, down into the city, and all its streets crowded with squawking, chittering, chattering humans.

If challenged, Nub would without question have asserted the singular proof of intellectual superiority as the ability to just . . . shut up. All this human babbling, like birds in a thicket, surely belonged to the careless phantasms of barely functioning brains. That said, most challenges made to Nub resulted in deadly violence, so there was that.

Few humans would stand in the way of a bull bhokaral, and so a path down the steamy street miraculously appeared before him as he knuckle-loped along Old Wall Market Street, angling sharply left between the high garden walls of two temples, then out onto the wider concourse surrounding the Temple of Va'Shaik. Around this domed edifice, thence to Wide Round and finally to the soot-stained facade of a temple that had seen better days.

Instead of entering this temple through its twin, but narrow, front doors, Nub vaulted onto the garden wall to the left of the entranceway, clambered over, and dropped down into the riotous greenery, scattering a covey of roosting doves. Plunging through the thicket amidst drifting feathers, he emerged into a small round with a fountain in the centre.

Where lingered a shadow cast by nothing.

*   *   *

G'danisban was a faded study in dun tones and weary paint in the waning afternoon light. Built of sandstone and mortar, blockish and chaotic as befitted a settlement born before the era of carts, much less carriages, almost every street was an alley and every alley a tortured, winding maze between buildings. Barring the cemetery mound of Bastran, a bird wheeling overhead would see little more than clotheslines on flat roofs, seemingly festooned with flags, every nation a home, every army a household, all in rich dyes and flapping in the hot wind.

The open concourse known as Blue Sky occupied the nominal centre of the city, flanked to the east by the Old Temple, its walled compound conjoined with the old Falah'd palace, dating back to pre-imperial times when the entire continent was under the complicated rule of a theocracy. The palace was thick-walled, as much a fortress as an administrative centre, a bastion of those priest-kings who eventually climbed to power, generation layered upon generation, addition upon addition, enforcing

13

the illusion of continuity which, should the bird fly ever higher, was not an illusion at all. But some things were too bitter to contemplate.

The Old Temple was now the barracks for the 14th Company of Malazan Marines, virtually empty at present, while the company's headquarters occupied the old palace.

Upon the flat roof of Imperium House, a little over two hundred paces to the southwest of the company headquarters, High Fist Jalan Arenfall sighed, his thick, scarred forearms resting on the low adobe wall, his slate-eyed gaze scanning the maze of drying clothes, stone and shadows of the city below.

What made this such a knot in the heart of Seven Cities? Barely thirty thousand souls dwelt here, every one of them besieged by seething acolytes of a score or more competing temples, with hands held out and dire warnings on their tongues. Extortion extending into the realm of souls, no less. *What manner of beast is man and woman?*

Most days, he bore his second name with just enough wry acknowledgement to fashion something like equanimity in the company of his staff, city and provincial officials, officers and clerks and all the rest of his daily entourage. *Arenfall.* Aren's fall to the Malazans was not, however, the origin of his name. His attribution referred to a later event. Namely, the day that Aren *did not fall.* When it held fast against the Rebellion, an island of life surrounded by death.

The fall, that time, occurred outside the city's walls. A detail of such significance that the great city had suffered a fatal shift in the regard and sensibilities of an entire empire. No longer Aren, but now *Aren Outside the Fall.* A mouthful to be sure.

So, how was it that one man's death could change the world? Or give a rebel's son his second name in the manner of an empty promise?

Over the city, almost level with where the High Fist stood, swallows spun and wheeled through the turgid, dusty air. Their presence, flying out from nests in holes built into Imperium House's high walls, made an eternal paint of guano down every side of the building, and occasionally, when the winds fell away, a fetid reek as well. Yet he did not begrudge them – was anything more glorious than their aerial dance and piercing song? And now that a freshwater sea occupied what had once been a desert basin, not too far away, malaria had returned to the area. Bats and swallows were welcome to eat their fill of mosquitoes, to the benefit of all.

He heard footsteps approaching and stifled a second sigh. Moments of contemplation were getting rare. Straightening, he turned to study the two men with whom he now shared the rooftop. The captain, Hadalin Bhilad, remained close to the hatch leading into the rooms below, thumbs tucked into his weapon belt, his off-white telaba's hood raised to hide his head and face. There was enough in his stance to tell Jalan that not all was well between the captain and the other man, who was now joining the High Fist close to the wall.

Jalan dipped his head. 'Adjunct.'

'I have unwittingly shattered your sanctuary,' Adjunct Inkaras Sollit said. 'Forgive me.'

'Pondering the city below yields little sanctuary,' Jalan replied, 'although this view is removed enough to offer some relief.'

'And, I would think, perspective?' Inkaras moved to lean on the wall, matching Jalan's pose of only a few moments ago. The dusky blue of his hands and bared forearms delivered a stark contrast to the magenta-dyed telaba he wore. While many foreigners struggled with the telaba as a garment, given its peculiar folds and bias cut, the Adjunct might well have been born in one, such was his apparent comfort wearing the traditional desert garb. And yet, he was no native of this land.

'Are you settled in your chambers, Adjunct? Given no announcement as to your pending arrival—'

'You did very well indeed, High Fist. The rooms are most satisfactory.' He paused, and a half-smile flitted across his blunt, battered features. 'The heat, on the other hand . . .'

'I would think the Napan Isles—'

'I was born on Malaz Island,' Inkaras interrupted. 'The city of Jakata, to be more precise, which began as a Napan colony. Or so it is said and given the predominance of blue-skinned inhabitants on that side of the island, it seems likely. In any case,' he went on, 'my family were fishers, living on Break Island facing the Inside Passage, where the winds from the south were icy year-round.'

Jalan Arenfall considered, and then said, 'Icy no longer, I would think.'

'True enough,' Inkaras agreed. 'The world of my childhood is not the world around me now. But then, can we not all say that? After all,' he continued, gaze still on the city roofs below, 'you were a child-soldier in the rebel army of Korbolo Dom, your father one of his most trusted commanders. I am curious – what does your father think of your life now? A High Fist serving the empire. Poet and musician. And utterly godless.'

Jalan was silent for a moment, wondering why the Adjunct had neglected to mention Jalan's most notorious trait: namely, his infamous propensity for violence. If baiting, then a dangerous game indeed, especially with the man within reach, and seemingly intent upon the scene below. Arrogance? Confidence? If both, then twice misplaced.

If he chose to kill this man, here and now, none could stop him. Not the captain ten paces behind them. Nor the Adjunct himself, since no magic need be called upon.

'"Arenfall",' Inkaras went on, still oblivious, 'is therefore a peculiar appellation. Then, of course, there is your other name, the one barely whispered in shadows, which I find . . . fascinating. What meaning, then, is "Blinker"?'

The question faltered on the last word, as the Adjunct now found himself staring at the point of a knife, hovering in front of his right eye.

'Ah,' Inkaras said shakily. 'In the blink of an eye, then. I comprehend.'

'Less than you imagine,' Jalan replied, slowly withdrawing the blued blade and taking a single step back – whereupon he felt the broad tip of the captain's sword poking through the cloth of his telaba between his shoulder-blades.

'We share the flaw,' the Adjunct murmured.

'We do not,' Jalan replied. 'Had I taken your life in that instant, Adjunct, your captain would have followed in the next. The point made here, Inkaras Sollit, had already been delivered.'

'And how do you imagine the Emperor would feel about you killing his Adjunct?'

'Upset, I'm sure.'

'Not enough for tears,' Inkaras said, apparently amused. 'But your grave would be unmarked.'

Jalan loosed a heavy sigh. 'Do you not think, Adjunct, we already have too many revered tombs? Too many venerated barrows? Why are you here, if not to address this seething cauldron of dead martyrs? No, I welcome a nameless hole for my bones.'

'Just not today,' the Adjunct said.

Jalan shrugged, slowly turning to stare down the captain.

'Return to our quarters, beloved,' murmured Inkaras to Hadalin Bhilad. 'For the discussion to follow, it must be the High Fist and myself and no other.'

The captain's cold gaze held for a moment longer on Jalan's eyes, and then he lowered and sheathed his otataral longsword, stepped back, wheeled and walked towards the hatch, down which he noiselessly went.

'Yes, he is fast indeed,' the High Fist allowed.

'But not fast enough.'

'At ten paces, no one is.'

'I am surprised the Claw did not pay you a visit long ago, with skills such as you have just displayed.'

Jalan Arenfall frowned across at the Adjunct. 'Well, the Claw are not likely to record their failures, are they?'

'At recruiting you?'

'No, Adjunct, at surviving the encounter. Did you not know? I used to hunt down and kill Claw for a living.'

Now it was the Adjunct's turn to stare. 'The Emperor was somewhat terse, it seems. How is it you are now a Fist? This makes no sense.'

'There is a perennial problem with the imperial secret assassins, enough to send cold sweat down the back of any emperor. Accordingly, periodically, a cull is required.'

Now the Adjunct's eyes were wide. 'The Emperor hired you to clean house?'

Jalan shrugged. 'There was precedent.'

'There was?'

'Kalam Mekhar did much the same for Empress Laseen. In Malaz City, in fact. After that bloody night, she could breathe easy for a time.'

'Hardly at all!'

'Well, other matters intervened.'

'What other matters?'

'The Crimson Guard's untimely return, I suppose.' Jalan then shrugged. 'Is this what we are to discuss, Adjunct?'

'No, but finding my feet is taking longer than expected.'

That was an honest enough admission. Jalan decided to ease out a notch. 'My father disapproves of all that I am, Adjunct. We do not speak and haven't in years. Accordingly, he knows less of me than he thinks.'

'And you are certain of that?'

'No, but in truth, it hardly matters. Leoman of the Flails' betrayal broke him. My father hasn't faced a day sober in many years. Not an uncommon fate for the broken-hearted.'

'You sound almost forgiving.'

'A preferred outcome to obsessive, murderous rage, Adjunct.' He paused, and then said, 'A world of broken-hearted people sounds . . . peaceful.'

Breath gusted from Inkaras. 'Blessed Laseen, you leave me rattled at every turn!'

'Apologies, Adjunct. Of all the titles given me, it is "poet" that cuts deepest.'

'Why is that?'

'It is the only curse among them.'

It seemed that the Adjunct had little to say regarding that, and a short time later he made his excuses and, with a distracted air, left the rooftop.

Arenfall returned to his contemplation of the city as dusk slowly arrived. With familiarity, he shifted his attention to the gloaming mass of Bastran Hill, watching the scores of bhokarala emerging from the holes, pits and fissures in the hillside's looted tombs. But it was not the sight of the feral apes that made him frown, this being a nightly occurrence. The source of his unease was a lingering one. Beneath that pocked surface with its odd gravestones was the Under Quarter, an occupied subterranean maze of crooked streets, sunken houses and chaotic passages.

The Under Quarter was ungovernable, utterly lawless. Thus far, all past efforts to cleanse it had failed, such failures going back to pre-imperial times. By default, toleration of its presence seemed to establish a kind of stability, but one based on the assumption that this hidden world was essentially changeless.

And so it would have remained, if not for the rise of the Raraku Sea. Now, the Under Quarter was slowly flooding. The subterranean realm was knee-deep with black, silty water in every passageway, treacherously deeper in the pits and old cellars. In a neighbourhood with a rough roof in place of sky, with that roof often being barely a man's height – or less – the rising water table posed a problem.

The bhokarala, after all, were not the only feral population down there.

Many settlements across Seven Cities were built upon older ruins. The sheer weight of new buildings usually crushed everything underneath, although not always. Some of the exceptions had become legendary.

This was a haunted land, the modern little more than thin skin over the bones of the past. Every city a clenched fist. Here, in G'danisban, the water flowing among the buried bones of Bastran was unwelcome blood, and it was on the rise.

Perhaps it took a poet to appreciate such notions on the cusp of an impending rebellion, with Bastran the singular symbol of an entire continent's bubbling cauldron of discontent. Or perhaps not. Some symbols arrived like a fist to the face.

*   *   *

When the Adjunct entered the room, Captain Hadalin Bhilad did not rise from the bed where he lounged. His sword was across his thighs and his hands rested lightly upon the blade. He did not lift his gaze when he said, 'He was right. I could not have reached him in time to save your life.'

'I know,' Inkaras replied as he strode to a side table and poured himself some wine.

Now Hadalin glanced over. 'The red is Tanno,' he said.

The Adjunct studied the wine in the goblet he held. 'Your point?'

'Hallucinogenic.'

After a moment, Inkaras set the cup down, untasted. 'The High Fist plays with us?'

'Not deliberately,' Hadalin replied. 'It is here for . . . ritualistic options.'

'For two men infused with the dust of otataral?'

'The brew is not magical, Inkaras. It is a mix of ergot, mushrooms and wine. Thus, a natural path into the Warrens. Consider Tanno Spiritwalkers. As children they take their first journeys with this wine. Facilitating the necessary comfort to devote their lives to spiritwalking.'

Inkaras removed his telaba and let it fall to the floor, a gesture clearly intended to irritate, since the robe was almost priceless, and a gift. Smiling to himself, Hadalin said nothing. He knew what this was about.

'I underestimated him,' Inkaras said, selecting another goblet and this time pouring out white wine. Holding it up, he shot Hadalin a look.

'Just wine,' he said.

Inkaras sipped. 'Musician. Poet. That dreamy expression.'

Hadalin studied his lover. 'Prefers women, I'm told. But you knew that.'

'A man who contemplates the scenery, blighted as it happens to be in this instance. Eyes tracking the dip and diving of birds. He moved uncommonly fast.'

'He is a killer. You'll not underestimate him again. Nor will I.'

'He tells me he has the matter in hand.'

'Are you satisfied that he has?'

'Well now, that is one of the reasons we are here. To ascertain his . . . management. Of the situation.'

Hadalin studied Inkaras, the pose held in contemplation, yet pensive nonetheless. 'And should he prove to *manage* too well?'

A faint twist of irritation in the Adjunct's features. 'The Claw has entered the city.'

'I'd wondered at that necessity,' Hadalin said. 'You've said nothing of your meeting with the Emperor.'

'Popularity is a dangerous thing,' Inkaras said. 'When combined with competence, more so. Add to that *ambition* . . .'

'I saw nothing so overt, if indeed he is ambitious.'

'Everyone is ambitious,' snapped Inkaras. 'And no one is more dangerous than one who hides it well.'

'The Emperor fears Arenfall?'

'Seven Cities has a habit of raising high its own.'

'Including Emperor Mallick Rel himself,' observed Hadalin. 'He would ensure the door remains closed behind him.'

'And barred.'

'So, should Arenfall fail in quelling this unrest, we are to intervene. And should he succeed, we are to intervene. Is this by the Emperor's own command? Or that of a faction?'

Inkaras shrugged. 'The Emperor holds a strange court.'

Grunting, Hadalin said, 'I was unaware he held any court at all.'

'Just so. Diffused, scattered. Disconnected. Neither hand knows what the other hand holds, or indeed, even where it is to be found. We are forever measured against unseen interests, not even knowing who our rivals might be. Enemies, friends, allies or not? All is flux.'

'Seems . . . clever.'

Head snapping round, Inkaras glared at Hadalin. 'You would think so, wouldn't you?'

And now at last the matter was exposed. 'You did not come in ignorance. At high tide you will find me a lover of men. At low tide, women. The tide, it seems, is low.'

'Still?'

'Still.'

'And have you found a woman to play with?'

'I have not. Perhaps that is the problem, an itch yet to be scratched.'

Not, it turned out, a particularly wise thing to say, as Inkaras's face darkened and then paled. He set the goblet down, kicked through the telaba at his feet on his way to the door. 'Scratched enough with me, then. Fine.' He left, closing the door behind him.

'Yet,' Hadalin whispered to the empty room, 'I remain privileged. Such largesse is ever seen as a curse by those who do not share it.'

Sighing, he rose, sliding the sword back into its scabbard and then shrugging into the belted harness. G'danisban was a sordid city, but no more sordid than the city he had been born in, which, by coincidence, was only thirty or so leagues away. Familiarity was not unwelcome, a world of streets, alleys, taverns and bars to slip into with a native's ease. Crawling with cultists to be sure, but even that was nothing new.

No, tonight he would wander.

Throwing on his telaba, he made his way out, pausing only briefly to take care of one detail before leaving the room.

*　　*　　*

'All the gods are destined to die! Upon their bones we shall stride, chained no longer, bowed never again, into a world of true freedom!'

'Freedom,' sneered the man seated opposite. 'Guiltless, you mean.' He jabbed with a finger. 'I know what you want, Boort! I've seen your snivelling, cowed self, but was no god bashed you about the head, was it? No, only your long-suffering wife!'

The others at the table laughed. More wine was poured.

Hadalin sat at the next table, his back against the gritty, sandy wall. This tavern was more pit than building, half carved out with brickwork doing little more than filling gaps in the walls. The smoke of rustleaf and durhang hung thick in the air, swirling beneath the ceiling and lit lurid by wick light. The stone floor underfoot was swimming in spilled wine the hue of blood.

'Sha'ik was the first to die. Then Poliel and then Fener. The gods toppling like dead trees in the wind! Their last dying breaths add to that wind, Xam! And more shall fall – they all will, you'll see!'

'No I won't, nor will you, Boort. You're only sore cos she stopped throwing you on the altar, stopped gettin' what she wants from you. Your usefulness as a husband, Boort, is at an end!'

'My wife is not a goddess!'

'And you said that out loud? To her face? No wonder she tossed you out into the street!'

Boort was waving his hands as if to dispel the laughter, without much success. 'I come and go as I please, damn you! Slave to no one, that's me!'

Hadalin's attention drifted away, to find a table on the other side of the pit. Crowded with women and almost obscured by the smoke coming from hookahs, mouths and nostrils. A table on fire, it seemed. Women with their faces in clouds, the flash of white teeth between glistening lips, powdered cheeks and gesticulating hands tipped with painted nails. For the moment, he had no desire beyond simply watching them, no pleasure beyond seeing their lively celebration of life.

A thing Inkaras simply did not – could not – understand. On another night, it might be a table such as the one at his side, crowded with men, and he would feel the same, luxuriating at a distance, the receiver of unintended gifts. Who needed gods when all the glory of living was right here, right now?

Did it even matter who mapped out the world, who set out all that existed and perhaps would ever exist? Clearly such a being wasn't interested in blessings and sacrifices, beseechings and prohibitions. Its joy was precisely what Hadalin was experiencing at this very moment. And if joy at this moment, then sorrow the next. If striving in one breath, then surrender with the one that followed. Running, dancing, leaping into the air in one moment. Stumbling, crawling, dying the next. All to be received, clear-eyed and unblinking, heartfelt in each and every instance. Such a being played no favourites, granted no boon, no pity, no punishment. No, all of that belonged down here, where mortals flirted with pleasures forbidden and costly, the tide ever rolling out and back again.

If time itself was doomed to end, so be it. In that final instant, not only the gods would fall.

Poor Boort dreamed of an end and called it freedom, as if the gods had any say in who was and who was not a slave. Only people made other people slaves, after all.

Now he caught a glancing gaze, kohl-wrapped eyes locking with his own behind a smoky veil, lingering, cheeks crinkling in the beginnings of a smile. Hadalin collected his clay cup, stood and made his way to her, the other women looking up or twisting to watch his approach. Strangely, it was at moments like these that Hadalin felt the most fearless.

Boort was a fool wanting this to ever end.

*   *   *

22

Inkaras paced the room, knowing his inconstant lover would not return this night, caring nothing for the bite of loneliness that left Inkaras bleeding, suffering – no, Hadalin was cruel in his indifference. Better to end it and cast him aside. Was not solitude an Adjunct's fate in the end? Look at those who had held the title before him. Doomed to dying alone, or simply vanishing into obscurity and who could say that death did not find them as well, in some colourless, unwitnessed fate?

To be the Will of the Emperor made unwholesome demands to be sure. He paused in his pacing, remembering once more the tip of the knife hovering before his right eye, so close that a blink brushed lashes upon the steel. The memory made him shiver . . . deliciously. Oh, to take such a man to his bed!

But even the universe felt cruel this night, to offer such luscious fruit yet deny the plucking, the tasting thereof. Perhaps there was some wisdom in Hadalin's open revelry in simply watching, seeing; in mere proximity to all that he desired, despite the ache of such impossible longing. *Not impossible for him, though!*

The High Fist would have a shadow in all that was coming, as the Emperor demanded. Was that enough to leave Inkaras satisfied? Assuredly not. Longing was torture, after all.

He had wandered the corridors after leaving the chamber, long enough for Hadalin to take his leave. Returning to his room confirmed his assessment, as the man was indeed gone, although Inkaras's telaba now sat carefully folded on the bed.

Would he spend the entire night pacing? No, he would not.

To the roof, then, and if perchance the High Fist once more lingered there, gazing at the stars, well, so be it.

And yet, am I not here to kill him? The blade for failure, the blade for success. Mallick Rel, this is an old imperial game. But do you heed the history? I think not. No, you imagine yourself an exception, the solitary puppet-master destined to succeed where all others failed. Such is hubris. Another lesson of history so easily discarded.

Jalan Arenfall, do you suspect why I am here?

*   *   *

Tholas, beloved servant of Va'Shaik, watched the tall man leave with the woman, and then slowly rose and followed. Word from Imperium House had proved accurate. The Adjunct to the Emperor had indeed arrived in the city, and while the Adjunct himself remained safely sequestered in a well-guarded wing – no doubt sleeping soundly even at this moment – the man's bodyguard had foolishly left the building.

And now, tonight, he would die. Another blow against the empire, a warning to the Adjunct, a reason to fear, perhaps even flee Seven Cities. And enough evidence would be left to incriminate Arenfall in this captain's gory death, to further muddy the waters. If the rumour was true, that the Adjunct and the captain were lovers – though at the moment that seemed unlikely – then High Fist Jalan Arenfall might well die by the Adjunct's own hand. What could be more ideal than Malazans killing Malazans?

Tholas would do what he could to ensure that. And for those who knew him, why, Tholas was skilled enough to succeed.

He followed the captain and the woman, whose name was Satala and known to all as both foolish and wanton, especially when deep in drink; and indeed, her death was overdue as far as Tholas was concerned. Her open indifference to whether her lovers were Malazan or native was enough to seal her fate.

The world promised by the ascension of Va'Shaik over this land left no place for Malazans. Nor a place for the godless, for that matter. Only the faithful deserved the rewards soon to be bestowed upon the pure-born, and the sooner Seven Cities was cleansed of all but the faithful, why, the sooner would paradise descend from the heavens to embrace them all.

Satala was leading the captain to her home, a single-room corner of a tenement deep in the heart of the Gentle Quarter. They walked a narrow, twisting alley. She was drunk, but not too drunk to walk if a wall was within reach of one outstretched hand. But it seemed that even this level of inebriation was now making the captain reluctant. He'd slowed his steps and she'd begun tugging at his arm. Distracting for the man, all this indecision, and her other arm, entwined about his waist, was now looped in the sword's baldric. How fortuitous!

Tholas increased his pace, drawing both knives. To such benighted unbelievers, what he was about to deliver was a mercy.

*   *   *

All tangled by the woman, Hadalin felt himself yanked hard enough to make him lurch to one side. 'Gods below, woman—' But already she'd somehow managed to get one leg trapping him at the knee, forcing him

24

into a stumble. With one arm around her hip, he felt his own weight dragging her down, but then she somehow slipped free, one hand lashing out in a strange gesture.

Then he felt her hands under his arms, lifting him back to his feet with surprising ease. 'Got you, lover,' she said, somewhat breathlessly, pulling him forward once more.

Hadalin straightened, hesitating. 'You're too drunk—'

'I'm not. I thought you wanted it that way.'

'You did? Why?'

'Well, rest of the table was pissed, wasn't it? And I'm the prettiest, you said.'

'Whispered, in your ear. I would never say anything to offend your friends.'

'Exactly. Oh, I'm sodden enough, but not so much I won't remember, right?'

'Are you sure?'

She laughed, tugged him forward again. 'Come on, we're wasting time out here!'

Relenting, Hadalin stopped resisting. He saw her glance back over her shoulder and wondered at that, so he did the same. Nothing to see in the alley, barring a mound of rubbish they must've stepped over, though he hadn't noticed.

'It's not far now,' she said.

*   *   *

It took some time, but eventually she stepped outside to light a pipe. High Fist Jalan Arenfall emerged from the shadows and walked up to her.

'Sleeping soundly?'

Smoke poured in a stream from between her lips, then she said, 'He's a loss to women . . . half the time at least.'

Jalan drew out a knife and handed it to her. 'Quite a throw. Straight through the eye and deep into the brain. Tholas likely never even saw it.'

'Happy to serve, High Fist,' Satala said, accepting the blade and sliding it back into its sheath somewhere inside her blouse.

'Any other news for me?'

'Something's stirring among the Va'Shaik crowd. Not quite worked it through yet. When I do, I'll let you know.'

'Very good.'

'One other thing.'

'Yes?'

'A brief flash of magic, upon Bastran Hill. Silver white, with a lingering after-plume, dull grey.'

'Imperial Warren,' said Arenfall. 'The Adjunct brought a Hand of Claw with him.' He pondered that for a few moments, then, glancing at Satala, saw her studying him intently. It was not difficult for him to guess at her thoughts. *By what measure does a commander survive? How thin the rope underfoot?*

Satala drew on her pipe, but it had gone out. She frowned down at it, then spoke in a low tone. 'Her orders were clear, High Fist.'

'And they were?'

'You have the Talon with you in this matter. We'll find that Hand. We'll leave it lifeless.'

'I'd rather you didn't,' said Arenfall. 'Find them, yes, but do not kill them. Do nothing to force the Adjunct into anything precipitous.'

She snorted, relighting the pipe with a sparker. 'Captain Hadalin might well do that entirely on his own.'

'Best leave that between them,' Arenfall said. He paused, and then added, 'It is unseemly in its carelessness, however. Both men are made vulnerable by their relationship. The disparity in rank doesn't help either, I would imagine.'

'You will make use of it?'

Arenfall shook his head. 'If anything, their display of common humanity is charming. I have no interest in exploiting the gifts they offer each other. It is, I suspect, not easy being an Adjunct.'

'Nor his unnecessary bodyguard and part-time lover,' Satala said. She was silent for a few moments, and then she asked, 'So, you were close?'

Arenfall shrugged. 'Not so much as to undermine your confidence, Satala.'

'Blinker close, then.'

He would not argue that. 'Tholas had a reputation.'

'Took his measure long ago, High Fist,' she said, pulling deep on the pipe. Smoke streamed. 'He saw me the way I wanted him to, and that made him careless.'

'All right. Send another Talon to shadow the captain back to the House. When he finally wakes up. You've earned a sleep-in.'

She snorted. 'Till noon at least.'

'Perks of the job.'

'Yes, he was all of that.'

Jalan smiled, clapped one hand on her shoulder and then left her to finish her pipe.

*   *   *

Sleepless and miserable, Inkaras spent the night on the roof, alone. Of course the High Fist did not return. The man slept, peacefully and no doubt dreaming of women. The Adjunct had the familiar company of himself and no one else, and as the sky lightened and the first of the swallows emerged from their nests to wheel through the air, Inkaras drew his telaba closer about his shoulders.

Hadalin was a fine swordsman, almost matching the Adjunct's own skill, which made for ideal sparring, keeping them both well honed with the blade. As for the rest – the complicated, messy rest – he was done with it. Leave the man to his love of women, and if that meant a closed door between them the rest of the time, well, why not? Failing that, why, he could find another bodyguard. Perhaps even a woman, to keep things strictly professional.

Yes, that was a good idea. He'd release Hadalin, send him back to the Red Blades, at soonest opportunity.

An Adjunct was the hand of the Emperor. Blood-splashed, hard as iron, unfeeling and uncaring. No place for weakness. No place for love or tenderness, or the heart opened to another.

And he had indeed been weak.

Never again.

'Adjunct, have you been here all night?'

He turned. 'You rise early, High Fist Arenfall.'

'To see the dawn.'

'How . . . poetic of you.'

'One of my many flaws, I suppose.'

'Oh,' murmured Inkaras, 'I think you have very few of those.'

'Will you return to report to the Emperor now?'

Inkaras shook his head, offering a sad smile. 'I am afraid you have my company for a little while longer. Until this is fully played out, High Fist.'

'Ah. Hopefully, not so close as to undermine my confidence.'

'Excuse me?' Inkaras asked, since it seemed such an odd thing to say.

'Never mind. I value your presence.'

Breath catching slightly, Inkaras said, 'Indeed?'

Jalan Arenfall nodded, gaze sliding past to take in the rising sun. 'This could get ugly, Adjunct. Keep that sword loose in its scabbard, sir.'

Sighing, Inkaras looked away from the man, away from the sun as well, and fixed his attention on the gloom still shrouding the west. 'As you say, High Fist. As you say.'

'And your bodyguard ten paces back won't do, either.'

'His carelessness begins to irk me,' Inkaras said. 'I may have to find another.'

'Hadalin judged that any threat to you could only come from the hatch leading to the roof, Adjunct.'

'Until you showed him otherwise.'

'He understands this land,' Arenfall said. 'That is essential. Besides, would you have him stand close enough to overhear our private exchanges?'

Inkaras smiled, for all the wrong reasons. 'No, leave him guessing.'

Arenfall tilted his head, and then shrugged. 'I will leave you to dawn's light, Adjunct. Until later.'

Inkaras nodded. 'I believe I would like to break my fast here – can you have a chair and table brought, and food and drink as well?'

'Of course, Adjunct.'

Inkaras watched the High Fist depart.

There was nothing in his rooms right now, anyway.

The cry of the birds was more screech than song, as if horrified at witnessing yet another day.

*　　*　　*

It was a common game among the bhokarala to mime the gibberish of humans. Yet, as Nub and his kin well knew, not everything issuing from the pink mouths of humans was gibberish. Excessive, always, but even so. Understanding was never as elusive as was conveyed by the witless expression a bhokaral displayed when being spoken to by humans.

It was dawn and Nub was sitting with his back against the olive tree in the garden of the old temple, his belly somewhat bloated since olives were dropping like rain on all sides, all too easily within reach. Perfectly clean pits lay all around him. While he wasn't groaning, his stomach was.

The whispering shadow was gone, its myriad commandments sinking into Nub's murky memory, to be resurrected when the time was right. In the ahead-time, not in the now-time, and thus not cause for anxiety or stress. Dawn's arrival had been relatively peaceful.

But now the lone human denizen of the temple emerged, no doubt on his way to the small storehouse at the garden's back wall, to gather up and pack whatever he would need for his journey. For indeed a journey awaited the High Priest. This much Nub knew. Shadowy commands always stirred things up.

The man paused upon seeing the King of the Bhokarala. 'I need some of your clan.'

Nub belched, then bared his teeth. Not in threat. More like mild contempt.

'Listen, you fat toad, insults are most unbecoming.'

'Ljalabalalaullamulajabig.' And now the witless expression.

'I'm hiring a wagon, and servants. Well, one servant, for the journey. And I already suspect you'll have a mob of your ugly minions following me, so let's just make it official, shall we? I'm to open a new temple. Far from here – which, I might add, will be something of a relief.'

'Yalalabalalalbababab.'

'Fine,' snapped the High Priest. 'Just take care of the place, will you?'

Nub farted, a most satisfying fart. Until up wafted the wretched smell. The King of the Bhokarala gagged, hands fitfully clawing the ground, scattering olive pits.

While the priest rushed past towards the storehouse.

In truth, it wasn't that bad, and only momentary besides. Still, Nub extended his thrashing about for a bit longer, then slumped over to lie on his back beside the tree, miming death by asphyxiation. Motionless, eyes staring up at the blue sky and its wheeling birds, he waited for the return of the human.

When the man did reappear, it was only to hurry past, offering a short comment as he did so. 'Melodramatic bastard.'

Decent servants, humans. But clearly they did not understand bhokarala at all. The melodrama, after all, was the whole point.

He held the pose of death inordinately long, seen by no one.

CHAPTER TWO

Have you ever wondered, dear reader, which time was the worst?
The rebels' slaying of Coltaine, or the Malazan betrayal outside
the walls of Aren? Was not his final moment one that saw him
as courage slain by cowards on both sides? Such is the fate of the
honourable and the worthy.

Now consider the great leader for whom every claimed virtue is
but a game of deception, or worse, a level of self-delusion breathless in its audacity.

Where the coward leads, only cowards follow.

Histories of High Thrones
Galabras

Inquisitor Vest Dyan considered it a modest expression of sorcery, but
it suited the moment. He stood by the trackside, watching as the last
struggles died away among the eight figures lying before him, then
turned to the rotund man beside the carriage. 'It is done, Holy One.'

High Priest Harapa Le'en drew out a silk kerchief to dab the beads
of sweat from his broad forehead. He paused, as if gathering himself for
an ordeal, though his eyes gleamed as his gaze fixed on the motionless
bodies lying across the track. 'There can be no forgiving false pilgrims,
Inquisitor. I regret what I must do. Too many the plethora of imposter
gods. That such foolish souls as these should so easily succumb is sad.'

Vest Dyan watched as the High Priest of Va'Shaik turned to the carriage and began, with difficulty, climbing into the high seat. Grunting,
slipper-clad feet slipping, his strangely short-fingered hands clutching
desperately at every purchase, pulling his substantial bulk upward as the
carriage tilted on its springs.

The two horses side-stepped suddenly, almost dislodging Harapa, their heads tossing.

At last, the man found his seat and gathered up the traces. 'Ah, see how eager my charges, Inquisitor! They well know the justice of what is to come!'

Vest Dyan was an Inquisitor in the faith of Va'Shaik. Until recently he had been ensconced in the First Holy City – still more a ruin than a city – of Hanar Ara, at least until the stirrings of unease and discontent across the continent provided an opportunity the High Seneschal could not ignore. Now in the company of the Seneschal's principal agent, High Priest Harapa Le'en, they were barely a day away from G'danisban.

If but one city could be said to possess the rotten heart of the Malazan occupiers, it was there. Residence of the Imperial High Fist, garrisoned by marines.

And are we to be the knife aimed unerringly for that vile heart? He had been entrusted to guard this High Priest, but beyond G'danisban, what other destination awaited them? Cleansing the city they now approached could only be the beginning of things.

In any case, Malazans weren't the only enemies to the liberation and unification of Seven Cities. The land was rife with apostates, heretics, unbelievers and followers of false gods. Some could be saved. Most couldn't. In this instance, the High Priest had not even offered them a choice.

The horses stamped and snorted, their eyes wild and showing white. Harapa Le'en held taut the traces in one hand, reaching for the brake release with the other.

'They have done this before,' Vest Dyan observed.

'I travelled the trader tracks surrounding Ehrlitan,' the High Priest replied. 'Sworn to my mission. Souls must be released. By this means do I feed the coming Apocalypse under the benign gaze of the goddess.'

Vest Dyan nodded.

Harapa Le'en released the brake and loosened the traces. The horses lurched forward, the high wheels beginning their roll with a jolt. The sorcery binding the array of false pilgrims held as their struggles grew frenzied. But they did not even cry out as the horses' stamping hoofs pounded into bodies, crushing ribs, skulls, limb-bones. Then came the bronze-rimmed wheels of the carriage.

Death, Vest Dyan reflected, was never pleasant.

As the carriage rocked and pitched over the bodies, Harapa Le'en's eyes were closed, his lips moving in fervent prayer.

So many unpleasant things in the name of the Apocalyptic. Was all of this a distraction? Possibly. An indulgence? Assuredly. Would it do to remind the High Priest of his proper mission? Well, not yet. There was no telling, after all, how things would play out once in G'danisban.

There was a temple of Va'Shaik in the city ahead. A High Priestess and an Invigil. Vest Dyan knew little about them. If devout, all would be well, the future seamless in its progression. If lax or lacking, the holy chamber would require cleansing. *Not Harapa Le'en's task, however. Mine.*

The horses halted of their own accord, hoofs and limbs spattered in blood and gore. Now they stamped because of flies and wasps. Their flanks were slick with the lather of sweat. As if drunk, the High Priest rose from the wooden bench, blinking, lips oddly slack. He made to descend. 'I yield to you the seat, Inquisitor. They are forgiven. I am spent.'

'Of course, Holy One. Best seek the comfort of the carriage. Today will be very hot.'

Grunting his way back down, Harapa moved to the side door. 'The track is stony,' he said. 'Take it slow, lest we damage the wheels.'

'We could descend to the Imperial—'

'No!' The High Priest rounded on him. 'Can you not see the seduction at work in using such conveniences? We shall hold to the ancient paths, Inquisitor, at all times!'

'Very well. Our journey will indeed be slow and measured.'

'Precisely. Let each moment remind us of the sacrifices we are bound to, my friend. Such sacrifices!'

'Holy One, I am curious. How did you manage your acts of justice in the absence of my sorcery?'

Harapa Le'en frowned, and then shrugged. 'The tracks surrounding Ehrlitan are crowded with pilgrims of all sorts. I simply charged into their midst to reap what harvest the goddess granted me.'

'Ah, I see.'

The High Priest opened the door and clambered inside. The latch clicked and the shutters snapped shut.

The loss of air-flow would prove a most trying sacrifice, Vest Dyan mused, as the sun rose to an inferno in the sky overhead.

He relinquished his grip on the sorcery where it lingered over broken corpses, allowed it to sink into the dead ground. The will of humans proved paltry in the end, when unseen threads wove into taut, bristling ropes of binding, constricting to seize the throat, squeezing out all the air from tortured lungs. Perhaps the High Priest believed his horses and his carriage were the deliverers of holy judgement. Perhaps before now they had been.

But Vest Dyan was the faith's Master Inquisitor. Murder in the name of the goddess belonged to him. At some point, Harapa Le'en would need to be reminded of that.

He had killed the pilgrims before the first hoof descended.

*   *   *

'Tholas is indeed dead,' said Invigil Ban Ryk.

Shamalle, High Priestess of the Temple of Va'Shaik in G'danisban, appeared to struggle making sense of the words. 'Tholas? The bug-eyed one?'

Ban Ryk winced but, knowing she would not notice, was not bothered by his own carelessness. 'One of my Appointed, High Priestess. Rather talented, to be honest. Under consideration for advancement, in fact.'

Shamalle blinked. 'Under consideration? Oh, that's interesting. Whose consideration, I wonder, or is this some disconnected, floating thing? Does it hover over everyone's head? Who can say? And advancement, you said? Why, to where and to what? From this side of the room to the other, an advancement in time, a shuffling of space too, I should think. Well, he advances no longer.' She lifted the mouthpiece of the water-pipe and squinted at it. 'At some point,' she murmured, 'I should take charge of things. Being the High Priestess and all.'

Ban Ryk considered refilling the potent liquor in the water-pipe's bowl. It was already near-lethal in its brew. But a dead High Priestess simply meant finding another to put in Shamalle's place. Not especially onerous, but time-consuming nonetheless, and then all the rituals and ceremonies and invocations . . . bothersome. Besides, Shamalle seemed strangely blessed, not to mention the source of occasional amusement amidst all the exasperation. 'Holy One,' he now said, 'upon unfortunate Tholas's forehead was carved two dog-heads in profile.'

'Oh dear, most temporary art, then. These heads, snarling at each other?'

'No, facing away from each other. It is the sign of the assassin cult of Karsi.'

33

'Is it? Tholas – the bug-eyed one, yes? – was killed by an assassin cult? I did not know of an assassin cult. Of course, they would be secretive, wouldn't they? What does the Malazan High Fist think of such a malevolent cult in our alleys and streets? Have you informed him?'

'Holy One, we do not communicate with the Malazan High Fist.'

'We don't? Why not?'

'He represents the scourge afflicting us all.'

'Us all? Who all? Who us? Is the High Fist not all as well, and us, too? You are forever confusing me, Invigil Ban Ryk.'

Requiring little effort on my part. 'Holy One, the Malazans are occupiers, oppressors of our freedom.'

She waved the mouthpiece dismissively. 'Oppression, oh dear. Before them, we were oppressing each other. Before them, oppression was the game in which we made up our own rules. The Malazan occupiers brought a new set of rules. Theirs, I should think. Better? Worse? Does the question even matter? You resent the Malazans because they stripped people like you of your power to oppress. Your freedom to oppress, that is.' Tilting her head back, she stared up at the tessellated, domed ceiling with its vast scene of unbridled, orgiastic activity, or perhaps at the layers of smoke drifting beneath it. 'And where will it all end? Where does one body cease and another begin? I see only flesh in expressions of ecstasy. If the world must die, better to be smiling than weeping, yes? My beloved goddess, after all, always knew the end was coming. What to do, what to do, oh my, when the game is filled with small-minded pricks like you, Invigil?'

These small flares of biting, stinging clarity always rattled Ban Ryk. He said nothing for the moment, watching her return her attention to the water-pipe, and a few moments later all light left her eyes again. He said, 'I shall endeavour to hunt down the Karsi cultists. We must show our ability to police ourselves.'

'Show? You show me, I show you, we show everyone. I'm sorry, who is it exactly we're showing again?'

'The native-born of our land, Holy One. Upon ascension, with our faith ruling over all, that we have no need of Malazans to keep peace and order, to see to the prosperity of everyone.'

'Oh, I do love prosperity. Are you prospering, Invigil? I should think so. Am I? Most assuredly. Shall we share in our largesse? Is there enough to go around? Too many tell us otherwise. "Not enough, never enough, only enough for me and people just like me," they say. It's all such a mess, isn't it? I have a sinking feeling that there is indeed enough of everything, only some people would rather there wasn't, as they profit greatly from controlling and indeed limiting the supply.'

'There is much to correct,' Ban Ryk said, eyes narrowing.

'Send in Pash and take your leave, Invigil, I grow weary.'

Ban Ryk bowed. 'At once, Holy One.'

Exiting the chamber, the Invigil waved over the small-faced, tiny woman seated on the stone bench opposite the doors. 'You, Pash. Be mindful of all she says and report it to me this evening.'

A quick, darting nod that made the colourless hair bob like a dandelion gone to seed, her strangely vulpine eyes avoiding his gaze, and then she was at the doors, opening one just enough to slip inside.

Ban Ryk stared after her, waiting until the latch clicked shut, and then he set off. Tholas dying was disturbing news. The twin dog-heads carved into the man's forehead could have veracity, or they could be misdirection. For all he knew, an entire cadre of Claw could be in the city, under the command of the Adjunct. The High Fist . . . no, too soft to be anything but what he was.

She'd probably like him. They'd even get on well. Poems sung to the five-stringed traitel, her eyes answering with sleepy, languid blinks. Formless conversations and probably ending in clumsy fucking on the bed. Shamalle was indeed a perfect embodiment of Va'Shaik.

Of course, the dissolute failed in most things, including all the mundane and yet vital tasks of managing a temple, an entire religion, a rebellion. In fact, living symbols were pretty much useless, beyond the personification itself. And yet Shamalle unveiled her contempt for him again and again. On that basis alone, it might be time to spike her drugs and see the end to her. An end from which all manner of symbolic meaning might be derived, if one could be bothered.

A final concern to ponder – he withdrew from his sash a small, rolled tube of papyrus and paused in the corridor to read again the words inked onto it. *'An assassin known as Blinker is believed to be in the city.'*

The killer of Tholas? A master killer from the Karsi cult? A Claw? Or someone new, someone yet to wet the blade here in G'danisban? His spies knew not, but in time they would.

In any case, with luck, the Adjunct would move on, or find reason to depose Arenfall or send him to another city. Malazan attention on

G'danisban would drift away. After all, the most dangerous swarm of hornets would be found circling Burning Y'Ghatan. And if all Malazan focus fixed upon the Flames of the Flail, all to the better.

The Sha'ik rebellion all those years ago had been flawed at the outset. Doomed to fail. Too chaotic, too blind in its ferocity. The lack of purity, and keen wit, had been its downfall. This time it would be different. The Malazans had grown complacent.

Sending the Adjunct, even a handful of Claws, won't do. No, they should be sending three, four, even five full legions. But they don't have any to spare. And even if they had, even if they did, well, the days of commanders like Coltaine are long gone.

This empire is vulnerable in ways like never before. The time has come.

His thoughts had carried him to his private office. His first task now was to assemble a Hand of killers, his very own assassins, and set them loose into the city. Judicious culling was necessary. For which the Malazans – and that Adjunct – would be blamed. It was also said that the Adjunct's bodyguard was a night-prowling womanizer. Easy to kill if necessary, but perhaps other options were possible. He would have to think on that.

*   *   *

Pash sat cross-legged at the High Priestess's feet. Somewhat rounded feet, with rounded toes, puffy ankles, but smooth and hairless, and a rainbow of colours spanning the nails of those toes, and, visible up almost to the knee on one leg, an equally smooth shin from which hung a heavy, fleshy calf. This ampleness, Pash knew, stopped just above the hips, as if Shamalle consisted of two bodies from two different people, carelessly mismatched.

Two or three seasons back, workers had been pulling up the flagstones of the temple's courtyard, only to find a mass of rubble and artifacts, including a dozen or so knee-high marble statues of uncommon workmanship. These had been assembled from composite parts, arms notched into shoulders, legs to hips, and upper body to lower body. This apparently allowed them to be positioned in a variety of poses.

A few of the city's scholars had taken an interest in the discovery, and for a week or two the temple grounds had been crowded with old men and old women of the studious sort, dusting-up corridors and stumbling into the wrong rooms and arguing late into the night. The High Priestess had delighted in their presence.

The hunt, it seemed, had delved deep into mystery cults, although even then the purpose of the lifelike figures with their solemn expressions remained elusive. The debates would have gone on for ever if not for the brief appearance of an itinerant Malazan historian who, upon first sight of the statues, pronounced them models for an art school.

So much for secret gods and lost religions.

The High Priestess had held a sumptuous dinner party in mocking celebration of the mystery's end, inviting not only all the scholars but also a dozen or so sculptors and painters, with the bemused historian seated immediately upon her right and therefore subject to her groping hand the entire evening.

This had been before the High Fist's arrival in G'danisban, else he too would have been invited, no doubt. Perhaps seated on Shamalle's left, within reach of her other hand.

Pash had been born in a hovel, abandoned by her mother when she was four. Collected up by an acolyte and brought to the temple, which was always in need of servants. She knew no other life. Hunger in her earliest years – before the temple – had left her stunted, her features uneven, the subject of no one's interest. Baited and bullied by other servants and left to the most menial, degrading tasks possible, her fate had changed only a few months back. An evening she'd spent picking through the temple's rubbish heap, as a particularly fine tessera had been lost from a prominent mosaic, assumed to have been swept up (it hadn't), and so she had been kneeling in the fetid garbage, surrounded by hissing oil-lamps, as she picked through the leavings, when the High Priestess emerged suddenly from a door Pash had not known existed, stumbling slightly, to then halt, gaze turning to fix upon Pash.

'Do we not feed you, darling?'

Eyes averted, head dipped, Pash said, 'A lost tessera, Holy One.'

'The Hiparian mosaic in the Vestibule? That ghastly thing. It's the gold paint. Glaze, I mean, only it isn't gold at all, it's pyrite. Do you know what pyrite is?'

Pash shook her head.

'Look up, dear, meet my eyes. I'm never a violent drunk, anyway. I was coming out to puke, but now you've distracted me. Still, the air's clearing my head, so I'm grateful. Puking also clears the head, but in a far less pleasant way. Now, pyrite is false gold, seducer of the gullible, a prettiness of no value at all. Yet see it glitter! Drawing every eye – even those of thieving idiots.'

Pash slowly leaned back, glancing back down at the rubbish surrounding her.

'Who set you this miserable task? Never mind, I can guess. The truly valuable tesserae in that ugly mosaic, by the way, are the rubies disguised as enamelled embellishments, gaudy and distracting. No one ever steals those. Tell me your name, sweet ruby.'

'Pash, Holy One.'

'Pash, now my personal maid. We shall have to clean you up, of course, but no effort to hide your other attributes. In time, I will show you their advantages. In time, you shall blaze unseen. Oh, now I do have to puke after all.'

Which she did, rather spectacularly.

And so began Pash's new life, new education, new tasks and duties both public and private, secular and secret.

Ban Ryk saw in her the perfect spy. This detail had amused the High Priestess, and in no way had Shamalle advised, instructed or in any way interfered with this secondary responsibility. So Pash did due diligence in memorizing all that passed between her and the High Priestess, and indeed, all that passed Shamalle's lips. Her discretion, such as it was, belonged to Pash herself.

Unknown, therefore, to both the High Priestess and the Invigil, Pash only reported what she wanted to report, which was in fact the cheapest of content and of almost no import. In many ways, Pash spilled into the presence of Ban Ryk an entire garbage heap of useless, often invented information, in which a precious tessera might or might not exist (it didn't).

As for her feelings for Shamalle, the High Priestess of the Va'Shaik Temple, who reminded her always of two body halves inexpertly put together, Pash loved her with all her heart.

Among all the voices that had assailed her all her life, only one named her a sweet ruby.

And how could anyone think that more was needed?

Be the one to cast rubies in all directions, and may your eyes slide past the world's false gold, so empty of worth.

'Darling Pash? Your mind drifts.'

A quick dip of her head. 'Sorry, Holy One.'

'More aphorisms? Poetic intrusions? Are these like considerations, I wonder? Hovering over the head, floating like cute, puffy clouds? It would not surprise me. The Invigil wants a report tonight, I'm sure. Well, what matters of grave import shall we discuss? And after your breathless words to the Invigil, what then for you? Will you in the darkest, most melancholy bells of night, prowl the rooftops with keen eye and even keener ear?'

'I will, Holy One.'

'Oh.' She appeared momentarily flummoxed. 'I was being melodramatic, possibly rhetorical. I was being, hmm, I don't know what I was being, but as instruction, assuredly not. Yet you take it as such. Very well. So be it. Make it so and so on. Prowl, sweet ruby. Rooftops and alleys, ducking under clotheslines and that sun-kissed scent of laundry on all sides. The linens and cottons, the silks and hemps, all the colours sucked away by the night. Do you live in a grey world, darling?'

'I live in this world, Holy One.'

Shamalle's smile was always breathtaking, like an orchid opening to moonlight. 'I see you as my sober self, I think. The quick-witted side of me, which I left on the divan, or was it the dresser? Made manifest by some amused spirit. Is this a disservice to your person, Pash? Your wretched history and each day in which you draw breath? Which would you prefer? My quick-witted self can always return to the dresser, or divan, after all.'

Pash said, 'To be your sober self, Holy One, is all that I desire.'

'Hmmph.' The sound was somewhere between a grunt and a sigh. 'She *would* say that.'

'I worry, Holy One.'

'About what?'

'The potions the Invigil mixes for your water-pipe.'

'Potions? Oh, you mean the poisons. Has it not occurred to him that he inures me to their effects? The ground leaves of wesp set fire to the nerve-ends, until the skin screams. If skin could scream. But the beneg seeds crushed into powder bring an internal silence. The pathil mushrooms paint the world in new colours and open doors into long-lost warrens, where sad spirits wander with shining eyes and glossy lips. Wine infused with mallik berries plunges my soul into deep waters. The rustleaf drops heavy anchors into the solid earth. The durhang stirs me into amusement without revealing the mad hilarity behind it. And drunkenness, well, drunkenness casts off the shackles of constraint. One must be careful with that one. Now, will you report my musings to the Invigil? When you do, take close note of his reaction. I would hear every detail of his floundering dismay, darling. Every detail!' And she beamed.

While the sober self looked back, a calm pool under distant stars.

* * *

A night of great agitation. Nub's displeasure hounded him. Again and again his lips peeled back as the King of the Bhokarala looked out upon the city, its smokes and firefly lantern glows, its hanging shrouds of laundry on rooftops and stretching over alleyways.

His children were out and about, watching, pilfering, fleeing when necessary. And tonight, it was most definitely necessary.

Magic, the bristling charge of something unseen, yet prickling the hairs of forearms, hands and nape – oh, Nub so despised magic! Was not the world meant to be constant, one day like the other, every night the same?

But now a shadow was speaking to him, a high priest had fled the temple, the waters of Under Quarter were rising, a veritable cascade of magical annoyances! That, all of that, yes, and the rooftops crawling with assassins.

Fangs bared in the night, in the face of this preposterous absurdity. Humans! He shook the tree.

* * *

The carelessness of Tholas might well be Satala's death. Gazes had lifted that night, eyes tracking the sudden departure of the assassin in the wake of the Malazan bodyguard and the woman who would take him to her bed. A body in an alley brought Tholas's pursuit to an end, while Satala was back in the tavern pit the very next night, drinking and smoking and laughing as if ignorant of how close death had been, and all of this was enough to fix attention upon her, along with sober consideration. Had anyone else died in that woman's wake? None known, but how relevant was that? The most successful killer is the one best at hiding her victims, after all.

Bodies were found all the time. The destitute slain by the cough thriving in weakened lungs. Drunks who took one swallow too many. Various addicts with their twitchy limbs and marble eyes, carving the last bit of brain from their skulls. Sickness and infections and perhaps the most pernicious killer of all: neglect. Neglect by society, by whatever remnants of family remained, this vast, devouring void that was the state of being unloved, uncared for, unacknowledged. All too often, that cause of death belonged to children, abandoned and cast out and basically wiped off the slate of a culture's regard, a nation's ledger of the useful. Small bodies huddled in alleys, around which rats danced.

Satala knew, with all the senses of a woman feigning weakness in the company of men, that she was now being hunted in earnest. Stalked. Fixed gazes indeed, assembling the components of a trap, each carefully sliding into place, building for the moment of ensnarement.

This night, then, about to throw up to the glittering stars a sudden violence, the heat of blood spilling out beneath their cold, lifeless reserve.

Four, perhaps five hunters slowly closing in, as she reached up, fingers curling over the gritty lip of a roof's edge, and pulled herself onto that roof, lying flat, breath held, waiting. Her heart thumped hard deep in her chest, suspended above the still-hot tiles by bone and fluids and the meaty flesh of her breasts and finally the supple leather of the tunic under the cotton shirt. Held, then, like a hot fist in the firmament, beats bridging the gap between breaths.

From there, she sent her senses outward. Night air was different from the air of the day. In its dissipation of heat came the coolness that did not rise, but pooled, deeper in shadows, sultrier in open spaces, but no matter where, forever reluctant to the passage of anything and anyone. Trembling, as well, to the unfolding of sorcery.

Her stalkers hunted with magic in addition to their mundane skills.

Were they the Adjunct's Claw? No, not yet. Nor would the Hand know that Talons were in the city. Of *course* the High Fist would have agents and spies. To be expected. The Adjunct would have instructed the Claw to settle in before making any overt move.

No, these hunters were home-grown.

Satala possessed her own sorcery, but to use it would be like lighting a torch in a cave. And that would not do.

She saw a vague shape dart across the far side of the roof, but it was just a bhokaral, quickly gone from sight, and was that not telling?

A muted scuff in the alley below that she had just quitted, then the faintest of breaths drawn as the man paused, motionless, gathering up a knot of magic. With her head turned away from that roof's edge, Satala caught the flicker of something larger than any bhokaral among limp clothes on lines opposite, one building away. The net closing in.

In one smooth motion, she rolled over the roof, back the way she had just come, fell a man's length, drawing both knees up in the instant before landing on the figure crouched below. Her knees crunched down on his upper back, breaking both collar bones and dislocating both shoulders. Her weight drove the man face-down into the cobbles below, shattering his nose and snapping back his head, whereupon she slid a knife-blade across his throat beneath the hinge of the jaw. Blood splashed out and began spurting onto the cobbles, making small pools that gleamed in the starlight.

The man's magic drifted like a sprite, then slowly dissolved.

Satala rose and quickly backtracked down the alley, hunting the next foolish lighting of a torch.

*　　*　　*

Pash possessed no skills, no talents. She was, in her mind, less than complete. Survival was only possible if she remained forever beneath notice, or, failing that, quickly dismissed. Irrelevance was her secret power. In idle moments, such as this one now, sitting on a rooftop in the Old Market Quarter, with bared feet dangling over a vine-knotted passageway only small animals and flitting birds could traverse, she could imagine a multitude of people just like her. Passing like ghosts through the world, their lives a brief, barely noticed spark that died unseen on an empty night. A night as empty as this one.

The tangled mess of vegetation below was an olive tree, twisted into itself by crowding walls and scant light. Whatever water fed it came from fetid runnels of spilled sewage in the canted, jumbled remnants of broken pave-stones amidst the riot of roots. The tree's triumphant crown of leaves was just beneath her feet. A dip of her toes could brush the highest ones, gliding lightly over their dusty-leather surface, making them dip and nod as she liked.

Below, bhokarala in the gloom among the exposed roots made skittering sounds as they hunted olives through dry leaves and shreds of bark that had peeled away of their own accord from the tree's trunk, the sounds furtive and chilling. Like her, the bhokarala lived mostly unseen. Like her, they witnessed things.

A brief flash of purple light caught her attention on a lower rooftop three buildings away, and her eyes narrowed upon seeing two figures seeming to embrace in some wild, silent dance. Spinning, cavorting, then springing apart, with one falling in a heap and the other suddenly

42

crouching, as if gathering breath. The air seemed to shiver, sending a cold rippling sensation through Pash. Quietly, she drew her legs up and moved into a low crouch of her own.

The world was one thing and only one thing. She knew this, had always known it. Things that seemed unconnected, unrelated, were in fact bound together, tighter than any woven net. Slipping between, touching not a single strand, was almost impossible. By the gift of her eyes, she was now linked to what she had just seen, and the motionless figure now lying alone on that rooftop was proof of that, even as the man's death flinched and twitched above the body it had once occupied, like a songbird born in a cage no longer caged. All the sensations of loss flittering away – and now the leap into freedom and the spirit was gone.

Across that rooftop, the long thread of the murderer's path. Emanations of violence now tattered, fraying, fading into nothing. Over the far side of the roof the killer had gone, and from what Pash could recall of that shadowy figure, it was a woman, her hot body forcing itself through the cool night air, the wake still swirling to her passage.

Pash sniffed the darkness and found more scents of magic. One very close, on the very rooftop where she still crouched.

Then a man's low voice spoke directly behind her. 'She sends you out into danger. No, best not turn around, maiden. I mean you no harm. It seems we are witnessing the same things this night, but between us, only I am forced to act. Although,' he added in an amused tone, 'so far she's needed no help at all. But a whole pack has been let loose tonight, so I will continue to shadow her, just in case.'

Pash remained motionless, her mind growing still and calm.

'And here we find you at last,' he then said.

She heard him move slightly, heard his breath now louder, closer, fluffing the thin hair above her left ear. Upon her right shoulder settled his hand – no, a coin it held, pressing down as if being carefully, delicately placed – and then withdrawing, leaving only the faint weight of the coin itself.

'A Runt for you, little watcher. Do you know Runts? The manifested coinage paying passage into the realms of Icarium?'

She shook her head.

'Ah, perhaps your mistress will. Root, then, cold-hammered copper, gnawed out of the rock itself and beaten flat. Etched upon one side, a tree-stump. Upon the other, well, could be anything. Pay heed to that tree-stump, see the axe marks. No natural felling, this. Yet the root abides, holds tight to the deep earth, and from the decaying thing above, the promise of flowers.'

Now she knew the voice. On more than one night, music had drawn her to a tavern and whatever shadows she could find nearby, to listen to a stringed instrument and a low, melodic voice in which hid all the sorrows of the world. The songs drifting out into the night, weaving things of their own. This was the High Fist. This was Arenfall himself.

'I need no coin from you,' she whispered. Did not the Invigil call this man evil? Was he not an abomination?

'Spend it or not,' he replied, 'but either way, a Runt is no simple coin, no matter how base the metal. Should you find the need to pay passage – not of the mundane kind – have it at hand, little watcher.'

'Why give me anything? I'll not spy for you!'

'I have no need of that, not from you in any case.'

Still she did not reach up to touch that coin. 'I don't want it!'

'The land forever abides. You are its unnoticed eyes, little watcher. Its beating heart too low, too faint to be felt. Here you are, listening to the night, the parting fabric tears and the magic spilling out, the lives ending.' He paused, and then said, 'I'm of a mind to make you a song. Perhaps, in some night to come, you will hover at a shuttered window, and hear me sing of the little watcher. Who sits at the Root of all that we are.'

'Leave me alone,' she hissed.

There was no reply. He was gone. Pash reached up at last and collected up the thing he called a Runt. She held it up for a close examination, difficult in the gloom. If it was indeed copper, it was blackened. The etching on one surface was as he had described: the raised relief of a tree-stump she could trace with a fingertip. She turned it over, squinting. A misshapen face looked directly back at her, one eye higher than the other, the rudder of the narrow nose offset to the right, with hollowed cheeks upon either side. A narrow jaw and jutting chin. Eyes almost lost in pits. She was, she realized, staring at her own face.

A whimper escaped Pash.

'This isn't fair,' she whispered.

He had spoken as if he expected her to report to the High Priestess, but how could she now? Arenfall had clearly cursed her, dragging her into terrible light. The Unseen should serve no god, should move to no force but one's own – tiny as a fluttering leaf dangling from a branch, only moments from silently dropping to the ground below, to lie among all the other tiny, dead leaves. She deserved no more than that. *None of us do.*

To be the land's eyes and ears – no, that was not a burden she could carry. No one could . . . could they?

He curses me. All my life, my face belonged nowhere, not in any room, not in any company. I dwelt in the background, forever in the background, a bare smudge upon the scene.

Now she looked upon her visage etched into a coin. Like some empress, some divine protector, some goddess. *Goddess of the Misfits. How can the land expect anything of me? How can anyone? It's not fair!*

Did it even matter? She did not know what to do, did not know what was being asked of her. It made no difference at all, in fact. Changed nothing. She was Pash, the dirt-smeared ruby, the gaudy bauble of no worth.

And yet, the sober self of a drunk High Priestess.

And yet, a woman with a coin.

Sudden thumps and scuffling behind her on the rooftop. She whirled round to see two figures, one sinking down, the dying flare of magic filling her vision with dancing orbs of light, half blinding her. Two quick footfalls, a shape stepping over a victim dying in a sprawl, the gleam of staring eyes fixed upon the stars.

'You startled me, child!'

To the woman's soft exasperation, Pash scowled. 'I'm not a child.'

The killer slowly straightened, still holding a knife that dripped black gore. She paused to look around, sniffing the air. 'Oh my,' she murmured, 'this has been a night of slaughter, and not all of it mine.'

'Arenfall helped,' Pash said, her tone surprising her in its lack of bitterness. The absence of outrage.

The woman approached and a moment later was sitting with moccasin-clad feet dangling over the roof's edge, idly studying the wet blade of the knife in her hand. 'Five on my tail,' she said. 'All accounted for by this Kanese dagger right here. There were others, then. Are you one of Arenfall's? I've never seen you before.'

No one's ever seen me before. No one ever sees me at all. Pash deftly slipped the Runt out of sight, and then sat down beside the killer. 'He was here. He spoke to me and then was gone. I am not one of his. I'm not one of yours.'

45

The other woman sighed and carefully scraped her knife's blade against the edge of the roof-tile on her right, whereupon she slid it into an unseen sheath. A moment later a pipe and rustleaf-pouch appeared. 'If you're not one of us, are you one of them? It would be . . . genius, seeing how ineffectual you seem at first, and even second, glance. In fact, a master assassin in your guise would be . . . devastating.'

Magical fire and the pipe was lit, the bowl glowing as the woman drew deep.

Pash's right hand drove a knife into the woman's chest, between two ribs just below her left breast, penetrating the heart.

Silent with death, the woman fell back, the pipe tumbling and rolling on the gritty tiles, spilling embers that flared and then sagged into a deep, ruby glow. The crunch of the back of her head was mercifully brief. Then, like the person farther back on the flat roof, who stared sightlessly heavenwards, this woman did the same. Smoke rose in idle tendrils from her slightly parted lips, her nostrils. Her soul was a brief flutter, then gone into the night.

Pash carefully cleaned her knife-blade. She whispered, '*I am her sober self, and I live in a grey world.*' She then had another thought, and added, '*The land abides, but sometimes . . . the land strikes.*' Drawing the Runt back out, she studied it with renewed interest. 'See that stump? Someone cut down the tree. Someone is going to get exactly what they deserve.'

There, in the background behind the stump, the bare smudge on the scene wasn't what it seemed. Not at all what it seemed. No, that smudge was a *blur*. Barely catching the eye. In the instant before it arrived. *Delivering death.*

No, she didn't tell Ban Ryk everything. She didn't tell the High Priestess everything, either.

She was Pash.

Only Pash, who once stumbled behind a man, a rope around her neck.

Encircling hemp, rasping burn of fibres with each and every tug.

The best disguises weren't disguises at all.

*   *   *

The rising sun was relentless, a burning eye setting on fire the eastern sky. Arenfall crouched beside the still, lifeless form of Satala, the body lying from the knees up on the flat rooftop, feet dangling, flies already clustering around the eyes, her parted lips seeming to seethe with buzzing madness.

His mouth felt full of ashes, his eyes stinging to grit both real and imagined. Was it coincidence that she had taken position here, almost matching that of Shamalle's homely spy? This very same rooftop, now home to two bodies? Setting her back to the last hunter left dead behind her, scraping blood from her blade on this tile edge, at such ease as to light her pipe?

This so-brief gap in Arenfall's attention, while he'd been busy killing another handful of would-be killers – accidental vagary of circumstance? Was it simple bad luck, the Lord's Push, the deadly conspiracy of chance?

And what of that little watcher? Witness to this, or had she fled shortly after Arenfall's own visit? Or was she . . . no, that seemed unlikely. Shamalle wasn't interested in assassination, or control of the streets, and by all accounts, tiny Pash belonged to the High Priestess, not the Invigil. And extending that thought, Ban Ryk simply wasn't smart enough to make Shamalle's spy into his shaved knuckle in this wretched game.

A gesture sent the body of Satala away with a faint pop of displaced air. Had he a High Mage Necromancer at his disposal, he would have his answer – the last things Satala had seen before dying. Echoes of sound or even voices. But this was wishful thinking these days. Necromancers were rare beyond measure now, many having shifted their interests elsewhere. The Grey Rider wasn't interested in bargaining, couldn't be bribed, and never faltered in attention, or turned away in indifference. No, Hood he was not, and besides, he had a damned army at his disposal.

Still, Arenfall would leave her where he had sent her. Bodily, at least, beyond the reach of decay. Of her spirit, well, likely already deep in Iskar Jarak's embrace.

Whatever that meant, and who could know now that the doors of death had so firmly closed?

Forgive me, Satala. I failed you.

Distant wails on all sides were greeting the discovery of the past night's slaughter. Arenfall opened his warren and slipped inside. He would have to report to the Adjunct, and there might be acrimony in the exchange.

Even so. *Adjunct, a High Assassin is at work here in G'danisban, and he or she is not named Blinker.*

The nights ahead would be a fucking mess.

*   *   *

47

One otataral sword was deadly enough these days. Two, to the Adjunct's mind, were overkill. Perhaps this was the reason for his reluctance to strap the damned thing on. Leave all that martial rubbish to Hadalin, his presumptive bodyguard, who was now that and only that. Setting aside the personal was a function of being the Adjunct, after all. A liberating notion, in fact.

At first chance, he would dismiss the captain, send him away – no, cut him loose. A supreme act of indifference punctuating the end of their relationship. Decisive, unambiguous.

Inkaras had commandeered a room to use as an office. Outrageous, truth be told, how much the role of Adjunct to the Emperor had become one of administration. From Master Mage-Killer to Master Bureaucrat. Overseeing agents in the field: spies and assassins, hands of Claw, infiltrators in cults and temples. In the absence of legions on hand to hammer down sedition, more clandestine means were necessary.

The challenge here in Seven Cities was the sheer proliferation of new cults and faiths, all competing for domination, for the fixed hand of social rule. That wretched arrogance dictating how everyone should be: this was the perceived goal, the crown of glory. As if a mind could be regimented, beaten and pounded into an automaton of belief. As if children were destined to be paragons of the doctrine, assuming one got to them early enough and was diligent in crushing their spirit into a quivering mess, begging for eternal guidance.

The slavery that was a mind in chains was far more powerful and pernicious than the physical version, and these teachers knew it. Their faiths would have it so, these very chains, this obliteration of the questioning, challenging mind. All the dictates of a soul's purpose, all the prescriptions and prohibitions, all the blasphemies, heresies and mutual vigilance, all the horrible punishments for the simple act of *objecting.*

Inkaras set his quill down. He read over what he had just written, and then frowned. A sudden flood of guilt and shame rushed through him. His philosophical musings were nothing more than a hobby, too shallow of thought to be of any value to anyone. He should be turning his mind to the grand scheme here, this most delicate plan that he and the Emperor had assembled. All on the matter of one too-popular, too-capable High Fist.

Another pause, another digression, taking him down alluring paths.

Arenfall. Now, and no matter what his fate, there was an interesting man. Fascinating, enlivening. There was a solidity about him that was dangerously seductive. Inkaras reminded himself to be careful. But then, not all attractions led to sex, did they, and love itself was a many-faceted experience. Indeed, potential pitfalls awaited him should he loosen his reins of control. But he could manage this, he was sure of it. To simply bask in the pleasure of the man's company would be more than enough. Until it was time to end it.

The soft chime of a bell from above the door made him quickly close his journal of thoughts, rising and turning in time to see the door open and Hadalin step in. With a faint smirk quickly hidden – that infuriated Inkaras – the captain said, 'High Fist Arenfall requests your presence, Adjunct, as soon as it is convenient.'

'That would be now,' Inkaras said. 'Where is he?'

'The Governor's Chamber, sir.'

As Inkaras made to leave – an act about to necessitate coming too close to Hadalin, deepening the Adjunct's irritation – the captain cleared his throat and said, 'As requested, sir, from now on,' and Hadalin's attention shifted to the weapon belt slung on a peg near the desk, 'I will, of course, walk three paces behind you to the intended destination, as always. Even so, the corridors we must traverse may not be as secure as we would like. The High Fist ignores the Commander's Residence, though it would surely prove easier to secure.'

Scowling, Inkaras collected up the belt and strapped it on, the sword in its scabbard feeling uncommonly awkward, the brass ring hard against the point of his left hip. Sparring was enjoyable, he allowed. Though perhaps less so now, since it was Hadalin he normally sparred with. And Inkaras knew he possessed uncommon skill with the blade. Still, there was something crass about it, as if the use of a sword constituted a fundamental failure. Strapped on, the weight there on his left hip seemed to do little more than remind him of past failures – past times when he'd no choice but to draw it out and use it. Concluding an argument, as it were.

'Very well,' he now said. 'Leave me room to pass.'

A hint of the smirk returning, Hadalin ducked his head and edged to one side.

He baits me. This is becoming insufferable.

Out into the corridor, forging a path through the comings and goings of clerks and servants, cleaners and messengers. There was something new this morning, he quickly discerned, a febrile tension. Hissed exchanges, whispered conversations. Here and there, expressions taut with fear.

Inkaras finally halted and turned to Hadalin. 'What has happened, Captain?'

'Killings in the night just past, Adjunct. Many killings.'

'Whose side?'

'I cannot say, sir. I have been at my station since you entered your office.'

'Yet you spent most of the night in the city below.'

'I was occupied for most of it, sir.'

Baits me!

Inkaras turned back and resumed walking. Arenfall had assured Inkaras that the captain's nightly peregrinations were not as solitary as Hadalin likely thought, a detail meant to put the Adjunct at ease. But increasingly it mattered less and less. If Hadalin's wandering cock got him killed, well, those were the risks, and this was a level of carelessness that would, sooner or later, demand a price.

Such unfortunate fates were to be expected. The Adjunct would simply find another bodyguard.

The double doors to the formal Governor's Chamber were flanked by two guards, eyes hidden in shadow beneath the rim of their helms. Ignoring them both, Inkaras halted before the entrance. After a moment, one of the guards pulled on the bell, and then opened the nearer door. The Adjunct strode in.

He found the High Fist sprawled on a settee to one side of the massive desk, forearm over his eyes, one booted foot on the floor. 'Take a seat, Adjunct,' he said to the ceiling in the weariest of tones. 'Forgive me my exhaustion.'

Turning, Inkaras bade Hadalin close the door, then added, 'Outside, Captain.'

Smiling, Hadalin stepped back and the door quietly shut between them with a muted click.

Inkaras found a chair and settled in it, pushing the sword out to the side to keep the belt from riding up. 'Was Blinker busy, then?'

A moment of silence, and then, 'Not busy enough.'

The High Fist remained as he had been, eyes covered, flat out on the settee. Should Inkaras take offence? Oddly, he didn't. The scene invited a certain intimacy, a firm step away from the formal. Not a High Fist behind the bulwark of his enormous desk, but an exhausted man unafraid of showing it. 'You asked that we speak. Here I am.'

'Hmm, yes. I did and here you are.' He paused, and then said, 'I admit I expected in a bell or two. I understand you are in the habit of pacing half the night in your bedchamber. A flawed assumption in imagining you sleeping late, since it seems that insomnia plagues you as much as it does me.'

I am not in the habit of pacing half the night. 'You have disquieting knowledge of my nightly activities, High Fist.'

'My palace, my house.'

'Yet one rife with enemy spies.'

'Just so, Adjunct, allowing me to dictate precisely what my enemies learn.'

'And assassins in the corridors outside?'

'Potentially,' said Arenfall, 'anyone can be an assassin. Granted, it takes a certain will, a kind of inner dislocation if you like. To make the victim an object. To make the act of killing effortless. At least,' he added, 'effortless in the spiritual sense.'

'Yours is a dangerous house, High Fist.'

Arenfall grunted. 'Any more dangerous than the Imperial Palace?'

'Hmm,' Inkaras said, deliberately echoing Arenfall a moment ago. 'Perhaps, in a different way.'

'I've never met the man.'

'The Emperor?'

'What is he like?'

Inkaras considered the question for a few moments. 'I don't think anyone knows, really, what he is like. As a man, a human being, that is. As Emperor, well, we have an empire to examine for the answer to that.'

'A most subtle rule.'

'Yet, on occasion, revolutionary as well.'

'He betrayed the Malazan Empire at Aren,' Arenfall said. 'Sacrificed ten thousand good soldiers. And would have opened the city's gate to the Dogslayers.'

'Yet now he rules the very same empire.'

'Formidable bastard.'

'Assuredly so, High Fist.'

Another pause, and then, 'Three cults, working in concert, sent out killers in the night. Some were hunting my agents. Others were silencing dissident voices within their own organizations, or rivals of the same. The unbowed among the city's citizenry, dying for their refusal, their defiance. Isn't it odd, how so many faiths resort to killing the dissidents among their own people?'

'The ones who dared to object,' Inkaras said in a half-whisper. 'We walk the same paths of thought, High Fist. Did you lose people last night?'

'One, a most precious one.'

'I am sorry,' said Inkaras, and he meant it. This exhaustion he was seeing, so openly on display, was the exhaustion of grief as much as physical weariness or lack of sleep.

'Not inclined to be careless. I cannot fathom how she was caught unawares, having just killed all five of her stalkers.'

'No, that is odd, and disturbing.'

'We have a master assassin in G'danisban.'

'Might it not have been just chance?' Inkaras asked. 'It seems an extreme conclusion you make here.'

'You did not know Satala. She was my best, Adjunct. My very best.'

'Satala,' Inkaras said in a low murmur. 'The name—'

'Your captain may have mentioned her. His lover the first night.'

'You were protecting him even then?'

'Of course.'

'And the women since then?'

'Other agents.'

Inkaras was silent, his mind assailed by waves of confusion and alarm, of startlement and something like awe. 'You, sir,' he finally said, 'are extraordinary. The very first night? The same day as our arrival? How could you have known the captain would leave the grounds, venture into the streets?'

'I couldn't, but I have faith in my agents in the city. Word went out ahead of your captain's departure.'

'So swiftly! How?'

'My magery, High Fist.'

'What warren?'

Finally, Arenfall pulled his forearm away from his eyes and tilted his head to study the Adjunct seated across the room. 'Otataral diminishes interest in warrens,' he said. 'You negate every one of them, after all.'

'Barring Elder Warrens.'

'Almost never seen any more. The Runts are a much quicker means for pretty much anything magical.'

'Does that bother you? Your tone . . .'

'It does, just not always.' Attention ended, head turning back, forearm settling once more over the man's eyes. 'Apologies,' he said, 'I have a headache and this morning light burns.'

'Are you a deliberate target, High Fist? Drawing the enemy here to G'danisban? Do we need to adjust the plan?' *The one between us, that is. The other plan remains unchanged.*

'Adjust? Mostly, no,' Arenfall replied. 'But it does pose an added opportunity. Still, I'm not convinced we'll find the rebellion's heart here, no matter what they may manage to achieve. Killing me, killing you, for example. Our plan is already in progress. It doesn't *need* us.'

'Well, I'd rather neither of us meet that fate, High Fist. Back to this imagined master assassin—'

'Leave him or her to me.'

'To Blinker.'

'Fortuitously,' Arenfall said, 'I've already seeded that name among rumours, an identity unknown but to be feared.'

'Yourself as bait.' *Again.*

'It's the best way of dealing with these things. Better than the master assassin proceeding with the slaughter of all my agents. No, I want to distract the bastard. Better still, I want to sting my rival's ego, make myself a challenge to his or her skills.'

'I still foresee mutual slaughter accompanying your plan.'

'I will quickly escalate things, Adjunct, giving my rival less time to damage us.'

Inkaras sighed, stretching out his legs. 'An assassin-war. Where have I heard this before?'

'Dear Adjunct,' Arenfall said in dry amusement, 'more than half the cities now in the empire were taken with assassin-wars. Claws infiltrating, commanders and leaders dropping everywhere, entire lineages of potential heirs wiped out.'

'All very true,' Inkaras allowed, 'but this city already belongs to the empire.'

'And that changes things?'

'Killing our own citizens? Because they choose to object? Where then the virtue of our stance?'

'I wasn't aware we had one, or needed one, for that matter.'

'A cynical side of you heretofore unseen, High Fist.'

'There are lessons inherent in religious upheaval, Adjunct. It's time to teach them.'

Inkaras snorted. 'As if they'll learn from them.'

'Now who's being cynical?'

*   *   *

Ban Ryk waved the smoke from his face. 'Holy One, we lost thirteen agents last night.'

'Lost? The city isn't that big.'

'Murdered.'

'Oh. Why didn't you say so in the first place, rather than have me wondering how locals should find themselves so unaccountably out of sorts? I mean, that wouldn't make any sense at all, would it? Followers of the faith so confused they don't know where they are. Who, then, are they following? Clearly, the wrong people.'

The Invigil struggled to remain calm, keeping his expression bland, but with just enough concern applicable – it must be assumed – to the dreadful losses of the night just past. 'Others died as well, of course, but these are of no concern.'

'They are of no concern. Well, that's a relief. Who were they, I wonder, to so slide off the polished sheen of your consideration?'

'Enemies, Holy One.'

'Yet now their souls walk hand in hand with our dead followers. What inference might we make of that? Indistinguishable in death, the peaks and troughs of each life levelled to the smooth surface of the Unseen River. So grey the waters, so reflective the mirror. This morning, Invigil, I have spent contemplating death. How apt your report.'

Teeth gritting, Ban Ryk said, 'It pleases me my words so entertain you, Holy One.'

'It is no entertainment to receive elaboration on thoughts of finality. I wonder, have I done enough? What is enough? Whose expectations are we implying here, that must be met or fail to be met? Did my life have a plan before it even began? Was I born to a path from which no deviation was possible?'

'As the Goddess wills, Holy One.'

'She wills nothing. That is her whole point, Invigil. Ephemeral as these scented clouds, wandering the room in the blissful bath of oblivion.'

Sighing, Ban Ryk looked away. The suds of the tub the High Priestess lounged in had indeed taken on a greyish tint, receiver of kohl and other paints. Its steam was indeed florid with the scents of petals and flower-heads. The smoke of her water-pipe *indeed* drifted lazily, thick enough on occasion to veil her eyes with mysteries their glassy state did not suggest as remotely likely.

Drunk and stoned and dreaming of death. Well, that definitely fell deep into the shadow of Va'Shaik. But it was no way to run a temple, a city, or a continent.

'Leisure,' Ban Ryk said, 'is the mark of privilege. Won by hard work, the collective efforts of a people.'

'Yet indulged by hardly any of them, this hard-won leisure.'

'There is an order to society, Holy One. Those who rule, for all their privileges, also know the burden of grave responsibility.'

'Yes, this burden simply crushes me. Uhm, where were we again?'

'A master assassin hunts us, Holy One.'

'If truly a master, shouldn't we have been found by now? The temple is hardly a secret, is it?'

The smaller door to one side of the bath-chamber whispered open and in came Pash, struggling under the weight of a bucket filled with steaming water.

'Pash! You found us! A deed the dreaded master assassin still fails at. Unless, of course, you are that master assassin – but wait, should that not be mistress assassin, at least in your case? Is there precedent for such a title? Does it send shivers through a quaking, terrified populace? And if not, why not? Who am I asking, anyway? Surely not you, Pash, and do pour slowly, lest you scald my honey-hued skin. Then the Invigil, clearly, who sits with clenched jaw and savage eyes – dear sir, partake of popping poppy seeds and the sizzling black oil of durhang on yon brazier, for your peace of mind if not your health, assuming a dichotomy indeed exists which I, of course, highly doubt. But who am I to challenge the latest sages with their brilliant brains formulating brilliance on a daily basis? Would we divide the indivisible, cleave a sphere of water? We must, they say. We must! Oh, Pash, dip the bucket deep here, then deluge my head!'

Stiff where he sat, trembling, Ban Ryk watched the maiden pour bathwater down atop Shamalle's head, while the High Priestess squeezed shut her eyes, her round face scrunching in the manner of a toddler about to wail, which she then did.

'Cleanse my brain, sweet water! Dissolve all tremulous doubts, I beg you – is there a god or goddess of water? Why yes, there is! Pour another deluge down, sweet ruby! In waterfall, do I call upon Nerruse? Or Mael? Do they even know each other? Which – pfagh! – excuse me. Mother or Father, who comes first? Is she his daughter, or is he her son? Or are both instances true? How is that possible? Even worse, what if they're married on top of all that? Or, hah, who's on top, hah hah! I would– *blurblubull* . . .' And the rest was lost as she sank down into the tub, her mound of hair bulging then flowing outward on all sides, a boulder covered in seaweed.

Ban Ryk lifted his gaze and met the eyes of Pash.

That proved strangely disquieting, as he saw not a hint of anything in them. 'Be sure she doesn't drown,' he said to her, rising from the narrow footstool he'd been perched on. He paused to stare down on Shamalle. Her face was a blur beneath milky grey water, bubbles rising in a steady stream since she was still talking. *Big lungs.*

The idle thought accompanied him out of the bath-chamber.

*   *   *

'This dildo, darling, is the perfect lover,' Shamalle said to Pash. 'Us women being too complicated, and men, oh, men! Inarticulate dullards who splash piss on the rim of the shitter and breathe heavily through oversized nostrils. No, ruby mine, here in this one hand is the universe's gift to women, and why wouldn't the universe give women a gift? After pushing out babies, we deserve it all. Oh, Pash, your drying efforts make my skin glow! Or is that oil? Oh, both, I see. Very good. I know you've never been pregnant, indeed, perhaps still a virgin too. Shall we do something about that? It is my thought that pregnancy and birth are a devil's seduction, with all the curses appertaining to their achievement. And the scars – oh, see the scars! Well, stretch-marks, then. Badges of dubious honour – shall we see you knocked up and waddling the rooftops at night? Er, not the best image. Unless under moonlight! Well?'

'I am blessed just as I am,' Pash replied, still rubbing the towel over Shamalle's substantial body.

'Of course you are, and what more poignant truth can be uttered by any of us? But I have concerns, desires to see you find all the fulfilment you deserve.'

'I have all I deserve, Holy One.'

'Then you are content?'

'I am content.'

'Woman deprived of leisure? Servant to the privilege of others? Buckets of hot water and thick cotton towels, the daily travails of service? This is all you desire?'

'I am blessed in all things, Holy One,' said Pash.

'What a strange little woman you are.'

Pash nodded, in complete agreement with that assessment.

'The night past was a busy one,' Shamalle now murmured. 'See much of it?'

Another nod, and then Pash said, 'It was . . . uneven.'

'Heed that naught, ruby mine. Be the balancer in all the tumult.'

That, Pash conceded, was good advice.

Sweet Ruby, the moon's belly is swollen and the birth to come, why, the night shall rain down with chaos. Until, at the very end, a most perfect balance is found. Oh Runt of Root, of Land, you shall receive this bounty of blood, as precedes every birth, in blessed deliverance.

Her sober self will take the night, then.

Like a throat between two hands.

*   *   *

He knew that there was so much that Inkaras did not understand. To see Hadalin's faint smiles as mockery, to see nothing of the hurt and the pain behind them. It was too easy to imagine this disparity of desires as just that, a wall raised between the two. The love of women on one side, the love of men on the other. From this flawed vision, it was no wonder that Inkaras saw him as incapable of commitment, when in truth that was not the case. Given the choice, Hadalin would make Inkaras his life partner, never again looking at a woman.

But Inkaras was the Adjunct. Even these strained bonds between them were a liability, a vulnerability to which no Adjunct should ever be subjected. This and this alone drove Hadalin into the arms of others. He could say nothing of this to Inkaras, however. The dismantling of his own heart that was necessary each time Hadalin walked away from

Inkaras, the false elation he rode into the night on the streets and in the taverns and bars of G'danisban – this was for him alone.

It had been Hadalin's own weakness in succumbing to Inkaras in the first place. A failing in his duty as bodyguard, as protector. Accordingly, no one else could fix this. The sacrifice belonged to Hadalin.

Inkaras would never understand. And now all was cloudy, swirling and treacherous between them, with wounds being delivered with venom and malice. All the wholly natural responses to being hurt.

Hadalin could not tell which of them was doing the most damage, or which of them held to the stronger defence, the righteous rationale for every word, every act committed against the other. How curious, how fraught was love. Of all the battlegrounds that could be experienced or imagined, surely the one belonging to love was the cruellest.

Standing as he was now, at the second-floor window of the brothel, with its thin pane of cloudy, rippled glass transforming the scene in the street below into something more dreamlike than real, he could not help but see every blurry figure passing within sight as the bearer of wounds from that battlefield. Love lost everywhere, burdens carried, all the scars behind calm, placid gazes, the fixed expressions, the common gestures.

To guard such a gift as was love seemed the highest calling. Yet all too often, blood flowed. All too often, weapons did their deadly work.

The woman in the bed behind him was stirring, a rustling of sheets and shifting of weight making the mattress squeal and the bed-frame creak. Then silence.

He slowly turned to face her.

She was sitting up, dark eyes fixed upon him. 'That was fun,' she said.

Hadalin smiled, and if the smile was a match to the one he'd offered Inkaras, well, so much for simplicity. 'I need to return to Imperium House.'

'Yes,' she said, 'you do.'

At that strange comment – and the sudden sharpness in her regard – he frowned.

She rose from the bed, sheets falling around her, and began dressing. 'I'll state this plain, Captain. You're risking too much with these jaunts. The Adjunct has a meeting with the High Fist and sends you away, and off you go. Although the High Fist has no direct command over you, he advises that you cease these activities. We're in an assassins' war, Captain, and shadowing you every day and night is drawing off valuable assets.'

She paused, now dressed in her plain shift, long hair tied back and looking nothing like the lascivious woman of the time just past, and then she said, 'The High Fist is tired of babysitting your careless impulses. Besides, you are making Inkaras less effective.'

He stared at her, momentarily at a loss for words.

Heading for the door, she paused again and looked back at him. 'But it *was* fun.' A wink, and then she was gone.

Reaching up, Hadalin ran shaky hands through his hair. 'Fuck,' he said.

Love, you make fools of us all.

*　　　*　　　*

Nub crouched on his branch, in the foulest of moods. The mysteries of the universe were infuriating. Any creature with half a brain knew as much. Yet, among his tribe could be found individuals devoid of natural angst, never once experiencing the binding knot of frustration, and most certainly never approaching the weary realization that indeed, some things could never be explained; that some questions would never be answered; that the universe was essentially confounding.

From whence such bliss among these select few? The answer, alas, was simple. Stupidity. Utter dullards, with their witless smile and unclouded gaze, their excruciating expressions of relentless happiness. For them, all was simple, all was explicable, never once experiencing even so much as an agitated ripple upon the smooth surface of their inner world.

If one required an obedient army, why, none better than brainless legions, the march of the dumb, the senseless rage of the unthinking.

Amidst the swirl of such thoughts, Nub reached out and cuffed Bort upside the head.

A head that then dipped, only to rise up again, brainless eyes blinking, only to spin round right back to their original boundless equanimity. 'Vlalaballalalalllalal!'

Nub raised his fist for another strike, even as Bort bared his teeth in a mindless grin, and then gave up, all inner torment collapsing into a mulch of despair.

Commanding such legions was a chore.

'Bavallala allub alabua buluah!'

Nub glowered at his minion. If only the words spilling from Bort's hairy lips made sense, actually meant something. Oh, what was the use? There was only murk behind those bright happy eyes, the bubbling brown mud of a brain lost inside itself. Contentedly so.

The miserable night was done, the sky blue once more, the crunchy little birds back in the air and singing. Bodies were being carried to and fro in the streets and alleys of the city, while others rutted in their rooms or attended to banked fires to make the second meal of the day. The flapping clothes on the lines were snatched down and folded to death. Dogs yawned and stretched, noses twitching to the light wind's myriad hints of piss and whatnot. All so normal, all so . . . senseless.

Did none but Nub understand? The waters were rising! Rising, you damned fools!

'Mmalalalub abbal ulhgggg alib!'

This time, when Nub swung his fist, Bort ducked.

CHAPTER THREE

In the days and weeks before the Quench, the XXXIst Legion's Fourteenth Company of Marines was being run ragged. It was no wonder, since it was the only marine company stationed in Seven Cities. That said, most of its activities escaped the notice of pretty much everyone, barring those whose actions necessitated their intercession. They noticed, the hard way.

An Informal History of the Malazan Marines
of the Late Empire
Tallobant the Younger

It was only an assumption, but Captain Dunsparrow was certain that once, long ago, she'd had a sense of humour. All these years of living had beaten, pounded, flattened, stomped, then ground it under one twisting heel. Nothing left, not even a smear. As dead as optimism, as dead as all hope, just plain dead.

Having just had these thoughts, she concluded that this was one of her better days. She reached for her tankard.

Opposite her, Captain Hung looked like he'd just tasted something sour, but then, he always looked like that. It was his face that was sour. 'Where are they now?' he asked.

'Mine? Equipment repair, resupply, healing.'

'Really?'

'No, not yet. I sent them to an outpost on the Odhan border.'

'We have an outpost on the Odhan border?'

'No. That's their job. Set up an outpost.'

Hung nodded, reaching for his own tankard. 'There's nothing beyond that border.'

'I know.'

After a long moment, Hung nodded again. 'Good move, then.'

'You? Where are yours?'

'Locked up.'

'Oh. That's a good move, too. Wish I'd thought of it.'

'Well, there's a few empty cells left over, but probably not a good idea.'

'No,' she agreed. 'That would be bad.'

'At least we're getting some rest.'

'Sure, some of us are.'

'They're getting some rest, is what I meant.'

'It won't last.'

'No, it won't.'

'One survivor from the Sixth,' Dunsparrow said. 'Now in my squad. Along with the corporal who isn't a corporal. He was in the Sixth too, I think.'

'No, he isn't, but he was. Still, who is he?'

Dunsparrow squinted across at the man, then shrugged. 'And that lone survivor is a sapper. Could have been anyone, but no, I got another sapper.'

'How did the Sixth dust out? I wasn't here, didn't get the details.'

'Almost none to give. Bandits, apparently.'

Hung's eyebrows lifted. 'Bandits?'

'I know. Doesn't add up, does it.' She paused to swirl the dregs of her wine around in the bottom of the tankard, and then said, 'If I had to guess, my new sapper blew the others up. Of course, he's not talking. Neither is the corporal who's not a corporal.'

'Sapper's feeling guilty, then, since that's the only thing that shuts them up.'

'That man's never known guilt. At all.'

'Oh. One of those. Makes for bad soldiering, in my experience.'

'Hence, the only one left alive in the Sixth.'

'Except for the corporal who's not a corporal.'

'And now mine. Technically, they both are.'

'Another round?'

'Gods yes!'

The Petals Tavern was empty, it being just past dawn. The two captains had only each other for company, such as it was. At a gesture from Hung, Obly the Boy came over with a clay amphora and refilled their tankards.

62

'This wine is shit,' Dunsparrow told the boy.

'Shall I leave the amphora here, Cap'n?'

'Good idea, do that.'

He did that and retreated once more into the back room behind the bar. What was in there that had him so busy? Who knew? Stuff, she supposed.

The door opened and in strode Captain Veroosh. He dragged a chair up and joined them, on Dunsparrow's right and Hung's left. 'It's official,' he said, just as Obly the Boy reappeared with a new tankard, collected the amphora from its ringed-metal stand on the table, poured, replaced the amphora and then left again.

'Glad something is,' Dunsparrow said.

The three drank.

'Bandits,' Hung muttered.

'Or friendly fire,' Dunsparrow countered, suddenly feeling belligerent.

'The Sixth?' Veroosh asked. 'Heard it was a mercenary company, a nasty one.'

Dunsparrow belched and the belligerence went away. Sighing, she said, 'Three sappers now for me.'

'Bad luck,' said Hung.

'The worst luck, Dunsparrow,' said Veroosh. 'Feelin' sorry for you right now and that's honest.'

'Thanks,' Dunsparrow acknowledged.

'Where are they?'

'Odhan border.'

'There's no outposts that way.'

'Not yet. The point is, they can do no harm, right? As far away from anything as possible.'

'Until the next mission,' said Hung.

'Even then,' said Dunsparrow. 'I'm waiting for my new recruits.'

'Oh, about that,' said Veroosh. 'They're here.'

'Are they?'

Nodding, Veroosh drank down the second half of his wine and poured some more into his tankard. 'That's why I'm here, getting drunk. Out of commiseration, Dunsparrow. Pure, genuine commiseration.'

'Don't be, Veroosh. Recruits can be worked into something.'

'Not these ones.'

'What do you mean?'

63

Veroosh squinted at her. 'Don't want it being me tellin' you, to be honest.'

'Where are they?' Dunsparrow asked.

'Barracks.'

'With the regulars?'

'Not any more.'

'That bad?'

'Yup, that bad. I mean,' and now he smiled at her, which was the most alarming thing possible, 'you just got to laugh, I say, and that's the honest truth.'

But Dunsparrow knew she wasn't capable of that, her sense of humour being extinct and all. 'Pour me another, then I'll go look.'

What was official? Veroosh never told them.

*   *   *

If the tiles, frescos and drains in the floor were any indication, this had once been a steam room, attesting to Imperium House's origins as a highborn residence. Now it was just clammy, badly lit by two oil-lamps on the lone table occupying its centre. On that table was a map of Seven Cities, the Feroot version, which made its accuracy questionable. That said, the Wessel version was even worse. Official maps had a way of being anything but. There was, in fact, no true official map.

It was a curious notion, Jalan Arenfall reflected, though the weariness fogging his mind threatened to make reflection formless, lazy and vague. Nonetheless, maps sought to make the ephemeral concrete, locked in time, attesting to a reality one could verify on the ground, as it were. Yet no map was truly accurate. Oh, it might record the indents, stretches and notches of a certain coastline, or the bend in a river, but the older the map got the less accurate it became. Change was the force of nature and it never slept.

Battles were won or lost based on maps. Empires rose and fell to the same. Errors of distance, or complete fabrications, could be pivotal to success and failure at any given moment, in any given place. The conceit was that the world could indeed be mapped.

Arenfall had his doubts. Not that it mattered. More often than not, the lie served.

The room was far below ground level, twenty-three spiralling stone steps down, in fact. The vents in the walls were high up, just under the ceiling, each one a circular hole covered in dusty bamboo latticework. Everything smelled of mould.

The door opened. Arenfall turned from his examination of the map. 'Corporal.'

'Sir.'

'Join me. Let us peruse the map.'

The man strode over, his footfalls soundless on the tiles.

Arenfall studied him briefly, then said, 'The décor does not disturb you?'

Thin brows lifted as the man paused and made a visual examination of the room as if for the first time. 'No, it's fine, sir.'

'The frescos. We're surrounded by capering nudes.'

'Yes, well, I've seen worse.'

Arenfall frowned. 'Not distracted even in the least?'

'Only where the limbs look wrong. The artist wasn't very good. As for the commissioner's taste in flesh, I really have no comment either way.'

'You are a strange one, Corporal.'

'Yes, sir.'

Stretching an arm, Arenfall pointed to a spot on the map. 'You'd think it will all kick off here.'

The corporal leaned forward, squinted. 'The Burning City. Seems the wrong precedent, sir.'

'How so?'

'Well, things end there, not begin.'

'Hmm. That may explain all the attention we're getting here in G'danisban.'

'These religious purgings are not uncommon, sir. Besides, there is a Claw now in the city.'

Arenfall's gaze snapped up, fixed on the corporal. 'You knew this how?'

'Your Talons should watch their backs.' The corporal's gaze lifted and met the High Fist's regard. 'You too, sir. Though the Adjunct might save you for himself.'

'I was advised to make use of you, Corporal. I begin to see why.'

'Sir, it may all kick off – as you poetically put it – here in G'danisban for the simple reason that you are stationed here. The notion being, cut off the head of the imperial command and chaos will ensue. That said, the Emperor's own Adjunct may be the one delivering some of that chaos.'

'By cutting off my head? Doing the rebels' job for them?'

'Irony abounds.'

'If it's to all start here in G'danisban, then the sooner we end it, the better.'

'Yes, sir.'

Arenfall tapped the map again, in the same spot as before.

The corporal sighed. 'I'll check it out, then.'

'You seem reluctant.'

'It is a thing maps cannot show, sir. Places where violence has soaked deep, age upon age. They're volatile, such places. At any one time, the people there may imagine their motivations immediate, bound to the present circumstance. They don't realize the power of the history beneath their feet, where violence folds and unfolds, endlessly repeating. It's a place of endings, sir, as I said, but getting to that end isn't pretty. And every end is temporary.'

'I'm short on marines.'

'Yes, sir.'

'I keep sending them out. They're getting whittled down, Corporal.'

'Not much longer, I think,' said the corporal. 'It's heating up.'

Arenfall frowned. 'Thought you said purgings are common events.'

'Aye, they are. But I'm getting hints that gods are stirring this particular pot.'

'Va'Shaik?'

He shook his head. 'Not yet.'

'Then who?'

'As I said, sir, just hints. It's damp in here. Not good for maps.' His gaze drifted back to the map. 'Shall I inform my captain?'

'Not yet. Just don't overstay, Corporal. One last thing, this rise in banditry in the countryside.'

Nodding, the corporal said, 'It's organized, yes. That and the rogue mercenary companies.'

'You were with the Sixth when they got ambushed.'

'Aye, sir. Definitely caught us by surprise. Some heavy magery was thrown around.'

'What were you doing during all of that?' Arenfall asked.

'Keeping our own sappers from blowing everyone up, and I do mean everyone.'

'It seems you failed in achieving that.'

The corporal shrugged, and then half-smiled. 'The nastiest magery came from the other side, sir. Distracted me for just long enough. Cussers are pretty indiscriminate.'

Now Arenfall was scowling. 'That level of carelessness is inexcusable. Why is the sapper still breathing?'

'As you said, sir, we're short and being run ragged. Besides, there's some question about what happened. The sapper who survived might not have been the sapper who threw the cusser.'

'He wasn't questioned?'

'Aye, that didn't help.'

'Does the Adjunct know about you?' Arenfall asked.

The corporal blinked. 'I can't think why he would, sir.'

'He asked me how I was managing to send my marine squads through the Imperial Warren.'

'Marines are mages, sir. He can't be unaware of that.'

'Of course. But his point was that it seems I somehow keep managing to send the squads in such timely fashion, quenching the flames before they turn into wildfires. It's my predictive talents he's questioning.'

'Good. Keeps him off-balance.'

'But I'm not the one with the uncanny timing, Corporal. That would be you.'

The man shrugged. 'Hence these scouting missions, yes?'

'The thing is, if you are to be my shaved knuckle in this game, maybe I shouldn't be dispatching you all over Seven Cities.'

'Got to throw the bones to play, sir.'

Arenfall paused, and then sighed and said, 'I may not be able to stop this uprising.'

The corporal nodded. 'Don't worry, sir. They can start it. We'll be the ones finishing it.' He glanced back at the map. 'After all, we have history on our side.'

*   *   *

Invigil Ban Ryk studied the tendrils of smoke rising from the censer on the altar before him. Some fools thought they could read the future from such things. Truths hidden in the curl of smoke, the wayward tug of unseen currents in the air, the play of shadows in candlelight. The cast of knucklebones or polished stones, the maddening game of tiles and Runts.

Oh, the patterns of the universe resided in everything, to be sure. All was connected, bound together in subtle, often unseen ways. At the same time, so much of life, of living in the day to day, clung to the illusion of isolation, an assertion of disconnectedness, where all that mattered was within reach, and all that existed beyond that reach didn't matter. Said reach could be a stretching hand, or a wandering mind. It was too easy to retreat to the moment, this immediate present where both past and future lost relevance.

Such was the surge of emotion, the impulse of the instant. His attention lifted from the smoke rising from the censer, to find once again the round, somewhat shiny face of High Priest Harapa Le'en. 'At the very least, allow me to send my servants out to cleanse your carriage wheels.'

Harapa Le'en smiled. 'I'd rather my conveyance continue wearing the tattered flesh of heretics, Invigil. It suits my chosen path in the world. Just as I travel only the old roadways and tracks, eschewing imperial abominations, nothing about me is without deliberation.'

Ban Ryk decided to drop the matter, though the foul stench of the carriage in the courtyard outside the window drifted in with every sigh of wind. 'Your arrival was unexpected, but fortuitous. We are locked in a quiet war in this city, High Priest.'

'By your design.'

'Initially, yes. I did not anticipate the prowess of our enemies, however.'

'Underestimating Malazan marines is beyond foolish, Invigil. Moreover, this is the seat of the High Fist, and now the Adjunct. It was premature to bloody their noses.' Harapa paused, and then added, 'I was perforce required to forbid the Inquisitor's presence here in this room, so vast his indignation. You acted too soon and now face the consequences. How many of the faithful have you lost?'

Ban Ryk scowled. 'You and the Inquisitor clearly misunderstand the situation, High Priest. My faithful were not targeting the High Fist, nor the marines. Rival cults constitute an insult to Va'Shaik. This land belongs to the Apocalyptic. Fools kneeling before a crow-feather or a dog-head amulet offend my eyes, and my faith.'

'Was not the Adjunct's bodyguard targeted, then?' Harapa asked, brows lifting.

Ban Ryk's scowl deepened. Too many loose tongues in the temple. 'A perceived opportunity, High Priest.'

'A flawed one, obviously. If that man wanders the city unattended, has it not occurred to you that he poses as bait? Does he not carry otataral?

So magic will not aid in the assassination attempt. No, assume he is shadowed, and that all attempts will be intercepted, thus effectively culling your faithful. Did you not receive clear enough instruction, Invigil? Let our bandits and mercenaries in the countryside do their work. Tell me, do marine squads patrol the streets of G'danisban? No, they do not. We are keeping them busy. We are wearing them ragged.'

Ban Ryk allowed a wry smile at that. 'Whilst your bandits wear them ragged, High Priest, the marines in turn kill them by the score.'

'Only the least reliable ones,' Harapa said with a wave of one hand. 'When offering coin to bandits, it is worth remembering that such people are venal, disgusting and treacherous, and once we win our freedom across all of Seven Cities, their corpses will adorn the walls of every city. Their use, therefore, is temporary. Are the marines killing them? They are. Do marines fall in the process? They do.' He shrugged. 'The lives of bandits and mercenaries are of little relevance. Unlike your faithful agents in this city.'

'A master assassin is here,' Ban Ryk said. 'Discovering this now rather than later is worth the lives already lost.'

'And what do you plan to do about this master assassin?'

'Why,' Ban Ryk said, smiling, 'set another against him, or her.'

Harapa Le'en snorted. 'You have a master assassin in your employ?'

'Not directly, though one such is here. That the two will seek each other out is foregone, since they are clearly not upon the same side of the matter.'

'Hmm, your city is in for interesting times, Invigil. In the meantime, my instruction to you is this: constrain your agents. By all means, clear the apostates and heretics. Drive out the false cults of the Crow and the Dogheads and all the rest. But leave the Malazans alone.'

'For how long?'

'You will know, without doubt, when the time has come. Now, I need to be resupplied. Our journey ahead will be a long, arduous one.'

'Ah, then the Inquisitor will be accompanying you.'

'Of course. Too dangerous to leave him here.'

'Oh? Is he at risk of losing all constraint so near the Malazans?'

'The Malazans? No. It is the stupid among the faithful who have good reason to fear. Please lead me now to the High Priestess, so that I may make acquaintance with her.'

'Of course, and shall the Inquisitor join you in this audience?'

'He shall. Does that concern you?'

Ban Ryk smiled. 'Not at all. Please, follow me.'

*   *   *

'What is that dreadful smell?'

Pash, holding above a flame the callipers with the tin basket filled with crushed, compacted rustleaf, paused before murmuring, 'The visitors' carriage and the horses, Holy One.' Enough heat ignited the cake and Pash turned slowly to set it down on the cup of the water-pipe. 'It is ready,' she said.

Shamalle began drawing in and blowing out clouds of scented smoke. 'There, that's better. If eye must water, let it be to sweetness. These horses you mentioned, are they undead? The carriage, did it once serve as a plague wagon?'

'They trampled unbelievers on a track outside the city.'

'Oh! How careless!'

'The unbelievers were likely ensorcelled, Holy One.'

'Where in the Book of Forms and Rituals can we find Trampling?'

'Nowhere, Holy One.'

'I fear I have no choice but to instruct this priest and his Inquisitor to write an amendment to the Book at earliest opportunity. He can title it "The Imposition of Faith by Hoof and Wheel, as Precursor to Funeral Rites". What do you think?'

Pash hesitated where she sat at the High Priestess's slipper-clad feet, then said, 'Unbelievers receive no funeral rites, Holy One.'

'Ah, of course you're right. Silence and indifference enshroud their unfortunate deaths, in itself a tragic observance. Unless, of course, their own chosen deities arrive to spiritually attend said release of souls from their mortal cages. So much for timely miraculous intercession. But then, does the possibility not invite an ontological crisis in the matter of who commands belief in the mortal realm? I am far too stupid to consider such things, thankfully. Leave it to sober men with happy childhoods, blissed and blessed with an easy life, to chew without end the gristle of nuance and interpolation, finding in said discourse all the rage and indignation humanly possible to bolster unto excess their manic zeal. But why, darling rose, is it that zeal so closely aligns with vicious cruelty and inhuman acts of violence? Shall we ask the undead horses?'

A bell sounded and a moment later the twin doors to the sacristy opened and in strode Invigil Ban Ryk and the two guests to whom the carriage belonged.

'Holy One,' intoned Ban Ryk, 'may I present High Priest Harapa Le'en and Inquisitor Vest Dyan.'

'High Priestess Shamalle,' said Harapa, 'it is a pleasure to look upon the mortal manifestation of Va'Shaik. May I say you are an exemplary representative.'

'You mean slothful and fat? Why, thank you, High Priest. And Inquisitor, why such a sour cast to your decidedly plain features? Nobody trampled yet today? Well, it's not even noon, is it? Have faith!' She straightened amidst her heap of pillows. 'Oh! Did you hear me? Have faith? Why, we are in a temple, no less. Yet even here, in the most sacred precinct of our beloved goddess, faith becomes a matter of discourse, if not challenge. How extraordinary!' Then she sat back, resumed smoking.

Inquisitor Vest Dyan bared his teeth in something not even close to a smile. 'My faith is absolute, High Priestess.'

'Spoken in tones of threat. Are you threatening me, Inquisitor?'

'I was charged to begin cleansing from the highest step of the Lost Temple in the Lost City, High Priestess. Outside of the House of Va'Shaik itself, in Hanar Ara, none are above my station. None are immune to my inquisition.'

'Well, thank you for elaborating upon that initial statement. For an instant there, I thought you a janitor driven to extremes. I take it "cleansing", therefore, is euphemistic for torturing and murdering and being as sadistic as possible in the name of our goddess. Who knew Va'Shaik was into splinters under fingernails and giant carriage wheels crushing hapless bodies in the road!'

Ban Ryk, hands clasped before him, his expression strangely benign, now said, 'Holy One Shamalle, vigilance and inquiry are sacred tasks within the church organization, as you well know.'

'Hence "Invigil" for vigilance and "Inquisitor" for inquiry. Now I see! How enlightening! I'd always wondered at those titles. I mean, might they not have emerged in mistaken interpretation of the slurred mumblings of our goddess? Given her eternally inebriated state. But no, it turns out their appearance was subsequent to churchly organization, or should we say "reorganization", or whatever you want to call it, as overseen by the man who sucks stones. Well, gentlemen, thank you for paying a visit. I fear I am drunk on rustleaf and red-stalk tralib, the latter being a most

71

obscure poison the Invigil is testing on my person. Alas, not even close to fatal – do add that to your secret notations, Ban Ryk. Ultimately, your compendium of poisons will be of such encyclopedic stature as to find copies in every assassin headquarters the world over. Think of your future fame! Pash darling, do close the door after them, won't you?'

'It is not for you to dismiss us!' snapped Vest Dyan.

'Isn't it? Oh dear. Well then, what else do you wish to discuss, Inquisitor? Assuming discourse with a drunk woman is your deepest desire. Personally, I find conversing with drunks very frustrating. I know I frustrate myself all the time. Even right now. I wonder how the goddess manages it. But you have been in her presence, haven't you? Oh, do tell me everything! Gossip from the feet of the goddess herself! I can't wait!'

Vest Dyan turned to Harapa Le'en, and then to Ban Ryk. Neither responded to his attention, their gazes fixed upon Shamalle. The Inquisitor frowned, and then cast upon the High Priestess his most disdainful regard. 'I see little value in continuing this conversation.'

Shamalle clapped her hands – somewhat clumsily as she still held the mouthpiece of the water-pipe. 'Exactly! Hence my sending you away. See how easily things become confused when you overstay your welcome? I know I've overstayed mine. Who invited me to this? Never mind. Pash, darling, see me feign weariness? Be a good dear and shoo them away, won't you?'

Pash rose to her feet.

With a half-snarl, Vest Dyan swung round and marched from the chamber. Harapa Le'en bowed and then followed.

Shamalle blinked sleepily at Ban Ryk. 'Invigil? How did I do?'

'Splendidly.'

'Very sweet of you to say so. I hear the purple-leafed variety of tralib is most potent.'

'I shall acquire some at once, Holy One.' And, with a bow, he too departed.

Pash returned to the base of the dais and settled once more.

Shamalle remained seated, smoking, pondering, one foot slowly rising and falling. Like the head of a serpent on a bedroom floor.

*   *   *

'So how fares the Fourteenth Company?'

Captain Hadalin Bhilad moved to seat himself opposite the Adjunct. 'It is as the High Fist said. Undermanned, overworked, exhausted. More to the point, the entire Legion is slowly making its way east to the coast. The Fourteenth Marines constitutes the last elements still active.'

Inkaras Sollit frowned. 'And that has certainly been noticed. This rebellion is too impatient to start. Five months from now, the imperial military presence in Seven Cities will be at its lowest point, in terms of personnel, since before the conquest.' He paused, looking away. It was difficult to look upon his once-lover, to see him at an imposed distance, with a gulf between them that would never again be crossed.

Life was complicated. Relationships never stood still, not for a moment. Those that did not end still changed, evolved, devolved, twisting away from whatever existed before. Sometimes, it was best to simply cut the tie. 'I am contemplating sending you away, Captain. At the very least, from now on, make your residence the Imperial Guard. Not too far away that you cannot be quickly summoned.'

Hadalin dipped his head. 'But far enough. Of course, Adjunct.'

'We were unprofessional,' Inkaras said. 'Both of us are to blame. But it falls to me to correct the matter. Divided loyalties pose a risk we cannot afford.'

'Understood, sir.'

'It was the Emperor's hope to establish a constabulary to manage the provinces of Seven Cities, keeping the military presence minimal. Instead, even before this transition is complete, we are facing yet another rebellion.'

'High Fist Arenfall's reports to the Emperor were accurate,' Hadalin said. 'It follows then that his request for keeping the Legion here was not a ploy empowering his own consolidation, nor a prelude to his challenging the Emperor.'

'Or establishing his own fiefdom,' Inkaras added. 'Does it not occur to you that Arenfall's growing popularity poses little threat once the Legion departs? Perhaps patience will stay the hand.'

When Hadalin did not reply immediately, Inkaras glanced at the man, noting his narrowed gaze.

'Dispense with that look, Captain. I will act if need be. If not me – or you – then the Claw. My point, however, remains. Without the Legion the High Fist is toothless, thus posing no threat at all.'

'This is what made the Emperor suspicious, Adjunct,' Hadalin finally said. 'Upon learning that the Legion was to depart, Arenfall rushes to warn us of impending rebellion.'

Inkaras frowned. 'You doubt him still?'

Hadalin shrugged. 'Fanatics stirring things up? Plenty of that, to be sure, Adjunct. But this land has always been a cauldron of dissent. Spawning religions and cults and rebels and revolutionaries every fortnight. It is, perhaps, ironic that in a more general sense, I happen to agree with Arenfall. Do not send the Legion away.'

Inkaras waved dismissively. 'That decision has already been made. The High Fist remaining determined to hold on to the marines until the last possible moment is what I want you to continue investigating. How are they stamping out spot-fires before the embers even take flame? And this seeming obsession with bandits and mercenaries – neither of whom regularly count among rebels and religious fanatics. There will always be bandits. Let the constabulary deal with them. As for mercenary companies, well, nothing is stopping us from hiring them, after all. A simple solution.'

Hadalin smiled. 'A simple solution to unemployment is employment. A worthy treatise.'

'Are you mocking me, Captain?'

The man's brows lifted. 'No. Not at all. Hiring the mercenaries to bolster the constabulary is indeed an elegant solution. Barring one thing.'

'And that is?'

'They'll end up abusing their power, and their excesses will stain the empire's reputation. Lastly, the constabulary may not possess sufficient martial capability to subsequently deal with them. The High Fist is right in eradicating them, Adjunct. Such companies lingering within the imperial borders are always trouble.'

'I don't disagree,' Inkaras allowed, shifting his regard once more to study the office he'd made his own. But even that notion was suspect, as nothing of his personality was visible in the room's desultory scatter of items and furniture. Still, better scanning the vacuity of his own presence than watching Hadalin Bhilad, the man still holding the knife thrust into his heart. 'Remain watchful, discover all you can about the company of marines. Is there someone among them of extraordinary power, sufficient to pose a threat? I begin to suspect so.'

'The High Fist has agents protecting me, Adjunct. My activities are already being reported to him, no doubt.'

'Agents? What kind of agents?'

'Spies of some sort. I suspect his people have infiltrated half the temples in this city, not to mention control of the streets.'

'Who would have observed the killings at night, yet done nothing to prevent them?'

'I can't say if they did nothing, Adjunct.'

'But not the marines.'

'No, no marines active in the city, sir.'

'This is most curious,' Inkaras admitted. 'You can go, Captain.'

Inkaras didn't look up until the door closed behind Hadalin, and when he did, it was with a wince at the man's sudden absence. What to do, when love was a ghost?

*   *   *

Three marines emerged from the barracks that had once been the Temple of Dryjhna. They descended the steps and strode down the colonnade with its double flank of unpainted limestone pillars on either side. The colonnade, once named for the temple it fronted, was now known as Coltaine Colonnade, at least officially. Local denizens of G'danisban did not call it such, of course. They didn't call it anything at all.

Beyond this was Well of Blue Sky, the nominal centre of the city, a broad expanse of mosaicked cobbles surrounded by a high wall bearing four gates. As soon as the marines exited the colonnade, they passed on their right the gallows platform, pretty much fallen into disuse since the conquest. They began crossing the open round, the well staying on their right as they headed towards Open Gate.

Even this early in the morning, people were gathered, mostly priestly acolytes, drawing holy water to take back to their temples. A few glanced over at the marines, then quickly returned their attention to the well.

One temple servant, upon turning and noticing the marines for the first time, lost grip of the amphora he had been about to lift over his head. It struck the cobbles and shattered, spilling water everywhere. His fellows swore and berated the poor man, but this was momentary, as the mob's attention was swiftly snared by the three marines, who had, in the instant of the amphora's explosive demise, dropped prone to the cobbles.

Now, as they climbed back to their feet, one of the soldiers, a woman of average height and weight, with ratty brownish hair jutting out beneath her skullcap helmet, strode over. She halted before the silent, attentive acolytes, and held up a roundish ball halfway in size between an ostrich egg and a common chicken egg. Every eye fixed upon it.

The woman said, 'You all almost died.' She turned to the servant who'd dropped the amphora. 'Bad luck on your loss. So. Behind the pillars back there you'll find all sorts of amphorae, not being used any more. Feel free to take one.'

Instead, the man bolted, sandalled feet flapping. A moment later, all the others did the same.

Sighing, the marine carefully inserted the sharper into its leather pouch on the webbing beneath her cloak and returned to her companions.

'This is why no one likes you, Fedilap,' Ormo Foamy said, wiping sweat from his brow.

'Oh, there's plenty more reasons, sir, I'm sure.'

'Aye,' said the other sapper, Pulcrude, as they resumed their journey, 'if either of us forgot to drop onto our hands first, why, this whole round would be a smoking crater right now.'

'First thing to learn,' said Fedilap. 'Since, if you don't, well, there ain't a second chance, is there? It's not like a thing you practise, I mean.'

'I hate sappers,' said Ormo. 'But then, don't we all? You two are the worst of 'em, too. You've given me a nervous bladder. It's chronic now. I curse you every time I squirt.'

'You squirt a lot then?' asked Pulcrude. 'I mean, you curse all the time, sir.'

'The smell's a bit of a give-away,' added Fedilap, nodding. 'Mind you, piss is better than shit. Isn't that right, Pulcrude?'

'I have a thesis about you two,' the lieutenant said, eyeing the sappers, 'which I'll expound upon once we get inside.'

'Inside' was the Petals Tavern, an establishment wherein all local business had dried up once the marines decided to make it their off-duty hole. The proprietor's sudden wealth likely eased the sting of being shunned by his friends, neighbours and family. At least, Fedilap reflected, the man hadn't bolted the doors, shuttered the windows and disappeared. Then again, maybe he *had* run off – she couldn't recall the last time she'd seen him. Just the serving boy these days.

Pulcrude snorted. '"Expound upon"? You jawing with the heavies again, sir?'

'I was, I admit it. I like learning new words, which, by the way, supports my thesis, as you'll soon see.'

'"Thesis"!'

They strode through Open Gate. The Petals was on their right.

'Lots of wailing this morning,' observed Pulcrude as they approached the door to the inn's main-floor tavern. 'Heard it even from our cell.'

'Hadn't noticed,' said Fedilap.

The lieutenant led the way inside.

It was early. The tables were all empty, still a bit smelly and sticky from last night. Ormo Foamy picked the table he always picked when given the chance. It was dead centre, the kind of table that made any sane soldier nervous, or, if not nervous, terrified. Fedilap suspected the lieutenant did it on purpose.

They sat. Obly the Boy arrived with a tray on which waited three clay cups of red wine. 'Saw you coming, good sirs.'

'You did?' Ormo asked. 'How?'

'Well,' Obly amended, 'I saw a buncha water-bearers run past.'

'Ah,' said Ormo, nodding. 'Makes sense. And yet, you guessed three of us? Why not six? Ten? Four?'

Obly's single, forehead-spanning eyebrow lost its straight line. 'I just did,' he said, shrugging.

'Really?' Fedilap asked.

Obly's gourd-shaped head bobbed. A moment later, he scurried off.

'Strange,' muttered Ormo, reaching for his cup of wine. 'An alarming detail of predictability, as Scatter might say.'

'No,' said Pulcrude. 'Flutter would say that, not Scatter.'

'Whoever, then. A heavy would say that.'

'Not every—'

'Right,' Ormo cut Pulcrude off, before they ended up at each other's throat. 'Here's my thesis.' He pointed at Pulcrude and then at Fedilap. 'You two.'

'That's your thesis?' Pulcrude asked, reaching up to scratch vigorously under her leather cap, then straightening in sudden attentiveness and throwing a smile at the lieutenant, whose gaze remained fixed on Fedilap, with leaden gravity.

'Yes, you,' confirmed Ormo. He glanced at Pulcrude, but her sudden attention had already wandered and she was now picking a fly out of her wine.

'Out with it, then,' grated Fedilap.

'Thanks. It's just this. You're both shallow.'

Fedilap blinked. 'Shallow? What do you mean?'

'Just that,' Ormo said. 'You're mere sketches, like someone seen from a distance. By someone with poor vision. There's a blurriness about you. But don't take it too hard. Not your fault. There's just not enough there, you know?'

After a moment, Fedilap nodded solemnly, and said, 'I think you may be right, sir. Is it because we're sappers?'

'Of course it is,' replied Ormo Foamy.

In the meantime, Pulcrude had retrieved the half-drowned fly from her wine, and it now perched, or maybe writhed, on the finger she held up before her.

'You destroy things for a living,' Ormo continued. 'It takes a certain kind of shallow to take pleasure in that.'

When Pulcrude flicked away the fly all three watched it sail haplessly to the floor.

'Really, sir,' said Fedilap, 'you think we actually *like* destroying things?'

'Yes.'

Fedilap waited for her fellow sapper to look over, and when she did, both women shrugged. Then she cleared her throat and said, 'But having said that, I would suggest that the others in the squad are even worse. Including you, sir.'

Ormo frowned. 'Now you're challenging my thesis. I should never have taken you two out for a walk. Should've kept you locked up. I could be sitting here drinking on my own, utterly content with my own shallow self. Instead, here I am having to share my puddle with you two.'

'Well,' Pulcrude asked, leaning forward, 'why did you?'

At that moment the inn door opened and in strode their captain. He walked over, pulled out the last chair at the table and sat facing the two sappers. 'Explained it yet, Ormo?' he asked.

Obly reappeared with a fourth tankard, then vanished again into the back room.

'No, sir,' Ormo replied. 'I would've, only I don't know why you wanted us.'

Captain Hung's sour face soured even further. 'Hmm, I might have forgotten.'

'I think so, sir,' Ormo agreed.

The captain thumped the table with one palm. 'No matter. You're all here now and that's what counts.'

'We like to think so,' Fedilap said.

'I'm thinking of sending you down into the Under Quarter.'

'It's flooding down there, or so I heard,' observed Pulcrude.

'Water table's rising,' Fedilap added, 'on account of the Raraku Sea.'

'You don't want us to stop the flooding?' Pulcrude asked the captain. 'I mean, we might be able to slow it down some, but there ain't no stopping it.'

'True,' agreed Fedilap. 'Of course, we can always divert it.'

'Oh, I hadn't thought of that. I guess I'm shallower than you, Fed.'

'You are. It's an engineering problem, so the least shallow among us should handle that kind of thinking. That's me. No offence intended, Captain.'

'What about me being offended?' Ormo demanded.

Fedilap sighed. 'I was hoping you wouldn't ask. Anyway, sir, we can divert things, but it'll be messy. I mean, there's people living down there.'

'And about a million bhokarala,' added Pulcrude.

'Actually,' Fedilap pointed out, 'the little apes only forage down below. They nest in the tombs above ground.'

Pulcrude frowned. 'Not what I heard.'

'Well, the tombs run deep, so you could say they're half in, half out. Above the ruins, but sometimes punching down into them. Personally, I never could figure out why tombs and barrows so often have steps leading down. What's wrong with ground level? Or even hilltops? What is it about holes, anyway? Oh sure, you might say holes and dead people go together. Still.'

'Bastran is a hilltop cemetery, Fed,' said Pulcrude.

'With tombs punching down, way down. Then again, maybe you need a hill to give you all that below-surface stuff to dig down into. Better than bedrock, right?'

'Are you two finished?' Captain Hung asked. 'Good. Now, this is just a scouting mission. How many cults are active down there? How many sanctorum-style temples and altar-chambers are there that we don't yet know about? Another question. How many people are living down there?'

'What about the flooding?' Pulcrude asked.

'Oh,' said Fedilap, 'I get it. That flood's going to bring 'em all to the surface. And that could be a problem, right, Captain? As in, swarms of bedraggled rats, only human and ape versions. And real rats, too.'

'Or a fly drowning in wine,' said Ormo, squinting across at Pulcrude. She scratched under her cap again. 'A mission of mercy, then.'

Fedilap, Pulcrude and Ormo all looked over to where the fly had landed. It hadn't moved. It was dead.

The inn door opened again and in strode Captain Veroosh. He halted suddenly, one step inside the room, eyes widening. 'Have you lost your mind, Hung? You let them out!'

Draining his tankard, Hung rose to his feet. 'Temporary. Any news, Veroosh?'

'Aye, it's official. Not quite settled, though. No, not that at all.'

Obly appeared with a new tankard.

CHAPTER FOUR

It is a conceit to imagine the realms of magic as fixed or static, as if immovable, as if outside of the ever-changing universe. All forces are in eternal flux, evolving by their own rules – if such things can be said to have rules. What the mortal mind can grasp is but a fraction of magic's reality. Exercise hubris at your peril.

It is also a conceit to imagine the realm surrounding you, for all its mundane familiarity, its plain and simple patterns of cause and effect, as fixed or static. More to the point, the mortal mind, even here, can grasp but a fraction. Hubris, in this instance, is not even subtle.

Opening statement in The Astari Bridge Collapse lawsuit, *Untan High Court Proceedings*, Advocate Burle for the Defence

T'Sual Tavern had a back room with no floor. Fedilap stood at the edge, just inside the door, her boots perched on the last few brick pave-stones before everything fell away to misty, damp darkness. She sniffed. 'Sewage.'

'This morning's sewage,' Pulcrude said. She turned and walked back through the larder, returning a moment later with one of her hands dragging along Chorb, the tavern-keeper. She shook him. 'Did you shit over this, Chorb?'

The scrawny man's eyes were bulging with panic. 'What if I did? It's a damned hole, woman!'

'That hole goes down into the Under Quarter! People live down there!'

'Not *right* down there,' Chorb retorted. 'That'd be stupid, on account of all the shit.'

Pulcrude released the man, who quickly scrambled back through the larder, muttering a string of curses. 'We need a different way down,' she said.

'Don't be silly,' Fedilap replied. 'Just be careful where you put your feet and hands. He ain't dumping right over the ladder, is he?'

'Begging the question of who has a ladder going down their shit-hole. Anyway, you're such an optimist.'

'Am I?' Fedilap frowned. 'Ever noticed how so few sappers are women?'

'Most of us ain't that stupid.'

'Hmm, hadn't thought of it that way. Makes sense.'

'Of course you didn't.'

'But you did.'

'No, I heard it from somebody.'

'Ah, that makes even more sense.' Fedilap pulled a pair of leather gloves from her belt and began putting them on, cinching tight each finger in slow, methodical fashion. 'The avoidance of said crap requires finesse.'

'That leaves us out.'

'Sometimes, faking finesse will do. Practice makes perfect, right?'

'What you're really saying, Fed, is "if only we weren't so stupid".'

'Witless with style, that's me,' said Fedilap, nodding.

Pulcrude moved up alongside her and stared down into the gloom. 'Not one of the obvious ways in, meaning nobody'll know we're even down there, snuffling around. But they'll know we've been if we end up smelling like shit.'

'Take it slow and careful, stay on the rungs, and don't even think of climbing onto the ladder before I'm down and clear.'

'That only happened once. I know better now.'

'I hope so, since I'm guessing you're loaded up. You are, aren't you?'

Pulcrude scowled. 'I don't like going anywhere unarmed.'

'We're not unarmed. We have swords, we have knives. I've even got a hammer.'

'Like I said, unarmed.'

'What have you got, then?'

'Two sharpers, three burners, three crackers, one spike.'

'Sharpers? Girl, listen to me. We're going to be in low-ceilinged tunnels and old alleys and streets, with piles of rubble over our heads. A sharper will bring it all down, killing everyone.'

'That's right. It's for a last stand situation. Take 'em with us, right?'

'Okay. But then, how come you got two of 'em?'

Pulcrude sighed. 'In case one's a dud, of course.'

'We almost never get duds, not with sharpers, anyway.'

'Just takes one.'

Fedilap looked down into the pit again. 'If you fall, your ghost better start running, cos mine's coming after it.'

'If your ghost runs like you do, you'll never catch me.'

Fedilap turned round and edged her way onto the ladder, carefully moving each foot down onto the first rung. 'I'm relieved to say he never uses this. Chorb.'

'Unless he's careful. Remember that heavy, what was his name? Bakkra? Used to study every dump he made? What was all that about? Never got the chance to ask.'

Fedilap moved down another few rungs. 'How'd he die anyway?'

'It was an off-duty accident. Him and that madwoman with the nauseatingly beautiful hair—'

'Stillwater.'

'Right, her. Broke into a barrow, right outside Unta.'

'Noble burial grounds? Those are still being used.'

'Used? The dirt covering the entrance was still damp. The family was so outraged they hired assassins, and a damned mage. Bakkra was knifed behind a tavern, too drunk to fight 'em off.'

Fedilap was halfway down, if the echoes and trickling water sounds below were any indication. 'Stillwater avenged him?'

'Probably. The offended family disappeared. All of 'em. Bakkra, the heavy who had to stop and smell all the roses. And we know his biggest mistake.'

Fedilap nodded. 'Don't be friends with Stillwater.'

A moment later, and in unison, both women said, 'Poor Bakkra.'

Fedilap stepped down onto broken bricks. Slimy broken bricks, and the slime was pungent. 'I'm down and I stepped in it,' she reported.

'Light the room up,' Pulcrude called down. 'I'm on my way.'

Fedilap pulled a pebble from her hip-pouch, glared at it for a moment until it began shedding greenish light. The expanding glow revealed a canted wall to one side, shattered furniture to another, and a black, fetid pool covering the rest. She moved away from under the ladder. 'Someone tried to seal the passageway,' she observed.

Pulcrude's voice drifted down, 'With what?'

'A dining room.'

'Well that's stupid. Never eat and shit in the same room. Everyone knows that.'

Fedilap made her way over to the wrecked furniture. The dining table, minus its legs, served as the principal barrier, vertically pushed up against what was probably a hole in the wall. Chairs and innumerable wooden legs held the table in place.

Pulcrude arrived without explosive mishap and joined Fedilap.

'That's a lot of legs jamming that table. Think something nasty was trying to get in here?'

'Looks that way.'

After a moment, Pulcrude said, 'I think we've gone far enough. Let's go back up and report to the captain.'

'Saying what?'

'Isn't it obvious? The whole Under Quarter is fucked. A nightmare of doom. Demon-ridden, dripping blood, floating bodies all bloated with piggy eyes. A reaper's feast of slaughter old and new.'

Fedilap glanced at her partner. 'You got all that from a barricaded door?'

Pulcrude nodded.

'And here I was thinking they didn't want their dinner interrupted.'

'Yours is a feeble imagination.'

'That's what makes me so practical, Pul.' Stepping forward, she started kicking away the angled legs.

'What are you doing?'

'Captain let us out of our cell, girl. Let's take advantage of it.'

'Oh, fine. I'll point out right now that me being armed is probably a good thing and you'll thank me for it before too long.'

'I told you before. If people are living down here and they are, everything will be fine.'

As she kicked away another leg, the table lurched suddenly.

Both sappers stepped back, Fedilap's right hand on her sword-grip, Pulcrude's right hand under her half-cloak.

'That's ominous,' Pulcrude said.

'What's ominous is you reaching for a damned sharper before anything else!'

'Maybe I'm seeing a last stand here, all right?'

'Already? And you call *me* the pessimist.'

'What you call "practical", you mean. I never call you a pessimist. Mind you, I'm not sure you're very practical, either. Despite your weak imagination.'

'So basically, what you're really saying is that I'm stupid.'

'I was carefully stepping around that word, darling.'

'You're so sweet, did you know that?'

Pulcrude shrugged. 'People have said as much.'

'We should be friends.'

'What? Fedilap, we've never been friends. We never will be. We hang out in different crowds.'

'What crowds? We're in a fucking marine squad. And when we're not working, we're locked up.'

'If we had crowds, they'd be different ones.'

'Maybe yours would.'

The door groaned, then a lower corner shifted and in came a stream of icy water.

'Oh, now it makes sense,' said Fedilap. 'No monsters, Pulcrude. Get your hand off that sharper.'

'No way a door pushed up against a hole in a wall can seal it from water.'

'It hasn't been, obviously. Look at that pool behind us.'

'That would've filled up, eventually coming level with what's behind this table.'

'Maybe it will. Especially now.'

The water was sweeping over their feet, gurgling and making other watery sounds in the chamber behind them. The back-flow brought a turd bobbing up alongside Fedilap's left boot. She sighed. 'Pull it right back. We knew we'd be getting wet, after all. Everybody gets wet down here.'

Together, they shifted the table enough to edge past it, entering a low passage that almost immediately intersected a narrow street running at an angle, where the ceiling overhead was slightly higher, though no less treacherous for its projecting bricks, wooden beams and sharp-edged, broken blocks of stone. The water filling the street was shin-deep, so too now in the room behind them.

'That's cold,' Pulcrude said as they stepped into it. 'You'd think it wouldn't be, with all that desert and sun above us.'

'This water ain't ever seen the light of day, girl. It's coming up from way down.'

'Doesn't smell as bad as Chorb's puddle.'

The glowing stone was still in Fedilap's right hand. The light it cast reached out no more than a few paces. But off to the right, twenty or so paces away, the street found another intersection, where ambient lantern-light gleamed on the rippled surface of the stream.

The sound of trickling water was everywhere, but a deeper echo accompanied it, filled with distant echoes that might be voices, shifting stones, splashes. The air was fetid, but cold enough to slow rot and decay.

Fedilap grunted. 'Chorb's daily contribution highlights the state of humanity,' she said. 'Someone higher up's always shitting on the heads of people lower down.'

'That's heavy's talk, woman. Stop it. But you're right. Chorb needs a punch in the face and a good rattling shake.'

'Revolutionary,' Fedilap accused. 'No wonder no one trusts you.'

'Wrong. The next time us lowlifes get fed up enough and rise up to drag down all established authority, why, you can *trust* me to be first in line.'

Leading the way, Fedilap began sloshing up the street towards the distant lamplight. 'People will live anywhere, given the chance.'

'No taxes, no tithes, no law enforcement. Just complete, utter freedom.'

Both started as a bhokaral bolted across the street a few paces head, splashing from a hole in one tilted wall and into a crevice in the other.

'Aye,' said Fedilap, 'the freedom to impose taxes, tithes and enforcement via protection rackets and nasty gangs.' She came opposite the crevice and peered into it. 'How did it fit through that?'

'Tiny heads,' Pulcrude said.

They resumed their sloshing walk.

'Besides,' she continued, 'coinage buys trouble every time. Makes things unequal, and that's when the bullies move in and take over.'

A few paces before the intersection, Fedilap paused and held out a hand to halt Pulcrude. 'So,' she said in a low tone, 'I know we're not friends or anything, and our orders were to check out the situation down here and all that. But we don't like bullies, right? I mean, we share that at least.'

'What are you suggesting, dearest?'

'Just a little exercise in social, uh, adjustment.'

'What for? Nothing down here's gonna last anyway.'

'Exactly. That makes it manageable. We build an empire that lasts, oh, I don't know, a month. Think of it. The usual sudden rise, explosive you might say, sweeping all else from its path. Sudden cultural flowering, wealth abounding. Then, in the second week, the consolidation, followed by the first cracks in the foundations. But it's all still good, good enough to ignore the warning signs.'

'Week three,' said Pulcrude, 'the beginning of fractionalization.'

'Regional disputes, local block leaders with swelled heads, thinking they could do better if they were in charge. Greed arrives. Corruption, the gathering close of muscle for protection, and then enforcement, and then threats and finally, violence. It all explodes!'

Pulcrude nodded. 'Civil war. Anarchy, chaos, blood in the streets.'

'That's week four.'

'Week four. End of empire, everything in ruins. Knowledge lost. The survivors forget how to light cookfires.'

'Start eating everything raw. Sickness. Plague.'

'Floating shit.'

'Beady bhokaral eyes glinting in cracks and crevices.'

Pulcrude smiled. 'Let's do it. I'll be Empress.'

'Hold on, it was my idea!'

'You can be the brains behind the throne. You can be my Dancer.'

'I'm not a subtle assassin, Pul.'

Pulcrude tapped the faint bulge of the sharper-belt beneath her cloak. 'More subtle than me.'

'Point taken. Besides, with me behind the throne, why, I'll be the first to betray you.'

'Of course. It always plays out that way. But like Kellanved, I'll just disappear. Presumed murdered, but no body ever found.'

'And I'll disappear too,' said Fedilap, 'leaving the necessary power vacuum for the sudden, violent dissolution of everything we built up. Fire and smoke, screams and mayhem.'

'Okay, but what then?'

Fedilap considered, then her shoulders sagged, and she sighed. 'Captain Hung does a Mallick Rel. He locks us back up in our cells. The rest of the squad glares their hatred at us.'

'Envy, you mean.'

'Precisely. We're not friends any of us.'

'That's for sure.'

'It'll be our last mission, you and me. He'll never risk us being sent anywhere ever again.'

'Not without supervision.'

'The lieutenant.'

'Ormo Foamy. I hate Ormo.'

'Me too.' Fedilap ran some fingers through her ratty hair. 'How about we just follow orders?'

'Smart decision, for a stupid sapper.'

'It is, isn't it?'

'Don't get complacent. You ready?'

Fedilap nodded. 'I am. Let's get stuck in, girl.'

They headed for the intersection, where the voices of commerce and life echoed from both sides, along with plenty of splashing and swirling and the occasional derisive hoot of a bhokaral.

*   *   *

'Captain Dunsparrow departed with her new recruits this morning,' said Captain Hung.

Arenfall nodded. Both men stood on the balcony overlooking the inner courtyard of Imperium House, a courtyard mostly overgrown from the huge potted plants situated here and there around the circular pool in the centre. Dead leaves and snaking vines and roots covered most of the pave-stones. All the blossoms in sight were past their peak, beginning to wilt and rot. Some kind of fly surrounded each flower in thick, spinning clouds. The pool was bright emerald.

'And Captain Veroosh?' Arenfall asked after a few moments.

'In the archives, sir.'

'Again?'

'Every chance he gets,' Hung said.

'And what is he looking for, Captain?'

Hung shrugged. 'Sometimes I wonder if even he knows. Without doubt, the rest of us haven't a clue.'

'Is he addled?'

'Undoubtedly, sir,' replied Hung.

'At risk of being problematic?'

'Oh, I wouldn't go that far, sir. His squad likes him well enough. Their efficiency gives no cause for concern.'

'Even though their captain's skull is full of scrambled eggs.'

88

'We're marines, sir. We're all a little off. Especially the officers.'

'Even Dunsparrow?' the High Fist asked, glancing over.

Hung met the man's gaze. 'She has no sense of humour.'

'Oh. That's bad.'

They stood in silence for a short time. Whatever was holding Arenfall's attention in the courtyard below had Hung baffled. He couldn't see much down there worth the time or the concentration. 'Thought I saw Corporal Hasten Thenu the other day.'

'Did you?'

'Half a block away, in a crowd. Not with his squads out west at all.'

'And what did his captain say about it?'

'She smiled.'

'Smiled?'

'Humourlessly.'

'Ah. Anything else to report, Captain?'

'I sent Fedilap and Pulcrude down into the Under Quarter. It would be useful to get a sense of how fast the water's rising, and what the people down there are likely to do.'

'Well, it won't come as a surprise, one assumes.'

'No, sir. But whatever disruption occurs once the threshold is crossed will start below ground, and when it erupts in the city streets, or even just around Bastran Hill, it will be full-blown.'

'And you want your sappers to report on their reading of that?'

'Aye, sir.'

'Captain, the city garrison will be the ones responding to the disruption, not the marines. Your task remains as it was. While you may be headquartered here in G'danisban, this city is not your responsibility.' Arenfall paused, and then added, 'But I'll welcome their report nonetheless.'

Hung hesitated, and then said, 'It's also possible that Fedilap and Pulcrude will cause some trouble down there.'

'In what way?'

'They may object to the myriad injustices and criminal activity they're likely to witness.'

'Object?'

'Sir, if they follow orders, they should be back out in a few days at most. On the other hand, if they take too much offence, they may go off-piste as it were.'

'I see. And when will you know which way they've gone, Captain?'

'As I said, sir. Back out in a few days. If not . . .'

Arenfall sighed. 'Why is it marines are so unmanageable?'

'Was that rhetorical, sir?'

'Not intentionally. But I imagine that is a question that's echoed down the decades.'

Hung nodded. 'Blame Dassem Ultor.'

'We all do. Of course, it then becomes self-fulfilling, in that recruiters send the odd ones their way.'

'Aye, sir. We know what to do with them.'

*   *   *

Fedilap dipped her sword into the water and gave it a shake. 'This is convenient,' she said. 'See how quickly all the blood washes off? You don't need to wipe it down or anything.' She lifted the blade and studied it. 'Anyway, I really hate protection rackets.'

Pulcrude was busy in the room with its watery floor and plank walkways and floating tabletops, using her own sword to prod the bodies bobbing about. 'No fakers in this bunch,' she concluded, sheathing her weapon. 'But I was cold iron. You, lady, weren't. You were hot.'

'I told you. These kind of operations offend me on a personal level.'

'Why?'

'History,' she replied, that old sour taste coming back along with all the memories.

'Fine. I'm asking because, well, are we really sure this bunch was working a racket here?'

'You saw the fear in the eyes of everybody on this block. Everybody but this crew. These ones, they looked . . . smug.'

'Maybe it's smugness that gets under your skin, Fedilap.'

'That too. But this brand of shit has a particular smell. Besides, they clearly objected to us kicking in their door. I'd lined up a whole list of questions I never got a chance to ask.'

'All that brain work, wasted.'

'That annoyed me, too.'

Pulcrude moved up onto the platform at one end of the room and sat herself on the damp settee with the fabric of its arms worn down to reveal the bony wood. She crossed her legs and lounged. 'Of course, wiping out this gang will just open up opportunities for neighbouring gangs to expand their own petty empires of graft, extortion and unwholesomeness.'

Fedilap nodded. 'A veritable cascade of criminality.'

'Feeding the furnace of your outrage, darling? Hot, hot, hot.'

'You just stay cold and it'll all balance out.'

'I'd like to propose we float these bodies out into the street and let the current take them away.'

'Away?'

'Somebody else's problem, right? Not to mention a subtle but not so subtle pronouncement to at least the downstream rival gang. Meanwhile, we set up here. Our very own protection racket. Only we don't extort money. We stick to the protecting side of things.'

Fedilap studied the other woman for a long moment. Then she said, 'You know, the legend goes that what you're describing is precisely what Kellanved and Dancer did, in Malaz City, from which the whole empire was born.'

'There's a delicious synchronicity to it, isn't there?'

'You want to be Kellanved.'

'That comparison should be obvious, even to you.'

Fedilap began the onerous task of dragging floating bodies to the doorway and shoving them into the street current. As far as currents went, it wasn't much, which meant the bodies crowded the front of the building for a while, which in turn drew in locals to stare down at them. Someone then got the idea to take a knife to one particularly hateful face – blissful in death notwithstanding – until it wasn't recognizable as a face any more. Then others joined in on select others, and the water flowed red for a time.

Fedilap watched from the doorway.

Eventually, a red-faced woman of spherical girth waded up to stand before her, scowling. 'You takin' o'er then? But we all paid this week and we ain't got nothin' t'spare.'

'I'd imagine you never have anything to spare,' Fedilap said.

'Sometimes excuses are true, y'know?'

'Right. Well, we don't want nothing from any of you. But we decided to not let anybody else move in, either. Somebody does, you send them our way. To our new office here.'

The woman's scowl was still there, but she was now looking downstream. 'Expect one of Sug's to come up for a look around, once that blood in the water reaches 'em.'

'Sounds . . . protracted.' Fedilap looked back into the room behind her. Pulcrude was still draped all over the settee. 'Sweetie, I'm thinking we should get ahead of this.'

'Okay. How so?'

'Well, by getting behind all this blood. Get off your big round butt. Let's go take a slow walk downstream.'

After a heavy sigh, Pulcrude stood up, pausing to adjust her sword-belt. 'A promenade? Arm in arm, darling?'

'Revealing your innermost desires is unseemly, Pulcrude. We don't like each other, remember? Now, get out here. We're off to see someone named Sug.'

*   *   *

Sug was having it good. One of his henchmen was even named Hench. Could it get any better? They were soaking up coin from the residents of six whole streets and two levels in three of them, the other levels being overrun by bhoks. All of the prostitutes were keeping their complaints to themselves, and none of the neighbouring jumpers had the clout to cause trouble. Meaning, they were scared. Meaning, Sug's plans of expansion were on pace.

In fact, and this was always bubbling and seething in the back of his mind, he was building something special down here. Almost a government. Running smoothly, too. He had his officers and they were loyal, keeping their corruption at low levels of coin-slipping, which in turn made justice negotiable, which was what seemed to make most people, if not happy, at least not unhappy.

People wanted to live as freely as possible. The constraints on that freedom needed in turn to be plainly good, obviously beneficial, in service to general well-being and all that. So long as the reasons for each and every rule were explained, people were okay with them. Poverty only went criminal when injustice got out of hand, especially coming down from high above. Nobody liked seeing others get away with stuff.

Granted, a certain amount of bullying was required on occasion. There was always someone who didn't like staying in the queue. Who figured the rules wasn't for them.

That's where Hench, Gryba, Stipple, Ance and Morco came in, and a half-dozen others Sug could call upon if required. His modest army of peacekeepers, and what greater virtue was possible than keeping the peace?

Civilization was a balancing act, and Sug knew he was good at it. Just the right amount of freedom blended almost seamlessly with the giant spiky fist of coercion. It was an art, in fact. Sug, the Artist. Sug, the benign dictator, the king blessed with the gifts of divine providence. Sug, the—

There was a ramp that led down to the doors at street level, on account of all the water, so when the doors were suddenly kicked in, a slosh of pink water rolled up, far enough so that Sug could see it, halting his line of thought, and a moment later two figures appeared on the ramp, coming up and into Sug's view.

Morco and Ance had been guarding the entrance. These two weren't Morco and Ance.

Sug, seated on his makeshift throne in his self-styled throne room with its brocaded tapestries positioned high enough to avoid the damp wooden floorboards, off to one side his work-table where he conducted deliberations and whatnot, the tall candlesticks flanking his chair with the candlelight casting a flickering, ominous play of light and shadow across his craggy features, and of course the crossbow alongside the chair which he now lifted into view, ratcheting it into its lock and now a thick-headed quarrel nestled in place, were all more or less accurately reflected in the roving eyes of these two women who now stood before him, not quite at eye level given the sloped floor.

'Which one of you wants to die first?' Sug asked.

The red-haired, beefy woman on the left looked across to her less robust, brown-haired companion. 'Was that a trick question? I occasionally dream of seeing your face all lifeless and un-irritating, Fedilap. So in that context, clearly you need to die before me.'

'After an eternity in your company,' the woman named Fedilap replied, 'that would be a mercy.' She turned back to Sug. 'It should be me, we've decided. I want to be the one to die first.'

'Granted,' Sug said, shifting the aim of his crossbow slightly. From the street outside, someone was shouting. Sounded like Gryba. In a few moments, these two would be between a whole lot of trouble. 'That blood in the water behind you, have you been unkind to my police officers?'

'Police officers?' the red-haired woman asked. 'That explains the uniforms.'

Fedilap then said, 'We're shutting down all the protection rackets.

That fug-house across the street with those little boys and girls sporting dead eyes and bruised bodies. Places like that.'

Sug sighed. 'If not me then someone else.' He could see the water swirling at the base of the ramp and that told him Gryba was in place. 'Now, my empire has been invaded before. You two are not the first barbarians trying to take down my entirely necessary and mostly just civilization. Because, you see, that's your problem. My subjects are content. Well, more content than most people down here. I'm not especially cruel. I like to think of myself as fair-minded. As for the fug-house, it's as much an orphanage that pays for its own upkeep as anything else. The world is an unkind place, alas.'

Fedilap was nodding through all of this. 'Yeah, figured you had it all worked out in your head. To not poorly reflect all that venal ugliness. Hence the smug expression.'

'Uh-oh,' muttered the red-haired woman.

Fedilap gestured, and then frowned.

Sug smiled. 'Was that magic you tried there? Too bad about the floor under your feet, those boards, and all the otataral nails in them.' He shrugged, then fired the crossbow.

Somehow, with barely four paces between him and the woman, his shot missed. She'd dipped a shoulder, slid to one side, impossibly fast. In the meantime, even as the quarrel shattered against the wall behind Fedilap, the other woman had ducked, spun and tossed something into the corridor that led down to the doors. A deafening *crack* sounded, rebounding back into the room. The numbed shock that followed was suddenly broken by Gryba's shriek, and he staggered into view, falling onto the ramp, a mass of shredded flesh.

The red-haired woman stepped close and drove her short-sword into the back of Gryba's head. The shrieks stopped.

Fedilap spoke. 'Best guard the doors, Pulcrude, in case anybody else shows up.' To Sug, she then said, 'Problem with crossbows, right? Miss and you're screwed.'

'That was a munition,' Sug said, licking lips that had gone cold and dry. 'You're marines. Or outlawed ex-marines. If the latter, can I bribe you to leave?'

'Well,' said Fedilap, 'if we were barbarians in truth, why, that'd work just fine. Unfortunately, we're not ex anything. It was a good try, though.'

'What would your High Fist think of his marines moving into criminal activities?'

'Ah!' Fedilap smiled. 'Then you acknowledge the criminality of your, uh, activities? Pulcrude, that sounded like an admission of guilt to me. How about you?'

'The crime here,' Sug said, 'belongs to you, not me. I am an organizer, plain and simple. It's not perfect – I'll be the first to admit to that – but it's better than the alternatives. Indeed, if you really want to bring law and order to all of Under Quarter, you'd do worse than to join me. After all, I possess knowledge about this benighted realm, whilst you clearly possess the, shall we say, explosive persuasion that might – no, certainly *will* – be required. What say you?'

From the doorway, Pulcrude said, 'Got a few more coming up on us, Fed. Hurry up, will you?'

Fedilap looked thoughtful as she said, 'It's an interesting proposal, Sug – you are Sug, aren't you?'

'I am.'

'But some pretty basic laws would need to be changed, before we could agree to any of that.'

'Such as.'

'Your fug-house, for one.'

'I don't run it. The proprietor simply rents the building from me.'

'We may have to kill that proprietor.'

'Be my guest. He's odious.'

Pulcrude backed from the doorway. 'Hey, Fed?'

'What?'

'We gotta whisper a bit, you and me. Right now.'

Frowning, Fedilap held up a hand to Sug. 'Negotiations in progress, right?'

Sug nodded.

Fedilap then joined Pulcrude. They put their heads together, but Sug could see that they did most of their talking using hand-signs. A moment later, both women moved to one side, and up the ramp came Hench and Stipple.

Meeting Sug's gaze, Hench said, 'We settling things out, boss?'

'We are, I think. That is, Fedilap, are we?'

'We are,' she replied. 'And yeah, we got a deal. Let's expand this empire of yours, Sug, until it's the only one standing.'

'You know,' Sug said, 'Ance, Gryba and Morco really didn't have to die, did they?'

Fedilap shrugged. 'Mistakes were made.'

As the tension drained from the room, Sug noted, in passing, the ferociously angry expression on Stipple's face, and wondered at it. It wasn't like Stipple was friends with any of her dead companions. Hated all four of them, in fact. Sug hadn't much liked them either.

But never mind that. Things were looking up. Sug's natural state of optimism had a lot going for it. Useful to remind himself of that on occasions like these, what with all the blood in the water.

Besides, marines in the pocket wasn't anything to sneer at.

*　　*　　*

Inkaras Sollit sat on the padded bench. To his left was Arenfall behind his desk. To the right was the office's door. There was no question in the Adjunct's mind that the High Fist was wary, some confusion stirred between them making this meeting slow to start.

A city gripped in fear, with mobs of fanatics on the prowl every night, and if the presence of a Claw remained unofficial, at least for Arenfall, certainly the suspicion had to be there.

As much as Inkaras offered up the pretence of solidarity, he suspected that Arenfall was beginning to feel isolated, a lone figure on a small island. The sensation could not be pleasant. Alas, putting the man at ease was not, for the moment, in the Adjunct's interest.

'The predations of the Va'Shaik cultists against other faiths is becoming an issue,' Inkaras now said. 'The empire's official stance is freedom of worship—'

'Barring a few exceptions,' Arenfall cut in.

'True, to a point. Domination of any single cult in the Malazan military is forbidden, for obvious reasons. Even the God of War poses interests that, well, let us say might not always align with the empire. Bloodthirsty expansion is a thing of the past, after all.'

'Sometimes,' said Arenfall, 'staying the hand can lead to extremes of violence, where no one is in control of anything. The Legion is both worn out and in need of recruits. Worse yet, its march to the east coast makes its imminent departure an open secret.'

Inkaras nodded. 'Clearly, there are some main players in the city who aim to expunge all rival cults.'

'Va'Shaik.'

'For whom,' Inkaras continued, 'both continental religious homogeneity and the collapse of imperial control are central to the faith, or at least its purported resolution.'

Arenfall shrugged. 'The doctrine is muddled, Adjunct. Once you apply holy words to secular interpretation, the very sacredness of those words becomes tarnished. Oppression of rival beliefs answers mundane needs, not godly ones. The same for political independence.'

'Of course,' Inkaras agreed. 'But that is the messy reality, and it's the messy reality we must deal with.'

'By sending away the last full legion on the continent?'

'There is a reserve legion at Aren Outside the Fall.'

'A long way from where the trouble will start, as Coltaine showed us,' Arenfall countered. 'Adjunct, do you think I would have chosen to move my headquarters here to G'danisban if I had known the Legion would soon be gone? Besides, the High Fist in Aren Outside the Fall is consistent with historical precedent.'

Inkaras frowned. 'What do you mean?'

'He's incompetent, corrupt, and probably a coward. Just like Pormqual: should things take flame, he'll probably sit tight and hold his army behind the city walls. Coltaine knew to not count on Aren and its army and so do I.'

'Which leaves you with the marines.'

'For now, and not much longer. Accordingly, I will use them.'

'They are too few—'

'Probably.'

'I can cleanse the Temple of Va'Shaik, High Fist.'

'Cleanse.' Arenfall looked away. 'Sure. Do that. Set fire to all of Seven Cities. I suppose that's one way to force the Legion to wheel about.' He was silent for a moment, and then he shook his head and met the Adjunct's gaze. 'I am no Coltaine. One legion won't be enough.'

'And if I take command of the legion in Aren Outside the Fall?'

'But you won't.'

'Why do you say that?'

'Because you are here, Adjunct, not there.'

'The uprising has not yet begun.'

Arenfall's sigh was a frustrated one. 'Adjunct, it began months ago. I imagine the Emperor has no experience of peat-fires. If he did, he'd understand. I do not send the marines by warren to places of modest dispute, or bare hints of smoke. I send them to crush the growing brood of firestorms, the children of the Whirlwind.'

'Your bandits and mercenaries?'

'You fear an army united by faith, Adjunct. Is it any different from an army hired by a single cult? Here on the ground, I see little difference.'

'We know the location of Hanar Ara,' Inkaras said, musing on Arenfall's words.

'Go after the goddess herself?'

'Well, who can say she's a goddess in truth, High Fist? A foundling from Sha'ik's desert camp, now grown into adulthood. But that woman is dissolute, so obese as to be bed-ridden, so bound in numbing fumes she rarely even so much as opens her eyes.'

Arenfall's gaze was level. 'You have agents in Hanar Ara.'

'We keep an eye on things.'

'You have positioned yourself well in advance of me, Adjunct. In turn, I conclude that you – or the Emperor – intend to act independently of my own plans. This puts both plans at risk—'

'This is what I came here to determine, High Fist,' Inkaras said. 'Fortunately, for us both, I see no possible clash, and give you leave to proceed as you intended.'

'I would know what your plan is, Adjunct. Assassinate Felisin Younger?'

Inkaras started. 'I had no idea you knew her name.'

'She had another one.'

'No doubt,' said Inkaras. 'Have you ever wondered, High Fist? This orphan child of Sha'ik's desert camp being given the name of Adjunct Tavore's lost sister? A sister who presumably died in the uprising at the mining camp? Was this some ex-patriot's bitter joke, do you think? Korbolo Dom, perhaps? Once he learned of Tavore's arrival in Aren, and her command of the retributive army? The one that eventually crushed the Whirlwind? Or Kamist Reloe, for that matter.' Inkaras paused, studying the High Fist. 'Your father was there. I suspect that you know far more than I, and certainly more than you are prepared to tell me.'

'You may unleash the rebellion, Adjunct. If her body now serves as the immobile, somnolent prison for the goddess herself, killing that body would be a terrible mistake.'

'The possibility exists,' Inkaras allowed. 'Hence my freedom to make

98

that call. That said, obliterating Hanar Ara while sparing the woman in its temple is possible. It would certainly shatter the insurrection's ability to orchestrate anything.'

'And this is the plan?' Arenfall asked.

'It is an option.'

'Assaulting Hanar Ara will require, at the very least, my marines.' ·

Inkaras smiled. 'So do not use them all up, High Fist. Can I ask at least that of you?'

'Divert the rest of the Legion to Hanar Ara,' Arenfall snapped.

'It would be a modest diverting, since Hanar Ara lies well east of here.'

Now Arenfall's eyes narrowed in suspicion.

Inkaras shrugged. 'None could assert that Emperor Mallick Rel was neither subtle nor a master of timing, High Fist.'

'Timing I'll grant you. But in this case, perhaps too subtle. To take Hanar Ara – a city within a mountain – sappers will be needed. My marines will be needed. Throwing the Legion without them at that fortress will yield only the annihilation of that legion.'

'As I said, High Fist, do not lose us the marines.'

A sudden knock at the door startled them both An instant later it opened and in strode a woman dressed in mud-spattered boots, trousers and blouse. The knife at her belt was as long as a short-sword. She glanced briefly at the Adjunct, then fixed her eyes on the High Fist.

'Fucking sappers!'

Arenfall's brows lifted. 'You'll need to explain that, Stipple.'

'The Under Quarter was about to be ours! We had Sug wrapped tight! Everything was going to plan, High Fist. Then you sent two damned sappers down there and they almost destroyed everything!'

Inkaras slowly rose. 'Your pardon – Stipple, is it? Interrupting this conversation in such an unseemly manner is clearly a breach of security in whatever mission you happen to be on. After all, is the Adjunct supposed to know of this?'

Stipple blinked, the colour draining from her face. 'You're the Adjunct?' Now she rounded back to Arenfall. 'High Fist, I've been down there for months – sure, I heard rumours but how was I to know what he – or she – even looked like? And you have agents all over the place that I've never even met! Damn, if your office isn't secure, well, sir, that's a failing I'm not responsible for!'

Seeing her anger back up – after the briefest of hitches – was impressive.

Inkaras looked to the High Fist and shrugged. 'Well, Arenfall, she's all yours, yes?'

Arenfall held up both hands, as if to forestall some pending physical assault. 'Stipple. Captain Hung sent the sappers down to survey the rising waters and, I was told, to check on the status of various cults and temples as might now operate down there.'

'Oh, that's sweet! Of course they weren't going to immediately attack all the criminal gangs down there! I mean, why would they?'

'You said "almost", Stipple. "Almost destroyed everything".'

The woman's shoulders slowly slumped. 'By the Lady's pull alone, me and Hench survived, so we can probably salvage this and complete the takeover. But Sug's three *other* lieutenants are all dead.'

'Presumably replaced, in some kind of partnership, by two sappers. I'd say that more than balances out.'

'They're insane! They think they're the reincarnations of Kellanved and Dancer! And that the Under Quarter is the modern version of Mock's Hold in Malaz City!'

Inkaras snorted. 'That would only be cause for worry if there was an Azath House in the Under Quarter.'

Stipple stared at him.

'Oh,' Inkaras eventually said.

*   *   *

'It was my thought,' said Vest Dyan, 'to scourge the temple, beginning with that infuriating High Priestess. Nor would I have spared the Invigil.'

High Priest Harapa Le'en stood outside the carriage door. The reek of rotting flesh and blood still clung to the wheels, axles and undercarriage, but it was now faded, dulled to the senses. It seemed even the flies had lost interest. A temporary lull, Harapa reminded himself, the thought interrupting his consideration of the Inquisitor's pronouncement. A moment later, he waved a hand. 'The time for setting upon our own kind, in judgement of their many failings, my friend, is still to come.'

'As you keep insisting,' Vest Dyan growled. 'They have offended me to my very core. Yet I am asked to abide?'

Harapa narrowed his gaze on the Inquisitor. 'You are far from un-familiar with mercy. Exercise it once more, good sir.'

Vest Dyan frowned at him. 'What do you mean?'

Tugging open the carriage door, Harapa lifted one foot to the step.

'Why, killing my victims in the moment before the hoofs find them, of course.' He paused, gauging the reaction his observation had triggered. Seeing the shock and then annoyance was most satisfying. He smiled. 'Mercy is a weakness in the person of an Inquisitor, of course. But the allowance for it, in the person of a High Priest, always has its place.'

As far as warnings went, it was subtle, perhaps too much so. But Harapa knew that Vest Dyan, for all his recalcitrant belligerence, was no fool. His frown, which had shifted into a scowl, now fell away like a mask discarded. In its place was something wry. 'The scourge can wait.'

Harapa's smile broadened. 'Indeed. Now, it is time to quit this city. The growing influence of our rival cult demands . . . correction. To do so, we must travel to its heart—' Halfway into the carriage, he paused again and tipped his head – 'its *smouldering* heart, we might say.'

He then entered the confines of the carriage, its smothering embrace of must and heat almost comforting in its oppression. Closing the small door behind him, he settled onto the plush bench, leaned back and closed his eyes.

The carriage rocked as Vest climbed up to take the traces. A dull echoing *knock* announced the release of the brakes, and then they were rolling forward in a clatter of hoofs and wooden wheels on cobbles.

Perhaps, Harapa mused, they would eventually return to G'danisban. To cast appropriate judgement upon the temple denizens, including that odious High Priestess. Propriety insisted upon respect, and it was indeed offensive to be subject to her careless dismissal of that respect. Clearly, some inner flaw existed in Shamalle, well beyond any hope of correction.

She would have to die, of course. Beneath the wheel. Sometimes, holy mercy made it quick. Far more satisfying when no such swift judgement was delivered. Lingering agony was itself a lesson to all who witnessed it, and surely to the sufferer herself. That seemed fitting.

The city sounds outside the shuttered windows were irritating, if thankfully muted. All that discord surely was symptomatic of deeper flaws in humanity. The future would be different. Constrained in all conduct, an extended pause in which chaos was held in check. A land locked in peace. Before the Apocalyptic's blessed gift of oblivion.

These thoughts, so satisfying, lullabied him into a doze.

*　　*　　*

Nub squatted on the branch that was his throne. His eyes flickered from scene to scene in the sprawling city below. The human herds, the sly shepherding bho-karala, the witless birds overhead, the exuberant laundry yearning for flight on the hot, dry wind.

All so delicious, in a ferociously dissatisfying way. Oh to be sure, Nub ruled with a light hand. That much should be obvious. His cuffing fist to the side of a head was relatively rare. The proper managing of civilization was, while at times onerous, mostly a dawdle. That said, dawdling itself was a talent, and Nub had it in abundance.

He lounged on his bark-skinned throne, idly picking lice and ticks from his crotch and taking them between his incisors where they popped most pleasurably. Then his roving gaze caught and fixed upon a carriage emerging from the Crimson Gate, and a terrible scowl clenched his leathery, wrinkled visage.

When the carriage turned off the imperial road, rocking and wending its way northward on a mostly disused old trader track, Nub's rage vanished, replaced by a lazy baring of his canines, then a yawn that wasn't a yawn at all.

The half-dozen minions clinging to branches below him all cringed, flattening ears and clutching their own tails. The fear of one resulted in the explosive release of gas from its anus.

At the braying sound, the King's rage returned and he half rose.

Yelping in terror, the minions scattered.

BOOK TWO

AWAKENINGS

Is this the day to reflect
when surrender became habit?
Is this the moment
to unravel every poignant memory
every gift once held precious?
Compromise is both negotiation
and bargain, balance's scales
neither solid nor seen,
and the measuring thereof
is done in private.
To contemplate the costs
and the rewards ascribes value
in an ongoing conversation
from which time itself is stripped
away, taking in one hand
past present and future
as if they were one.
But the scales will shift
in such a volatile scheme,
between self and the other
in myriad unspoken ways.
This is the day to reflect
the surrendering of the past
to the revised present,
and of the future, why,
no bargain obtains.

When it Ends
Hiyant

CHAPTER FIVE

'I have no need for warriors. My army does not march in rank. My army carries no weapons, wears no armour. In conquering, my army kills not a single foe, enslaves no one, rapes none.'

The Book of Salvation
Va'Shaik

Some days the wounding seemed far away. In other moments it crouched in her shadow, demonic and gibbering, half-child and half-corpse. Delivering heat and pain for outrage, lifeless chill for what had been lost. The sensations rocked between the two extremes, from blood to bloodless and then back again, a seemingly endless cycle that she now knew to be memory.

Felisin Younger, Va'Shaik, the Goddess Reborn, had been thinking of that wretched old man often of late. Bidithal, the deliverer of wounds, his face lit with a zealot's madness, a zealot's conviction. She wondered if that conviction still blazed in the instant Bidithal's severed cock and balls were shoved down his own throat.

What the skin wrapped itself around was more than just muscle, bone and organs. Skin made for a self-contained world to all that it held. That world took what it needed from outside. If unopposed, it also took what it wanted. It had a habit of confusing the two, and from that habit was born war, murder, theft, misery, suffering, cruelty, envy and hate.

When the gifts of indolence were first heaped upon her all those years ago, here in her Holy Temple in Hanar Ara, the First Holy City, she had set out to stretch that skin unto bursting. Appetites unleashed expanded her inner world in a gluttony of sensation. In this manner, she realized even then, she had made herself the personification of true Apocalypse. Consumption unto destruction.

It wasn't complicated, was it? It was, in fact, not only simple but also glaringly obvious.

To make of herself a most unambiguous symbol, she had imagined consuming until her excesses killed her, and this indeed had been her intention. She had devoured every morsel within reach – and they were always within reach, surrounded as she was by sycophants. Drunk every offering of heady herb-soaked wine from cups that never emptied. Smoked all that could be smoked. Fucked all that could be fucked until fucking was no longer possible. Her world was made immobile in slabs of fat, a vast body oiled and pampered, its excretions instantly cleaned up and all signs and smells eradicated, bodily shifted about by a half-dozen servants on a regular basis to free the skin to breathe and to change the bedding beneath her, her long hair combed out, her lips and eyelids painted. Before long, all other exigencies disappeared. With the needs removed, she soon lost the common abilities that had once belonged to her; no longer could she stand, walk, or, finally, even so much as sit up.

Inside her bloated, sated world, her mind swam through thick, viscid waters, barely able to keep its figurative head up, and in this place – where dissolution was a state of being, not a process – she had watched her ambitions drown, only to give final blessing to each and every one in its moment of sordid demise.

There was a state that came to her then, incrementally, so subtle as to be at first beneath notice. An emptiness of spirit that slowly pulled her away from her flesh, her body and all its desires and needs and ceaseless appetites. At some point, she realized that something strange was happening within her, when no amount of wine or durhang could blunt the keen awareness growing within her. The belief that all places within her could be escaped had proved to be false, a delusion. And when at last her intellect snapped free, she had at first thought this to be death. The severing of the mortal tie.

No such luck. Instead, she found that she could float free of her body, could wander unseen out from the chamber that had become her prison, could drift like a ghost, out among the corridors and rooms and cells of the temple, all its precincts, its apse and altar room, its cloisters where dwelt all who served her, the scribe room where sat the Book of Salvation, only a dozen or so pages written upon in the ancient Holy Hanarian script, left open on a high pedestal and layered in dust.

The proclamations of the goddess, it seemed, were few, leaving Felisin to wonder when precisely she had stopped speaking. Years ago, she now suspected. The devouring maw needs no words, after all.

And out, eventually, into the mostly hidden City of the Fallen, a city that reached so far into the battered mountains that many tunnels, subterranean avenues and chambers were now forgotten, lightless and lifeless and the air befouled.

Her intellect, thus freed, grew keen. Such alacrity soon proved more of a bane than a blessing. Clarity of vision, she now understood, was no gift. She was witness to the venal pursuits of her priests and priestesses, all overseen by that half-drunk madman, Kulat, who now spoke in her name and had, in effect, assumed rule in the First Holy City and all the outlying regions that fed it with grain and livestock. The temple's holdings had grown as bloated as Felisin's body, until its hoarded wealth now rivalled any great city in the Malazan Empire.

It further startled her to see that Kulat was considered Hanar Ara's Va'Falah'd, or High Fist, and that trade had been formalized, which in turn meant that the First Holy City had been recognized as a province by the empire, and thus tithes and taxes were expected to be paid to the Imperial Seat in Aren Outside the Fall. She saw too that Kulat was paying but a fraction of what was properly owed.

These details of corruption were hardly uncommon. Seven Cities was one of those conquests that wore the mantle of loyalty loosely at best, and in certain matters not at all. Imperial rules were adhered to when and if they were useful to local holds on power; otherwise, they were simply ignored.

Felisin was mostly uneducated in these affairs, and indeed indifferent. But something about Kulat's behaviour bothered her. On one level, he was but an embodiment of her: avaricious and acquisitive of all within reach. For her, it had been food, wine, rustleaf and the pleasures of the flesh. For Kulat, it was mostly wealth.

Matters to ponder, as she floated through the world of her making, all-seeing as any goddess, if not quite all-knowing, and in no way at all all-caring.

But this assignation, this title, this thing called 'goddess', remained a mystery to her in so many ways. Did she possess power? Power beyond her symbolic presence – still breathing, still living, if only barely so? Did she possess sorcerous might? What warrens swirled in her temple? Were they aspected to her, and if so, could she make use of them? And if she could, what might she do?

The impetus to act required that she give a damn, about something, anything. Did she?

Floating, spying on her so-called followers, so-called interpreters, so-called mouthpieces to her holy will. Discovering also all that had become of the temple's Open Wing, with its lone human occupant, dwelling amidst a score of mongrel dogs. A survivor of the plague. A child she had renamed *Crokus*. Now a man, a very strange man indeed.

Her journeys returned her, at last, to her disease-scarred followers. Her worshippers. Seeing them for what they were.

Disappointing.

And her personal servants? Well, they left her disgusted, and with good reason. Desirous and desperate to see her massive body expel its last breath, and the sooner the better. She could hardly blame them for that. It was all very well to be the personification of worldly appetites, but the curse of the clean-up was all too real, too personal and, accordingly, unpleasant in the extreme.

Felisin considered killing that body, as an act of divine mercy to all concerned. Only to discover that her link to it was not quite as severed as she had believed at first. Something of her own freedom began imposing its will on that somnolent, drugged form lying amidst silk pillows and deeply padded mattress. Fat melted away, gradually, and it was a week before the servants who rotated her body about noticed – and of course they would be the first to do so, as she had not had visitors in years – not even Kulat – and had been too fat for anything resembling sex for almost as long.

The detail was eventually reported to someone, noted and otherwise ignored. Felisin Younger was not a child any more. She was a woman now, an ageing woman, a dying woman as well. Some dread cancer perhaps, growing amidst the folds of fat, or in damaged organs. Liver, lungs, whatever.

The servants were delighted. Final proof of the flesh at last failing in earnest.

Yet, unlike the victim of tumours and cancers, Felisin Younger's body still sought sustenance, although nowhere near past appetites. It was fed as normal until, one morning, it began feeding itself. More hasty reports travelled outward at this seeming miracle – and those half-lidded eyes buried deep in the creased folds of flesh on her face, why, they seemed almost lively.

Still, no one cared to investigate, and this pleased Felisin Younger.

There came a time when she regarded her reduced self and was displeased to see how the skin now hung about her, loose and bearing old stretch-marks and the purple traceries of veins and arteries. A morsel of vanity within her intellect stirred awake, and it proved efficacious, as day by day that skin tightened, restored itself to resiliency.

Thus. The goddess, it seemed, was not entirely helpless. Her rule, her command, why, it oversaw – with acuity – that minor temple that could be called her body, her mortal expression. This was not only pleasing, but also something of a relief, and perhaps a lesson as well. To command the self, after all, struck her as redolent of the sacred. A notion wrapped in competing impulses of discipline and guilt, will and weakness, self-love and self-hate – and what could be more religious in essence than all of that?

By now, of course, not only was she sitting up and feeding herself; not only was her gaze alive and roving, and even occasionally acknowledging the baffled attentions of her closest servants; but she had begun moving her legs in ways preparatory to standing, perhaps even walking.

This last report, delivered (her formless intellect had observed) somewhat breathlessly, had at last elicited a slight surge of alarm in Va'Falah'd Kulat. He immediately began preparations for a formal visitation to her sacred precinct, and indeed the Holy Chamber of her Repose. These preparations she watched with some interest.

At last, after some more days – days in which he commanded those servants attending Felisin to probe her growing capacities, to attempt in fact to awaken her sufficient to speaking (which she wasn't inclined to do, yet) – Kulat was finally ready.

His first order was to empty the precinct of all attending servants and acolytes. He would see her alone. How could the mortal voice of the goddess do otherwise?

Awaiting him, Felisin sat upright in her bed, flowing silks of green and orange about her upper form, her auburn hair – absurdly long, a detail she would deal with soon – combed out and then oiled and braided and now more or less out of the way, revealing a face mostly smooth and suited to a woman of about thirty years of age, still plump and rounded as befitted her body which remained far from thin, her eyes lined in kohl and powdered malachite, her lips painted in gold-flecked vermilion.

Now at last he approached, select accoutrements in hand, and then paused just outside the door. His old habit of rolling and sucking on rounded pebbles in his mouth remained, and her hovering intellect could hear the soft, liquid clatter. As a long habit, the damage it had done to Kulat's teeth was excessive. Healers had mitigated what they could, but for some reason Kulat had yet to find a High Denul healer to restore the ravaged mess of his mouth. A curious detail.

In any case, she could see that he was steeling himself. Then he reached for the latch.

At that, her freed mind returned at last, fully, to her body. Blinking, she felt herself spreading back into her flesh, rediscovering her form, her weight, the tidal ebb and flow of her breathing. Pain flashed like sparks in her limbs, her joints, and her vision spun, momentarily filled with motes.

The door opened and in came Kulat, the Va'Falah'd of Hanar Ara, Voice of the Goddess. In one hand an unstoppered vial, in the other a fistful of red silks he intended to push down her throat to prevent her from throwing back up the poison.

A gesture from her pushed the stones in his mouth down his throat, lodging them there. Gagging, head rocking back, he fell to his knees. The vial fell away and rolled, spilling its deadly contents. The silks unfolded where they now lay on the floor, like a flower greeting the sun.

Eyes bulging within a darkening visage, he stared at her.

She spoke, her voice thin, almost a whisper from disuse. 'It began with such promise, didn't it? Trust between us. Faith, even. Of course you could see how broken a child I was. As broken as the T'lan Imass who delivered me.'

He was getting some air into his lungs, but not enough. His face was now the hue of ash. He clawed at his own throat, pushed a finger into his mouth, but neither effort succeeded in dislodging the stones.

'Stealing what the empire is rightly owed. You thought yourself so clever. I've seen the opulence of your chambers, Kulat. I've seen you raise up High Priests and Inquisitors who dream only of sharing such wealth, as you send them out to bleed dry the poor in every city, every village. Promises of salvation? Indeed, but whose? Surely not that of the poor.'

110

She gestured again, to take away the last whistling path of air into and out of his lungs.

'The Goddess has returned,' she said, watching him die. 'And it seems that there is work to be done.'

He finally fell forward, sliding onto one side, his dead eyes seemingly fixed upon the red silks lying wilted upon the floor.

Life, she reflected, was so very short.

*   *   *

Master Librarian Bornu Blatt was in his chamber, surrounded by scrolls and tomes and tablets of fired clay. On his desk was stacked at least a dozen small wooden frames containing wax, each one meticulously covered in tiny script, written in his own hand.

It was an unfortunate detail that the dust of the past made his prodigious nose drip incessantly. Sneezing was not uncommon, also streaming eyes. Papyrus and vellum and other skins of dubious origin were a beloved curse, with all the confused sentiments entailed.

But he was not a man at ease with others. A face judged pugnacious, details misaligned and oversized, a shock of unruly black hair that was . . . shocking. His body fared no better in estimation. Gourd-shaped, with large flat feet at the bottom, knobby knees and bulging belly. Ugliness was his companion; one he had lived with all his life. It had been said, indeed, that he had been born homely and misshapen, and thus destined for either the village cesspit on a dark night, or to be sold to whatever local temple would have him.

Was it compensation then that his mind was a thing of such breadth and wonder? Or some unknown entity's idea of the cruellest joke imaginable? After all these years, he remained undecided.

Gift for languages, gift for observation, deduction, all the subtle truths hiding beneath the crass lies of lives lived on all sides. A maker of maps, surveyor of monuments, gleaner of ancient secrets. A fair hand as artist, wise advisor to merchants on matters of economy, a man prone to prescient and therefore unwelcome commentary in all manner of company, it was a wonder he still had his head atop his crooked shoulders.

Not destined following birth for the cesspool, then, but to a temple. And, after many years mostly indifferent – devoted as they'd been to the task of self-education – he now found himself in Hanar Ara, the First Holy City, serving as scribe in the Temple of Va'Shaik. His initial responsibility had been to record the holy words of the goddess. That had been short-lived since she'd stopped talking not long after his arrival.

Thus freed of the onerous task of recording the mumblings of a woman barely past childhood, in all her drug-fuelled liberation from the necessity of making sense, Bornu Blatt set out in pursuit of his true interests, none of which had anything to do with divinity. Unless, of course, one could view knowledge itself as divine. Which he did on better days. On days not better, when his frustration at all he did not and could never know overwhelmed him, knowledge was positively demonic.

In either case, he was more or less left entirely alone to his pursuits, barring the assistance of a half-dozen servants whom he had trained in the arts of surveying, copying, recording and collecting things of possible interest to him from places all over Seven Cities.

Bornu Blatt was sitting at his desk, holding a wax tablet over a flame to melt away the clutter of words he'd spent the previous day scribing, since all he'd expounded upon he now saw to be rubbish, the ravings of a madman, when his assistant arrived. Bornu Blatt's small eyes flicked up to regard the woman. 'Yes, Salabi, what is it?'

'Portentous news, Master.'

'Is it?' He set the tablet down to cool. 'Kulat's purchased another dozen slaves to wear out in his bedroom? More false accounts devoted to the Great God Embezzlement? His absurd dreams of religious revolution one step closer to disastrous fruition? Out with it, beauteous one.'

For she was indeed beautiful. Bornu Blatt had stolen her from Kulat's clutches long ago now. Years and years past. And still, after all this time, her beauty remained. If anything, more wondrous now than when she'd been a nineteen-year-old third daughter, flung at the temple in lieu of family debt. In any case, Bornu had been newly appointed as Scribe of the Goddess back then, and that had meant something, and he'd seen the quickness in Salabi's bright eyes and had known her for what she'd proved to be: very, very smart. So he'd managed to keep her from Kulat's clutches – the first of a dozen or so modest victories over Kulat's tyranny and his insatiable, licentious appetites.

For this alone, Bornu Blatt's personal servants remained loyal to him; of that he was certain. Why else remain in his ugly company?

'Va'Shaik has returned to us, Master.'

'Didn't know she'd left. I mean, how could she, having turned herself into a beached dhenrabi?'

112

Delicate brows rose. 'Master, did I not report her growing transformation?'

'Her what? Oh, I vaguely recall you mentioning weight loss. Thought it was a fatal illness. Then again, how can a goddess get sick, and no, I don't mean spiritually sick, which I now believe to be not only common, but inevitable, but physically so?'

'No illness, Master. A true, miraculous transformation, the fullest return to health.'

Bornu Blatt studied Salabi, seeing at last a strange confusion writ there in her perfect face. 'If so, then why does she still live?'

'Master?'

'Kulat.'

'Ah. He has gone to her chamber, Master. After sending all her servants away. He speaks with her alone.'

'Right now?' Bornu Blatt rose, rubbing his hands together vigorously to get rid of the patches of wax on his fingers and palms. 'How long has he been with her all alone?'

'Since this morning, Master.'

'Then she's dead, and he's busy concocting a grand proclamation of his own ascension while arranging the evidence to support it.' He sighed. 'Well, I see little change in the near future, as he has essentially played that role for years now.'

'But the Summoning Chime has sounded from her Holy Chamber.'

Bornu Blatt nodded. 'Then he's ready.' He collected up a few wax tablets and his bone stylus. 'Let's go record the grand event, shall we?'

She followed him out of his room. Halfway down the first corridor, Bornu raised a hand to halt her a step behind him, so that he could blow his nose. The handkerchief he used had been boiled clean so many times all the dyes were long gone, leaving it grey, with more than a few yellow stains no amount of sunlight could bleach out. It was the fate of an ugly man, he knew, to possess ugly afflictions, and he well imagined Salabi's carefully concealed expression of disgust at his back – not that he would embarrass both himself and her by turning to look.

Resuming the journey, Bornu Blatt tucked away the handkerchief. Dust, he observed glumly, dust everywhere.

Va'Shaik's personal servants were huddled outside the double doors leading to her chamber. The Summoning Chime had sounded but once, then, as twice would have sent them hurrying into her room to attend to her. He arrived and paused to regard them. 'It may be your responsibilities are at an end.'

The mixed array of expressions confused Bornu for a few moments. He had expected to see nothing but relief. Well, perhaps it was the sudden end to all that was familiar – even if unpleasant – to them, leaving their roles uncertain now, their futures unknown. 'Be at ease,' he added. 'I can set you to reorganizing my library – no small effort, I assure you – and in time I should have no trouble adding you to my staff.'

It was that, after all, or into Kulat's clutches. Now he saw unalloyed relief in their faces and was satisfied. Turning to Salabi, he said, 'With me, please.'

He lifted the latch to one of the doors and into the chamber they went.

When Bornu heard Salabi close the door behind him, he realized that he had halted but a single stride into the room, nailed in place by the scene before him.

Va'Shaik stood near the high, narrow window to the right of her massive bed. She had drawn back the curtains, which had in turn sent sheets of dust cascading down from the stiffened fabric, and now that dust roiled lazily across the entire chamber, lit by the sunlight streaming in.

Between the goddess and Bornu was Kulat, prone on the floor, his body twisted but utterly motionless, and from where he stood Bornu could see the dusty glint of an eye, fixed open and staring sightlessly. He saw, too, the vial amidst a stain of all it had contained, and then the silks on the floor.

'You are the High Scribe of the Faith?'

Blinking and then bowing, he replied, 'I am, Goddess. Bornu Blatt, of Caron Tepasi Province, your devoted scribe of all that is holy.'

She regarded him levelly, still partly turned towards the window. '"All that is holy"? From me?'

He bowed again. 'You've little said of late.'

'Are such words as you have recorded me saying, Scribe, implicitly holy?'

He shrugged. 'I doubt it. But then, such considerations are for the Devoted Scholars to decide.'

'Not me?'

'For you to elaborate presumes initial imprecision not suited to a goddess, I'm sure.'

To his astonishment, she snorted. 'And you are not among the Devoted Scholars? Is that not unusual, given your station here?'

Again he shrugged. 'In that I have failed you, Goddess.'

'How so?'

'I am not by nature religious, I'm afraid.'

This time her laughter was a near yelp. She swung round fully now to face him. 'Bornu Blatt, will you now record with accuracy the words of the Goddess, Va'Shaik?'

'Of course.'

'Good.'

He saw her pause after he'd readied his stylus over the first of the wax tablets.

Then she spoke. 'For his long devotion to me, I have released Kulat from life's suffering. He now dwells in the promised paradise as befits the purity of his service–'

Bornu Blatt coughed. 'Pardon, Goddess. The dust.'

'Of course, the dust. To continue. I now proclaim a synod and do recall all the High Priests and High Priestesses of my faith, to attend me here in Hanar Ara, in two months' time, upon the day of the Equinox within the pool of Deathdreamer's influence – a moment, have I that correct, Bornu Blatt?'

'You do, Goddess. The constellations will indeed be so arrayed in the night sky, which is fortuitous above such an auspicious gathering.'

Her brows lifted. 'Will it be? Auspicious? Have I misremembered? Is not Deathdreamer the one known as Leoman of the Flails? And does not the pool in this year represent the Queen of Dreams?'

'Precisely so, Goddess.'

'Leoman, who betrayed the faith.'

He tilted his head. 'Leoman, who delivered the greatest sacrifice in Sha'ik's name the world has ever seen.'

She frowned. 'Ah, I see. When did this, uh, interpretation gain ascendancy, and by whose command?'

'Perhaps two or three years past,' Bornu replied, 'and no source known to me lays claim to it. Public sentiment is a muddy sea, Goddess, stirred by unguessable currents. The Burning City is second only to Hanar Ara as a place of pilgrimage among the faithful.'

'Is it now.' After a moment she gestured that he resume scribing, and said, 'Within the pool of Deathdreamer's influence, as I said. To continue: Until such time, all temples are instructed to redistribute such alms as they receive to those in greatest need, and to devote excess funds to repair and building projects in the poorest quarters of their precinct, village or town. These efforts are to be diligently recorded, said accounts to accompany temple retinues attending the synod. Va'Shaik has spoken these words, faithfully set down by the High Scribe of the Last Temple.'

He completed writing and looked up to see her studying him.

'Your thoughts, Bornu Blatt?'

'Mine, Goddess? Whatever for?'

'Perhaps, I am curious?'

'That seems a dangerous thing, Goddess.'

'Why?'

He held up the tablet. 'Holy proclamation, not in the least ambiguous nor imprecise. I would think, indeed, that even the Devoted Scholars will struggle for wiggle-room within this assembly of words.'

Her smile was quick, momentary, and then gone again. 'It is not the proclamation's wording I am asking you to consider. Rather, its content.'

He was silent for a long stretch then, as he considered what to say, what not to say, until he took note of her growing irritation and impatience. 'Goddess, your faith is in possession of two holy sites, two places of pilgrimage. The date of your synod explicitly seeks to unify matters, to perhaps determine a final hierarchy with respect to the Last Temple here, and the Burning City.'

'Go on.'

'You are the Living Goddess, the formal inheritor of Sha'ik. Leoman of the Flails, presumed dead or even fully ascended, is neither living nor the inheritor of Sha'ik as such, and certainly not in any formal sense.'

'Correct.'

'I foresee a schism,' Bornu Blatt said – hearing a gasp from Salabi standing behind him, 'in which you will probably lose. Not only your place as the repository of all faith among your followers, but quite possibly your life itself.'

'Why would I fail this contest?'

He shrugged. 'A living saviour stands no chance against a dead one. Or a missing one.'

'Gather your things, Bornu Blatt.'

'I am to be exiled?'

'Why would you think that? No. Kulat's death has created a vacancy, which you will now fill.'

'Goddess, how can one devoid of faith be the Voice of that goddess?'

'No faith at all, Bornu Blatt?'

'None. Yet I do not reject the existence of immortals, of gods, spirits, ghosts and the like. It would be presumptuous of me to assert that the universe is defined by the limits of my perception – and worse, my interpretation of said perception. The blind man does not see the flames yet they will burn him nonetheless. And are we mortals not mostly blind?'

'Yet you call me Goddess.'

'As you have been named so I call you.'

'Has it not occurred to you that, returned as I am, I no longer have need for a Voice?'

He tilted his head. 'Then, I admit to confusion. Kulat's role is now clearly unnecessary.'

'As one who speaks for me, yes. But he possessed other functions, did he not?'

'He did. Treasurer, arbiter in the elevation of aspirants to the priest-hood. Various edicts and proclamations of the church. Management of the church hierarchy.'

'And Inquisitor?'

He said nothing for a half-dozen heartbeats. 'Kulat, for all his excesses, Goddess, saw no need for assuming the responsibilities of that role.'

'Well, I would imagine not, if by the loosest affiliation to my faith the treasury continued to grow.' She walked now to seat herself in the high-backed chair once intended for her scribe in those times of recording holy words. Though still a heavy woman, she moved with sinuous grace. She sat, legs crossing. 'Yet my faith has Inquisitors.'

He nodded. 'Just mostly not stationed here.'

She studied him for a few moments, and then spoke. 'You do not deny the existence of immortals. As such, you must also acknowledge the powers of such beings.'

'I do,' he answered. 'But faith is another matter.'

'Elaborate, please.'

'In standing – or kneeling – before one of greater power, is not faith but euphemistic for hope? The hope that one not be hurt, subjected to suffering, or simply indifferently crushed – as one might crush a tick or louse? Or the hope that one be granted gifts, healing, salvation, or social elevation with all the wealth that might come with that?'

117

'You describe a faith without the mutual recognition of love.'

'One loves a pet dog and the dog in turns loves its owner. That owner has in many respects god-like power over that pet dog. Is the relationship one of equals? No. More akin to a slave and master, I should think. All sustenance to the dog comes from the owner, and indeed life and death decisions reside mostly with the same owner.'

'But who said anything about equals?' Va'Shaik asked.

Bornu Blatt smiled. 'You spoke of love.'

That made her frown. 'There are many kinds of love,' she finally said.

'Yes, Goddess.'

A slow flush came to her features. 'Bidithal spoke of love, even as he sought to damage me.'

'Nothing of that is known,' Bornu said. 'Nothing of your past, beyond your presence in Sha'ik's camp in Raraku, is known to anyone, Goddess. No details, that is. Kulat managed such knowledge.' He paused. 'Bidithal was one of Sha'ik's lieutenants, yes?'

'I have need of a proper Inquisitor, Bornu Blatt, to scour clean the sanctity of my name, my evocation. My power is such that I can sense all who cloak their deeds in my name. Daily, nightly, I am stung by their crimes. While bloated, drunk and drugged, I was able to remain virtually senseless to these wounds. This, as you can see, is no longer the case. Bornu Blatt, I am in pain.'

'The synod is a beginning, Goddess, but I mentioned a schism, and your likely fate.'

'And you think my death will bring an end to my pain? It is no wonder you are not religious, since you understand nothing.' Her eyes glittered, hard and cold. Then she looked away. 'Leoman is alive and well.'

'Ah, Goddess, that changes things. Can you summon him?'

'To the synod?'

'Is he ascended?' Bornu asked. 'Does he even now luxuriate in all who pray to him? Is he your rival in truth?'

'As to that,' she said, 'I have no idea.' She waved a hand, somewhat dismissively. 'My strongest memory of Leoman was the pit he called home in the camp, a place so wreathed in the smoke of durhang one's eyes burned without surcease. Oh, I know what he did, eventually. Word was brought to me of Y'Ghatan, the trap he sprung against the Malazan army, that failed. The news horrified me.'

'Is its failure even relevant, Goddess?'

She met his gaze again, and once more that smile flickered for the briefest moment. 'Let me tell you of my holy birth, Bornu Blatt. And you as well, Salabi – for I have need of you in other matters. Seat yourselves at the bench there, you two.'

'Shall I record your words, Goddess?' Bornu asked.

'No. Find your own words for what I say here. To begin, I will tell you what my questing senses have told me, once I began to awaken within, once I made the choice to turn away from the chasm I had found myself crawling towards – to reject the dissolution I had so willingly embraced. Sha'ik's power, as Whirlwind Goddess, was born of a woman scorned, infused with the sorcerous damage of the T'lan Imass and a rendered warren. Fed in turn by the torment and agony of the Crippled God. And, lastly, she was served in her fury by the restless spirits of the Holy Desert Raraku – what all saw as sand and waste those spirits remembered as the bed of a sea. What all suffered as unrelenting heat and desiccation, the spirits recalled as the sweet caress of cool waters. What curses so afflicted ancient Raraku? Only the insatiable thirst of mortal empires.

'But Sha'ik had no interest in seeing her desert home made into a sea. She simply used the spirits to create and feed the Whirlwind. She betrayed them. Is it not an irony, then, that a foreign army ended up freeing those spirits and so transformed a desert into a vast freshwater lake as big as a sea, eager to become the womb of new life?' She fell silent, her eyes seemingly fixed on memories, or perhaps visions, and then she shrugged. 'The Crippled God is gone, never to return. The Imass woman scorned finally knows peace. Perhaps as oblivion, perhaps as forgiveness. Thus, all that empowered Sha'ik is no more. Where then the rise of Va'Shaik? This twisted resurrection of Dryjhna the Apocalyptic?'

When it struck Bornu that her questions had not been rhetorical, he sat straighter, considered, and said, 'Two things sacred, perhaps, and one profane. The first, your elevation – but there it seems that our official account of that is mostly . . . apocryphal?'

She shrugged and then nodded.

He resumed. 'The second, also to be considered sacred, was Y'Ghatan. Thus, Leoman's dire act.'

'And the profane?'

'Ah, Goddess, we are an unruly lot, a land of tribal peoples, a vast stewing pot of beliefs, faiths, schools of philosophy, feuding academies, too many old men arguing about the universe over hookahs and strong honeyed teas, too many old women drinking the Wandering Wine on moonless nights. It is, I believe, in our nature to speak of apocalypse, while dreaming of salvation.'

'When you describe it so,' Va'Shaik said, gaze half-lidded as she regarded him, 'the profane strikes me as more sacred than does opportunistic ascension and burning cities.'

He could not help but smile. 'In this, Goddess, and at last, we find agreement.'

'Do you finally understand, Bornu Blatt, the nature of the schism?'

That caught him off-guard. 'Goddess?'

'The Burning City of the Apocalypse upon one hand, and upon the other, the Book of Salvation. Where else but in this scorched land with its unexpected seas and restless spirits and restless souls, could such a faith arise?'

'Then,' he said, 'not a schism at all, but two forces in both opposition and balance, mutually dependent. You seek to *unify* the cults. And for that, you will indeed need Leoman of the Flails.'

'Do you not now wonder, Bornu Blatt, at the source of my power? Because I do. Is your profane stewing pot sufficient? What other legacies do I now feed upon? What of my own rage, the scorned self, the wounded child I once was? What of Bidithal, who sought to carve out all hope of pleasure from between my legs?'

Bornu heard Salabi's sharply indrawn breath beside him on the bench, but could not pull his eyes from the goddess, as power began swirling round her form, a growing, incandescent rage.

'And what of Leoman himself, who left me to that fate even as he planned to flee everyone, and planned – let us not mince words here – to gather the last and most fanatical believers all in one place, and then incinerate them? Was that the Queen of Dreams' solution? A question I intend asking.

'And lastly, what of Toblakai? My too-late avenger and slayer of Bidithal? Am I to thank him for delivering justice? Or shall I curse him for leaving the camp when he did, for abandoning so many children to Bidithal's twisted desires and whims?'

The power now engulfing the seated form of the goddess was blinding, fierce as any firestorm, and yet white as the heart of a sun. Somehow, Bornu was able to see the woman nonetheless, amidst that coruscating conflagration, as she slowly leaned forward and said, 'When it is time,

I will have words with Karsa Orlong of the Shattered Face.' She stood and raised both hands. 'Salvation or Apocalypse, which of my gifts will he choose, I wonder?'

A most chilling question.

'Leave me now, Inquisitor Bornu Blatt, Chief Scribe Salabi.'

Bornu found himself half lifting Salabi from the bench, and he wondered at her sudden weakness. They reached the doors and a moment later found themselves standing in the hallway. The servants who had been waiting there were nowhere to be seen.

Salabi was leaning against him, head hanging, her entire body trembling.

'What afflicts you?' he asked.

She shook her head, and slowly he felt her strength returning as she straightened, the shivering falling away, her breaths deepening, settling. 'Not for you,' she whispered.

'What is? What is not for me, Salabi?'

She shot him a sharp look, and then stepped away. 'No matter. I should not have spoken.'

'Tell me, Salabi.'

'You would not understand. Forgive me. I do not mean to offend.'

'Very well, I choose no offence. But I still wish to understand.'

'Did you see her power?'

'Of course.'

'Did you feel it?'

He frowned. 'More seen than felt, I admit. Is it because I have no faith?'

'No,' she said.

They were walking now, returning to the temple's library wing. 'Then why you and not me?'

She snorted, not looking over as they continued down the corridor. 'A woman's rage you may witness, Bornu Blatt, but never truly know. Best leave it at that, Master.'

'Master no longer, Chief Scribe,' he replied. 'I hear you, however. I may not know it, Salabi, but I will honour it.'

She nodded her thanks and said nothing more.

'I have no wish to be Inquisitor,' he said after a time.

'Better reluctant than eager, I should think,' she replied. 'She will send you out now, into the world beyond. I will miss you.'

121

Now it was his turn to smile but say nothing, and likely for the same reason. She was finally free now, after all. A scribe in her own right, and no longer bound to his company. Of course she would say something kind, to take away the sting. He would not resent her dissembling, even if he had not dissembled at all in his vow to her.

That said, the thought of being sent away from his beloved scrolls, tomes and tablets was most depressing. What could the world beyond offer him to replace the loss? Scant little, he suspected.

The Goddess had set upon him a task, and that was an inescapable truth.

The ugly man sent out into the world. He sighed. What a miserable fate for everyone, himself included.

CHAPTER SIX

Will you sing of success and choke on failure?
Polished pebble to one side
Broken brick to the other
Have you laid out his every deed
Pored most scrupulously over this and that
Making order the language of god?
Are these the garden gatherings
In slumbering temples beneath leafy shade
Tap-tapping agreement in measured chants
From place to place oblivion between each breath-fall –
All you voted to cast away slipping down unseen
As if truth is mere democratic currency
Meaning bowing before unanimous chorus.
And a new holy book supplants its predecessor
Over which you clap hands to shed dust
Expunging all uncertainty *at last at last!*
But you understand nothing.
His successes are without relevance
His failures less so.
The Historian will tell you of the hollow shell
Of the man who stood before them all
And how each witness so eagerly filled it.
Such is memory's rank slurry worthy of recoil
Let's see your reduction the gold pooled
In the crucible – to think of glory as blinding
Is only fear's secret cowering self –
But in the name of Duiker
Mine is the hand of promise

Destined to flay you to the bone
Upon this the poet and the historian agree:
Faith is not what you think it is
And look not to find it
in words

Prelude to

Lay of Duiker the Historian
Fisher kel Tath

A man without faith is given the regulatory task, made into a walking symbol of the will of a goddess. Her faith in him had become Bornu Blatt's burden. Broken-faced arbiter, travelling from village to city, from town to hamlet, crawling slow as a beetle in the dust along tracks and paths, imperial roadways and trade routes so old they had no name – and, more than once, no living destination.

He had begun to see himself as a pilgrim, not embodying the mortal quest for anything spiritual, no, not in that way at all. Instead, his wandering served the dubious purpose of filling empty spaces on a map, marking out the ruins of forgotten linkages between forgotten places. His was a mind obsessed with details and precision and if so, why did this leave him so melancholic?

To complete a map, to measure out and inscribe every detail, divesting all mystery, transmuting the unknown into the known, was this not the task of a devoted cartographer? Wax tablet after wax tablet, inked and stamped onto papyrus sheets, filled with copious notations: estimations of a hamlet's population, the ratio of child to adult, male to female, the necessary professions of sustenance. Was this not of value and relevance, the very foundation of governing? To mark out temples and shrines, parcels of land given over to monks, nuns, priests and priestesses, counting heads of sheep, goats and cattle. All of his obsessions, his great loves, were now bound to this endless, dreadful, soul-crushing journey.

Did the goddess observe through his eyes? If so, he wondered what she now thought of her charge upon him, her desire, her demands.

He leaned forward, grunting as he pulled the axe-blade from the skull of the body lying at his bared feet. Blank spaces on maps offered more than enticing mystery, it seemed. They were also refuges. For the cast-out, the dwellers on the edges of society, civilization's lawbreakers, the myriad shadowy creatures who could never manage a life within an orderly and ordered world. Bereft of talent, emptied of ambition, skittish and hungry, opportunistic and murderous.

The blank face he now looked down upon, with its cloven-in forehead, blood-blasted eyes and flopping tongue, had been without secrets only a few moments ago. Enlivened with need, with the sharp attention of killing intent. And now, he could see, all mystery returned. Chilling it might be, but death was surely a mask. One all were destined to wear eventually, offered up to the living and feeding their fascination with its every detail.

Every mortal soul, upon this wretched earth, took on – without thought – the task of the cartographer, when solemnly regarding the lifeless mask, and all its confounding, infuriating mystery. Death, what are you? Cold, motionless face, what do you hide? Dull, flattened eyes, where did your life go?

He stepped away from the corpse, feeling like its watery reflection, mercurial and agitated, troubled still by what had cast it.

'I forget,' said Gilakas behind him, 'your curious talents, so ill fitting a scholar.'

'I was a child brought up among the followers of a forbidden faith,' Bornu Blatt replied, eyes now fixing on the bloody strands of hair snagged on his axe. 'Outlawed. Or so it was believed. The need to defend ourselves was but one lesson among many.' He stepped forward, bent down and used the dead man's filthy tunic to clean the blade. The reek of excrement and urine assailed him. He quickly straightened.

Death without dignity was surely the cruellest death of all. But did the soul even care, as it sobbed free of the body that once held it? 'It is said blessed relief awaits us all,' he said. 'In mists of white, we are greeted by those who went before us, bereft of judgement, filled with joy.'

'Rewards of the Apocalypse,' murmured Gilakas, cleaning his own blade on the rags covering the narrow chest of the youth he had cut down. 'The son and the father now stand side by side, hands clasped, drowning in wonder.'

Bornu Blatt shot the man a look. Gilakas, his self-appointed guardian, probably an ex-soldier, alarmingly pious in his newfound faith in the goddess. Tall, long-limbed, clean-shaven and so hiding nothing of his creased, flame-marred face. His eyes were too bright, too sharp, his air of fanaticism making Bornu Blatt's skin crawl. 'Unwitting servants of the goddess, were they?'

125

Gilakas shrugged and then sheathed his sword. 'A village must be close. This track leads somewhere.'

'I find it odd,' Bornu said, 'this sudden ambush, this absence of demands. Most who would rob begin with threats.'

'Easier, I suppose, stripping a corpse.' Gilakas collected up his satchel, shrugging into it with a grunt. 'Inquisitor?'

Nodding, Bornu collected his own pack, and they resumed their trek along the rocky, narrow trail.

The broken face of the cliff to their right, bleached white in the sunlight, was pockmarked with small caves, before which were heaped tailings and rubble. Here and there along the cliff-side, older, darker, harder veins of stone were visible, pushing through the sandstone. This stone displayed streaks of raw tin.

'In ages past,' Bornu Blatt said, 'this place rang with the sound of picks, voices echoing. Children wearing ankle-shackles disappeared into the shafts. Some of them never returned. Or were dragged out from under fallen rocks, by their ankles, limbs loose and covered in dust.'

'You paint a grim picture of progress, Inquisitor.'

Progress. Yes, many would see it as that. Mining tin, mining copper, making bronze. The myriad tools of industry, every ingot wiped clean of sweat and blood before being sold on. Less than a whisper, the voice of child-ghosts lingering in places like this one.

One day, the veins were tapped out. Silence returned, the hollowed ways into the rock left to unrelieved darkness. The crews with their scrawny, dull-eyed and malnourished workers moving on in search of more places to keep civilization heaving onward.

'I am beleaguered by history,' Bornu Blatt said. 'By knowing. Will there come a time in my life when knowledge ceases to wound me? When all the patterns become clear, rightfully placed, no more and no less than the embrace of a welcoming universe?'

'There will,' answered Gilakas. 'But only after your last breath.'

'Then why strive until then?'

'I ceased my striving – for anything – long ago, Inquisitor.'

'Then what urges your next step, Gilakas?'

'Idiotic momentum. It's a habit we all share.'

How could the minds of others not be fascinating? Wondrous, terrifying, pools of wisdom and pits of stupidity, with the barest hints of revelation exposed by a word or two, an expression or gesture, while the

126

deeper world within remained unseen by anyone. And was Bornu Blatt any different? He was not.

We are all we have. Alone and together. 'I do not understand you believers,' he then said, as the cliff on the right gave up its caves, the last of the darker rock vanishing, the sandstone showing unbroken, tilted layers rising ever higher, even as the track began descending. Somewhere ahead, Bornu suspected, they would find a small spring or pool, frond-swallowed with humming clouds of insects over it. Or a stone-lined pond with paved paths leading to and from a village or hamlet. The air would smell of livestock and dung. Animal tracks in the dried mud.

'Many are the ways of surrender,' Gilakas said. 'You, of course, refuse them all.'

'The goddess is far from perfect.'

'Making you the strangest Inquisitor ever.'

'I am more clerk than inquisitor, I fear.'

'You speak in her name. She calls her children back into her embrace. A momentous event.'

'How can you deny all suspicion, Gilakas, when a fellow human stands before you, professing to have all the answers? Do you not look back, into yourself, seeing all the wretched flaws and foibles, and realize that the fool standing before you is no different, no matter what he says?'

'Va'Shaik is a goddess, not human.'

'She once was.'

'And no longer.'

'The flaws and foibles left behind? She would tell you otherwise.'

'I appreciate her humility.'

And so it went, day after day, this exchange less than a conversation, doomed to never find common ground. Bornu Blatt had begun to see Gilakas as a divine punishment, Va'Shaik's mocking enigma manifested in human form. Impenetrable in every way that mattered. There was no hope of abandoning the man. Gilakas wasn't interested in obeying the commands of the Inquisitor. He answered, apparently, to a higher authority.

And yet Bornu Blatt had never seen the man before, nor even heard mention of his name. If he had been a citizen of Hanar Ara, he had made anonymity an art.

Perhaps Va'Shaik had conjured him from a lump of clay, to take on the role of dubious conscience, or deliverer of faith's terrible pressure, making this a performance of sorts, inviting Bornu Blatt into formulating a thesis on the nature of belief in the divine, or some such thing. Not that he had any interest in doing so. The subject did not inspire him. Perhaps Gilakas – and by extension Va'Shaik – did not understand him. When he said things like 'I do not understand you believers at all,' it was not meant as an invitation to explain. It was, instead, nothing more than exasperation.

You serve a cause no one can agree on, by rules sundered insensible by clashing interpretations. You claim a single light, yet each and every one of you holds a different candle, which alone you pronounce true. You declare your belief unimpeachable, even as you damn your neighbour's. And yet, despite all of this, a holy army will see itself unified in its purpose, and indeed act so, at least until the day is done, and in the dusk following, why, it rips itself apart.

The wonder of it all, in fact, is that not every god drinks and smokes itself senseless in the wake of all that.

Va'Shaik, you should never have returned to your senses. Better by far the sweet dissolution of the flesh inside which you were trapped. You remain a child, I fear, dragged into our presence by your ankles. We mortals are your doom.

They say many gods are stepping away from mortal affairs.

I'm not surprised. The pertinent question is 'what took you so long?'

In all this time, perversely beneath notice, the left side of the trail had become a slope of shattered bricks and splintered bones, leading down to a salt-flat that stretched away to a blurry horizon. Not that it was disinterest that had Bornu Blatt avoiding even a glance in that direction. Rather the opposite, in fact, because no map of this region showed any salt-flats at all. And the bones, well, the bones belonged to giants.

Gilakas had yet to comment on any of this.

'You have ceased making notations, Inquisitor,' he now said. 'Is this route familiar and known to you?'

'I am suspending judgement,' Bornu Blatt replied.

'Counting paces?'

'Not that, either.'

A scent of blossoms in the air, a hint of humidity, and then, ahead, greenery and shade cast down by the cliff-side, which now made an overhang – and this too made no sense, as the cliff was on the north side of the track, the sun's light ahead, or it should have been, but Bornu now saw the sun directly overhead, strangely blushed in hue.

Low ferns awaited them in a thick sward. Beyond it, bits of a low stone wall could be seen, and beyond that, dragonflies wheeled amidst thousands of rising mayflies in a feeding frenzy. Passing through the ferns, they halted.

A woman was seated on the low wall to their right, barely visible in the deep shade. One hand was dipped into the pool they could now see, the wall forming a perfect circle around the water. The pool, about thirty paces across, bore a dusty surface, as if layered in a patina filled with rainbow colours. The mayflies, breeding madly in the air amidst the slaughter, had begun clouding the water with their dying selves.

Bornu Blatt bowed. 'Goddess.'

The woman glanced up, pale eyes sleepy, distracted. 'A momentary interlude, but necessary.'

'In what way?' Bornu Blatt asked.

She gave the water an abrupt stir, sending ripples outward. 'Tell your goddess I have no idea where Leoman has gone.'

'You tired of him so soon?'

That caught her attention, an acuity coming to her gaze. 'Bornu Blatt, your guise is most unfortunate.'

'So I have been told.'

She shook her head. 'You misunderstand. None see the lesson you offer them. We are surface-dwellers . . . most of the time.'

'"We"?'

'Excuse my generosity. I was speaking of mortals, of course.'

He nodded, hearing the harsh breathing of Gilakas a step behind him. 'Of course.'

'You know not to trust us.'

'"Us"?'

She smiled. 'Gods.'

Bornu Blatt sighed. 'You imagine it gives me peace, Goddess, this . . . scepticism of mine?'

'No, I would think not. Rather, its gift is freedom.'

'Again, no peace comes from that.'

'The man behind you is an agent of the Malazan Empire. He would have killed you already, but you have proved fascinating. He wonders at the goddess choosing a non-believer to deliver her edicts.'

'I too have wondered, Goddess. Perhaps Gilakas will find the answer before I do. One can only trust in curiosity to continue staying his hand.'

The Queen of Dreams tilted her head. 'Leoman would have liked you, Bornu Blatt.'

'Oh dear, misunderstood, was he?'

'In ways you cannot even imagine,' she replied.

'And his sacrifice at Y'Ghatan?'

'That wasn't sacrifice, Bornu Blatt,' the goddess said. 'That was murder.'

'Why? Why did he do it?'

After a moment, she shrugged. 'You will have to ask him that. But consider Sha'ik's camp, in the heart of Raraku. The nest of vipers – his own words, by the way. It might occur to you, then, that Leoman was simply sick of fanatics.'

'I admit,' Bornu Blatt said, 'Gilakas had me convinced of *his* fanaticism.'

'Agents of the Claw are talented indeed. But his fanaticism is no illusion. Alas, not in service to Va'Shaik.'

'She has reached out to you?'

'Here, now, through you.'

'Does she hear us speak?'

'You think I would permit such a thing? No, but upon your return to Seven Cities, she will know of what has passed between us.'

'Then you interrupted my journey to simply tell me you don't know where Leoman has gone?'

'Saving you future pursuits in my direction.'

He studied her for a moment. 'Faith in you is fading from the world,' he said.

She nodded, gaze returning once more to the pool, her submerged hand distorted, elongated beneath the wrist. 'We pass from mortal minds. Generations of gods and goddesses, some abandoned, others transmuted, diluted. We linger in faded script on weathered stone. Our symbols plague shards of pottery. Etched into corroded blades. Strange pendants in graves, statues . . .' Abruptly she lifted her hand out of the water and shook it, scattering droplets that made dragonflies dart down hungrily. 'But this is not our history, it is yours. The fleeting devotion of mortal beings – do not mistake it for the weakening of gods and goddesses. Think more of your indifference delivering to us the gift of freedom.'

Bornu Blatt frowned, a thought occurring to him. 'I wonder then, Goddess, is the time of worship your penance?'

'The price we pay for being one day forgotten? Released?' It seemed the idea amused her, at least momentarily. 'I would think our leaving the mortal world – and your mortal minds – is for most an exhausted retreat.'

'And are you exhausted, Queen of Dreams?'

'Perhaps.' She paused, and then said, 'Even within my temple, there is debate as to the meaning of my title. By "Dreams" is it meant a reference to the dreams of sleep? My means of visiting them, my delivery of fraught meanings, symbols and metaphors? Is it therefore the priestess's task to offer interpretations of dreams, to become students of human nature, cartographers of the mind?' She raised her glistening hand. 'Or by "Dreams" is it meant a direct reference to the ambitions and desires that define so much of a human life? Is my primary task one of making the dreams of mortals come true?'

Bornu Blatt shrugged. 'Why not both?'

She smiled. 'Indeed, why not both?'

'Yet the debate rages on?'

'Blood is spilled, in fact.'

He shook his head. 'Madness. But then, if not some esoteric debate about your aspect leading to murder, then some other equally banal point of contention, having nothing to do with you or any other immortal.'

Sighing, she then said, 'Shall I kill him for you?'

'Who?'

'Gilakas. Shall I wash his fate from my hands and so turn red this sweet water? Your goddess can consider it a favour. Besides, if I send you away as you two now are – knowing the killer at your back – will she not wonder that I did nothing about it? Will she, in fact, become deeply offended? Do I invite acrimony?'

Bornu Blatt swung round to regard Gilakas. It was almost immediately clear that all capacity to move had been taken from the man. He stood, trembling, eyes wide and filled with rage.

Facing the Queen of Dreams again, Bornu said, 'I'd rather you did him no harm.'

'He will now seek to kill you at the first opportunity.'

'I doubt it.'

That startled her. 'Are you a fool?'

'You named him an agent of the Malazan Empire.'

'He is, yes. A Claw assassin, in fact.'

'But also a spy, yes? You told me earlier that what has stayed his hand to this point is his curiosity about me. Do you think that curiosity personal or professional? Would it not be useful information to discover what Va'Shaik intends with her synod? The direction she seeks for her

131

worshippers, for the temples and the priests of her faith? After all,' Bornu Blatt continued, 'what the goddess seeks may yield the very solution the Malazan Empire desires. Namely, peace.'

This clearly left the Queen of Dreams astonished. 'Are these your thoughts, or hers? If hers, then tell her from me: she is a fool. More to the point, if she would deliver such a message to her congregation, they will probably reject her, in anger, and disperse in furious, bloodthirsty indignation, to find other deities they can bend to their murderous impulses!' She leaned forward. 'And if from you, then why, I invite the man behind to do as he pleases. Because, dear Bornu Blatt, you are too innocent to live – not in my world and not in yours!'

Bornu Blatt heard a gasp from Gilakas and turned to see the man stumble forward, arms wide to regain his balance.

When Gilakas looked up, his face was dark with fury, but fixed on the Queen of Dreams, not Bornu. 'You cow! *Of course* the empire wants to know what Va'Shaik intends! *Of course* I have stayed my hand and will continue to do so. In fact, there is nothing about Bornu Blatt that's earned my knife's deadly kiss! The man is indeed innocent! And yet, she *chose* him! Why, if not in the hopes that a killer such as me would quickly ascertain the message she wishes to deliver to the Emperor?' Straightening, he made a dismissive gesture. 'Go away and be forgotten, Queen of Dreams. You'll not be missed.'

'If I kill you now,' the goddess said in a cold voice, 'it will not be as a favour to anyone but myself.'

'The next Claw to find Bornu Blatt may not display my sensitivity,' Gilakas retorted. 'In which case, you will indeed earn Va'Shaik's acrimony. But go ahead, do as you will.' He crossed his arms and waited.

After a long moment, the Queen of Dreams looked away, waving one hand, and slowly vanished. With her departure, the low stone wall encircling the spring was now little more than overgrown fragments, and the bank to the left was a muddy, rank quagmire of hoof prints, animal piss and dung. The overhanging cliff was smoke-blackened on its underside, just above a jutting ledge where a beehive-shaped brick oven was visible, caved in on one side. Beyond the spring, the track descended a hundred or so paces to a huddle of houses to either side of a single, wide street. At the far end of this hamlet stood a temple on a raised mound. Opposite it was a pilgrim's hostel or tavern.

The temple, Bornu Blatt saw, pre-dated the rise of Va'Shaik, and perhaps even of Sha'ik herself. Nor was it a temple more recently consecrated to any new faith. He continued studying it in growing wonder.

Gilakas was swearing under his breath, in some foreign tongue, as he checked his gear, including his weapons, of which apparently many were secreted about his person. Then he looked up and grinned at Bornu Blatt, but added nothing to the smile.

The Inquisitor returned his attention to the distant temple. 'What make you of that, Claw?'

'Please, Gilakas will do. That . . . oh, *that*.'

Grunting agreement, Bornu nodded. 'Yes. That.'

'You know – and I say this knowing you will not be offended, Bornu Blatt – I have always considered both Sha'ik and now Va'Shaik as being minor players in the realm of . . . well, in the realm of the apocalyptic.' He jutted his chin towards the squat temple. 'Here, of course, we have the real thing, and I admit, just seeing it has sent shivers through me.'

'And now we will pay it a visit,' Bornu said.

'Must we?'

'Failing in your desire for adventure, Gilakas?'

'It looks abandoned.'

'Yet not the hostel, if all those horses behind it are any indication. We shall go there first.'

They made their way down into the hamlet. The residences were in a sad state, several clearly unoccupied. A few locals were about, glancing over in surprise at the appearance of two strangers coming down from the spring trail. One, a tall man with hunched shoulders and a long, narrow face, approached them.

'They sent you down?' he asked.

'And who might that be, good sir?' Bornu asked.

'Kraelas and his son, Ulpan.' He nodded towards the spring trail. 'A bandit is hiding somewhere up there, and they went hunting for him. We chased him out, y'see, for–' he nodded towards the hostel, 'the pilgrims. Though now they're saying they want him alive.'

'We saw no one,' Gilakas said.

'Now that's strange,' the man said worriedly.

Gilakas then turned to Bornu. 'Inquisitor, I feel the need to investigate the trail we have just walked. Will you excuse me for a time? With luck, I will return before the dawn.'

133

Bornu Blatt studied the Claw, wondering what he was up to. His own shock and grief kept him silent. The father and son had somehow mistaken them for this bandit. Not the other way around. A bungled ambush, and now both were dead. Even so, things sounded confusing – something else was at work.

Gilakas set off. Turning back to the local man, Bornu Blatt said, 'Is there room within the hostel?'

'Called you "Inquisitor",' the man said, eyes narrowing. 'You have found the wrong temple, my friend.'

'We are not so inimical in our faiths. I will pay my respects.'

'The pilgrims might be less inviting.'

Bornu Blatt shrugged. He moved past the man, weathering the hostility of his regard, and felt that hard gaze on his back as he passed the remaining houses. The hostel was an adobe-over-grey-wood upper level above a stone-walled tavern, the roof clay-tiled and sharply angled, the windows shuttered against the sun's light and heat. Just visible behind the structure was a horse-crowded corral and stables.

As he drew within ten paces of the tavern entrance, two figures emerged, a woman and a man.

Bornu Blatt halted. He glanced to his left and studied the facing of the temple. His dread deepened as he peered up at the vertical lines of text carved into the stone framing the central frieze. Many of the glyphs had faded into illegibility. The frieze showed a row of robed individuals in bas-relief, their faces beneath the hoods hacked away. Here and there, remnants remained of the black paint that once adorned the robes. Huddled before this row was carved a naked man, kneeling and bent over in profile, head facing west. The patches of paint left on this supplicating figure were dusty green, and Bornu could see a tusk curling up from the corner of the man's mouth.

He turned back to the two pilgrims. 'This is . . . unlikely.'

'This is no place for you,' said the woman. Her black robe hung like an overcoat, open on the front to reveal a surcoat of chain and a weapon belt with the hilt of a long-knife visible above her left hip. Her face was pale, as if dusted in chalk, making her dark eyes seem even darker. Short black hair, cut as if mimicking a helmet, made a fringe that hid her eyebrows. She was neither young nor old, but somewhere in between, though Bornu was never a good judge in such matters.

The man beside her, also robed in black, was leaning on an ornate staff he gripped with both hands, and many of the fingers on those hands had been truncated. His face was round and strangely smooth and childlike, utterly hairless. His fleshy lips were set in a smile that did not reach his small, blue eyes. His lank, mousy hair was cut in similar helm-fashion, though far less successfully.

Bornu Blatt shook his head. 'This is preposterous. The cult of the Nameless Ones died out centuries past. You play at this, understanding nothing.' He gestured to the temple. 'Do you even know the Jhag on his hands and knees?'

'Icaras,' the woman said, baring her teeth, her face twisted with contempt. 'We understand far more than it comforts you to think.'

Straightening, Bornu Blatt said, 'Very well, let us challenge our mutual depths of knowledge on such matters, shall we? And for such a task, is this street the best place?' He nodded towards the tavern. 'Invite me in, if you dare.'

The man spoke in a piping voice, 'We have already consecrated—'

'I'm not interested in entering the temple, I assure you. Perhaps you are not even aware of this, but the sorcery you have awakened there is not even human.'

'Jhag—'

Bornu cut the man off again. 'No, not Jaghut either. Do you not see the foundation stones? They are thousands of years older than the construct raised atop it, and that latter construct itself is two or three thousand years old.' He pointed at the frieze. 'The Nameless Ones re-carved a much older scene, and in turn were themselves deposed, and now you thought to resurrect them here?' He shook his head.

The man's tight smile had grown strained. Now he said, 'We awaited a proper sacrifice to complete the consecration of the altar. You will do.'

'Ah, the "bandit" you ordered the locals to hunt down? Came with you, that one? But then managed to escape. Telling the locals your intended victim was a bandit was a terrible mistake. They planned on just cutting the hapless person down. Besides, blood sacrifice is an abomination.'

Now the man's smile was entirely gone, and the woman had her hand on the grip of her long-knife.

'In any case, that too would have been a mistake,' Bornu said. 'An unwilling victim is, in this instance, a very bad idea.' He sighed. 'I am thirsty and hungry. I will utter my challenge a second time. Invite me in if you possess the courage.'

135

'To challenge our faith?' the man snapped, his voice pitched even higher.

'No,' Bornu replied. 'To dismantle it.'

The woman asked, 'Where have you come from?'

'Hanar Ara. I am the Inquisitor in the name and service of Va'Shaik.'

Spitting onto the ground, the man then said, 'And who granted you that title?'

'She did.'

'Kulat—'

'Kulat is dead. The goddess has returned.'

'A heap of gasping blubber—'

'No longer.'

'She sees through your eyes?' the woman asked.

Bornu shrugged.

After a moment, the woman let her hand fall away from her weapon. 'Come ahead, then. The service within is spare but will serve.'

Her companion turned to her. 'Why believe anything he says? Kill him now, Gracer.'

She looked down at the man at her side. 'We leave him to Melok to trap him in his lies. I for one look forward to the battle of wits. Tell me, Stult, has a false soul ever withstood Melok?'

The man's smile slowly returned. 'No, none. Why, by shock alone, most confess their sins. This I will delight in seeing.'

Stepping back, Stult now bowed and made a sweeping invitation with his staff.

As Bornu strode past, he paused and said, 'The invocation you carved on that staff is filled with errors, rendering it both meaningless and powerless.'

Seeing the smile vanish a second time pleased Bornu Blatt.

Entering the tavern, Bornu paused until his eyes adjusted to the gloom. The woman, Gracer, remained directly behind him, and now she said in a low tone, 'Where did you send your friend?'

'I sent him nowhere,' Bornu replied.

'Will he return?'

'I don't know. Will he?'

Then she moved around him, followed by Stult, whose childlike face was filled with venom, though his eyes glittered as if in anticipation. 'Come stand before Melok, Inquisitor.'

Six other black-robed people occupied the tavern, along with two shadowy figures behind the bar who Bornu judged to be a husband and wife, proprietors of the hostel, and the manner in which they clung to the shadows beneath the sagging shelves indicated abject terror.

Only one of the six commanded Bornu's attention, this being the heavy-set man seated on a chair directly opposite the door, back to a wall, a small round table to his right on which sat a clay jug of wine and a cup set on its side and still dripping. Something glittered in the centre of the man's wide forehead, and as Bornu approached, he was startled to realize that it was a third eye – not a set gem in facsimile, but an actual, clearly functioning eye, blinking to match that of the other two.

'Why invite him here?' the man – undoubtedly Melok – now wheezed. 'No supplication. He believes nothing.'

'And yet,' piped Stult, 'calls himself Va'Shaik's Inquisitor!'

Bornu broke the uncanny stare of three eyes and spoke to the pair behind the bar. 'Ale, if you have it, and what passes for a meal, please.' He then shifted his attention to his immediate surroundings, found a table he could drag close, and then a chair. Setting his satchel down he positioned the chair on the other side of the table, facing Melok, and then sat.

'You perceive yourself as my equal?' Melok asked, adding a raspy chortle that shook his upper body. 'Did I invite you to sit? Whatever did you interpret in my demeanour suggesting such a thing?'

'Alas,' Bornu said, 'I wasn't paying attention to your demeanour, leaving me nothing to . . . well, interpret. You are Melok, yes?'

A slow nod. 'I am the Holy Destriant of the Nameless Ones, consecrator of temples and shrines, sire to the faith reborn.'

'You have delved in strange sorcery,' Bornu said, 'with that third eye of yours. I am trying to recollect if I have ever read of anything similar. Well, not in the surviving texts attributed to or about the Nameless Ones, to be sure. Pilashin? The Gleaner Sect? Travellers among the caravans, devoted to divination. Said to drag their spirit-god with them everywhere.' He shook his head. 'But no spirit-god trails you, Melok, in chains or otherwise. Or rather, not the one you think.'

This was answered by silence, but animation had left all three of those eyes. In the suddenly motionless tableau, the woman from behind the bar crept up to set a tankard and a plate of boiled vegetables on the table in front of Bornu. He smiled his thanks, but she'd already turned away, seeming to shrink as she went.

'Anyway,' Bornu resumed with a faint sigh. 'Pilashin, I think. Requiring a victim, or someone willing to give up a living eye, which is why the one in your forehead is different from your regular ones. A child, perhaps? Or that of a woman – it's certainly prettier than the other two. The conceit was soon revealed, of course, that a third *real* eye grants nothing of the properties of the *inner* third eye. But it did yield ferocious headaches, requiring potent numbing drugs – usually blended with wine.' He retrieved a wooden spoon from the satchel at his feet and then began eating.

'The headaches are the price I pay,' Melok said, licking his lips, 'for the gifts I receive. Your arrogance leaves me breathless, your presumption infuriates, and I do not think you will leave this room alive.'

'Well, resorting to violence means the challenge Gracer spoke of is already won, by me. I was invited to match wits with you, Melok. You to defend your faith and me to dismember it and reveal it as invented hogwash. You see, I am a scholar of religions old and new. In many ways, I have devoted my life to such pursuits. But please, do attempt to convince me that you are indeed Destriant to the Nameless Ones. The rest of your claims I do not question. You indeed consecrate temples and shrines, and as for being sire to the faith reborn, well, yes, I suppose you are. Just not the faith of the Nameless Ones. And the temple across the street? The Nameless Ones who occupied it were squatters, and probably paid the price for their trespass with their lives. That said,' he added, 'your blood will be welcome.'

Slowly, all the other black-robed pilgrims had left their seats. Weapons were drawn. Alone among them doing no such thing, Gracer waved them all back. 'The goddess sees through him,' she said. 'Witnesses all that happens here. What we do here could invite a war, and we are not ready for that, not even close. Melok! You know I am right!'

'I doubt he knows anything,' Bornu Blatt said. 'That very real eye likely destroyed the gland behind it, a gland most definitely essential to spiritual awakening. Melok is a charlatan. And like the best grifter, he understands human nature and exploits it for effect. He indeed discovers liars – knowing well the face in the mirror – and this talent has always served him well. The Pilashin are pretty much extinct, by the way. The Malazan Empire does not look kindly on mortals chaining and torturing earth-spirits.'

The woman returned with a hunk of bread, which Bornu now used to

138

wipe up what remained on the plate. 'The temple opposite,' he said, busy soaking up runny grease, 'belongs to Dessimbelackis, in his Deragoth manifestation. Continue consecrating temples and shrines, Melok, and you may well resurrect the bastard. Of course, I doubt it. His time has passed. The Nameless Ones who tried claiming the temple didn't last long. Besides, they had their own problems. They couldn't hold down what they created. And one day, their creation turned on them.'

He paused, and then sat back, reaching for his tankard and looking at the pilgrims facing him. 'Va'Shaik, goddess of the apocalypse, will of course dip her head in humble acknowledgement to the Lord of Annihilation. Best you do the same, though you cannot hope to impose order upon that Lord.' He glanced over to Gracer. 'Icaras is the degraded version of the name, by the way.' He faced the others again. 'But I assure you all, no mortal or god has any hope of controlling the Jhag named Icarium.'

*   *   *

The boy had drunk from the wrong side of the spring and now lay on his side in the mud, convulsed in cramps. He observed this from a distance, as if hovering above his own frail, small body. This was the place he retreated to. It was silent, cool and calm, and it was clearly a place no one else could see.

Months could pass without his ever leaving that refuge, even as he watched himself walk, run, eat, sleep, and all the other things a body did. He could observe the people around him, a hand grasping tight his upper arm, dragging him along a grimy alley. People gathering round him and speaking to each other. He listened to their words and understood them. He observed all the things their faces gave away, and understood that, too. There was no need to speak. What they wanted to do with him was no secret. Of course, the variations were many, keeping him curious.

The body writhing in the piss-splashed mud was where he once lived, in the time before the refuge, the floating, invisible place of hiding. There were memories in that body, fractured, scattered things. As time passed, more drifted away, out beyond his reach, dissolving into nothing. He did not miss them, never longed for what he lost. The remaining fragments were mostly unpleasant.

Barring one memory. A tall man, possibly his father, as he understood the idea of 'father'. He remembered emerging from him, like a thing spat

139

out. And so, he knew that some part of him was his father. If other parts existed, something bound to the thing called 'mother', that was gone. But in truth, he did not think he had ever had a mother. His father made him from his own body.

How did he lose him? He did not know. One moment his father's large, callused hand enveloped his tiny, soft one, and everything seemed possible. Then he was alone, and all the rest was inevitable.

The world was strange, in that it had never welcomed him. How could a world exist that did not welcome those who came to live within it? And why did all the people in that world fight each other for what they could never possess? The world simply was. No one could own it. No one could rule it. It was not a place to be bent to any will. Instead, it resisted, and then broke. To imagine resistance to be the same as relinquishing was a mistake. Was this not obvious to everyone?

The three-eyed man wanted to cut the throat of the body he sometimes lived in. Over an altar, and as his blood pumped out to fill the runnels in the stone, the three-eyed man would intone sacred words in the name of the Nameless Ones, imbuing with power the place of killing.

This was silly. Killing imbued every place with power. But mostly that power was a mix of smaller powers, because dying was confusing to the one dying. Besides, the Nameless Ones were gone. He did not know how he knew that. He thought it might be a fact held by his father, and his father was, he suspected, very intimate with the Nameless Ones.

People called him Mute, so this must be his name. If his father had another name for him, he'd forgotten it. Memories, after all, were not to be trusted, and without doubt, *that* came from his father.

So, all his past was scattered and fading away and none of it counted for much anyway. The moment of 'now' was all that meant anything, because it was full, filling out all his senses until it seemed he would burst.

Hands dragging him down alleys.

Rope looped about his neck, the knot drawn tight.

Into daylight, out of daylight, into night, out of night. Winds from the north, winds from the south, the west and even the east (where storms came from).

Meals to eat, liquids to drink. The body had needs.

It was poisoned now. There was lots of pain.

These were the things of now:

Right now, he slipped free from the rope, a woman's face hovering.

Right now, he ran into the night.

Right now, they chased him on horses.

Right now, he slipped among crags and rocks where the horses could not go.

Right now, a father and son came looking for him and he hid from them.

Right now, he found them both dead and did not know how or why.

Right now, beside a muddy pond, he was dying.

'Ah, lad, that was a mistake.'

Hovering over the strange man now crouching over the body, Mute nodded in agreement to his words, but his body did not do the same. Too busy with all that pain.

'Not much of a bandit, are you? Why did the boy and his dad try an ambush? What was there to fear from you? Half-starved as you are. Not even a paring knife on you. Just a damned leash – gods, these people are fucking savages. Pardon my language. But then, abandoned children are hardly unique to Seven Cities. Get enough people anywhere and some are going to be deemed expendable. Weak ones, poor ones, little ones. The real wonder is how we let it happen and keep happening.'

As he'd been speaking in the now, he had gently lifted the moaning, twisting body from the mud, carrying it over to a bank of grasses, then – seeing all the ants occupying that spot – over to a flat-topped remnant of stone wall, where he set the body down.

He then turned Mute onto his side and pushed a finger down his throat.

Foaming, yellow liquids gushed out, heave after heave. Coughing, spitting, and then, slowly, the pain began to loosen its tight clench on his gut, uncurling his body.

The man was mixing into a small clay cup a paste from some powder and water from a flask. When he was done, he lifted the body's head, forced open the mouth, and poured the liquid in. The body swallowed, coughed, and then relaxed.

'You can open your eyes now,' he said. 'I know you're in there.'

But he wasn't. It was a common mistake people made around him.

He watched the stranger lightly slap Mute's face, to no effect. After a time, in which he could track all the details of the man's indecision, the man collected Mute up in his arms and set off back down the trail.

In this particular 'now', he realized – with shock – that he was no longer alone in his refuge. And this had never happened before. *Never ever!*

A woman's sigh, and then, *'I won't stay long. It's pretty, however, and so very clever in its design – is this truly your own making? Or a gift from the one who made you? No matter, it is all yours, now.'*

She was *with* him, as invisible as Mute was in this place.

'Memories are indeed a curse, especially for one such as you. Still, do you know what happens when you turn your back on your body? When you release it from all attention? How quickly the hunted becomes the hunter – had you not paused to drink, they would in their fright have led you down into the hamlet, and had you followed, why, everyone there would now be dead. Including those foolish pilgrims.'

He knew his body did things when his wandering thoughts took him away from it. He would discover that it had travelled far, that it was among different people. That seasons had passed, and he was thinner or fatter, a bit taller, his hair cut short or grown long. Sometimes, he returned to find himself splashed in blood, none of it his own.

But 'now' was an easy place to be. Did it even matter that situations changed?

'I begin to suspect,' the woman's voice said, *'you were an accident. There is . . . precedent. But listen, child, return now to your body – it recovers. I would rather you not harm the ones you will find yourself among.'*

Mute thought about it. He thought about all of it. Then, with a flick of an invisible hand, he sent the woman spinning away. Her startled cry quickly faded, and Mute was alone again. And no one, no one ever, ever again, would sneak into his refuge. *Never ever!*

He returned to his little body so that it didn't feel little any more, so that it became the *whole world*.

It was dusk and the air was cool, and the man's arms were strong.

Mute decided to sleep.

Dreaming of nothing.

*   *   *

No doubt knowing that stoning or worse was imminent, Melok fled in the night, taking an extra horse and all the coin intended to fund the resurrection of the cult of the Nameless Ones. Abandoned by their leader, things quickly devolved for the pilgrims.

Three set off with the dawn, with murderous intent, hot on Melok's trail. The others wandered off singly or in pairs, until only Gracer and Stult remained in the tavern, sitting at a table near the door and deep in whispered debate, occasionally casting glances at Bornu Blatt where he sat at a table near the back stairs, eating a hearty breakfast – the same boiled vegetables and stale bread, but plenty of it this time around.

The proprietors, Saegis and her husband, Nulri, appeared convinced that Bornu had been responsible for driving the pilgrims away, and though that meant a potential loss of income, the prospect of a reawakened temple on the other side of the street, filled to the brim with the boiling blood of human sacrifice, pushed Bornu into the guise of hero, a deliverer of salvation no less. When he assured them that no new arrival of pilgrims was imminent, even this momentary disappointment vanished when he explained the temple's cursed origins. By the end of that explanation, Saegis was determined to see the old temple knocked down, stone by stone, and every stone shattered into rubble. The fire in her eyes made Bornu believe she would manage just that, even if she had to do it herself.

Still, he felt uneasy taking credit for shattering the cult. True, Melok and his ilk – imposters and swindlers – often thrived within the cosy, slippery realm of religion, with no end of gullible, desperate followers eager to surrender all will to a leader's whims. Such leaders were usually mad, of course, or at least perverted beneath their veil of piety, and exposure was inevitable. But being gullible was not the same as being a fool. Things were more complicated than that.

That said, Melok and those like him always knew when it was time to bolt.

Bornu had simply hastened things along. A word here, a word there. No special prowess required.

Still, this was a place for regret. The sad killings up the trail. A father. A son. The failure of communication so often the cause of calamity. Silence and misunderstanding as the lynchpins of history, assuming one saw history as nothing more than disaster heaped upon disaster, with the shining truth of human resiliency burning through it all with every passing moment. To his mind, then, this was the struggle of existence, this dichotomy, the warring of every singular soul against a universe they barely comprehended.

Was it not the responsibility of the gods to reach down a helping hand?

Quite possibly, this was Va'Shaik's desire. That made it noble to Bornu's thinking. Without that conviction, he would not be here. Yet, in his absence, a father and a son would still be alive.

Pushing the clay plate away, he grunted to his feet, collecting up his satchel as he did so. A passing nod to the two remaining pilgrims, and then outside into the sunlight, where he halted.

Just now emerging from the temple opposite, Gilakas, and with him was a boy of nine or ten, sleepy-eyed and streaked in dry mud.

Bornu Blatt walked towards them. 'Gilakas, that was . . . risky.'

The Claw shrugged. 'Haunted, aye. The antics of the ghosts and spirits, Inquisitor, left us little reason to fear them.'

'Why is that?'

'They danced all night.'

'I did not think you'd delight them, Gilakas.'

'Not me,' he said.

Bornu saw the Claw's gaze slip past him, and he turned to see that Gracer and Stult had emerged, only to pause, as if waiting for something. 'Your pilgrimage is at an end,' he said to them. 'Where will you go now?'

Gracer tilted her head. 'With you, of course.'

'But, why?'

It seemed she had no ready answer. Bornu looked to Stult, who shrugged and said, 'Where she goes, I go.'

'I have no destination, or rather, many destinations,' Bornu said. 'Besides, is it really fitting that you present to us such fickle allegiance?' After a moment, he added, 'Well, I doubt Va'Shaik would be bothered, to be honest.'

But Gracer was now scowling. 'I give no allegiance to your goddess, Inquisitor.'

'Then why accompany me?'

Her gaze flicked to Gilakas. 'I thought you might have need of a bodyguard. But it seems you do not. Still, we shall all be upon the same road for a time. You came from the east and the only road out leads west. So.'

'We have spare horses and pack-mules,' Stult added, leaning on his staff, favouring his left leg. 'Melok knew he couldn't steal them without waking everyone. The mules complain loudly when disturbed in the middle of the night.' There was a faint sheen on his visage, from whatever unguent he used to remove all hair and whiskers from his face. 'And tents and cook-gear and food.'

144

Bornu nodded. 'It does seem reasonable that we travel together for a time. Very well.' Dismissing them for the moment, Bornu went to Gilakas for a more private conversation. The boy paid him no attention at all.

'Is he addled?' Bornu asked.

Gilakas hesitated, and then nodded. 'I think so. Mute—'

At the word the boy's attention snapped to him, expression now alert and expectant.

'—so far. Hardly,' he added sourly, 'a bandit.'

'Well, no,' Bornu agreed. 'An intended sacrifice, for the temple you just spent the night in.'

'Tavern door was locked up when we finally got here,' Gilakas explained.

'And now, Gilakas? Can you leave him here? No, I don't think you can.'

'Agreed, Inquisitor. But Va'Shaik is the protector of waifs, is she not?'

'Among other things. Orphans certainly. A temple will take him into its care. Still, he looks malnourished – you may end up carrying him all day, Gilakas.'

'He can ride my horse,' Gracer said behind them, having drawn closer. 'I was never happy with the whole idea. Blood sacrifice and all that. But Melok said—'

'Melok!' snarled Stult, spitting into the dust. 'Lying bastard.'

Bornu turned to study the boy again. He was staring at Gracer, showing no fear at all in his eyes. 'It seems he has no objection, which is odd. I would think just seeing you two would be traumatizing.'

Gracer snorted. 'Mute fears nothing. He's barely there most of the time. Empty as a coconut husk, that skull.'

'Yet he escaped you.'

Nodding, Gracer frowned at the boy – whose name, it seemed, was indeed Mute – and then said, 'Melok found him in Estaramon. Bought him, I mean.' She paused, and then added, 'He bites.'

'I'll bring the horses and mules around,' said Stult.

Gilakas said to Gracer, 'I am Gilakas, and yes indeed the Inquisitor is under my protection. Be mindful of that. I'll not hesitate in killing either of you, or both, if you give me cause to think you a threat.'

'Gilakas,' said Bornu, sighing, 'this is a joining of convenience, hardly unusual among travellers in these wastelands. Customs obtain, including mutual pacts of defence against marauders, the sharing of food and meals and tasks in maintaining a camp. These are common across all Seven Cities.'

'Malazan,' Gracer suddenly said in a growl, glaring at Gilakas.

'Foreigner,' Bornu corrected. 'Do you have a problem with that, Gracer? If so, best you and Stult journey on your own.'

'Is he Malazan or not?'

Bornu frowned. 'We are in the Malazan Empire. Accordingly, we are all Malazans.'

'You know what I meant!'

'I did and have chosen to pretend otherwise. Will you take the meaning of that?'

Through all of this, Gilakas simply smiled at Gracer.

'Well,' continued Bornu, 'this has started out as expected. Is it any wonder the wars never end? At the very least, I can observe in detail the root causes of human conflict, as personified by you two spitting cobras.'

Stult reappeared, leading four saddled horses and two pack-mules.

The boy, Mute, left Gilakas's side and scrambled up the flank of the lead horse. Gracer went to them and began cinching up the stirrups. Stult busied himself adjusting the bulging, glistening waterskins slung down the sides of the mules, and Bornu was momentarily startled by the strange likeness of those waterskins to Stult's own head and face.

Then, recollecting himself, he turned to Gilakas, keeping his voice low. 'The ghosts danced around the child last night?'

Gilakas nodded. 'As he slept, aye.'

'In a frenzy? As if compelled to do so?'

Frowning, the Claw shook his head. 'No. More like dancing in pleasure and delight. Protectively, as well.'

'Oh, that's not good.'

'I would have thought frenzied and compelled to be a worse option,' Gilakas murmured, rubbing his jaw. 'Since that would've meant the child's dangerously powerful in his madness. But I felt and saw none of that.'

'Yes,' Bornu said. 'That would've been bad indeed. But this is much worse, Gilakas. The boy is aspected.'

Gilakas swung round to scowl at the temple, head lifting to study the frieze. 'Nameless Ones?'

'Forget the Nameless Ones,' snapped Bornu. 'This temple belongs to Icarium. The child is aspected to *Icarium*.'

*   *   *

146

Astride the horse, his legs barely able to bend down to slip into the stirrups, Mute remained in his body for a time, as they all set out on the road leading west, back the way he had come when Gracer had held his leash. Gracer, who when no one was looking, took a knife to that rope and let Mute rush off into the darkness. And Stult, who saw all of that and could have shouted to wake the others, but didn't, because his love for Gracer was a deep, all-devouring thing, like a root longer than its tree was tall.

Poor, doomed root, forever searching for a single drop of life-giving water from Gracer, but that would never happen, because Gracer knew nothing of what love meant.

The ugly-faced man they called Inquisitor, he knew about love, but maybe in the same way as Stult. His root stretched many, many leagues, and seemed in no danger of ever snapping. The heart well-cupped in strong hands could withstand a lifetime of anguish, and the Inquisitor's hands were strong indeed.

His saviour, Gilakas, had made a habit of breaking his own heart, but all of that was long ago, and now he filled himself with imagined loyalties. Giving one's own heart to a cause rather than a person. It was the saddest sacrifice among them all.

Eventually, Mute left his body and retreated to his refuge. He had so much to think about. All the stories of the ghosts, all the revelations of the dancing spirits. And now, at last, the name of his father.

The Nameless Ones had always known they would fail, would lose in the end. It was part of their scripture, in fact, this final promise fading into silence, and empty temples with dust skirling across the floor, mocking all that had gone before, and all that would one day come.

It was good to be travelling again.

Especially since he now had a father to find.

147

CHAPTER SEVEN

It is a shallow mind, carelessly gliding over all the senses to which we are gifted, to see nothing in a desert. To look upon flat lands or even a distant rumple of grass-hided hills, and utter the pronouncement that nothing of worth is to be seen, that the wind is empty and devoid of voice, that the scents of the air bespeak of dust and naught else.

Within, two glorious gifts have been silenced. The first is the imagination, left so deadened by disuse as to yield an inner landscape far more denuded and lifeless than any desert or plain. The second is the gift of stillness, wherein wonder expands to every horizon; where, in mindful awakening, this stillness is revealed to be alive with motion, with the subtle play of hue, light and shadow, with the faint ticking of stones baked by the sun, with the hum and hiss of winged insects, with the waving grasses at the feet of wind-bent trees in valleys and dried stream-beds. And here wanders yet another ghost, named Time, so willing to meet your eye and, perhaps, wink.

The shallow mind turns away from all of this, charged by other things inside its inner world of colourless absences, with its one voice listing without pause the boredom of its own failing.

I weep for those flat eyes that see so little of what can only be described as a feast of revelation, of beauty, and the forlorn melancholy singing its eternal aria.

Is it only me then, whom you may see if you care to, out on that land, standing alone, drunk on wonder?

The Lie of Nothing to See
Musings of the Wandering Woman
Anonymous

'These lands,' Gilakas muttered, 'endless wastes in every direction.'

'What lands would those be?' Bornu Blatt asked. He and Gilakas rode side by side on the stony trail. Behind them was the train of horses and mules in the company of Gracer, Stult and the boy, Mute. The bitter cold of the night just past was boiling off in the burgeoning heat. The last hamlet was two days behind them. Even the herders with their flocks of sheep and goats were absent.

'Seven Cities, of course,' answered Gilakas. 'Where people scrabble for whatever water they can find. Nothing around but goats and the occasional sheep, wild asses and wheeling vultures. Withered plots of wheat. And rock, lots of rock. And sand. Lots of sand.'

They were approaching a serried vista of crags, cliffs and upthrust layers of sandstone. The trail they were on was centuries past its era of regular use, hinting of lost ages when the land was more fecund, its people flush with its gifts. Now, almost none of that remained. Grey branches littered the ground to either side, attesting to a stand or row of trees long ago, their stumps like stubby, rotted teeth. Stult was busy collecting the branches into bundles for the cookfire.

There had been warning of roving bandits in the last settlement, so Bornu had elected to lead his troop off the trader track. What he could recall from a scattering of very old maps had indicated a possible short-cut to the next region of habitation, but faint scratching on frayed vellum gave away virtually nothing of the reality on the ground. This was less a trail than a shallow gully carved out by run-off from some past thunderstorm.

The trio behind Bornu and Gilakas were still a bit of a mystery to the Inquisitor, their stories mostly unknown. The need to belong to something, be it a cult or any other company, was perhaps universal. The rewards of solitude always held a taint of pathos, after all. Rarely was its virtue not diffident. It was clear, however, that Gracer had been, if not a soldier, then a mercenary. Stult's attachment to her was not subtle in its reason, making its hopelessness all the more poignant. As for Mute, the boy was broken inside, and, having tired of sharing Gracer's saddle, would now sit astride one of the mules the entire day. At times when they halted to eat or rest, Gracer would have to lift the boy from the saddle, and even when left standing, he seemed barely aware of his surroundings.

The track climbed slightly as it approached the bluffs fringing the mesa, the bright sunlight making the sandstone glow as if lit from within, and a dozen paces later they found themselves moving through a channel with hollowed cliff-faces rising to either side. As the path cut deeper into the ridge-line, the sheer walls of sandstone began showing the signs of carvings and red paint, with more images appearing on boulders squatting in hollows on the ground. Among the paintings, Bornu could see the outlines of hands surrounded in red mist, many of them missing digits. The carvings made geometric, maze-like patterns that shifted in plays of light and shadow as they rode past.

When a wide cave opened out to the left of the trail, Bornu drew in the reins. 'We will rest here,' he said. He slowly dismounted, every joint in his body reminding him of half a lifetime of inactivity.

Stult pulled the mules into the shade of the overhang and began readying the sloshing skins of water for the beasts. Gracer slipped down off her horse and gathered up Mute, seating him on a boulder outside the cave. The boy reached down and began collecting shards of flint and chert from the glittering ring of shattered stone encircling the boulder.

Gilakas carried the various bundles of dried foodstuffs to the level area outside the cave where a ring of stones marked an old hearth, and flat stones had been dragged into a vague circle around it for seating.

Bornu walked into the cave.

He had imagined this journey out from Hanar Ara to be one taken in solitude, indeed a solitude in which diffidence was a lifelong companion, all its heat long since cast off. He had been at peace with his ugliness, having made his own hollow of isolation. He knew that his appearance was an unwelcome imposition upon the sensibilities of others, making his excusing himself from their company a gesture of mercy on his part. There was no point in being bitter about any of that. If his considerate nature held any bite, it was on the soft parts of his own soul, not anyone else's.

But then almost immediately Gilakas had joined him on this journey. The Malazan spy and assassin, for whom the offence of his intended victim's unwholesomeness was irrelevant. And now Gracer and Stult, exchanging Melok for Bornu, and in terms of comparison, it could be argued that a man possessing three eyes was far more disconcerting than a man devoid of symmetry. As for Mute, well, now was not the time to focus attention on the boy, and in any case, the outside world rarely impinged upon Mute. At least, not yet.

At the back of the cave, almost lost in the gloom, there were three

150

distinct passages. The one on the left was the narrowest, a crack rising at a slight angle, its upper edges smeared with old soot. The centre opening showed a dip in the stone floor, from the passage of feet across centuries, if not millennia. The one on the right was half-blocked with rubble, and atop that heap had been placed a head.

Bornu stood studying it, his mind struggling to make sense of its details.

Gilakas spoke from the hearth-ring ten paces behind him, 'Inquisitor, will you eat?'

'Not yet,' Bornu replied.

He moved closer to the head on its perch of rocks. At first, he had wondered if it belonged to a beast of some sort, since a pair of what looked like horns jutted out to either side. Now he saw that the horns emerged from a helmet, fashioned from the skullcap of some creature unknown to Bornu. The face beneath it was more or less human, covered in patches of withered skin over strands of tendon. The eye sockets were unrelieved holes of darkness beneath heavy brow-ridges. The lower jaw was missing.

Sighing, Bornu dipped his head slightly. 'T'lan Imass.'

After a moment there came into Bornu's mind a rattling, dusty reply, 'Why assume I have anything to say to you, mortal?'

Bornu shrugged. 'You just did.'

'Why have you not gone into the centre passage?'

'Why would I?'

'No reason. Only, it is better if you do, like so many others have done.'

'Why is it better to do that?'

'Because then, mortal, you do not return, so I need not recall how to speak, and all the unpleasant confusion that is conversation need not happen. Your hesitation has disturbed my eternity of pointless contemplation.'

Bornu shifted his attention to the passageway on the left. 'And the smoke-blackened passage?'

'I think we should ignore it.'

'Why?'

The T'lan Imass was silent.

'I should tell you,' said Bornu, 'most of the curiosity I am feeling is not mine. I am under the geas of a goddess.'

'Imagine elevating scorn into divinity,' the T'lan Imass said in a tone of infinite weariness. 'That part of her, at least. The curse that was an artist's roving eye. So often, alas, aesthetic beauty is but a reflection of sexual desire.

Does the flaw belong to the artist? Is it the artist's impulse to corrupt the beauty being worshipped? Do you see the problem, mortal, when worship and desire become one?'

Bornu shook his head. 'I do not know what you are referring to,' he said.

'He painted the woman he loved,' the T'lan Imass explained. *'A crime sufficient for, at worst, banishment. But the crime that sundered a world, why, that was the crime of painting the* wrong *woman.'*

'My goddess is Va'Shaik. Sha'ik *reborn.*'

'Not the first time I'm sure.'

'No, that is true. Yet, this Va'Shaik knows nothing of painting, or lost loves, or betrayal. None of the events you seem to be talking about have any connection to her. This one was adopted as a child by Sha'ik. And sent away before that Sha'ik's demise. The Book of Dryjhna was not passed to her. That book, in fact, has been lost.'

'Your point, mortal?'

'My goddess is here with me now, T'lan Imass. I sense her . . . confusion.'

'She forgets, then.'

'Forgets what?'

'She was taken by T'lan Imass and delivered to Hanar Ara. She was brought to the temple in the rock, in the city we carved from the heart of the mountain in the time of the First Empire. She was left there to gather up the remnants of madness that is scorn, the Imass bloodline burning a path through every Sha'ik and every Sha'ik Reborn. If she is confused, mortal, it is because she has not yet found her own cause for rage and madness. A betrayal waits for her. This is the power of Dryjhna. Not a book. Not the mewling complaints of spirits in the desert. Not the blind fury of sandstorms. Betrayal, mortal. The madness of scorn, the fury that cannot be stopped.'

The undead creature's words, hissing like sand over stone in Bornu's mind, left him chilled. The memory of Salabi's ordeal in the white fire of Va'Shaik's anger returned to him. While deeper inside, he felt his goddess recoil. He felt an impulse to defend her. 'She recalls your kind's role in her delivery to the First Holy City. Nor is she unfamiliar with anger. But scorn and betrayal? I think not. The Apocalyptic, T'lan Imass, emerged from the land itself, here in Seven Cities. It came from the heat, the blinding sun, the dust of drought, hunger, disease and death. It lies within us all, a fever only temporarily dormant.' He paused, and then tilted his head to regard the T'lan Imass. 'What has any of that to do with you?'

'Tell your goddess, mortal, to await the betrayal. It may be her who strides the world in the time of madness. Or perhaps the one to follow her, or generations still to come. The Apocalyptic does not belong to this land you call Seven Cities. It belongs to the world. Accordingly and in turn, the betrayal and its answer will be a world-devouring fire of destruction.

'The secret lies in the painting. Go, then, into the smoke-blackened cave. See for yourself. And show the goddess within you. I did warn you that all conversation would only serve to confuse.'

Sighing, Bornu turned away. He strode back to his horse, now standing among the other beasts in shade, and withdrew from a saddlebag a lantern. At the hearth, Gilakas had already lit a fire, the flames being fed sticks by Stult kneeling before it, the bundle at his side. Bornu walked over, reached down to the fire's flickering edge and collected up a burning twig, using it to light the lantern's oil-soaked wick. He sensed the eyes of the others upon him but felt no inclination to explain himself. Straightening, he returned to the cave.

'Goddess,' he whispered as he studied the crack in the wall with its old smoke stains, 'shall we see for ourselves?'

She made no answer in his mind. It seemed that she never did. It was even a possibility that he but imagined her presence within him, but he doubted that. Imagination was not one of his strengths.

He strode forward, shifting sideways to slip through the fissure. Beyond, in the yellow glow of the lantern's light, the passage opened out into a cavern. To either side, stacked vertically side by side like giant ribs, were rows of ivory tusks anchored by rocks. The floor was limestone, its pattern resembling that of flows of dried mud. In parallel rows to either side of the central track, elephant teeth had been set inside hollowed pits. A few paces ahead, the walls closed in again.

The fissure wended downward, ever narrowing and forcing Bornu to edge along sideways. High overhead was the occasional glimmer of sunlight but that vanished after another dozen or so paces, and before long the ceiling descended in a jumble of broken rock, close enough now that should he reach up, he could touch the smoke-blackened stones.

If there were currents in the air, Bornu could not feel them. The smell was musty, with no hint of moisture. Yet a strange pervasive heat raised sweat on his skin.

Thirty paces on, he came to another cavern and halted. Here, the walls bore paintings, image overlying image, a chaotic profusion of lines, stains, streaks and dots in black, yellow and red paints. Gouges and runnels made cross-hatch patterns here and there, seemingly intended to obscure or perhaps destroy whatever image was behind it.

On all sides, then, he saw the shapes and likenesses of ancient beasts, from a time when the desert was savannah. Nowhere did he find handprints or their outlines; nor the common stick-figures of spear-wielding hunters.

Holding up the lantern, Bornu made a slow turn in the centre of the chamber. The play of light set the beasts into motion, flickering with life and seeming animation. Bornu's slow circle almost completed itself, then swung back. His breath caught. A place of smudges and faint stains, lying upon a bulge in the stone wall, the bulge itself revealing dips and hollows.

It was the scale that had initially thrown him. Whereas all the beasts were illustrated from a distance of perhaps twenty or even thirty paces, and whereas they occupied flat, even stretches of stone, the bulge in the wall, at a height level with Bornu's upper chest, or chin, was the size of a human head, and in deft blushes of hue and ground hollows and angles, a face stared back at him, its eyes buried in shadow.

He approached, astonished by the talent that had fashioned this. Among the Imass, she would have been beautiful. The black paint above the forehead seemed to float, drifting away and then into the rock itself, denoting a raven mane of long hair swept back by a wind this place had never known. The broad, flaring cheekbones below her hidden eyes seemed made for laughter, plump and faintly flushed with red ochre. The bulge had been shaped to add details and depth, until it seemed that the face projected from behind the stone wall, transforming rock into the thinnest, translucent skin. Carved, then painted, then polished smooth.

For an instant, Bornu believed that should he reach out to touch this face, he would feel its warmth, its life. 'Gods below,' he muttered.

From somewhere, perhaps deep within, he could hear faint weeping. *The wrong woman.*

*　　*　　*

Gilakas glanced again at the fissure in the back of the cave, where the Inquisitor had vanished. The others had gathered to eat, and to drink hot water flavoured with mint leaves and aspar root, since Stult complained of an upset stomach. It may have been nothing more than Stult's complaining nature, but the medicine would do no harm to the others.

Sighing, Gilakas then rose to his feet. 'Stay here,' he ordered, setting out for the cave.

Of course, Gracer objected to that simple instruction. 'You do not command me, Mezla,' she said, moving to join him, one hand on the handle of her long-knife.

Before Gilakas could reply, a stranger's voice in his head spoke. '*You should fight over it. I've not seen pointless blood spilled in a long time. Remind me, you two, of my kind's legacy, our blood-gift.*'

Gracer hissed a curse and searched the cave, and then pointed. 'There. That skull speaks.'

'I heard,' Gilakas muttered.

'A spirit-god of the cave, or a demon.'

Moving closer, Gilakas said, 'I have never seen one, but I think this is the head of a T'lan Imass. Their bones, or skulls I mean, are said to haunt the places they reside.'

'*Haunting is a matter of perspective, mortal. Nor do I precisely "reside" here. My enemy retreated until her back found a wall, and she could retreat no longer.*' The voice paused, and then added, '*I wish she had. Oh, those four words have certainly haunted me. But I should be grateful. After dismembering me, she was kind enough to set my head atop my cairn, to bear eternal witness to . . . well, whatever happens past. I think you should all take the middle passage. This is my sage advice, mortals.*'

'The Inquisitor elected the one on the left,' Gilakas observed.

'*It goes nowhere you want to be. If he stays on the path, he should return. Eventually.*'

'And if he leaves the path?' Gracer asked.

'*He will meet her, and never return.*'

'Who?' Gilakas demanded.

'*You wield magic. Why not quest inward? Begin with the track behind me. She hasn't had need to build a new cairn in a long time. Though your head resting beside mine will prove poor company, since immortality is my curse, not yours. Or follow your sceptical Inquisitor and stay on the path. My advice, of course, remains the middle passage.*'

'He mocks us,' Gracer said. 'I'll retrieve the Inquisitor. You, Mezla, can do as you please.'

Gilakas hesitated, watching her march forward and vanish into the fissure.

'*She has no light. A step off the path would be unwise. If you hear a scream, it is already too late.*'

Gilakas shrugged at that. 'Stult can grieve,' he said. 'Who dismembered you, T'lan Imass?'

'*It was a war, mortal. I never asked her name.*'

'A war you lost.'

'*Personally, why not? And here I remain, imprisoned. And her? Why, she dwells in her own prison. In truth, neither of us won, and neither of us lost. On a flat stone close to the hearth outside and behind you, mortal, you may find the faint carvings of a playing surface. Thousands of years ago, traders plied this route through the hills. Often, at night, two would sit with the playing surface between them, engaged in a game of walnuts and knee-caps that looked complicated.*'

Scowling, Gilakas said, 'What is your point?'

'*In similar fashion, she and I face each other here, locked in a contest without hope of it ever ending. Me upon the threshold, her within. It is maddening and delicious both. Neither can cross to the other. We were fools. Never once did it occur to either one of us that a third player would join the game, fashioning an arena to snare us both.*'

'This place is a trap of some sort? Who was the third player, T'lan Imass?'

'*What, not who. You stand in front of an Azath House, mortal. Your Inquisitor – and now the angry woman with the narrow-bladed knife – have entered it upon the lined path. The centre passage, meanwhile, leads into the yard, in a manner of speaking. None return from there. Behind me is a doorway, one of many here, since this particular Azath House is very, very old. Caves, mortal, are but an early variation of houses. Besides, the Azath embraces a host of warrens. Thus, the passages may take you into unexpected realms. Or not.*'

For a long moment, Gilakas considered the deathless creature's words. He knew of Azath Houses – who did not? Dread places of murderous magic. Cursed and cursing, lifeless yet mysteriously alive. He had even stood before the Deadhouse in Malaz City, wondering if any truth could be found in the legend of Emperor Kellanved's brief residency there; eventually concluding that it was unlikely. The man had begun as a thief, after all. His first conquests were against rival gangs on the waterfront. Mock of Mock's Hold had very nearly killed him and Dancer both. Thus, no evidence of ascendant powers in either man. While it was held that, could one successfully traverse an Azath House, all manner of magic prowess followed, or so went the tale.

Gilakas stepped back. 'I'll choose none, T'lan Imass.'

'And think yourself wise in that, I'm sure. Your caution, mortal, confirms your innate mediocrity. Now, the child in your company is another matter. Bring him no closer. Not a step.'

Gilakas glanced back. Mute remained seated atop the boulder, holding in his hands sharp flint shards that he seemed to be trying to piece back together. Had there been any point to saving the boy? Gilakas returned his attention to the head of the T'lan Imass. 'I see no contest here,' he said. 'Your slayer can leave at any time. In your state, you could not stop her.'

'Not personally. Rather, it is what I represent. The fate awaiting her, of being hunted down and slain by my kind.'

'I have heard, and it's commonly known, that your war has ended. The T'lan Imass are no more. Returned to dust.'

'Am I dust? I am not. You either lie or are misinformed. The war will only end when the last Jaghut has been slain.'

'I think your people changed their mind,' Gilakas said.

'That is not possible.'

'Trapped here, T'lan Imass, you have missed great changes in the world. No one has seen your kind in over ten years. Except for forgotten pieces of them, such as you.'

'As the bearer of ill tidings, mortal, you have my curse.'

Gilakas laughed, somewhat harshly. 'Not the first curse thrown at me and likely not to be the last. But if you will curse the messenger, so be it.'

'I will. I'm shallow that way.'

*   *   *

Hearing scuffling behind him, Bornu turned to see Gracer emerge into the lantern-light. She had drawn her long-knife, the blade's blued steel gleaming like water on ice. The kohl encircling her eyes reminded him of the stone-woman's sunken orbs, barring the faint glitter at their centres. Any other similarity proved difficult. He said, 'I don't think it is safe for you to be here.'

'Not safe for you either, Inquisitor.'

'The T'lan Imass spoke to you as well?'

'And your Mezla.'

'Then where is Gilakas?'

She shrugged. 'I guess he listened to the warnings. That man is all about self-preservation.'

'And you are not, Gracer?'

'Finished exploring?'

Bornu pointed. 'The passage continues. My goddess is in need of answers. Well,' he amended, looking back to the carved face, 'beyond the obvious.'

Gracer approached, her gaze now on the carved face. 'This thing?'

'What do you see?' he asked.

The tone of her reply, when it came, was dismissive. 'Obsession.'

Grunting, Bornu faced the passage beyond this cavern.

'Just another man,' Gracer continued behind him. 'No woman's hand carved that. Not even a woman in love with her would do that.'

That assertion made him curious. 'Interesting. Is not all love obsessive, in its own way?'

'This man carved to trap her here, Inquisitor. He sought to possess her beauty.'

'And succeeded, it seemed.'

Her laugh was harsh. 'Yes, by turning her beauty into a curse.'

'The T'lan Imass said this . . . crime, relates to Va'Shaik.'

Gracer frowned. 'This woman was the first Sha'ik?'

'No. At least, I don't think so. If I understood the T'lan Imass, two women vied for the love of one man. This carving signifies his choice. From the decision was born the Whirlwind Goddess.'

Gracer laughed again, but longer this time. When it finally fell away, echoes lingering, she sheathed her weapon and reached out to take the lantern from Bornu. 'Here, then, let me lead the way, Inquisitor. But tell me, is your goddess urging you to destroy this carving, by any chance?'

'If she is, I refuse. I have been standing here, contemplating the tragic lives of three Imass, not just one. And how their fates, this scene of love and fury, of woundings in stone, how it all never went away. Like an echo reverberating down the bloodline. To be reborn to this every time is indeed, as you say, a curse.'

'Every generation must cast off the chains of the one before it, Inquisitor. If you can, that is. You'd think a goddess would have the power to do just that. Unless,' she added, 'it's all useless and escaping our legacy is impossible.'

Bornu studied Gracer for a long moment. 'You have set high standards in your search for something – or someone – worth believing in.'

She snorted. 'And you haven't? You said that you do not worship your goddess – the one riding your soul right now. How does that even work, Inquisitor? And see it from the other side. If you from her very own temple will not meet her eyes, what hope has she in the world beyond? No wonder she dreams of apocalypse.'

Her words shook Bornu. He found he had no reply to them. He gestured her towards the passage.

She lifted the lantern and strode forward.

He followed.

*   *   *

'Where did she go, Mezla?'

'After the Inquisitor,' Gilakas replied, returning to the hearth and seating himself on one of the flat stones.

Stult stared at him, and then asked in his high, thin voice, 'You do not fear she might kill him?'

'Why would she? Unless you know something I don't.'

'Only that you're a careless bodyguard. Where did they go?'

'Deeper into the cave.' Gilakas grimaced and fixed his gaze on the dying fire. 'I don't like caves.'

Stult said, 'And so the great Mezla assassin pauses at the threshold, frozen like a hare. All because he fears small places.'

'You'll never have her, you know,' Gilakas said in languid tones. 'You're just a stray pup. One with a limp at that. Have you no mind or will of your own, Stult? You followed her into the company of Three-Eyed Melok, a bastard worth less than the goat-shit under my boot. You think her driven, when she's even more lost than you.'

'Should you be wounded on the trail, I'll proclaim you dead and see you buried in the smallest cairn,' Stult said, his fleshy lips curved in a smile. 'You'll open your eyes to darkness, and none will hear your screams, since we'll be long gone on the trail.'

'The delusions of your wishes are no surprise to me,' Gilakas retorted. 'But now I wonder if you're even worth our pity. That said, pity's the best you can hope for, the alternative being contempt.'

Both men were startled by the sudden arrival of Mute. Cradled in his hands was an almost complete cobble of stone, made from all the broken

159

shards he had collected. The slight motion of this assemblage made faint, grinding whispers as he sought to continue holding it up before them.

'Missing bits,' said Stult after a moment.

Mute dropped the cobble. It broke apart all over again. Then he walked back to the boulder and sat once more.

Gilakas stared down at all the sharp-edged slivers of flint. 'That will cut up someone's feet sooner or later, this close to the hearth.' He paused, and then added, 'Not us, though.' With that conclusion, he made no move to clean up the mess.

*   *   *

'I think she died of her wounds,' Bornu concluded after studying the gaping rents in the withered flesh of the Jaghut. The corpse was sitting, legs sprawled, back to the stone wall of this, the last cavern. The sword lying beside her left hip was a mass of calcretions, less a blade than a lumpy, misshapen bar. The handle of an Imass chalcedony knife jutted from her right side, halfway down her ribcage. The grip still bore remnants of its hide wrapping. 'With that thrust,' he continued, 'she likely drowned in her own blood.'

'I thought they were sorcerors,' Gracer said. 'She couldn't heal herself?'

Straightening, he looked around. The cavern was four or so paces across in any direction, more or less circular, crowded with rotten furniture, none of it intended for a Jaghut's size or weight. The Jaghut's crossing the room to her final resting place had been in a stagger, scattering the chairs and knocking over the small dining table, the blood-scrape of her feet still visible on the stone floor. Considering Gracer's question, he finally said, 'She may not have wanted to. The T'lan Imass were relentless in their genocide.'

'Whoever heard of a cave with furniture?'

'It would be foolish,' ventured Bornu, 'to assume that civilization arrives but once in any given world. As if the single known example of progress negates its repetition going back, and back, into ever deeper recesses of time. That said, the Imass were far from civilized. While the Jaghut . . . well, who knows what the Jaghut built for themselves. Towers. Not much else. That survived, anyway.'

'Your fascination with history bores me, Inquisitor. Can we now leave this place? The air is uncommonly cold, especially since the passage leading into it was so hot.'

160

He glanced across at her. 'The cold tells us that her spirit lingers. But clearly, for us she has nothing to say. Nor for my goddess, it seems.'

'Presumptuous to expect otherwise.'

Bornu grimaced. Gracer was right. 'Perhaps that is not so surprising. The self-inflicted crimes of the Imass are their business. Why should this Jaghut ghost care? The hardest lessons to stomach, of course, are the ones that humble us.'

Gracer walked over to the corpse, reached down and pulled out the Imass stone knife. The rippled chalcedony of the blade was almost translucent, the hue of honey.

'Is it wise to loot this place, Gracer?'

'I'd think she'd thank me,' she replied, tucking the weapon into her belt.

The chamber's already cold air suddenly sharpened. Among the scattered chairs, wood splintered, hoarfrost visibly spreading across every surface.

Bornu stepped back.

A wretched gasp from the corpse, the chest creaking as it expanded for the first time in millennia. The body's desiccated flesh swelled, sloughing dead skin, the gaping wounds closing. Life gleamed in the sunken sockets of her eyes.

They watched the Jaghut woman slowly climb to her feet, rotted clothing falling away. Reaching up to pull a crusted braid of hair from her face; it came away from her scalp. Holding it up, she sighed. 'Vanity,' she said in a rasp, 'is the last thing to die.' Flinging the braid away, she dipped her head to regard the corroded wreck that had once been her sword, then kicked it away.

'Do not impede me, mortals. I am leaving this place.'

Bornu bowed.

As the Jaghut woman - so tall she had to duck beneath the curving ceiling - strode towards the passage, she paused and turned to Gracer. 'You have no idea how long I have waited for someone to do that.' Her gaze twisted further until she regarded Bornu. 'The Azath were never a prison for the Jaghut. If we are found within one, it is by choice.'

As she passed into the narrow fissure leading out, Bornu set off after her, taking the lantern from Gracer as he did so. Cursing under her breath, she followed a few steps behind him. They passed through the gallery with its carved face, the Jaghut ahead of them not sparing it a single glance, and continued on.

161

Emerging into the hollow with its camp beside the old trail, they all paused. Before them at the hearth that was now nothing but ashes, Gilakas and Stult slowly rose from where they'd been sitting. The Jaghut woman seemed to be studying the landscape beyond, its falling-off slope leading down to a blasted plain of scrub.

'Well,' she muttered, 'that's changed some.' Then she turned and spied the head of the T'lan Imass on its perch of rocks. She strode over to stand before it.

Neither spoke.

Then, with a sudden flashing back-hand, she sent the T'lan Imass head flying. It struck the wall of the hollow, the horns shattering, the skullcap snapping free to fly across the trail and down over the edge, ending in a series of clattering sounds growing ever more distant. The head itself thumped on the ground, rolled a bit, and then came to rest face-down.

Without another word or gesture, the Jaghut woman set off, crossing the trail and then down onto the slope, heading south.

Bornu walked to the edge to watch her departure.

Moving up alongside him, Gilakas said, 'Inquisitor. Best avoid caves from now on, I think.'

*   *   *

By the day's end, the trail had left the ridge behind, descending back onto the flat-land. At the base an old camp marked by boulder-rings spread out to either side, and here they halted for the night. A tumble of sharp rocks marked an old spring, long since dried out. Water was growing scarce.

Stult built a small fire. A desultory meal followed.

Little was said. Bornu remained trapped in his thoughts, ignoring the growing tension between Gilakas and Stult, while, after bedding Mute down, Gracer drew out the stone knife and began wrapping its grip in fresh rawhide.

Bornu's final act in the place of the Azath Cave had been to return the head of the Imass to its perch, the gesture eliciting a weary sigh rasping through his mind, and then the words, '*Any other vantage point would have felt wrong.*' He wasn't sure if this constituted gratitude from the Imass.

The presence of the goddess within him felt pensive, remote. Most of the time now, when she came to him, it was while he slept, or lingered in the place between wake and sleep. If lying on his side, he would feel her close up from behind, curling her form against him like a lover. But she possessed no substance, nothing material. She arrived in a non-corporeal form, undeniably feminine, and in the snuggling up against him from behind, her energy – which seemed to be all that she was – would then flow into and through his body, delivering a tingling chill he was beginning to find pleasurable.

A few nights past, whilst on the bridge between awake and asleep, she had drawn up close as before, only this time she had spoken in his mind. *'I'm here.'*

He had been startled to find himself aroused, anticipating that flow of energy, but instead, he had felt her move to straddle him. Eyes closed, still lingering in something like sleep, he had rolled onto his back to receive her. And without his eyes opening, he found himself looking up into Salabi's face. The shock snapped him awake.

Lying in the dark, staring up at countless stars, he had sought to make sense of the event. The voice had not belonged to Salabi. The sense of that body, less than water yet palpable, was that of a large woman, a woman such as Felisin Younger. The desire, therefore, must have come from him, from that helpless core of love for Salabi, to clothe this amorous apparition in the guise of his desire. The sudden shock had possibly belonged to both him and the goddess.

Gracer's words from the cave returned to him now. *'If you from her very own temple will not meet her eyes, what hope has she in the world beyond?'* There were layers to the mortal mind, to be sure. Some responses were not conscious at all. Did that make them somehow more truthful? He wasn't convinced. When upon the bridge between sleep and wakefulness, either could be reached into, to fashion something in the immediate moment. His imagination, after all, had for years composed an endless succession of scenarios, of love professed and love fulfilled between himself and Salabi. Thus, a repository of images to draw upon when clothing in flesh the beginnings of consummation.

Was the goddess, in her desperation, seeking to seduce him? Another form of worship?

How much of his inner world was being shared with her, all without his permission? Were even these thoughts, and all that followed them, nothing more than a monotonous commentary to which she was witness? Was this the miserable bargain between god and mortal? If so, it was a wonder not all gods were utterly mad, driven there by the repetition of banality without end.

'Firelight,' said Gilakas.

Bornu looked up. The others had all bedded down while he had indulged in self-examination, gaze fixed unseeing on the ebbing coals of the hearth before him. He twisted round to study the line of hills to the north, in the direction Gilakas had indicated with a nod, where he saw glowing pockets beneath gold reflections painting the rising smoke.

'Do maps mark that as a settlement?' the Malazan asked.

'Not that I'm aware of,' Bornu said. 'Of course, maps of this region being what they are, that's not saying much.'

'Well, even bandits need a camp, a stronghold.'

'I imagine so.'

'Worth noting,' Gilakas continued, 'that they will have seen our fire, too.'

Bornu nodded, and then sighed. 'We'd best rise with the dawn and not linger.'

'I would not count on the others in a fight, Inquisitor. Just because someone carries weapons, even many weapons, doesn't mean they're good at using them.' Gilakas paused, and then added, 'In my life I've seen enough to know that mediocrity is common. And there will be some who, when facing a true fight, will run away given the chance. Or at the very least will act only to defend themselves, not anyone else. There are many paths to preservation, after all. The smartest path, that of fighting together and supporting each other, isn't a natural inclination. Its logic is not the kind that's understood instinctively. It takes training, and even then, some who are trained simply go through the motions, without ever intending to use them.'

Bornu studied the man's shadowed visage, the muted glints of red here and there, reflections from the last few remaining embers, and said, 'Uncommonly loquacious, Gilakas.'

'Words to chew on, Inquisitor, before a fight. Better now than in the moment. I'm good with my weapons. I will fight to defend you.'

'And the others among us?'

'The boy, perhaps.'

'He's in no need of defending,' Bornu said.

'Why do you say that?'

'Mute survives. It's what he does. You and I, Gilakas, have fought side by side before.'

'Against two fools. It was over so quickly there was no time for anything else. Tomorrow, we'll likely be accosted by a half-dozen, maybe more.'

'You said you would fight to protect me. Why?'

'I now believe you are Va'Shaik's gamble, Inquisitor. She throws you into the game, knowing well how close things are to boiling over, all across Seven Cities. And knowing, too, the central role her purported worshippers intend. She flings you out to scatter the pieces.'

'And this complements the desire of the Malazan Empire?'

'Any chaos in your cult is a good thing,' Gilakas replied.

'It seems,' ventured Bornu, 'this gamble is more yours than anyone else's.'

'Va'Shaik repositions the game. I adjust accordingly. All the temples and high priests and high priestesses; all the Invigils and Inquisitors out there – none of them are even aware of the game's change. Unaware of her and unaware of you, both now out on the field of play.'

'Do you not report to your superiors, Gilakas?'

Bornu couldn't be sure in the gloom, but it seemed that the Malazan shrugged before saying, 'Not always necessary. In my line of work, some independence is expected, and among a select few of us, even encouraged.'

'Eventually, however . . .'

'Aye. This route you've taken, Inquisitor, will lead us to G'danisban.'

'It will?'

'The seat of the High Fist.'

'Only relevant,' said Bornu, 'in that he is likely being targeted for assassination.'

'What of it?' Gilakas asked, hinting at something Bornu had not expected. Impatience? Irritation? After a moment, the Malazan leaned back and said, 'Oh. By a cultist's knife, you meant. From the temple of Va'Shaik in the city. If that is your fear, Inquisitor, this overland journey is taking too long. She should send us by warren, drop us in the city as soon as possible.'

'I expect my goddess is more aware of external situations than you might think. The blessed among her servants can be her eyes and ears.' Bornu kept the tone casual, even as his mind raced in entirely another direction. Gilakas, on the subject of assassination, had not even considered the danger as coming from cultist fanatics, or agents from the temple seeking to unleash chaos on the Malazan occupation. No, the notion of the High Fist's assassination had taken the man's thoughts elsewhere.

Gods below, is Arenfall targeted for in-house killing? These Malazans . . . why do we bother fomenting rebellion at all? The fools keep cutting their own throat.

165

Or was chaos precisely what the Claw – or indeed the Emperor – desired? *A lot of fat can be trimmed in all the confusion of the aftermath, after all. So now, I must wonder, Gilakas, is it your knife I'm delivering to G'danisban? Not to drive into the back of any high priestess or Invigil, but Arenfall himself? And if so, am I also now in your game, set up to take the blame on behalf of my temple, my goddess?*

'We could always yield to the bandits,' Gilakas then said. 'Most prefer robbery over killing, since those left alive can be stolen from again and again. Whilst the dead give up their gifts but once.'

'As the goddess wills, Gilakas. Now, it's time for sleep.'

'I'll take the first watch, then. And wake Gracer for the second.'

Bornu smiled, knowing the detail was unseen by Gilakas. 'The goddess never sleeps.'

*   *   *

'Do you know he loves you?' Va'Shaik asked Salabi.

The woman, summoned into the presence of her goddess, appeared confused by the question. 'Holy One? To whom do you refer?'

Va'Shaik offered up a wry smile, 'He did delight in the precision of language, didn't he? It's no wonder his most cherished apprentice should so closely emulate his manner of speech. Inquisitor Bornu Blatt, Salabi, is to whom I was referring.'

Salabi was without doubt attractive, although Va'Shaik suspected – no, now knew, intimately – that Bornu's feelings for her had long ago left behind the merely physical. Indeed, in the absence of both hope and consummation, the man's love had in itself become a shrine, with an unreal, even impossible version of Salabi at its heart. This pathos was not uncommon among mortals. What that said about the plight of mortals, on the other hand, was less clear.

'Not once,' said Salabi now, in even tones, 'has Bornu Blatt hinted at such matters. He has always displayed the decency that is his nature, and indeed his generosity. Our relationship has always been simple and direct, entirely professional. Even his eyes, Holy One, do not stray.'

'Sometimes fear of rejection will prevent overt displays of desire, or intention. It only *appears* to be decency.'

'And sometimes propriety and integrity invoke a wholly natural discipline, Holy One.'

Va'Shaik blinked. 'It seems, then, you understand men better than I do, and I do not count that unlikely. Come closer, Salabi. Seat yourself – that chair, drag it closer, yes, good. Better. How is it that so many holy rituals undertaken by my worshippers insist that I absent myself from the proceedings? Beyond some final wave of the hand denoting blessing, or perhaps benediction. Or my head tipped in mere acknowledgement? My point being, I am most often left alone.'

Salabi, now seated only a few paces distant, fixed widened eyes upon Va'Shaik. 'It is assumed, Holy One, that such rituals are in service to the faith itself, rather than to you. Acts affirming communion find strength in the sharing. A mortal need, perhaps, as much social as anything else.'

Va'Shaik studied the new temple librarian for a few moments. 'You and Bornu must have had many enlivening discussions, Salabi.'

A quick nod. 'We did, Holy One. In exercising my mind, he was an exemplary teacher.'

'Yet you gleaned nothing of his love for you. His finding you worthy of worship? For that is what he has done to you, in the absence of all else.'

Something fluttered momentarily in the woman's eyes. 'If so, then, it seemed,' she said, slowly, choosing her words carefully, 'a shrine best not entered.'

'Because you could not return such love. Bornu being such an ugly, bent and misshapen man.'

'No, Holy One. Because I could not be equal to his version of me, the one within that shrine. And so, I did not wish to disappoint him.'

'You are my rival for his worship,' said Va'Shaik. 'But in truth, that contest was your victory long ago. I may be his Goddess, but he is not devoted to me.'

'I think his devotion to you is absolute, Holy One. Is there but one way to worship? One way to believe? One way to love?'

Va'Shaik was silent. Neither spoke. Then the goddess said, 'I was a woman once. Rather, a girl, then a young woman. Past that, things are unclear. Physical intimacy wasn't intimate at all. The pleasures of the flesh were first taken away from me, and then returned. Neither state involved anything like love. I think of sex as a weapon, a knife in hand. I lost the desire to use it before I knew anything of it. Then it was placed into my hands once more, but blunted, dulled into clumsiness. Such a weapon is of little value when one is floating upon an insensate sea.'

Salabi seemed to be examining Va'Shaik with peculiar intensity. When

167

the goddess finished speaking, the woman blinked a few times, and then spoke, 'Holy One, sex is not a weapon.'

Va'Shaik scowled. 'He used a knife to kill it. The analogy seems entirely apt.'

'You were wounded, but as a child, Holy One.'

'I was denied something. Told it was for my own good, lest I lose control of myself. Lest I cease honouring the covenants of service. There is nothing wounding in correction.'

'And when you were healed?'

'I fell into the very thing he sought to prevent. This is my belief. And yet, within me, I feel . . . rage. Blame the knife or the hand wielding it?' She waved dismissively, the gesture almost a chopping motion. 'Does it make any difference?'

'Holy One, I am a woman of few experiences in this matter. Of sex and pleasure. There was curiosity, and opportunity, and I took advantage of both. I hear your words, and I am confused. In the histories, there are instances of the practices you appear to be referring to, though most were long ago and mercifully short-lived.'

'Bidithal sought to resurrect it,' Va'Shaik explained. 'In Raraku Oasis, among the orphaned daughters of the Whirlwind.'

'Among the—' Salabi's mouth shut, lips thinning.

'Speak,' commanded Va'Shaik, her heart thudding hard in her chest for reasons she could not yet comprehend. 'Show me what I am not seeing.'

Instead, Salabi's eyes glistened, filling with tears.

'You give me pity?'

The woman mutely shook her head.

'Then speak!'

Though tears flowed down her cheeks, the woman composed herself. After a moment, she spoke. 'Bidithal's name is known, in temple records – not temples of Shaik, however. Other cults. Holy One, the man was not a man at all. Just a vile, despicable creature, twisted and sadistic. His inner world was so lifeless he was driven to every excess in the desperate need to feel something, anything. He found a position of power in which to indulge his pathetic needs. Alas, we let him.'

'We?'

'As my teacher once told me, Holy One, a society founded upon absolute freedom is a flower-bed inviting every plant, no matter how poisonous, no matter how evil. If freedom means nothing but the privilege of washing one's hands of all responsibility, then evil will indeed thrive, in abundance.'

'Bornu Blatt's words?'

Salabi nodded. 'Holy One, this was not "correction". What he sought to deny in you was only a reflection of what he never had, never understood, and could never hope to achieve.'

'Karsa Orlong killed Bidithal, or so I was told.'

'Karsa Orlong? The god known as Toblakai?'

'But is he truly a god now? I wonder. I have contemplated, given my awakened powers, reaching out to him, in the manner of gods conversing with other gods. But I admit, I am not sure how to do that. Nor do I know what I would say to him, beyond the simple truth that he acted too late. My flesh may have been healed, but flesh only, do you understand?'

Salabi nodded. 'You could never regain the innocence of pleasure.'

The innocence of pleasure. Now it was Va'Shaik's turn to feel a sudden welling of emotion, a turmoil of grief, fury, and a sharp pang of something like . . . 'Salabi, is it possible to be nostalgic for what I never had a chance to be?'

'Holy One,' Salabi suddenly pleaded, even as she seemed to fold up into herself on the chair, 'I beg you, please, you are crushing my soul.'

Yes, that is what it's like, isn't it? 'You may go, Salabi.'

The woman struggled to her feet. 'Yes,' she said in a ragged whisper. 'It is.'

'It is what?'

'Possible.'

'I imagine, then,' said Va'Shaik, 'that Bornu Blatt longs for a world where he is handsome and desirable, a world in which he has won your love. Well, far be it for even a goddess to think she can remake the world. His propriety, as you say, is indeed a natural quality, though I would think, such a quality can only be born of past wounding. In his case, the persistent anguish of his ugliness. A difficult thing to carry, to be sure.'

Salabi stood, only two steps back from the chair. Va'Shaik's resumption of the conversation had halted her in place, and now once more she looked upon her goddess, her face blotchy, eyes puffy and red. The helplessness of her expression and pose was painfully raw. 'I have always loved Bornu Blatt,' she then said.

169

'Including his formidable sense of propriety.'

Salabi's expression shifted into anger. 'Forgive me, Holy One, but you, above all others, must understand the distinction between the surface and what lies beneath. No doubt Bidithal offered you a kindly face, and benign words to soothe the troubled but trusting child. Within, however, a monster.'

Va'Shaik flinched as if struck. Her gaze broke away from Salabi's steady regard. 'If he be monster on the outside,' she eventually said, 'not a dangerous one, our Bornu Blatt. I understand your confusion,' she added. 'You see, I sought to couple with him a few nights past. The essence of my presence and will, at least. It delivers a most ecstatic touch, apparently. An arousing one. He welcomed the sensation – I am certain of that. But I failed. His mind took over the moment, and before I could settle onto him, he fashioned me in your image, Salabi. Then,' she concluded with some bitterness, 'we both awoke. I felt his shock and, one presumes, he felt mine. So I must ask you, does ascendancy into godhood demand an excising of all physical pleasure, all hopes of love, even?'

Salabi's face was ashen, her lips looking dry, almost lifeless. 'You are in love with Bornu Blatt?'

'He doesn't worship me. How could I not?' She shook her head. 'So here we are, the three of us.'

'The three—'

'And oh yes,' Va'Shaik continued, barely hearing Salabi's words, 'love is most certainly a knife.'

*   *   *

It was mid-morning before the bandits came within sight on their back-trail. Two hundred paces ahead was a small village, perhaps a dozen buildings in all. There was an outer wall enclosure, barely waist-high, situated fifty or so paces from the nearest house. This wall, Bornu suspected, belonged to an older manifestation of this settlement, a time when it was not a struggling village, but a city. Just past this wall, with its myriad gaps, rounded humps and sinkholes gave away all that was now buried by drifting sands and rubble.

Their track cut through the wall at one of the gaps. Not a proper gate, just missing stones.

Behind them, the dozen or so bandits clearly dismissed the putative safety of the village, as they closed at a steady canter.

'It's my thought,' opined Gilakas, 'the bastards rule the whole area, this town included.'

The meagre wall behind them, they continued towards the straggle of low houses and humped mud-brick grain silos, the latter long abandoned.

In reply to Gilakas's words, Gracer snorted and said, 'Once again the Malazan Empire fails in protecting its own.'

'More like its own fails in protecting themselves,' Gilakas snapped. 'The empire, after all, offers organized law and the right of policing, but if the citizens can't be bothered with any of that, who really is to blame?'

'How about both?' Bornu answered. Just off to the left was a hostel of some sort, half-closed by a fenced area for horses, which he led his party towards. 'We will assume nothing is awry,' he continued, 'and take our meal at the inn.'

'Just keep your weapons close,' Gilakas said.

Bornu dismounted at the corral's gate, slipped the loop of rope from the side-post, pushed the gate open and led the way inside. Gracer slid down to gather up reins from all the horses while Stult prodded the mules closer to the trough on the opposite side of the inn, Mute weaving as if half-asleep in his saddle.

Gilakas loosened his sword in its scabbard. 'We may not even get the chance to order if we don't hurry.'

Two adolescent boys ran out from the inn, clearly brothers, and took charge of the beasts. Shrugging, Stult pulled Mute off the mule and set him down, where he stood unmoving, the light wind stirring his unkempt hair. Gracer moved to stand by the door leading into the inn's main room, her hands resting on the pommel of her long-knife.

The thump of horse hoofs was growing louder with each passing moment.

Sighing, Bornu waved Gilakas and Stult after him as he headed inside.

'Mute!' Gracer called. 'Over here, quickly!'

The boy didn't move.

Cursing under her breath, Gracer set out to collect him, even as Bornu edged past her and entered the inn.

*   *   *

Mute felt her approaching, eager to take him inside where the others had already gone, but most of his attention was on the cruel knot of malice fast approaching in the thunder of horse hoofs. Something cold was

171

rising within him, and in the wake of its sudden birth, he realized that it was familiar to him, guiding him to a place he had known many times.

Only two paces from him, Gracer was halted, as if slamming into an invisible wall. Mute heard her startled curse. He could have explained it to her. He could tell her that this had awaited Melok, that no knife would ever pierce his chest. That all the sacrifices belonged to the ones seeking him harm. But that threat had passed. So his awakening was new to her.

But now the riders were arriving. Mute gestured, sending Gracer flying back, all the way to the wall of the inn, where she collided with the adobe, the back of her helmed head clanging like a bell. She slumped to the ground and slowly fell onto her side.

He could hear her heartbeat and so knew that she would return to her senses. When it was all over. Which was probably for the best. And as for the others inside the inn, well, he wrapped the building in impenetrable silence, and so too stole the will of Bornu and the others to return outside, to seek the fate of himself and Gracer. It was likely they had not even heard Gracer's collision with the wall.

Mute's senses expanded, taking in this village, including the sunken, pillar-lined entrance to a long-abandoned oracle, with its tunnels and hidden passages and chambers buried deep beneath the earth, which lay on the settlement's other side, close to what had once been a salt mine. He noted all the graffiti carved into the pillars, the generations of desecration, and this irritated him.

Attention returning, he faced the fourteen riders who had just pulled up beyond the corral fence.

Malice. The lust to harm, to deliver terror. The drunken pleasure of intimidation, see it shining in their eyes, eyes already bathed in the tears of others. So sure of themselves. So sure in their right to violence. So eager to reduce their victims to begging.

But I am the bound frustrations of the weak and the vulnerable, a world's worth, an eternity's worth. The child gives way. I am the cold core rising.

Where is my family? My kin? The Tiles are scattered. I am disassembled, by my own will I am disarticulated and cast to the winds.

This cold core, clothed in the flesh of a child, why, upon awakening, it remembers.

It remembers everything.

Mute heard himself keening, a wordless, stretched-out sound. It caught their attention, these fourteen killers, caught them and made them dismount.

They desired to enter the inn. To murder Bornu Blatt and the others. There was no reason to stop them. Their targets were not relevant. Not even the goddess cowering inside Bornu Blatt was relevant, though one day she might be.

But that malice. That cruel hunger. *That* was offensive.

The leader said something and many of the others laughed. They were drawing weapons. The villagers holed up in their homes knew they were safe because the bandits needed them. But travellers, strangers, no, they were not safe at all. So, the entire bargain made in this place was wrong.

Is a man's rage a child? That ferocious unleashing of wordless will?

I think so. I made it so, made all of it into the body of a child, then set him to wander the world in the way all of me once wandered. Seeking the past, seeking the truth. Seeking proof that no matter where I walked, I once walked before. All my mechanisms of time, constructed in opposition to the child and his blind rage.

It all makes sense now. I never needed to find my father. I am my father.

Mute's keening grew even louder. The fourteen killers now showed troubled expressions, pained expressions, as it seemed Mute's voice caressed them with the sharpest talons imaginable. And the flesh of their faces fell away in ribbons, blood everywhere, and they were screaming. Shrieking as all the horrors and terrors of their lust were turned back, turned onto them, and there was nowhere to hide.

A few sought to run away. But the keening voice sliced into them, through clothing, through heavy leathers, through armour. Flailing ribbons of flesh, spraying blood, the horses bolting – they deserved no pain, after all, and so none was delivered to them. Mute's voice was enough to panic the beasts and that was well. They had just learned to run from the beckoning hands of humans and for these beasts, never again.

But now his voice was gathering up all the ribbons, stripping away the last few still trying to cling to the bones, lifting everything into the air. In the village, walls exploded, roofs collapsed. Distant shrieks, the tumbling cascade of destruction rippling outward, riding his voice as like a giant fist it battered each and every building, down to cloth-snagged, wood-splintered, brick-shattered rubble, here and there the leaking bloom of blood and fluids. Dogs fled. Rats poured from the old silos as they collapsed.

It was a dangerous thing, to love all of this. He knew that. He regretted that. But regret belonged to love, so he was not surprised.

The village was flattened, beneath thick billowing clouds of dust. Above it, rising ever higher, the spinning cloud of red ribbons inside its pink mist that was all that remained of the fourteen killers. Apart from bones scattered outside the corral fence, and bits of twisted metal and brittle leather and cloth.

Dead. All dead.

He felt a sudden pressure, a buffeting sensation that drew him round.

The oracle. Someone is there.

He could feel waves of outrage, of shock, of growing fury.

Scowling, Mute set out, down the now-choked main street of the village, stepping over tumbled adobe bricks, older foundation stones knocked about in scattered disarray. The stinging clouds, the chalk reek, the drifting fist-like currents of shit and piss. Death's acrid wake, all intimately familiar, all crowded up like memories surrounding him. Oh yes, he could wear this redolent attire. Again.

Before him and off to the left a shallow hollow, the graffiti-gnawed pillars crowded with rude carvings, so many biting knife-tips defacing this and that, the mind behind every destructive, defacing act of such murky mediocrity as to pose in itself an offence to the gift of intelligence. That something blessed with awareness should choose to be so unaware . . . why then this unknown god's outrage directed at Mute? It made no sense. The desecration belonged to others, so many others, and now they and their descendants were no more. Obliterated for their disrespect.

Why your rage, nameless god? There, in the sanctum of your oracle. Can you not even see how the priests performed in the passages within the walls, throwing their voices through the gaping mouths of stone statues, fraudsters one and all? How they cheated all who came in desperate need of divination, dreaming of speaking with dead loved ones, fathers, mothers, wives and daughters – and do you see the remnant of the dovecote? How by dove and pigeon and swallow they learned first all the distant news, the great battles, to so frame their prophecy into truths?

Do you not see the charade, turning worship of you into a damned business enterprise?

Mute pushed aside the rubble that blocked the entrance to the oracle. His shifted his still-keening voice to eradicate the fill of dust, sand, gravel and boulders from the passageway carved into the bedrock. If the god in its fury would face him, so be it.

It wouldn't be the first time he'd killed a god, after all.

Deeper, the passage angling down, fifty paces, seventy paces, into a domed cavern carved out of tufa, with a spring-fed stream cutting across. Whatever boat or raft or bridge had once provided a way over this divide had long rotted away.

Mute simply used his high-pitched humming to carry him across, and he walked on, down the single passage. Twenty more paces.

The shrine, its wide tholos entranceway and womb-like domed sanctum, all pointed to a pilgrim's return to the world before birth, and there indeed – perhaps to the shock of every priestly ghost still lingering in this place – waited a god.

Mute stood before it, weathering its indignation, its savage grief.

It was not human. Nor Jaghut, nor Imass. The truth of it could only be guessed at, but Mute attempted the guess. He ceased his humming. 'Azathanai, I greet you.'

'You little shit!'

'You are forgotten in the outside world,' Mute said. 'Your time of worship is long past. Shall I put you out of your misery, Azathanai?'

'Icarium was no Azathanai,' the god snapped. 'It was not in him to do what he did. His blood could not flow for ever. His sanity could not hold together for eternity. Then he wanted to be K'rul but he never was K'rul. How do I know all this? Because you reek of it. His name, his every choice, his every insane justification. Look at you! Walking nightmare. Utter abomination. He plucked out his blind, idiotic rage and personified it into a *fucking child!*'

'It is for me to wander the world, delivering justice.'

'Justice!'

'I think,' said Mute, 'I should kill you now.'

The god, whose form seemed to evade resolution in Mute's eyes, now said, 'Ever met an Azathanai, child of Icarium?'

Mute cocked his head. 'Perhaps not. But a god is a god, and gods can not only die, they can also be killed. I will know regret, of course. That is my fate, to regret things I have done.'

'Oh, and that salves your soul?'

'So I tell myself.'

'Well,' said the Azathanai. 'Your arrival is timely, after all. The outside world will know nothing of my act here. Only that it has been saved from you. That's fine. Accolades are overrated.'

'What are you talking about?' Mute asked.

'Azathanai, you piece of cruddy nacht manure, can't be killed. You, however, most certainly can.' With that, the ancient god reached out, grasped the child as would a hand taking up a doll.

Mute struggled as he was lifted from his feet, disbelief rushing through him. He keened to awaken his rage – but the hand closed tighter, squeezing his chest so that he could draw no breath, and without breath, he had no voice, and without his voice, he had no power.

His astonishment burgeoned as the hand began crushing the frail sapling bones of his body.

'I know,' muttered the Azathanai. 'It's our plight to live such thankless lives. That said, better this than the alternative.'

I am dying! This is not possible – how can I die?

The question burst into that final flash of death, and as the flash faded, so too the question.

The Azathanai dropped the mangled mess that was all that remained of the child. 'Step away for a time and everything out there falls apart,' she grumbled. 'Well, that explains the end of worship. But damn me, those priests were entertaining.'

*   *   *

Dust was coming in through the slats of the inn's front window. The proprietor now stood frozen with indecision. He'd listened to their requests for food earlier, but had done nothing in answer, simply continuing repairing a chair leg just outside the storeroom at the far end of the kitchen, the clay-bricked oven left cold, the rectangular grill-basin heaped with lifeless ashes.

The two boys who had tended to the horses were now huddled in that kitchen, their trembling visible even from where Bornu sat.

A fog lingered in his mind, a sense of time lost and with it, vague disquiet. Eventually, certain details shook awake and he sat up in sudden alarm. 'Where are Gracer and Mute?' he asked.

Stult lurched to his feet, grasping his staff and limping quickly to the door. He flung it open and hobbled outside. Lunging to the left and out of sight, he cried out, 'Gracer!'

The cry seemed to snap through Bornu. He rose, as did Gilakas. Together, they hurried to the doorway and stepped out into the yard.

Stult was kneeling over Gracer's motionless body. Off to the far right, their mounts all waited in the roofed stables, heads dipped, tails swishing. Mute was nowhere to be seen.

Neither, Bornu realized, was the village.

'The bandits never arrived?' Gilakas asked. His sword was in his hand. He jogged over to the corral gate, his steps slowing. 'Gods below,' he hissed, eyes now on the ground. 'I'm finding . . . bits of them.'

'Everyone's dead,' said Bornu.

Gilakas turned to him. 'What – Fener's fucking grave – was there an earthquake? No, we felt nothing. That is, inside . . . I dozed. Did I doze? Gods, those bandits were on our heels! That innkeeper better have some answers,' he finished in a growl, setting off back towards the inn.

'Leave him,' Bornu ordered. 'He's knows nothing.'

Glaring, Gilakas walked up to the Inquisitor. 'Your goddess manifested? Is this – all this – her rage?'

Bornu shook his head. 'Not hers. Mute's.'

'What do you mean? Just an addled little boy—'

'He was never just that.' Bornu hesitated, then added, 'A manifestation of some sort. My goddess was . . . wary.' He looked back to the destroyed village. 'I think he's done this before.'

'Then where is he? Out walking the road?'

'I don't know.'

'She's coming round,' Stult called from beside the inn entrance. 'Gracer, my love—'

'Oh, leave off, Stult. I just knocked my head, and I ain't nobody's love.' Pushing him away, she lifted herself to her hands and knees, reaching up to tug off the dented helmet. 'Look at that – it's a wonder my skull ain't cracked wide open.'

Bornu approached. 'What happened, Gracer?'

'Mute. He sent me flying.'

'How?'

'Sorcery, I think. I've never been punched so hard in my life. Gods, my head aches. Stop fussing, Stult! Give me room to breathe!'

Now the innkeeper emerged, his boys close behind him. The man, belly round and sagging, feet splayed beneath knock knees, was now staring at what remained of the village. 'What have you done?' he shouted, swinging to face Bornu. 'You murdering bastards!'

Gilakas stepped up to the man. 'Murdering? More like the wrong people got murdered. Besides, we were inside, just like you. You saw us sitting there.'

'Mages! Your kind should all be hung! Gilap, Thrud, get them horses and mules out of there! We don't take these kinda people. They can camp in the salt pits, damn 'em! You wanted food? Forget it! Go away! And I'm sending word out about you! Callin' the Malazans on you!'

'That's easy enough,' Gilakas said, with a humourless grin. 'Here I am, toad. Here to tell you your friends are all dead—'

'Gilakas,' Bornu cut in. 'Leave him be.'

'This damned inn of his is nothing more than a honey-trap, Inquisitor, and you know it!'

'Not any more.'

'I was just surviving!' the innkeeper retorted. 'Got a family! What else was I supposed to do? And now you went and killed everyone!'

'It would appear so,' Bornu said. 'A better outcome would not have seen all the villagers dead. Just the bandits. An end to their extortion.'

Gilakas snorted. 'As if they had to extort anyone.' He pointed with his sword. 'This man didn't get fat on innkeeping.'

'Enough, Gilakas. Let's mount up – we'll find somewhere to camp past this place.'

'He's gone, isn't he?' Gracer asked. 'Mute. He's gone.'

'For now, it seems so,' Bornu replied. 'It may be we were merely at his convenience. Just because he would not or could not speak, it does not follow that he was not fully cognizant, when he chose to be, that is.'

'You had suspicions about him,' Stult said. 'I could see it.'

'More questions than suspicions.'

'I took care of him,' Gracer said. 'I even helped him escape. From Melok. And he damn near killed me.'

They returned to their mounts, ignoring the innkeeper and his boys. In the saddle again, they set out, back through the gaping fence-gate. Passage through the village was made slow by all the rubble spilled into the main street. Dogs were howling somewhere to the north, not too far away, but not drawing closer. The dust was slow to settle.

Opposite the extended approach to the oracle temple, Bornu halted his mount and fixed his gaze on the ruin. He frowned.

Beside him, Gilakas said, 'Your curiosity is a curse, Inquisitor. Leave it be.'

'Mine. My goddess's.'

'Leave it.'

'Look at how the passage was cleared. He went in there, I think.'

'Who? Mute? Well, he's not yet come out, so take that as a warning.'

Bornu grunted. 'Good point.'

After a moment, Bornu then kicked his horse forward again. Behind him, he heard Gracer muttering, too low to make out the words. Stult's reply was uncharacteristically cool in tone, short and also too quiet to make out. He recalled their exchange outside the inn. Gracer's careless dismissal had done damage. Perhaps she regretted it, or perhaps not.

'This journey,' Gilakas said after a time, 'is not what I expected.'

'And if my goddess had killed everyone back there, Gilakas?'

The Malazan shot him a blank look. Then he said, 'There are limits to the empire's forbearance.'

'For you to call?'

'Aye. My call.'

'I will keep that in mind, Gilakas.'

'Be sure your goddess does, too.'

'Not for me to say,' Bornu replied. 'Now, I believe a substantial settlement awaits us a few days hence, wherein I must pay a visit to a temple.'

Gilakas snorted. 'I so enjoy your temple visits.'

*   *   *

Even as the party rode on, Va'Shaik remained, facing the ancient oracle. Not substantial enough to stir the dust, nor block the faint, acrid wind drifting out from the destroyed city. Her sense of Mute's power lingered, a thing blind to itself, its own voice the only thing it could hear. She had felt – even as he pushed her away – his enjoyment of killing, made pure by an unwavering sense of justice.

For the bandits, he'd had a point. For the villagers, trapped by fear into passive servitude to those selfsame bandits, the matter of justice lost its purity. But he'd made no distinction.

'Do not enter my sanctum, goddess.'

The voice belonged to a woman, her language that of the oldest spirits of the land. 'The child's fate?'

'Destroyed. Few are capable. His bad luck was in finding one.'

'Truly destroyed?'

'Seems I've done Icarium a favour. He will never know it, scattered as he now is. Spawned into pieces, no less. Woe the fool who gathers all the Tiles and seeks to bind them into one. Mind you, the resurrected Icarium will be empty of rage. But so too empty of justice, or righteous anger, left standing outside all

moral imperative. Think of the monstrosity of that, goddess. Hold it up, if you dare, as a mirror.'

Va'Shaik recoiled. 'A mirror?'

'My priests invented divinations, made up prophecies, played the game of delusion and deceit, quenching hope's endless thirst. Do not begrudge them the comfort they gave. The age of oracles in this land has passed. The secret paths in the sky are forgotten, all those missives on the wing.'

'And in all that you did nothing?'

'I never said that, goddess. I was plenty busy.'

'Doing what?'

'Admittedly, I can't remember. But my words here were but prelude to this: I shall now give you a prophecy. None of that Dryjhna nonsense, mind you. None of the kind the priests flung out for a handful of coins. Will you hear it, goddess?'

'If it arrives as a riddle, I'd rather not.'

'You will walk the earth, goddess. But know this. When you do, you will not walk alone.'

Va'Shaik sighed. 'I said I didn't want any riddles.'

'What can I say? Habit.'

BOOK THREE

GHOSTS OF THE LIVING
AND THE DEAD

Glorious solitude
how I treasure
your company
No longer alone
at last freed
of clamour
not a single shadow
swinging my way
Blessed solitude
how I treasure
your company
and these that you see
are absences
emptied and departed
my triumph
stands alone
how glorious
how blessed
how – solitude
you arrive
in sublime echoes
of nothing and no one –
meet triumph's eyes
I beg you

Solitude
Fingal Bast

CHAPTER EIGHT

Bury me in coins
But do not think me churlish
In this shroud of
Unreasoning greed – no
You misunderstand
I so drag into my pit
All the wealth I have
To spite every one of you
Such are heaven's
Heavenly rewards

Let my cold limbs
Embrace in eternity
This meaningless hoard
The gleam'd treasure
You seek with shovel and pick
Each coin stamped with
My likeness in profile
Is a currency only valid
Here in my precious
Hold of the dead

Where, unseen by all,
I freely spend
All the tomorrows
I never saw
Who am I
To call them worthless?

And who are you
To steal my futures
Yet heed nothing
Of the debts inherited?

Poet's Legacy
Kulvinas

The silk that at first felt cool in his grip had now turned slick with sweat. Smiling at the face dragged close across the desk, Bornu Blatt said, '"*Alms given seek blessing. Blessing in turn is given.*" You will spend to feed the poor. You will heal the sick. You will build homes for the homeless. You will pay no heed to the beliefs of those you help, no heed to anything but their wretched need. This is as the Goddess wills.'

The face close to his, well-fed and perfumed, now bore a sheen as it slowly reddened, reminding Bornu that the man might well be choking. He slowly relaxed his grip, easing the High Priest back across the desk, then released him to thump back in the chair.

Gasping, the High Priest plucked at his robe's crinkled collar, wiped the beads of sweat from his forehead. 'I simply queried the wisdom of emptying the temple treasury, Inquisitor.'

Leaning back in his own chair, Bornu Blatt muttered, 'More of a bleat than a query.' Raising his voice, he continued, 'I have assessed the monthly costs associated with you, your priests and priestesses, and upkeep of the temple, along with the schooling. This has been set aside. The rest is to be redistributed, into your community, without favour, without graft, in the manner I have described.'

'Of course, Inquisitor! It shall be done.'

'Your second can handle all of that. You are to journey to Hanar Ara at once.'

A quick nod. 'The carriage will be readied and I shall depart on the morrow.'

'There will be regular audits conducted by my agents, to ensure no one gets . . . adventurous. Please remind your flock that the last town I visited, and the last temple I investigated, revealed such levels of corruption – both financial and moral – that fully half of the priests and priestesses were ejected from the temple, permanently, their fates left to the abused citizens of the town. As for the High Priest, he managed to take his own life before justice could be properly served. Needless to say, his corpse lies buried in unconsecrated ground.'

A grey hue came to the High Priest's visage. He licked his lips and nodded a second time. 'We may have been lax in our generosity, but in keeping with the directions given us by the First Temple—'

'From Kulat, yes, but Kulat is dead. The awakened Goddess takes a more direct interest in her children.'

'This pleases me.'

No it doesn't. It doesn't please any of you. 'I'm sure,' he said, rising to his feet. 'You may take two servants and one scribe with you. The rest will be needed here.'

'Understood.'

'I hope so.'

It was a relief to leave the office, although some pleasure remained from the act of dragging the man across his damned desk, ever closer to what he knew to be an unaccountably ugly face – his own. Few did not quail at this.

In the corridor outside sat Gilakas on a stone bench, legs stretched out before him. He quickly rose. 'Didn't need me then?'

'Not this time,' Bornu replied. 'We're not staying another night, however. Camping under the open air is always preferable after such meetings.'

Gilakas grunted. 'If you say so. There's a bloodfly infestation in the marshes north of here.'

'We continue west, and with most of the day ahead of us, we should be well clear of that by the time dusk arrives. Where are the others?'

'Gracer said you wouldn't want to stay, Holy One, and she was right. They're with the horses.'

Horses. I don't like horses. No, that's not quite accurate. I still don't like horses. Especially the one I ride. Then again, I suspect the dislike is mutual. 'Lead on, then, Gilakas.'

It wasn't far. The group was close by the temple's gate, blocking about half the width of the narrow street, with the locals keeping a wary distance. Gracer stood, wearing her usual black overcoat covering chain surcoat despite the heat, although she'd taken to wearing a broad-brimmed leather hat to shield her face. But it seemed the shadows only sharpened her features and their pallid hue. The dark pits of her eyes were of course the product of thick kohl generously applied, as if to mimic a skull's eye sockets. Beside her, leaning on his staff, was Stult, his round visage the colour of muddy clay, his small blue eyes darting nervously as was his habit. An anxious man, easily agitated, making him a target for Gilakas's attention.

Pausing before approaching them, Bornu Blatt sighed. An unlikely party of followers, none of whom he seemed capable of leaving behind. He'd not asked for any of them, not even Gilakas, the self-appointed bodyguard who'd be the first to betray him.

After a moment he resumed walking, drawing up alongside his mount as Gracer handed him the reins.

'You should admire her beauty,' she said. 'A horse likes to be admired.'

Bornu snorted. 'I am a man who gives back what he's offered.'

'So it's a battle of wills, is it? As to who is more stubborn, why, the horse usually wins.'

'We'll see.' Boot in the stirrup, Bornu pulled himself up and settled into the saddle. 'Domestication troubles me in principle,' he said as the others quickly mounted up, Stult heaving himself astride one mule and holding the reins of the other. Gilakas would fall in behind Bornu, followed by Gracer and then Stult and the train.

They set out up the street. The midday heat had driven most of the residents indoors. A few stray dogs briefly followed them, hopeful and shy – or hungry and opportunistic – Bornu could never tell with dogs. While various shorthaired cats lounged on window ledges watching them pass.

'Pets I understand,' Bornu continued, mostly to himself. 'Even abandoned ones. The dogs learning to scavenge. The cats hunting rats, mice in the grain. A kind of reciprocity at work. Goats and sheep stay safe in the care of shepherds. Again, something mutual at work there, at least until the selfsame protectors turn on their four-legged charges. Imagine the betrayal in the minds of those poor beasts. Fools to trust predators, especially clever ones. But mules, oxen, donkeys and horses? Slaves, nothing but slaves.'

The west gate loomed ahead, open and unguarded. The road beyond was worn, rutted and rocky.

'Dumb beasts,' Gilakas said behind him.

'My pity seems unappreciated,' Bornu pointed out, as his horse tossed her head, as if comprehending every word and suitably affronted. 'My horse understands me all too well.'

'That makes one of us,' Gracer said behind him.

'Consider this journey from settlement to settlement,' said Bornu, 'one of exploration. The ways of corruption in infinite variety. Venal self-interest, avarice, acquisitiveness, nepotism, the desperate coveting of influence and power, and all of that in just the innkeeper this morning as we settled the bill.'

Gilakas grunted a laugh. 'He was anything but subtle.'

Bornu shrugged. 'Ganabal of Bloorgris believed the soul to be multi-layered, like the rings of a tree, with each year of life marked by a thin line, a modest breadth of experience. Failure and success alike can accelerate growth, or, if no lessons are learned, begin the process of rot. Thus, the soul consists of an entire pocket of time, from birth to death – and, it is understood, beyond death as well – in which time can be said to be meaningless.'

'Now you make no sense,' snapped Gracer, her tone making a point of her impatience with this kind of talk.

'Consider your memories, Gracer – the layers beneath the layers. They remain to give you a sense of the past. Consider then your hopes and desires, launched into your future, a projection into the yet-to-be. Your thoughts dwell in your present, yet prove adept at mining memories and inspiring ambitions, of flowing freely between the past and the future. Yet they dwell, exclusively, in the present.'

'I'm not a tree.'

'Indeed, you are not.'

These final observations seemed to provide a natural conclusion to the conversation, and Bornu was content with that. Gracer was an intuitive sort, suspicious of complexity, dismissive of the abstract. Refreshing, at times. Most discussions with her ended abruptly.

The trader road led them past the outskirts of the town. Devoid of any natural impediments, such as gullies, gorges or crumbled mountains, settlements tended to sprawl. Ragged lines of foundation stones here and there marked old buildings and houses, mostly robbed out as the town's centre migrated over the centuries. The grasses and sedges that preferred disturbed soil now filled the interiors of these foundations, thicker and greener when rooted in cellars and sinkholes. Patches of once-tilled ground showed rows of stones pulled up by ploughing, the earth little more than angular lumps of rock-hard clay, bleached grey and lifeless, with all the topsoil long since blown away.

A faint rise of land fifty or so paces south of the road was crowded with grave-markers, although the cemetery appeared obsolete, both in style and relevance. Left behind by the town it once served. Bornu judged it to be at least fifteen hundred years old, the tall, narrow, obelisk-style tombstones characteristic of the age of bronze metallurgy, although even then, the first use of iron had begun elsewhere in Seven Cities and would soon arrive in this place as well.

Some historians posited that the shift from bronze to iron triggered some kind of economic collapse. The town's present state was indeed poorer, much reduced, if the extensive ruins in the fields on either side of the track were any indication. Then again, plague had swept the region not too long ago. Another kind of economic upheaval.

Even so, later burial practices were so different that Bornu suspected a complete turnover of population had occurred here, long ago, not long after the end of bronze, in fact. This, he knew, curiously coincided with rumours (and evidence) of some kind of catastrophe in that distant past. A catastrophe named *Icarium*.

Now, ahead, where the land rose out of the vast basin sprawled out behind them – which they had been crossing for days now and in which the town just quitted was but one of a score of settlements dotting the shore of what had once been an enormous lake – more substantial ruins were visible.

There were few maps of this region, at least none in detail. An early Malazan cartographer named Wessel had surveyed the area, followed by a rival named Feroot, and nothing of these two versions was at all alike. Worse yet, neither version matched what Bornu himself was seeing.

The ruins ahead looked strange. After another long moment squinting at them, Bornu said, 'This needs closer inspection.'

'The road bends away,' Gracer pointed out. 'That's usually a sign.'

'A sign of what?' Gilakas asked.

'Cursed. Haunted.'

'Ghosts are not to be feared, only pitied,' Gilakas pronounced.

Stult spoke up. 'Gracer is right. We should avoid the ruins. Nothing good comes of it.'

'Says the man eager to squat in a temple of the Nameless Ones.'

'Different,' Stult retorted.

'Well, sure,' Gilakas said. 'Gracer wanted to go there.'

'Enough,' Bornu cut in. 'You are, as always, free to do as you please.

While my main task is as Inquisitor, I am also a cartographer. Neither Wessel nor Feroot make mention of such substantial ruins, and that has me curious. Granted, they weren't very good cartographers, despite both claiming imperial charter. But this omission is noteworthy.'

'Perhaps another illusion,' Gilakas muttered. 'Another realm with a pool in the centre, a goddess with one hand in the water.'

'I doubt that,' Bornu replied. 'But then, one can never be sure.'

They reached the place where the road turned away, northward, to level out along a terrace running the length of the basin's rim, before climbing the slope once more. A few goat-tracks led off from the bend in the road, heading straight towards the ruins, and even from this distance, Bornu could see wild goats atop some of the ruins' outer walls.

'A city,' Gilakas observed. 'That should be known. Did the High Priest mention—'

'He did not,' Bornu replied. 'Although, not inclined to casual discourse under the circumstances. But I see signs of well-cut stone, and given the proximity of the track, the ruins should have been robbed long ago. One could back wagons almost right up to that outer wall.'

'True enough,' Gilakas said. 'This is indeed strange.'

'Ruins are boring,' announced Gracer.

'I agree,' chimed in Stult.

'Ride the track then,' Bornu said. 'We'll meet you on the other side.'

Gracer's eyes narrowed, but she nodded.

The ruins belonged to the abandoned cemetery they'd passed not long before, built and occupied in the same age of bronze. This was the period that followed the collapse of the mysterious First Empire, a time of confusion and anarchy. But people survived, rising again from flames and smoke. Still, written accounts were scant, the ancient cuneiform script poorly understood.

The city had once possessed a wall, but barring a few places, most of that wall had tumbled outward, forming an overgrown berm of rubble. The goat-tracks converged on a gap that had been a gate. A few of the feral beasts stood atop nearby wall fragments, warily eyeing Bornu and Gilakas as they approached.

'Never liked goats,' said Gilakas. 'Demon eyes.'

'Not all demons possess eyes with vertical pupils,' Bornu pointed out. 'Very few of them, in fact. Dragons, on the other hand . . . and K'Chain Che'Malle, or so I am led to believe.'

'Still don't like goats.'

'An omen?'

'You tell me, Inquisitor.'

Bornu said nothing as they guided their mounts through the gap. Just beyond rose broken humps where buildings had once stood, now collapsed and seemingly crushed in place, as if each one had been squeezed by some colossal hand, reminding Bornu of the village Mute had destroyed, but on a much larger scale. In between the mounds, avenues and streets remained uncluttered for the most part, clothed in yellow grasses that only greened in lines following buried gutters. On the main track directly ahead, more buildings were visible a short distance away that looked to be less damaged, although none bore intact roofs. Such tiles as he could see were dusty red, the heat making things blurry. Frowning, Bornu reined in.

'Something?' Gilakas asked, hand drifting to settle on the sword at his belt.

In growing alarm, Bornu stood on his stirrups, twisting round to study the gate they'd just passed through. 'Ahh, again?'

When Gilakas turned to look back, he swore. 'We didn't pass through that!'

'And see beyond?'

'I was right, then! We're in another realm. Damn whatever god lured us in here!'

The gateway behind them was complete, with a high arch on which was a frieze bearing, at the centre, martial figures gripping swords in one hand, severed heads in the other. At either end of the panel victims knelt before more soldiers, meekly awaiting beheading. The words carved in a curving banner above this scene were unlike anything Bornu had ever before seen.

Through the gate's opening, the land beyond was also unfamiliar, with rolling, stubbled hills and stands of strangely tall, narrow trees. No sign of the goats remained, and the walls to either side of the gate looked complete, undamaged. When Bornu faced forward again, even the collapsed buildings were gone, and in their place squatted two-storey edifices made of fired bricks. The architectural style was severe and unadorned barring rows of scallop patterns just beneath the peaked roofs, all of which bore the same red-clay tiling.

'From ruined city to a living one,' Gilakas said in a frustrated rasp.

190

'Living? No. Still empty. Inquisitor, let us return the way we came – back through the damned gate. Piss on all this.'

'Curious indeed,' said Bornu. 'No birds, no sound at all. Even the wind has died.'

'Died, aye. This is a necropolis. We do not belong.'

Bornu kicked his horse forward, eliciting a hiss of displeasure from Gilakas, who nonetheless followed a moment later.

From the grassy sward's thud under hoof to the clop on time-worn cobbles, the horses seemed indifferent to the miraculous transformation as they walked on. The main avenue continued, flanked by buildings with successive entrances, each entrance devoid of doors and revealing, through passageways, terraced gardens and fountains beyond. The sound of trickling water from the latter reached them, riding breaths of cool air streaming from the passageways. At the avenue's far end stood a monumental painted temple of some sort, again in a style Bornu did not recognize.

Now, as if rising from the ether itself, rubbish was visible on the streets. Broken pottery, scattered foodstuffs, including hazelnuts and spilled flour, olives and unfamiliar fruit. Signs of flight, panicked and desperate.

'We approach a moment,' said Bornu. 'With each step deeper into this city, Gilakas, we draw ever closer to that which constitutes "now" in this world. See how the details appear, filling in where necessary, to build for us this instant, this scene, a place between drawn breaths.' He paused, repressing a faint shiver. 'Do they pass us even now, the citizens, as they flee whatever calamity approaches? Are we but fades to them, less than ghosts? Mere shimmers and blurs to their fear-filled eyes? Or is their panic such that they do not notice us at all?'

'The world trembles,' Gilakas said, and even as he made the observation, both horses suddenly shied, ears flattening, hoofs snapping on the cobbles beneath them. Distant thunder sounded, but instead of fading the roar remained, growing. Reining to a halt in front of the huge temple with its brightly painted columns and friezes, Bornu glanced to his right, in the direction of that burgeoning thunder. The sky there was a rising wall of black, swallowing light.

Bornu dismounted. 'Join me, Gilakas,' he said. 'And we lead the horses inside, lest they bolt on us.'

Gilakas grunted. 'This temple should shield us from the storm, aye, though it too lacks doors.'

Glancing across at the man, Bornu said nothing.

They led their mounts up the broad, shallow steps, between columns, and then through the wide doorway into the temple's precinct.

To look upon walls of beaten gold and jewels. Above was a dome on which figures had been painted, engaged in mysterious activities. To either side stood niches occupied by statues painted in lifelike hues, the artistry breathtaking.

Directly ahead, at the end of a circular expanse bearing a gleaming mosaic, was an altar on which sat a man smoking a pipe and studying them with hooded eyes. He clearly did not belong, as much an interloper as Bornu and Gilakas.

With a faint sigh, Bornu tilted his head. 'Milord.'

The title set a scowl on the man's dark, weathered features. 'Listen well, child of Va'Shaik. I mean to speak plain. Besides,' he added, as the roar outside continued building, 'we haven't much time.'

'You have words for my goddess, milord?'

'The world is full of bastards, men and women both. Fanaticism breeds in stupidity like maggots in a pile of shit. I saw it, suffered in its midst. I decided I would give them exactly what they deserved, what they wanted, in fact. The great, glorious snuffing out. Make her understand. I was doing the Malazan Empire a favour, but that was incidental to my true intent. For a brief moment in the history of humanity, I made the world a little saner.' He lifted a hand and showed a gap between two fingers. 'This much. All I could do.' He used the altar to knock embers and ash from his pipe-bowl, and then stood. 'My worshippers . . . well, I may have to gather them again, all in one place. And deliver one more great, glorious *snuffing out*.'

'She would still wish to speak with you, milord.'

'Wasting her time.'

Now the entire temple was shaking, dust rising on all sides.

'Even so.'

'I am here to be reminded of something.'

'Milord?'

'My efforts? A mere piss in an ocean.' He paused, and then bared his teeth in something that wasn't a smile. 'Best not linger.'

'And you?' Bornu asked, turning to climb astride his horse – Gilakas quickly doing the same.

'So many are hiding in their homes. Others crowd the docks. Alas, not enough ships, not enough time. Fire was . . . clumsy. Here, here my friends, is *artistry*.'

Without another word, Bornu swung his horse around and kicked the beast into startled motion. Mosaic shattering with every crack of hoof, they rode out of the temple—

Into a gloomy world of descending ash.

Looking to his left, Bornu saw the black cloud filling half the sky, a swirling maelstrom of ash and burning rock.

'Gods below!' swore Gilakas.

'Follow me!' shouted Bornu, driving his horse recklessly down the steps, onto the street, and then, kicking the beast into a gallop, back towards the gate they had entered.

A wave of scorching heat swept over them. The roar of the world was deafening, the ashes tumbling in wild curtains of grey and white and then black. Flaming rocks rained down on all sides, shattering roof-tiles, bursting on cobblestones in explosions of molten stone. From somewhere close by, as they reached the gateway, rose a wailing scream, as of a thousand voices rising in dread chorus.

Smoke falling in a spark-filled curtain—

And then, suddenly, they were through, their horses stumbling at the slope, fighting to stay on the narrow goat-track - goats scattering from their path with baleful bleats - and Bornu twisted round, looking over one shoulder - that cloaked shoulder smouldering and scorched - to see the denuded bank of tumbled walls and dull yellow grass, a day swiftly falling into dusk, the western sky a smear of red and orange.

Loosening the reins of his horse, he left the mare to slow of her own accord, which she did. Alongside him, Gilakas appeared, brushing still-glowing embers from his mount's mane and head.

'Who the fuck was that?'

Bornu glanced at him in surprise. 'You did not hear him speak?'

'Saw his mouth move, but the roar swallowed every word.'

'Ah, not for you then.'

'Who, I asked, Inquisitor? I almost died back there!'

Bornu was silent for a few breaths, and then he said, 'Another city-killer, Gilakas. By fire, of course. Always by fire.' He paused, and then added, 'Do a thing once, and it follows you.'

*   *   *

'Are you dogs, then?' Gracer asked. 'Rolling in slag heaps or greasy hearths? You're filthy, the both of you.'

'You were wise to avoid a visit,' Gilakas said in a sour rumble. 'Gods playing miserable games, and us mortals in the usual role of being utter fools.'

This side of the ruined city, even the walls were little more than wrinkled ribbons, mostly obscured by sage and lumps of spiny cacti. The collapsed buildings beyond rose like round-barrows, picked clean of plants by the voracious goats.

'We've lost most of the day waiting for you,' complained Stult, standing near the hobbled horses and mules. 'An ill place to camp. No shade anywhere, beds of cactus and poisonous snakes as well, no doubt. Nor are we far away enough from the marshes. If bloodflies find us without any shelter, we may not survive the night.'

'Aye,' said Gilakas with a sober expression. 'Bad way to go. Best kill yourself now, Stult.'

The man scowled, looked away.

'I agree with Stult,' said Bornu. 'We'd best ride through as much of the night as we can manage. Mount up.'

Instead, Gracer walked closer to him. 'Not dogs. You're scorched, and . . . smelling of smoke.'

'Some cities take centuries to die, Gracer. Others, an instant.' Bornu shook his head. 'The one you see behind us has known both kinds of death, I fear. The ruins you see belong to Icarium, and that curse is potent enough to keep everyone away, to this day. Those ruins lie atop older ones to be sure.' He paused, and then added, 'But Gilakas and I rode through a different city, a city belonging to another continent, or even another world. And we barely escaped with our lives.'

'Perhaps the curse is within you, Holy One.'

He considered the possibility, and then nodded. 'That may be true.'

She glanced over towards the others, gaze lingering on Gilakas, and then said in a low voice, 'I don't think it's safe around you.'

Bornu hesitated, and then shrugged. 'You and Stult, of course, are free to depart our company.'

She walked over to her horse and climbed into the saddle, sparing a single glare towards Gilakas, who grinned back.

Stult mounted up and then fixed his attention resolutely, seemingly nailed to the setting sun.

Moments later and with Bornu in the lead once again, they set off, chasing the light.

*   *   *

It would be G'danisban, the goddess decided. Her attention lifted free of the Inquisitor and his curious entourage. Such were the gifts of faith that her attention could wing westward, to the city where her power seemed to wax with formidable energies. What awaited her in that city's temple of Va'Shaik?

She would see for herself.

*   *   *

'Well,' murmured High Priestess Shamalle, 'this is an ugly rumour. Summoned to Hanar Ara? To kneel before the goddess herself? To answer for my crimes? Rather, my noble deeds, I meant. Oh very well then, my crimes! What excuses shall I assemble, beloved Pash?'

'You have committed no crimes, Holy One.'

Shamalle glanced down at the strange little woman, who was working oil into her holy feet, in between the holy toes, and around the holy ankles, and so on. 'That's lovely.'

'You have nothing to fear,' Pash added, nodding.

'Hmm? Oh, the matter of my execrable litany of the unspeakable. The "lovely" comment was referring to your ablutions, darling. As to your assertion of my ineffable innocence, alas, your opinion is shared by no one else. Not even Invigil Ban Ryk, I should say. Surely the inferences implicit in the dictates of Kulat seemed to invite liberal interpretation, with plenty of wiggle-room, I add with a wink. But then, have I not embraced the very essence of Va'Shaik's . . . uhm, essence? Her physical manifestation, I mean. See the continental quivering of my thighs? The mountainous heaving of my upthrust . . . mountains? Curses, I am failing with descriptives this jangly morning! Rumours are cruel by any measure. Too blurry for detail, too slippery to grasp, much less hold down. Worse yet, when compounded, misery doubles – the Invigil's agents last night fared poorly again, I gather. Poor Ban Ryk is running out of them!'

Pash moved on to the other holy foot, which had been silently crying for attention all this time. 'He's not running out of agents, mistress.'

'He isn't? Well, how many does he have?'

'Each devotee of the faith is a potential agent,' Pash said. 'Many.'

195

'That's curious. And fairly alarming, to be honest. I need to give that some thought.'

While she gave it some thought, Shamalle looked around the bathing room. Glazed blue tiles surrounded her and Pash, beaded with condensation, some of the beads getting fat enough to suddenly burst, making crooked trickles down to the porous terracotta floor. Walls holding back tears, or something like that. She wished she was a poet. Or talented. But no. Steam made for droplets of water clinging to the tiles, finally defeated by fatness. Look at them down there, forming puddles. A woman could slip walking across this room. Imagine the crushing thump of that! She shivered.

'The floor drains are clogged.'

Glancing back at the puddle Shamalle was frowning at, Pash said, 'That's spilled oil, mistress.'

'From when I kicked that bottle over?'

'Yes, mistress.'

'And then I said, "Oh well, we have plenty more."'

Pash said nothing to that.

Shamalle pursed her lips. 'The indolence bred of excess, not just of flesh, but also wealth and all its material accoutrements. When one values nothing then nothing has value. Do you see the problem?'

'Mistress?'

'The Invigil's profligacy, of course. If one has, say, three agents, why, one must use them carefully, protectively, even. But when one has hundreds, if not thousands, why, it's like throwing handfuls of seeds, or something, into a seething pit of pigeons. Mice, I mean. Starving mice. A careless toss is my point. And what of loyalty? Three agents can be tested daily, in all that they do. But thousands? Evil spies must abound within such heaving mobs.'

'They get caught, Holy One.'

'Do they? I am clearly oblivious to all the nefarious doings here in my own temple. Are these spies who are caught expelled, sternly lectured to, given the heave-ho?'

'They are executed, Holy One.'

'Is this common?'

The scrawny woman at her feet shrugged.

'And the bodies? Never mind. I see the problem. Our enemies – whoever they might be – are equally profligate, and so we wager gains and losses over mere seeds of virtually no value. This life here, that life there. Gutters running red every night! Methinks this war unending, darling.'

Again, another observation worthy of no comment from the vigorous maiden whose hands were appallingly bony, the fingers appallingly long, and seemingly in no need of rest as they rubbed and massaged, from foot to foot and back again.

'The war for souls, one supposes, will never know peace. Barring death, presumably. But then, it's not like souls are fixed, nailed to the temple door for all time. I mean, they move around, flit this way and that. They wander through foreign halls and toy with unfamiliar things. Things are done that dismantle the virtue of all that went before, in that ledger of good and evil. The ledger trailing every soul like a strip of ass-wipe. The point is, save and indeed claim this soul today, but tomorrow? Who knows? You see my point? Unless you reduce everyone to quivering, mewling, submissive wretches, and keep them that way with terror and torture . . . well, let's face it, you can't win. No one can.'

Shamalle lifted a finger. 'But isn't that what our dear goddess has been saying all along? Or did she? I really should read some scripture. But . . . it's just so *dry*.'

Even to that, Pash had nothing to say.

'Dearest rose, you have been busy at night, out and about and so on. Do you suffer from angst? Ennui? Do you long for resolution, pine for peace?'

From this angle, the wiry bush of the top of Pash's head was all Shamalle could see of her servant. To her queries, the bush wagged from side to side. 'Suffering,' Pash then murmured, still bent over and working on the holy feet, 'is for others.'

Shamalle licked her lips, fidgeted slightly on the sweaty stone bench. 'Mhmm. There is this to consider. Rather, having considered matters, there is this. Imagine success for our Invigil. Imagine that odious Harapa Le'en and his wretched Inquisitor, Vest Dyan, successfully igniting all of Seven Cities into a new rebellion. Victory arrives! The Malazans are ousted! The rival cults obliterated! A unity of belief settles like a vast blanket over all the land! Glory be! Can you imagine all of that, Pash?'

A bob of the bush.

Thus encouraged, Shamalle continued, 'We dance in the streets, singing Va'Shaik's name, revelling in the imminent apocalyptic apotheosis. In the pantheon, the rejected gods reel back, struck to wonder and fear.

197

A sudden silence descends upon all of Seven Cities. Hallelujah! Well . . . what then?'

'Holy One?'

Shamalle noted the slight slowing of the hands massaging her feet, a growing hesitation. 'Let us examine the nature of us, shall we? People, I mean. In general. The vagaries of the human condition blah blah. Tell me, is your belief my belief, Pash?'

The hands slowed further. 'We serve the goddess, Holy One.'

'Mhmm, yes. But in exactly same way?'

A pause, and then, 'No.'

'Is my way better than yours? Or is yours better than mine?'

'They are different.'

'Difference! Oh no! Distinctions of faith and what it all means must be worked out. Consensus reached. But now there are sects within the singular faith, each choosing a different path, and in consequence diverging from one another. Leoman's frothing fanatics. Va'Shaik's Dissolutes (of which I am surely a member, possibly of high rank!). Harapa Le'en's over-armed army with blood in its eyes, and no one left to fight. Vest Dyan's mob of delinquents – pardon, inquisitors, in fervent need to police the populace, lest some fool stray into perversion of the faith, or rather those perversions not sanctioned by the church. Local variants in interpretation of holy text, a sudden burgeoning of beliefs! And then, alas, and of nauseatingly common historical precedence, conflict. Fistfights, rude gestures, arguments in the taverns, the flash of knife-blades. A riot, crowds seething and heaving, a library is rushed, occupied, texts lit to flame, the whole thing burns down killing dozens of screaming hooligans – excuse me, martyrs. The Inquisitors crack down, but only on non-inquisitors, of course. This upsets the Army of the Apocalypse, but only initially, because now they have someone to fight with! Entire cities fall out, raise defiant banners. The Army itself forms camps that start fighting each other. The Dissolutes lift heavy heads, blink myopically, and wonder what the fuck is going on? Meanwhile, the Manifest Goddess, Va'Shaik herself, looks on, first in horror, then disappointment, but at last in fullest understanding. Apocalypse, after all, is a seed within us. All of us, each and every one of us. We carry in us our own individual destruction, the disordering within the mind, leading to disorder of the flesh, and in worship of said potential, our faith can be said to narrow itself down, seeking first, disorder, and finally, the place where it ends. Namely, death.

Can it not then be said that all faiths worship death? When all the clutter is cleared and swept away? And that the ways of living, of proper comportment within the tenets of the faith, are but modes of preparation? None of which in any real way obviates the inescapable demise that is, you know, death? Hmm?'

The hands had stopped moving by now, were lying still as lifeless birds upon Shamalle's feet. Scrawny, starved, lifeless birds. Or dead mice, poisoned, but not as furry as real mice, the comparison being more symbolic than actual. As if that needed explication.

'And,' Shamalle resumed after a moment, 'since divisiveness lies in our nature, does it not follow that all religions – no matter the immortal eponymous head, its aspect, its variations – are one and all expressions of the implicit apocalypse dwelling within the human soul? And that, accordingly, mundane conflict between them is in fact utterly absurd? Not one religion, after all, defeats death. Not in any practical way, that is. The soul's journey beyond the flesh, well, can it not be said that we the living are the least authority imaginable in arbitrating its nature? And thus capable of nothing but empty, unprovable and distinctly unexperienced assertions therein?'

'Then,' whispered Pash, 'even non-believers cannot help but serve.'

'Either we all serve, or none serve.'

'And agents of death are the only true servants.'

'Oh, sweet rose of mine. Death needs no servants. Nor agents. Nothing you do makes a difference, except among the living, to whom Death is of course indifferent, yes? Besides, Death is equally indifferent to the very notion of faith. Faith in the inevitable is wasted effort, because, being inevitable, it requires no faith. Now,' she added, 'if one could invent a religion promising eternal life, not of the soul, but of the flesh itself, why, that would be a money-maker indeed! Perhaps the sciences will one day offer such a thing, through purely mechanical means, in which case, look out! Now, do find me a towel or robe, darling. It's suddenly chilly in here.'

*   *   *

Alarmed, bewildered, infuriated, the goddess fled the temple. But perhaps, she reflected some time later, this was precisely why gods and goddesses eschewed undeniable manifestations within the mortal realm, where nothing was simple, nor easy.

This Shamalle was a conundrum.

Well, we shall meet again soon. When I shall give answer to the annoying woman.

In godly fashion.

*   *   *

Confusion redounds in the moment of dying. Nothing is understood. The sudden separation of self from the flesh yields bewilderment. If fear embraced the soul in the instant before, or for the span of a hundred or a thousand heartbeats, that fear has now vanished. Instead, there is calm, leaving one floating within a universe of strange hesitation. A universe that dwells solely in the now.

Until, by some breakage of rules, it doesn't.

It was a long time before the woman came to herself, enough to recall her own name, enough to recall the sudden murder that was her death, sitting on the edge of a building's roof, feet dangling over the edge, with a dark, narrow, overgrown alley below. A wisp of a woman sitting beside her, one she'd first thought to be a child, but was not a child at all.

'That little bitch!'

Satala sat up, wearing a body identical to the one she remembered. Absent the slit from the knife-blade over her heart, absent the pain in her head that flashed – oh so briefly – when she fell back, skull crunching, bouncing once, even as her last breath escaped through her slack, lifeless mouth. Absent weariness, absent aches in the joints, the burning soles of her feet following an entire night on rooftops and everywhere else. Absent, too, a host of life worries.

She glanced down, saw that she was not naked. Indeed, she was dressed as she had been. But no knife in the sheath.

It was time to look around, to see where death had brought her. *Because I did die. I know I did. I saw my own body, there below me, whilst I hovered. I died all right. Tired, relaxed, careless. No one looking at that little woman would look twice. My apologies, High Fist. I saw you grieving.*

She found herself in a verdant glade, surrounded by jungle, or some overgrown garden. A spring-fed pool was to her left, its edges sodden and muddy and covered in yellow-winged butterflies, their wings slowly fanning the still air.

Momentarily fascinated by that fluttering carpet of motion, she started when a voice spoke close by. 'Your first words implied an unexpected end to things.'

Head turning, tracking the source of that voice, Satala struggled to make sense of what she saw.

A man, or most of a man. He was buried from the hips down. At first, she thought him propped up against a tree-stump. But no. The wood belonged to roots, as if the stump had been inverted, and they held him tight, wound around one arm and his torso, round his neck and diagonally across his mottled face. He was, as far as she could tell, human, or near-human, in any case. Still, the cast of his features struck her as foreign, somehow. His dark eyes returned her intense study without flinching.

'I know,' he said, 'it's not pretty.'

Satala rose to her feet, shifting her attention to the thick jungle on all sides. 'Where are we? Where is Iskar Jarak? The Soldiers of Death – why haven't they come for me?' She glanced over at the man. 'For us?'

'You, I can't say. As for me, why, I'm afraid I know nothing of your faith, or your expectations upon dying. Iskar Jarak? Never heard of him, or her. Soldiers of Death? Nor them. Death, I fear, remains a stranger to me. So too its realm.'

'How long have you been here?'

'I don't know. It never gets dark. The jungle itself never changes. The blossoms you see on the lianas never drop away. Those butterflies encircling the pool, there on the mud, they never take flight. Only their wings move . . . back and forth, back and forth. I've tried shouting. Waving my one free hand, but nothing startles them into flight. That said, you can move around. I'm curious to see what effect you might have on them.'

She studied the pinned man, trying to imagine being so imprisoned there, trapped in a realm beyond time, alone. 'Does it matter?' she asked.

A flicker of hurt, then disappointment, and he looked away. 'I suppose not.'

She stepped towards him, drawing his attention back. Only now his eyes had narrowed.

'By all means,' he said, 'try and kill me. I doubt it's even possible, but you never know.'

'Those roots seem intent on devouring you.'

'They're patient. But so am I. I did manage to get one hand free.'

'Someone buried a tree-stump upside down.'

'You think so? I don't.'

'What do you mean?'

'First off, it's not a stump, but a living tree. That means, somewhere down below, there's leaves, and sunlight, not that I can feel any of that. My legs may well have ceased to exist. No feeling there at all. Makes trying to free myself a bit pointless, I suppose.' He managed a half-shrug. 'Something to do here in our upside-down world.' He lifted his free hand and looked at it. 'At least now I can wave goodbye when you leave.'

She turned back to the jungle. 'No trails. I'd have to claw my way through.'

'You'll do that, eventually.'

'I will?'

'You're not the first to show up here, freshly dead. They all wander off. I'm poor company.'

Her attention returned to him. It was proving difficult not to, but not in a pleasant way. Not that at all. 'None tried to help you?'

'One or two, but not for long.'

'Why not? Are you so odious?'

'I might be. It is down to comprehension. Theirs, that is.'

She frowned. 'What do you mean?'

'I will make it easy for you, then. You see here the roots of a tree in the yard of an Azath House. This is the realm beneath Azath Houses. If you understand anything about such houses, you'll conclude that my imprisonment was probably a good thing – for everyone else.'

She stepped back involuntarily. 'Do you know . . . which Azath House?'

His brows lifted. 'Location? That's an interesting question to ask. Why, how many Azath Houses do you know of?'

'Only rumours. I've never seen one.' Her attention shifted slightly to study the roots of the tree. 'Is this one in a city? Do you remember anything?'

'A city. Yes, I think so. It stood in the very heart, revered as a temple. Source of faith for the inhabitants of that city. They sacrificed to it. Often.'

'Sacrifices? People like you? Fed to the demonic yard, to be devoured by the demonic trees?'

He made no immediate reply to any of that. In lowering his one free hand to rest upon the ground, she saw in the gesture something listless, defeated.

Satala was not by nature considerate of others; she knew that much about herself, the way in which she seemed different from most people.

It was neither a flaw nor a virtue. It was, she believed, simply a product of a life mostly spent in solitude. And, perhaps, of how seldom a hand had been extended to her in times of need and distress. High Fist Arenfall was an exception. He had won her loyalty and – strangely – that fierce binding remained, as if indifferent to her death.

She was thinking of how she might find her way back to the realm of the living. Since Iskar Jarak clearly had no interest in her. She was thinking of a scrawny woman in G'danisban.

'They leave to find the Gate,' the man said. 'Eager to shed the flesh of mortality. Fed up with it, usually. Weary of life. Impatient to see lost loves, family, parents, all those who died before they did.'

Satala grunted at that. 'Or resume old arguments,' she said, mostly to herself. 'I lost my knife.'

'You didn't. It lies in the moss, to your left. It was in your hand when you appeared. You'd just drawn it, I think.'

Turning, she scanned the ground until she found it. A faint shiver rippled through her when she bent to pick it up and took the weapon into her hand. Was this truly her knife, or its ghost? It felt right, familiar in every way. Sighing, she sheathed it. 'Whatever dragged me here was . . . considerate.'

'A unique perspective.'

She drew the knife again and approached the imprisoned man.

There was a hopeful flicker in his eyes as he watched. 'Mercy at last? Perhaps you will succeed where others have failed.'

'Some tried to free you?'

'Free me? No. Murder me.' Now his regard was quizzical. 'You would save me? Shouldn't we bargain first? The value of my gratitude surely must weigh in the wager. Besides, I may well be malign, twisted into insanity by this imprisonment. Or perhaps that evil was always within me, justifying my delivery into the grip of the Azath.'

She paused for a long moment, before shrugging and saying, 'I'm dead. What can evil do to me?'

'That is a question neither of us can answer.'

'Do you feel evil? Are you filled with malignant thoughts and desires?'

'No one feels evil, even when they are undeniably so. As for my thoughts, well, many are indeed self-serving, which makes them suspect. But I seem to harbour no enmity for anyone else.'

Satala found she was hesitating, not quite within the man's reach.

Something was wrong with what she saw when she looked at him. 'You have told me little of your past. Not even your name. What do you have to hide?'

A wry smile. 'Plenty. Then again, you've not told me your name either. What of your life? Since no details at all are forthcoming, what have I gleaned? Very little. You died suddenly, stabbed in the chest given your initial self-examination. You knew your slayer. That betrayal shocked you, but also made you angry with yourself. For being so careless. This tells me of a life spent guardedly. For dying you blame yourself as much as you do the one who stabbed you. And that knife settles sweetly in your hand, like an old, loyal friend.'

She loosed a long breath, and then shook her head. 'Is that all? Gods below.' She took a step closer to him, and then halted again, frowning. 'That is odd. I seem no closer to you, though I just took a stride.'

'You are closer. Try another, little one.'

Little one? She stepped again, and her breath caught. 'Some illusion at work here.'

'No.' And to prove it, he lifted his freed arm and brought his hand closer to her.

She stared at it, aghast. *That could wrap easily about my thigh.* Satala quickly stepped back. 'You are Fenn, a giant.'

The man withdrew his hand. 'Fenn? I do not know that name.'

'Tartheno.'

His eyes narrowed faintly. 'More . . . familiar.'

'Toblakai.'

'Ah! Yes, that will do. Toblakai. I am he.'

'That's not a personal name – well . . . never mind. It's a name for a people. Giant people, such as you.'

After a few breaths, he nodded. 'This helps. I recall a few more things.'

'Such as?'

'The city surrounding the Azath. I remember seeing it from high above, as I fell.'

'Fell from where?'

'From the sky.'

'You fell out of the sky?'

He nodded. 'Yes, very much so. I was already wounded. Dying, in fact. But no . . . that dying had been interrupted, somehow. For . . . for a long time.' He visibly struggled to recall more, his scowl deepening. 'I landed in a street. Broke all my limbs – the three not already broken, I mean. Yes, a leg wound, septic, killing me. The locals panicked. Dragged me to their temple, to the Azath. Gave me to the yard. I was too damaged to resist them.' He looked over, met her eyes. 'Then here. That is all that I remember.'

'Not your name?'

'No. Do you know yours?'

'Satala.'

He nodded. 'That is a nice name. Satala.'

'It's just a name,' she said. 'There was a . . . a creature like you. Who took for himself the name "Toblakai".'

'Presumptuous?'

'Yes, he was. His name was Karsa Orlong.'

The giant snorted.

'Something amuses you? You know Karsa Orlong?'

'No. But the etymology is . . . well, as a name, much devolved. Karfal was the highblood name of those who served in the household of a royal line. A palace guard if you like. Oralangal is a highblood term for a breed of lawless outlaw, of no surviving clan. Thus, a guard with no throne to defend. Karfal Oralangal.'

'It is said he has become a god,' Satala added.

'Poor bastard. What aspect does he claim?'

'Aspect?'

'Some iteration of a life's condition. A theme, a characteristic. A flavour. The aspect of war, for example—'

'I knew what you meant,' she cut in. 'Your question surprised me for another reason.'

'Which was?'

'I had no answer. I do not know the aspect of Karsi, as his cult is called. But those who belong to it are known to kill in the name of justice. Lynching. Stoning. Their symbols include two dog heads on a single chain. Or cracked glazing on a fierce mask. Shattered tattoos. Karsa Orlong was once a slave, then an escaped slave who was recaptured and branded. As Toblakai he was a loyal guard to Sha'ik, the Whirlwind Goddess.'

'Toblakai,' the man mused, and then said, 'Thel Akai. As opposed to the Thelomen. The Tartheno Thelomen. Avowed enemies. Lazy, useless, vicious raiders.' He looked up at her. 'I was a Karfal, once, to a king. A . . . beloved king. Well. I loved him, at least.'

'If I come within reach,' Satala ventured, 'will you attempt to grab me?'

'What for?'

'To slake some hunger or thirst, perhaps. Some savage need. Bloodlust.'

He shook his head. 'I'll do nothing, even if you scratch behind my ears.'

Satala smiled. She approached. 'You've dug in the ground around you.'

'Where I can reach, yes. To no avail. Rather, when I attempt to do more, the roots tighten.'

Sheathing her knife again, she walked a slow circle around him. He twisted his head as best he could to follow her, and then stopped as she began a second pass. Directly behind him, she halted. 'I see a weapon's edge,' she said, reaching down to drag away clumps of moss, revealing a broad, curved flatness of pitted iron. 'An axe. A huge, double-bladed axe.'

'Ah! Yes, that is mine. Once belonged to a Thelomen king. I killed him for it, I think.'

It took some effort to pull the weapon free, and once its full weight was in her hands, she gasped. 'I can barely lift it.'

'Drag it round, Satala, to my free hand.'

She paused. 'Dare I?'

'You can leave the glade then, get as far from me as possible. I've no interest in harming you. Indeed, you shall have my eternal gratitude.'

'You mean to cut yourself free?'

'I mean to try.'

'You're more likely to injure yourself. In fact, I don't see how—'

'My first change in circumstances in . . . in a long, long time, Satala. To simply hold the weapon once more. It is beyond words, the immensity of your gift.'

'Oh, very well.' She tugged and pulled the axe by its thick, wire-wrapped handle, until within the Toblakai's reach. As he lifted the axe – seemingly effortlessly – Satala moved well back.

'You can leave now.'

'I may not.'

He grinned at her. 'You wish to see?'

She nodded, crossing her arms.

He brought one edge up against the thickest root binding his chest, began cutting the thick, twisted wood. The sap that suddenly smeared the blade's edge was red.

It seemed the roots wrapped round the giant all flinched, and the man's face darkened as he fought for breath. His sawing motions grew frantic.

'Gods below,' Satala hissed, knife out again, moving close to start cutting away the thinner roots. They snapped when they parted, sap spattering across her hands. She moved to the root around the man's neck. 'Stay still, lest I cut your throat and save the tree the bother!'

Her warning was not needed. The axe fell with a heavy thump as the Toblakai sagged, losing consciousness, his face a mass of blue and green blotches, his eyes bulging and filling with burst blood vessels.

She nicked him for all her efforts not to, as the thick root round his neck finally came away. But that sting of pain restored the Toblakai to consciousness. Drawing a ragged gasp of breath, he reached back down for the axe. She pushed his hand away. 'I'll finish that one.'

He'd managed to saw through most of it, and a moment later it split apart.

'The knife is better for this,' she said, her attention now on the roots binding his left arm.

His voice was rough. 'I feel blood.'

'Aye, you bleed. I don't think you were ever dead at all. Not like me.'

'My kind are hard to kill, it's true. Blame the goddess who birthed us.'

'Oh?' she murmured, only half listening. 'And what goddess was that?'

'Why, Kilmandaros, of course.'

Satala paused, edging back when he reached over and began tearing away the lesser roots. Straightening, she took a few more steps to give him room. 'That's a very old name,' she said.

'Ah, but you know it even so.'

'A mention or two. Not much more than that. Epic poems.'

She watched him try to arch his back, pushing down on the ground in an effort to pull his legs free. The hacked tree roots and stump creaked and quivered. The blood-like sap had leaked everywhere. Fluttering motion startled Satala and she gasped to see butterflies now in the air, circling the giant and the wounded tree. They began settling on both man and bleeding wood. To feed.

The giant grunted a laugh. 'Clearly,' he said, slowly raising one arm covered with butterflies, 'in matters of patience, these creatures are without equal.'

*   *   *

207

As it turned out, the giant still had his legs, although barely recognizable, covered in roots that proved to be fused with his flesh, making his skin into something like gnarled, knotted armour. The tree he left behind was clearly dying, the streaming flow of red sap slowing in ever-weaker pulses. The giant's motions irritated the butterflies enough that they abandoned him to feed on the tree's sticky exudations. Retrieving his axe, he stepped clear. When he looked down to study his bared legs, he grimaced, but then nodded. 'This, then, brought the infection to an end. My fever, I now recall, was an eternal thing. For all the time my soul sealed the gate, I knew pain and delirium.' He paused, and then added, 'That delirium may well have saved my sanity.'

Satala struggled to make sense of his words. His soul had sealed a gate? A gate in the sky? A dying body forever dying – until he was spat out. How? When? 'In this place,' she now said, 'all is now. Dying, living, sickly and healthy. Bound and unbound. You and me. We are open now to all that is possible.'

He glanced down at her from his formidable height, half of his grin still in place. 'No matter how improbable. Satala, you have proved to be the hand of my liberation. I shall stand beside you now, as your Karfal Oralangal.'

She snorted. 'I am no royalty.'

'No matter, I see a crown, nonetheless. A circlet of virtue.'

She regarded him. 'Do you always speak in such flowery language?'

He shrugged. 'I speak in the common tongue.'

She started, only now realizing that they had been conversing in a language not her own.

Seeing her confusion, the Toblakai said, 'You are the dead one, Satala, not me. Your soul resides in a place of knowing, it seems. Your first words, cursing the bitch, were in my common tongue.'

'A common tongue shared by whom?'

He frowned, and then said, 'Thel Akai and Tartheno Thelomen. Jheck and Jhelarkan. Dog-Runners and the Tiste. The Jaghut, and even the damned dragons. That said, I believe it was a contrivance of the Azathanai gods. Conflict from mere ignorance lacks spice.'

Conflict from mere . . . 'These Azathanai gods. We're here for their amusement?'

He looked around. 'Might be still. But, in my time, surely the answer must be "yes". Precisely. For their amusement. The curse of immortals, I should think. That said, it too must pall eventually. This, you see, is not my world. Nor is it the world beyond the gate of Starvald Demelain. The Azath Houses are their own thing – never mind the Azathanai taking their name for themselves, being arrogant assholes.'

'You mentioned a gate – the one your soul once sealed?'

'Yes. Starvald Demelain. I remember that much, for now. What I don't remember is the name of the bastard who put me there.'

'And what of your own name?'

His frown deepened. He shook his head.

'Well,' said Satala, 'I'll not call you Toblakai. That would just confuse things and we can't have that, can we? I fear even Karfal Oralangal could prove problematic. No, you need a new name.'

'I will take a title. The Grey Shore.'

'Oh. What shore?'

'Creation's shore, Satala. To see one's youth restored, one must walk away from it, you see.'

'No, I don't.'

He drew a deep breath, filling that massive chest, and loosed it in a long sigh. 'I do feel . . . younger. Enlivened.'

'Lucky you,' she snapped.

He looked over, gaze sharpening. 'Satala, don't we have a little bitch to track down?'

'I doubt that threshold is easily crossed.'

'True. I knew a storyteller once, word waxer, who told tales of the unlikely.' He paused, evidently musing, and then said, '*The Lay of Satala and The Grey Shore*. Shall we weave ourselves a story?'

She scowled. 'For the edification of whom – gods take me, I'm starting to sound like you.'

'Never mind the audience, they rarely have anything good to say. That storyteller I knew? I was his worst audience by far, hah! Yet now we must step forward, to win the possible from the improbable. I foresee a grand adventure.' He then raised an admonishing finger that looked little different from the roots of the Azath tree. 'But you'd best know this now – you travel with a man whose heart is broken. Don't bother trying to mend it. You cannot. None can. Leave the river of tears upon your left, knowing it will never waver. My life to guard your soul, Satala.'

She stared at him, this giant of giant gestures. *Gods below.*

*   *   *

209

High Fist Jalan Arenfall stood in the cryptorium, his private, timeless warren, wondering where her body had gone. This mystery was leaving him more shaken than he cared to admit. He drew from a pouch the small, blank, coin-shaped Runt that signified the warren Oblivion. Blackened and pitted with impurities, the tin Runt sat cool and unusually heavy in his palm.

Oblivion defied time. The eternal pause between breaths. He had used it to shape this pocket warren, making a realm where nothing could change, nothing could age or decay. A place for all his indecisions. It was his suspicion that such things existed within everyone. Icarium's genius lay in his mapping of consciousness itself, that self-referential, self-contained builder of worlds. Mapping, then dividing, separating its component truths. In this respect, he suspected, consciousness itself was a natural builder of warrens. In an unawakened state, such warrens possessed little efficacy, firmly lodged within the mindscape, subject to every manner of deluded belief and doubt, as befitted the realm of the mind. Once awakened, however, they could alter reality itself.

This was a dangerous truth, something that, perhaps, Icarium had not considered. Unquestionably, reality resisted change, in the manner that a stone resists the chisel. All things were connected, but the strength of that binding varied.

Someone or something had broken into his pocket warren, his timeless crypt that had held Satala's cold, lifeless body. An impossible looting of a barrow, or, rather, what should have been impossible. Now he stood uneasy, as if the solid clay beneath his feet had suddenly turned into sand. The will of a mind could break anything. Icarium had shown as much. From the pieces, he had then reassembled them somehow, creating the Runts. Now, the constituent parts of human nature could be rearranged.

As an artist, Arenfall viewed those parts as themes. To be sure, there was no sharp delineation between each theme. Instead, all the edges blurred. The desire to sharply categorize such aspects of human nature was unsurprising, since confusion was, for the most part, universally unpleasant. The artist saw this confusion, however, as *potential*, a place where anything was possible.

If art was to have a god, surely it was Icarium. A broken fool forever seeking his memory, finding instead blank spaces within, where the only thing that could thrive was his imagination. His mechanical constructs, scattered all over the world, belonged to his obsessive need to fix his absences in both place and time. Seeking patterns, perhaps, and from those, some hint of understanding. A doomed effort, and what artist did not eventually reach the very same revelation?

No two minds were alike. Every mindscape was unique. It had always been so and so too would it for ever be. At the thought, arriving so awkward in its construction, Arenfall grunted in amusement. There was no Runt called Failure. The closest, thematically, was Ambition, signified by a gold coin with the image of a crypt on both faces. Unquestionably, Ambition and Failure were linked; in fact, he could not think of a more solid union. To reach skyward was to weather a storm of arrows. *Eventually, you bleed out.*

The flat clay ground still bore the faint impression of her body, where he had left her lying in repose on her back, arms folded and hands on her chest. This in itself was a shocking detail. The sign of what had been but was no longer present constituted an assertion of time. Its passage, its state of that leading to this.

My warren has been broken.

Existentially, of course, every time he visited, brought something here or took something away, he was imposing temporality, but such states left no impression. Presence or absence entailed re-creating the warren.

Not this time. Now, the realm was itself a corpse.

A gesture cast sharp light upon the immediate area, and Arenfall crouched to study the ground. *There. Footprints. Barely hinted at, but these I can track.*

Straightening, he hesitated. Back in G'danisban, a full dozen high priests, seneschals and abbots were awaiting him in the Communal Chamber, all eager to beg protection against one of their own. The persecution in the streets and alleys of the city was out of control. Something had to be done.

It will be, damn you all. But I ask every one of you: if it was your cult winning the war, would you be here?

They would have to wait.

Jalan Arenfall set out, tracking the footprints. They did not belong to Satala: too wide, too heavy. Some of that weight must be the body of Satala herself, of course. Still, likely a man. *If a woman, then a big one. Fenn? Possibly Barghast. Or Trell.* The prints were wide from side to side, suggesting a shambling gait, rolling hips. Something of a lope as well, denoting haste. Understandable, since Arenfall wasn't planning on a friendly conversation when he caught up to the body-stealing bastard.

The breaching of his pocket warren became quickly evident, as the trail continued on, and on. The edges had disintegrated entirely, and the land he now traversed was unfamiliar to him.

A thousand paces later, the footprints lost their human appearance.

Arenfall slowed down, a chill tracking up his spine, his mouth suddenly dry.

Reptilian. Three taloned toes splayed forward, one back, beyond the heel. And fucking big.

He was well read, a listener of epic poems and songs, a delver into all things strange in this world. He was in possession of details referring to things he had never seen. Such was the gift of language and an active, lively mind.

These prints must be K'Chain Che'Malle.

He found that he had stopped walking, the lure of what lay ahead losing its appeal. A wry grin twisted his lips. Hesitation might well come from confusion, but sometimes, hesitation came from certainty. *If I continue on, I could end up deader than Satala. Am I such a fool? Anger gives way to curiosity. Set aside the indignation, taking offence at this intrusion. Something more is at work here. What significance Satala's lifeless body?*

This unknown warren's landscape was bleak, flat, with every horizon seeming to dissolve into grainy uncertainty. Overhead was pallid, empty sky. The air was cool, cooler than it had been, carrying no scent Arenfall could detect. *An old world, or a world waiting to be built.*

At a sudden gust of wind, then the leathery thud of beating wings directly above him, Arenfall cursed and threw himself to one side, rolling over one shoulder, knives in both hands. He came to his feet even as the winged creature landed facing him. Wings slowly folding behind its back, it straightened, towering over Arenfall.

It then spoke in his mind.

'Apologies.'

He drew a few more breaths, waiting for his heart's beating to slow down, and then he said, 'I can't yet accept that until I know what you've done.'

The creature's elongated, reptilian head tilted to one side. *'I now recall.'*

'What do you recall?'

212

'My legacy of misunderstandings. Rather, it is my fate to be misunderstood. I apologized for startling you.'

'Not stealing a body from me?'

A pause, and then, 'I did not know you owned it. For what purpose? Supper? The sexual allure of utter indifference?'

Arenfall snorted. After a moment, he said, 'Forgive me, the twisted absurdity of that left me shocked. And that's not easily done. No, neither of those. She was a friend. I grieved for her death.'

'A grief you would then indulge indefinitely. I understand. Self-pity is ambrosia, is it not?'

'No, to, uh, everything you just suggested. I am responsible.'

'You killed her?'

He shook his head. 'Not directly. She worked for me. I put her in danger. That kind of responsibility.'

'I in turn needed her, to right an old wrong. This is done. Rather, she did well. My need for her is at an end. That said, it's not quite gone as intended. He elected to accompany her, you see. Worse yet, he appears to harbour ill-feelings towards me, despite the mercy of my efforts in seeing him freed from his abject state. Which, it must be pointed out, was not the original abject state I left him in. A different abject state, consequential but only indirectly related to the first one. I fear I have confused the situation for you. Not my intention, but surely you see my dilemma.'

Arenfall sheathed his knives. 'Not quite,' he admitted.

'He probably wants to kill me. This is common among past acquaintances, but I detect no obvious commonality beyond being acquaintances.' A moment's hesitation, and then the creature continued, 'There have been exceptions. Rather, an exception. Do you know K'rul?'

Arenfall said, 'Not personally, no.'

'No need to regret the absence of opportunity.'

'Very well. That's a relief. In any case, you were saying?'

'Many things. Can you be more specific?'

'Him wanting to kill you, whoever he is.'

'I believe his name would be unfamiliar to you. The confounding issue here relates to his accompanying your woman – who in death surely no longer works for you? Unless, of course, you are excessively demanding of your employees. In any case, she seeks to return to your world. For a purpose unrelated to you, as I understand it. More to avenge her murder at the hands of the one who murdered her, which seems logical enough on the surface. But you do see our problem, yes?'

Arenfall shook his head. 'I don't. If she died, then she has no capacity to return. The Soldier of Death plays no favourites.' Then he frowned. 'That said, you took her body – you somehow shoved her soul back into it?'

'If I did such a thing, was that a wrong thing to do?'

'You're admitting—'

'I admit nothing. I have found this response useful in the past and so I employ it again, here. It irritated K'rul but never angered him. I deem this a viable tactic in discourse.'

'I have a question – I did not know K'Chain Che'Malle had wings.'

'They didn't. Until I decided it would be fun if some of them did. Therefore, I created the Shi'gal Assassins. I found the form useful, personally, particularly when in Starvald Demelain.'

'You've come from the realm of Dragons?'

'We negotiated. At length. But this is now concluded, and if one side is pleased with the result, I am happy for them. They can always rebuild.'

'You have restored life to Satala's body,' Arenfall said, having arrived at the obvious conclusion despite this strange creature's evasiveness. 'That is a traumatic event.'

'Is it? I wouldn't know. She seemed fine, although she almost stabbed me the instant her soul returned to its mortal residence. That was . . . impressive.'

'And where are they now? Satala and this friend of yours.'

'Not a friend.'

'I was being facetious.'

'Ah. Well, that is indeed a valid question. I am not sure. Indeed, I hoped you might inform me, being such an obsessive employer. Unless, of course, she was merely renting the crypt you put her in?'

Arenfall pinched the bridge of his nose, then rubbed at his eyes. 'Then we are at an impasse since I have no idea where she could be. Nor how she could get from wherever she now is back to the world of the living.'

'I am familiar with this sort of impasse. It seems to accompany the conclusion of most of my conversations. I'm not sure why. If not impasse, then disagreement. I prefer the former, being far less violent than the latter.'

'I think I'll return to my world now,' said Arenfall.

'I will accompany you.'

'What?'

'Or, you have a better idea?'

'More than I can count! Can you not track the one with Satala?'

214

'He would sense my proximity. I'd rather not for the time being. Once his ire has cooled sufficiently, I am happy to find him, and remind him of the specific circumstances of our initial meeting. It seems he has forgotten some salient details. That said, I have not been in your world for . . . well, hmm, I correct myself. I have never been to your world and therefore know nothing of it. Tell me, do you think I would be welcomed?'

'Are you a god?'

'If I said "yes"?'

'Then no, as we have too many gods already.'

'And if I said "no"?'

'That depends. Would the K'Chain Che'Malle welcome you back?'

The creature was silent for a few moments, and then it said, 'Oh. I was hoping they'd died out by now. Do they swarm your world? I could always eradicate them for you. A matter of, as you clearly understand, guilt-laden responsibility.'

'They don't swarm anywhere,' Arenfall said. 'They may well be extinct.'

'I am relieved, if doubtful. Look under the wrong rock . . .'

'If this Shi'gal Assassin is merely a guise, then what are you?'

The creature sighed, and that sigh was a bellowing gust from at least four lungs. 'Azathanai. But don't hold that against me. It was all K'rul's fault.'

Arenfall did not know the term 'Azathanai', but he quickly gleaned its associations. 'K'rul is known as an Elder God in my world,' he now said.

'That makes sense. He bled for you all, the fool. It may be that he still does. We Azathanai are hard to kill. I could elect to pay him a visit, then. As I recall, our last meeting concluded with an impasse rather than disagreement, a rarity I have learned to treasure.'

'We know of other Elder Gods,' Arenfall said. 'Perhaps you are one of them?'

'I am Skillen Droe. Does that elicit the light of recognition?'

'I'm afraid not.'

'I have no reason to be disappointed, and yet I am. Popularity was never a talent of mine.'

'What was?'

'I'd like to believe negotiation, but all evidence is to the contrary.'

'I'll take my leave now, Skillen Droe.'

The Azathanai dipped its head. 'We depart on an impasse. I'm pleased.'

'And I in turn am relieved,' said Arenfall, bowing and then opening his warren, quickly stepping through and snapping it shut behind him. The transition, made in haste, left him momentarily bewildered, staring without comprehension at the room he'd found himself in. A few heart-beats later, familiarity returned. His private chamber. And across the corridor, down a side-passage, waited a mob of panicky priests.

He took a moment to gather his thoughts, and then set out.

*   *   *

In a mostly dissolved pocket warren, that Skillen Droe had casually ripped asunder to allow his own warren to flood in, the Azathanai stood studying the still-glowing reddish rent the strange human had stepped through only moments earlier.

Having deftly tied an almost invisible thread to the man, it would be no difficulty following him into that other, unknown world.

But he was undecided. Negotiators were valued additions virtually everywhere, were they not? What might he mitigate in that stranger's world? Why, virtually anything. Ending wars and other grand forms of conflict was not that difficult. The simplest approach was to eliminate one side of the disagreement, comprehensively. Predicated on an assessment of which side was the least objectionable. If equally objectionable, then killing everyone was by far the simplest solution of all, yielding an extended period of tranquillity. But, alas, a lonely tranquillity.

Smaller arguments were more complicated, more challenging. Mitigating those ones usually resulted in failure, but failure was no reason to stop trying, even unto applying the same methods which, though they failed the first (and second, third, and so on) time around, remained both logical and elegant. Conceptually. Failure, he'd long ago concluded, was reality's fault, not his.

In fact, in his long life, he had stumbled upon one civilization after another wherein this paradigm blossomed. Repetition based upon erroneous assumptions leading to catastrophic failure was, it seemed, an attractive lifestyle. For a while. Blossoming, after all, could refer (metaphorically) to a flower in one moment, then blood in the next. Poetic, no?

As Skillen Droe stood considering his options, permitting the fullest fulmination of notions both relevant and not – an indulgence he delighted in – he detected a rhythmic trembling of the damp clay underfoot. Head lifting, he looked around and almost immediately saw its source. A monstrous, six-limbed beast was loping its way towards him. Its weight was such that each lift of a foot tore clumps of clay from the ground. Festooned in weapons, its upper arms were readying a long arrow in a long bow.

The apparition's intent was plain, leading Skillen Droe to wonder if they'd met before. Certainly not in its present form – he would have remembered.

Suddenly, that arrow was in the air, racing towards the Azathanai. A mere blink from its striking, Skillen Droe shattered the arrow with a gesture.

This gave the attacking beast pause. Its pace slowed, weapons lowering, head cocking to one side. With fifteen or so paces between them, the creature halted.

Skillen Droe narrowed his gaze, which had the effect of expanding the range of light and heat his eyes could detect (a detail of biomechanical ingenuity he was particularly proud of). *'I no longer doubt. You are indeed made of stone. A statue, miraculously animated. You have outdone yourself this time, Spingalle. Utter genius.'*

The head cocked further.

Skillen Droe sensed waves of confusion emanating from his old frie— well, friend was perhaps inaccurate. Companion? No, absolutely not. Associate? Acquaintance? Oh dear. Fellow Azathanai, then. *'I fear your memories are equally indurated. You have forgotten who, and what, you are, haven't you? Your name, too? Spingalle, the Dancing Jackal. Lord, sometimes Lady, of the Hunt. Clearly, in your present state, you have acquired a dislike for K'Chain Che'Malle. Understandable. They are quite unlikeable. But I must express yet again my admiration. To manifest as a statue of stone, to dwell for untold ages in a godly guise well suited to being comfortably worshipped without fear of any interference on the god's part, being made of stone and all, well, brilliantly obviates the interminable ennui of eternal wandering. I would think—'*

'The fuckers chained me!'

Skillen Droe blinked at the savage rage in that bellow. *'They chained a stone statue?'*

'I am Spingalle! Lord of the Hunt!'

'Sometimes Lady,' Skillen Droe added, in the interests of precision.

'They chained me and then ran away!'

Skillen Droe nodded. *'Infernally unpredictable, those mortals. And ungrateful too, most of the time. Rather, gratitude of limited duration, leading inevitably to resentment, followed by hatred followed by murderous intentions. What was the problem just staying with plain gratitude? What is so bad having that gratitude*

217

persisting in perpetuity, generation upon generation, veneration and admiration unending? What is wrong with mortals, anyway?'

Spingalle began sheathing stone weapons through the stone loops of his stone belt. *'Memory returns. I know you, Skillen Droe. I don't think I liked you.'*

'This is true,' Skillen Droe admitted. *'Although, not actively so. I believe we were in the habit of irritating each other. Never escalating beyond that, thankfully. As for gratitude, well, you may express yours to me, in that I have been instrumental in returning you to yourself. I wait with calm equanimity.'*

'Keep waiting,' Spingalle said in a growl. *'Mindless rage unending is far more satisfying a state of being than . . . than this.'* The Lord looked about. *'Where the fuck are we? I have memory of a northern forest. Before that, scrub desert. Before that, a glade under the shadow of Sky-Keeps.'*

'Haven't you been busy, for a chained stone statue!'

Spingalle shrugged. *'A mortal hunter freed me. To him I was grateful.'*

'Oh, where is he now?'

'Dead.'

'I no longer seek your gratitude.'

'Wise. The hunter and the hunted are in a complicated relationship. That said, he understood in the end. I think. At least, let us say the bear did.'

'What do you intend now?' Skillen Droe asked.

'I am not sure.' Spingalle faced him. *'I recently killed many K'Chain Che'Malle. Are you offended?'*

'No.'

'Oh. Too bad.'

'Residue of your violent nature, this regret of yours.'

'Possibly. What of you?'

'I was thinking, back into a mortal world, filled with verve and zeal and the desire to mitigate and so on.'

'I may have just come from that world.'

'Indeed?'

'Like rotted cheesecloth, the barrier between here and there.'

Skillen Droe nodded. *'I suspected as much. These warrens are young. Fresh. I wonder who made them, and why they bothered. Not K'rul, to be sure. There is a hint of the Jaghut about them.'*

At that, Spingalle flinched.

Noticing, Skillen Droe nodded in commiseration. *'Hence my hesitation. It remains a subject of some contention. The Azathanai and the Jaghut. Did we* create them? Did they create us? Either way, their presence in this adjacent mortal world . . . and the hint mentioned a moment ago regarding the new warrens . . . well, I'm sure you can understand my indecision.'

'I should hate the Jaghut,' said Spingalle in a rumble.

'You do not?'

The Lord shook his head. 'But I fear them.'

'Ah. Complicated. Fear, with grudging admiration.'

'Just so. But listen, if together, we need not fear them at all!'

'Hmm. If together, not together long, thus stranding us both in a strange land filled with Jaghut. I am being realistic here, Spingalle. Given our history of mutual irritation.'

'And this is why we end up ruling nothing and no one! We could master every universe! Instead, we can't stand each other!'

Skillen Droe nodded a second time. 'Nature is diabolically clever.'

'I am leaving you now.'

'Where are you off to, Spingalle?'

'To find a pedestal of stone, fool.'

'Beware chains.'

'Shut up.'

Skillen Droe watched his fellow Azathanai thump away at something like a jog. Leaving him alone once again, contemplating his own indecision. A mortal world in need of mitigation. Occupied, at least in part, by Jaghut.

Such a dilemma!

Why, this could take years to decide!

He decided to squat on the ground, tail curling to one side and wrapping round, a length of it settling across his long, taloned toes. Like a posing cat. Unappreciated by anyone . . . and just consider the injustice of that!

* * *

Some anxieties can silence the will to live. Adjunct Inkaras Sollit stood on the roof – now a favoured location for contemplating his angst – and stood looking out over the city as the day slowly surrendered. When chopped up into palatable pieces, time offered the illusion of seamless continuity. One day into the next. Minor variations in the distant cries of hawkers in the market, in the lowing oxen and squealing mules and braying donkeys. The same clothes drying on the same lines, the same tall amphorae perched alongside rooftop pools of yellow and red dyes. The same damned swallows and rhizan in the air. The return of shadows to their old paths as the sun descended more or less where it always did. It could indeed feel like the world was unchanging, and all who dwelt upon it were also unchanging.

Yet age crept in, beneath notice, the slow grinding away to dust. Of buildings and monuments, of mortal lives. Exigencies of the moment could blind one to this, the crumbling of every border. And so, while he stood unmoving as he faced the sunset, the world within his mind was in turmoil. For most of his life, anxiety had been a stranger to him. Well, this kind of anxiety in any case. This soul-gnawing cloud in his head that he could feel undermining his entire life to this point, as if nothing was certain any more, not even his sense of himself, of who he was.

No need to think of love, or desire. These were surface indulgences. Distractions. This haunting unease went deeper, much deeper, and whatever emotions it launched upward were ephemeral, fleeting. He could not pin one down. *Ah, not true. I can, but I don't dare. Instead, I shy from every one of them, these venal urgings, because I sense well the rage bubbling beneath them. And yet, this rage is not me.*

There was another continuity lingering in his thoughts, one he could approach with a clinical, contemplative eye. The history of Adjuncts was uniformly sordid. The hand to the Emperor or Empress had a way of breaking, each and every time. No exceptions that he knew of. Brutal deaths, more than a few hinting of suicide, or at least indifference to death's arrival. The path for each Adjunct led to the same place of paucity and pathos. The only exception was perhaps not an exception at all. None knew the fate of Adjunct Tavore. A hand cut off from the limb, and if she had escaped the fate of all Adjuncts, perhaps it was this violent separation that had saved her.

But Inkaras had doubts. In his present state, he could see no likelihood of salvation, whether as Adjunct or once-Adjunct. To live so intimately with violence was to understand that all that existed on the outside was also inside. Enough years of this soured the imagination, rotted the soul, until it could not help but long for an end to this mortal farce.

Day after day, night after night, this same air of madness gripped the world. The peace or at least normality he looked upon now, in the fading light, was an illusion of sanity. Anger seethed in unseen places.

And this was the fear. The loss of control.

The hand of the Emperor was the hand of control. This and nothing more. And it failed, again and again. Social conventions of decency, decorum, consideration and constraint were all fragile. Only a fool could not see that.

And even now, in the streets and alleys below, in the homes and temples, people gathered in the name of the worst within them.

It was a challenge, to be sure, to recognize such potential in every human life. Not one hand, but two. That alarming impulses were part of a soul's eternal battle with itself. In those moments when it lost sight of its life-story and whatever legacy would live beyond its end, yielding to acts that could never be taken back.

Existential horror was a dire companion, here in his head, in his swirling cauldron of thoughts, feelings, dreads and fears. In resisting the constraints of civility, people spoke of freedom and so stoked their anger, making it a thing of indignation and outrage. But the failure did not belong outside such people. It was wholly inside, wholly within.

Freedom to do what? *What laws and rules impede you? Or is 'freedom' a bullshit word masking a selfishness so profoundly anti-life that its expression demands a disguise? Obfuscation inside a concept the meaning of which no two people can agree? Freedom? What the fuck is it? And to use that word to mask your resentment at the world, which in turn arose from your disappointment in yourself, is where it all begins to go wrong.*

Adjuncts were hardly unique. Presumptuous to think otherwise. Any clear-eyed observer of the world would eventually reach the same place. Or not. In truth, he had no idea.

So, you would serve your god? Be a chosen one? Be your god's hand in this mortal world? Well, take it from a veteran in this fool's game, every hand breaks.

'Do you wish company?'

Inkaras turned and it took all his will to fashion a smile. 'High Fist, I have suborned your habit here, on this rooftop.'

Stepping forward, Arenfall shrugged. 'No one soul can claim dominion of the day, nor the night. Nor this moment of hesitation between the two.'

'Will there be an end to this?' His question arrived abruptly, surprising even Inkaras. An instant later, he began to sense the desperation beneath it, and his growing helplessness in ever finding an answer. He saw Arenfall's brows lift.

'This immediate crisis will indeed end, Adjunct.'

221

'Yes, of course,' said Inkaras, nodding, 'the crisis.'

'If,' Arenfall resumed, 'your question referred to something more . . . existential, well, a thousand sages have pondered the same question, offering a thousand answers, no two alike.'

'As you say,' said Inkaras. 'At least dying brings an end to the ordeal.'

'Perhaps in ending one ordeal, a new one begins.' He shrugged a second time, gaze now on the gathering gloom. 'It would be pleasing to think that beyond Death's Gate, at the very least the torments plaguing one's life come to an end. That certain answers will reveal themselves. That, indeed, we are given a sort of context. An explanation.'

Inkaras studied the High Fist, wondering at his percipience. 'You see the truth of me,' he finally said. 'I am beset.'

After a glance back at the hatch, Arenfall regarded Inkaras again and asked, 'Where is your bodyguard, Adjunct?'

'In his chambers, I should think. It is a conceit, you know. My need for a bodyguard. My easy offer of two otataral blades instead of just one. He was my lover, after all. Now, that is over with. I am inclined to send him away. It is ironic, is it not, that Hadalin Bhilad was actually born and raised not far from here? Of course, he would return to imperial service. The Red Blades, perhaps, or a soldier of the palace in Unta. Somewhere, in other words, far away.'

'From you, and from his home.'

Inkaras sighed. 'Aye, I am doubly cruel. Indeed, let us call it vindictive and end the prevarication.'

'The sting fades, Adjunct.'

'This is love, then? The venom to the sting?'

'A thing of heat destined to cool,' Arenfall said, as if contemplating the notion. 'It may be so. It has evaded me thus far. Blessing or tragedy, this ignorance of mine?'

'Blessing, to be sure,' Inkaras said. 'Tell me, when do we act? When do we crush this foolish uprising? It had better be soon, High Fist, if only to spare the lives of the innocent.'

'And the civil comportment of empire, aye.'

'The Temple of Va'Shaik needs to be scoured clean,' Inkaras continued. 'Then levelled.'

A score or more voices could be heard in the distance, one of the cults announcing the vanishing of the sun. Other voices shouted in challenge or irritation. The city seemed to be seething. After a long moment,

Arenfall spoke. 'Your sentiments are not too dissimilar to what a host of high priests said to me this evening, when I met their cohort and listened to their disputation. Yet many were quick to qualify their desire. The temple High Priestess is unaware of the persecution being conducted in Va'Shaik's name. *Blissfully* unaware, you might say. It is her Invigil who is the focus of collective ire.'

'And incompetence serves as an excuse, High Fist?'

'I have not yet decided. Accordingly, I have set in motion a meeting with her. This High Priestess Shamalle.'

Inkaras snorted. 'You expect to find her sober?'

'I am informed that a synod has been called by the First Temple. Presumably, this will entail Shamalle departing the city to attend the gathering. As for sobriety, we will see the extent of her incompetence.'

'The synod is ideal as far as this Invigil is concerned, I'm sure.'

Arenfall nodded. 'True enough. Although I suspect she proves no impediment whether resident or not.'

'Kill him.'

Arenfall sighed. 'And this answers the unrest? The dissatisfaction?'

'Spurred by the man's rhetoric! Him and all those just like him! They *yearn* for apocalypse, High Fist.'

'An end to all this?'

Inkaras both felt and heard his teeth click as his mouth snapped shut. He looked away, was struck by the sudden onslaught of stars prickling the black sky. Where had they come from? Had it not been only moments ago that Arenfall joined him here? *I am losing grip. Nothing but sand beneath sanity's feet.* 'I will join you in speaking with the High Priestess,' he announced. 'While there, I may also pay a visit to Invigil Ban Ryk.'

'By the hand of the Emperor, then?'

'You question the value of that?'

'That depends, Adjunct. Will you quench the spark, or set ablaze all of Seven Cities?'

'I doubt his martyrdom has that power.'

'You gamble much on that assessment,' Arenfall said. 'Might I suggest you decide on the matter after we speak with Shamalle?'

'If you think it matters, very well.'

The High Fist dipped his head in a faint bow, and then departed.

Inkaras remained, gaze now searching the sweeping spray of stars high above. Perhaps some god beyond all other gods resided there. Not as an entity, though. Rather, all the Adjunct now looked upon, in that immense blackness, was itself the essence of that god. A distributed consciousness, scattered into a multitude of seeds, each one a life, each one doomed to its brief flare. Only to fail in the end, sidling defeated and broken back into the heartless womb. Over and over again, for all eternity.

Such a god . . . such a god. Will you have answers for my questions? Is your very existence meant to be answer enough? Because, you see, I look around me. Here, now, down on this wretched earth. If experience in all its myriad forms is our purpose, is your sole intent and desire; if free will is to be the playground of eternal variance to delight and entertain you, then your obsession with suffering troubles me.

No, speak plain, it terrifies me.

I wondered at the horror and the rage beneath my surface. Not understanding them was the lie I told myself.

This seed will one day return home. This seed will arrive like a slingstone of fire. Free will, dear god, with a vengeance.

Like a slingstone of fire. I swear it in your name.

CHAPTER NINE

I sense the settling
An unseen blanket
Dampen'd all ardour
Dulled the lust
For life's wild wonders

Madness abounds
In the muffled confines
The suffocating close
Grey'd swelter
In sackcloth weave

My shout escapes
What flesh cannot
Harkens the crowds
Who search the gloom
For god's birth in the world

Desperate words
Ride ether's currents
All that is solid
Parts ways
In fevered repetition

I call out 'who's there?'
They cry 'the Lord speaks!'
Roll'd down the plank
Cold a'splashing
In weltering seas

Silence comes
To the sinking god
The cloth'd divide
Between flavours
These kinds of dark

Sacrificing God
Sulthe Aes

A strange silence permeated the village. Even the dogs supine in the shadows looked cowed, all curiosity beaten from them. The few figures within Bornu Blatt's sight seemed to retreat from his attention without moving from where they loitered. Perhaps the oppressive heat alone was cause for this, yet something raised the hairs on the back of his neck.

Scattered across Seven Cities, like gnarled old warts on the landscape, were settlements built in a style that had not changed in a thousand or more years. In these places, buildings squatted, none more than two storeys high. Made of mud-brick and clay-hued plaster, they had the appearance of being half melted into the ground. Subject to constant repair but never knocked down or rebuilt, they were thick-walled, the sills of the squarish windows forearm deep, corners rounded, the threshold stones at every doorway worn into slumping depressions where countless feet had walked over centuries of occupation.

Such villages bore one main street, with only a scatter of side alleys intersecting it at seemingly random intervals. Each building held many families, with no internal passages connecting them. Access came from holes in the roof above each home. The single doors, one to each major stretch of wall, all led into an inner communal garden surrounding a well. The inside of this compound bore ladders to the roof. In essence, each building was a village unto itself.

Riding into such a place felt like a journey into the past, and the past, alas, was just as sordid as the present. Bornu frowned at the thought. It need not be sordid, after all. More like exhausted, worn out, weathered into lethargy. It was his own state of mind that was sordid.

'I see no temple,' said Gilakas, riding up to flank Bornu on the left as they walked their mounts down the wide, mostly empty street. Behind them and trailing in single file, were Gracer and Stult.

'You'll find no building of worship,' Bornu said. 'Not here.'

'Then . . . who, what?'

'In each home, Gilakas, there is an altar.'

The man grunted at that, and a moment later said, 'Household gods? How quaint. Inquisitor, this land of yours continually shocks me. How can such pockets of feeble ignorance persist?'

'Because few visit, and rarely,' Bornu explained. 'Their closest neighbouring villages are no different from this one. Together, there's enough variation to keep the inbreeding under control. Or not. There will be a dialect, as well, amounting to a private language. These people, Gilakas, are content enough with how things are, enough to resist changing much of anything. They manage communally owned herds. They keep gardens and have festivals and gatherings. Everyone knows everyone else and strangers aren't to be trusted. The occasional trader comes through to barter for whatever crafts the locals produce, and in exchange they get iron tools, cookware - do you see a stable or smithy? So, not even that—'

'Just my point,' Gilakas interrupted. 'No one thought to bring civilization here. Proof of the disorganized mess of your pre-imperial ways.'

Bornu shrugged. 'They seem organized enough, in what they need. But then—' He drew up short, halting his mount. Gilakas did the same.

Twenty paces ahead, off to the left where a side street was visible, stood the hollowed-out remnants of a building. Its irregular brick and plaster walls were barely man-height, often less, and the facing wall had been knocked entirely away to make a wide, gate-like entrance. The rest of the structure - all the rubble of rooftop, upper floors and interior walls - was missing. The vast space enclosed by this square was crowded with a half-dozen caravan tents, long and peaked, while off to the right, taking up nearly a third of the space, was a canopied stable under which many horses stood, heads down, tails swishing.

'Traders?' Gracer asked, pulling up beside Bornu on his right. But there was little conviction in her tone.

He glanced across at her, watching as her expression closed up.

'I don't think so,' she answered herself.

'No,' Bornu agreed. 'Not traders.'

'Mercenaries? Bandits?'

'Often,' Bornu murmured, 'they are one in the same.'

Gilakas spat to his left and then said, 'Waiting out the hot season. I doubt it's a peaceful occupation, though.'

'Rarely is,' Bornu said quietly. 'I felt the tension here, wondered at it.'

Two figures in the camp had taken note of them. One, a hulking man, had turned to enter the largest of the canvas tents. The other, a woman, now approached.

Bornu studied her. Her broad face was seamed in ritual scars. A south tribal, then, with a single scar to match every life taken by her hand. By his quick estimate, a hundred or more souls trailed this woman. Her long, badly braided hair was a blend of red and gold, in which black-wire fetishes were knotted. Her upper garment was a worn gambeson with no sleeves, once red or crimson but now faded to the hue of watered wine. Thick hardened-leather flaps rode her shoulders, and her weapon arm was protected by a vambrace from wrist to elbow. Her skirt was studded leather, ending well above her knees. The scabbarded sword slung from straps was just under her left arm, the pommel thrust forward. Riding boots of rawhide completed the attire.

The woman spoke. 'You can water your horses. Do that and then move on.'

Bornu asked, 'How goes the recruiting?'

Her eyes, pale and empty, narrowed. 'Not your concern, priest.'

From the tents inside the square more figures were appearing, many of them donning armour or checking weapons. The hulking man who'd entered the main tent had re-emerged in the company of a tall, thin man in grey and black leathers, and these two were on their way to join the woman.

'I don't recall telling you I was a priest,' said Bornu.

'Word travels. Kicking ant-nests. Well, nothing of that here for you. No temple, no priestly residents. Va'Shaik has no presence here, nor need for one.' She offered up a feral smile, revealing sharpened teeth. 'These souls aren't for you to save.'

'Still,' said Bornu, 'I imagine the walls are far from silent on the matter.'

That cut through her guard and one hand moved up to caress the grip of her sword. 'Water your horses or don't. Either way, you're moving on.'

'Problems, Arat?' enquired the tall man in leathers as he came up to stand beside the woman. His dark eyes slid past Bornu and Gilakas and fixed on Gracer. 'That you, Gracer? And Stult, too? Damn me, woman, pretty sure I heard you'd jumped on Melok's thigh to hump your way across the land.'

'One look at you, Futhar, and I ran straight off in search of salvation.'

The man, Futhar, turned to grin at Arat. 'Tried recruiting her a few years back. She insisted on Stult too and I agreed to that and then what does she do? Disappears herself, leaving me disappointed, even offended. Needless to say, I won't repeat the offer.'

Gracer said to Bornu, 'Holy One, we should water the beasts and go, like they say.'

Bornu counted fourteen in all. Two were hanging back, close to one tent in particular. The rest had emerged and were fanning out on the street in front of the broken wall. Bornu could not recall having ever seen a rougher bunch. 'I wish I could, Gracer,' he said.

'Oh, priest,' said Futhar, 'you don't want our kind of trouble. Besides, we took note of the Invigil's call to stir things up. In that sense, you should have no problem here at all. Not with us.'

'I know nothing of the Invigil's call and in Va'Shaik's name I so refute it.'

'Still none of your business.'

'Robbing villages of their children is an imperial crime,' said Bornu.

'Then let the Malazans deal with us.'

Bornu shrugged. 'Detachments are few and far between. Something cowards like you depend upon.'

Futhar smiled. 'It's not cowardice that has us avoiding imperial marines, priest. More like wisdom, and a healthy survival instinct. Now, I'm done talking. You can use our well's water or not. I think there's another one just west of Rethik – the village's name in case you didn't know.'

Bornu nodded. 'Yes, that one seems ideal. We'll camp there.'

Now Futhar scowled. 'For how long?'

'Can't say,' Bornu replied.

No further words were exchanged as Bornu nudged his horse into motion, the others following him up the central avenue.

As soon as they were well beyond range of hearing, Gracer said, 'Arat's also a mage. A good one. If we stay too long, Inquisitor, she's likely to come for me and Stult. Seems Futhar's still offended.'

'Understood. Then I suggest you part ways with us.'

Gracer was silent for a long moment, then she said, 'My problem exposed.'

'And that is?' Gilakas asked.

'Curiosity will be the death of me one day. Maybe soon.' She shifted her attention back to Stult. 'You don't have to share my fate.'

'Your fate is my fate,' Stult said in a growl.

Bornu caught the helplessness behind the promise. The man's unrequited love was painful to witness.

'How long?' Gracer asked Bornu.

'I am not sure. I will seek haste.'

'What does that mean?' Stult asked in exasperation.

'It all depends,' said Bornu, 'on the will of my goddess.'

An answer sufficient to silence them all. Bornu was content with that. They continued on through what remained of the village. The few figures watching them from shadows were now, to Bornu's eye, no different from the dogs. Beaten and cowed, and for the mothers and fathers among them, grieving as well.

Rethik dwindled in the way of all such villages, in heaps of rubble marking abandoned buildings, and then mounds that had begun as heaps but were now places where the refuse of the living village was dumped. Long-legged jala birds stepped carefully among the rubbish, darting down to pick at whatever they found, their black dagger-like beaks glinting like obsidian.

The well was in the centre of a flattened rise, ringed in rough stone, surrounded by a squared low stone wall about twenty paces across. A single date tree, a few centuries old, rose from one inside corner of the outer wall, its roots bulging the stones there, its dusty leaves casting shade over half the enclosure.

Gilakas said, 'You'd think this worth occupying. But even the trail's not been used in decades. Might be a poisoned well, Inquisitor.'

'Easily determined,' Bornu answered.

They left the main track, crossed a slumped, shallow ditch, and then traversed the scrubland until reaching the entranceway in the facing wall, whereupon Bornu halted, his eyes fixing on a symbol carved into the gap's left cornerstone. 'Ah, our reason.'

Gilakas cursed in Malazan, and then said, 'Dogheads take Seven Cities and all these mysterious carvings! What's this one mean?'

Gracer said, 'I've seen it, but not often. I don't know what it means either.'

Dismounting, Bornu said, 'It's very old. Belongs to the people who live in places like Rethik.' He looked back towards the village. 'Those walls are thick for a reason. Families bury their loved ones in them. The walls of every home are crowded with ancestral bones. Under the floor, too.' He faced the well again. 'There was a building surrounding this well, once, no different from the ones behind us. It was then razed, right down to the ground, leaving nothing. The enclosing wall was built to keep the curse dwelling here. The symbol is a warning.'

'So why the gap leading in?' Gilakas asked, 'Who'd want to visit a cursed place?'

'A hopeful exit for ancestral ghosts, I should think.'

'Ghosts carrying curses are invited to wander?'

'Likely to make them happier than being trapped, wouldn't you think?'

'Who cares what they think?' Gilakas said in evident frustration. 'And now you expect us to camp here? Where'd they put all those bones? As if I can't guess. That Futhar screwed us.'

'Hoping that, having gone this far, we'd just continue on.'

'We should do just that,' Gracer said. 'Fine,' she added, 'I can see we won't. But water from that well will at best give us nightmares, at worst kill us and the mounts. All those bones.'

Bornu led his horse through the gap in the stone wall. 'Horses and mules under the shade by the blessed tree,' he instructed. 'Cookfire close to the downwind wall. We'll sleep opposite. Please set all of that up.' After tying his horse's reins to a low branch of the tree, he strode over to the well, where he knelt before it, closed his eyes and lowered his head.

'Va'Shaik,' he murmured under his breath, 'I have two boons to ask of you.'

*   *   *

A scrawny waif of a woman ushered Adjunct Inkaras and High Fist Arenfall into the presence of High Priestess Shamalle, this following the gauntlet of a belligerent Invigil Ban Ryk whose fury was born, apparently, of personal insult. Not just the outrageous arrival of two Malazan officials to the sacred temple, but also the affront their very existence imposed upon the Invigil's sensibilities. It was a wonder the man didn't command every member of the temple to set upon them with tooth and claw.

Inkaras was still shaking off his astonishment that such an order was not given. Not that he'd seen too many acolytes and functionaries, much less armed guards, so perhaps the Invigil was short of people, or the timing was such that most of them were out in the city, offering up promises and terror in equal amounts.

No matter, all past the moment now, as Inkaras paused one step behind the High Fist when they halted facing the High Priestess on her well-cushioned dais. She was, he reflected – dourly – all woman, this Shamalle.

'How delightful,' she enthused, raising high a bejewelled silver chalice with such verve that most of its contents splashed out in a heavy dollop to land on her silk-covered thigh. 'Oops! Well, plenty more where that came from.' She gestured to the low table between them. 'Have some wine and succulent treats! Dates, olives, honey-dipped locusts and crickets, roasted carpenter ants, a variety of scorpions and sweets. Failing those, some of the night's supper is surely left over. Sage-wrapped chicken, I believe. Along with glazed eberfruit and a delightful garnish of . . . oh dear, I see that such pleasures are of no interest to you this evening.'

'Bellies already full,' Arenfall said with a dip of his head. 'But thank you for the offer, High Priestess.'

'Not even wine? You put me at an obvious disadvantage, since I'm drunk.'

At this first hint of the disingenuous, Inkaras narrowed his gaze on Shamalle, for those eyes were sharp as cut diamonds.

'We will endeavour to match your pace in our conversation,' Arenfall said.

'I foresee a turgid evening ahead,' Shamalle replied. 'Pash dear, do refill my cup, won't you, sweet ruby? There, yes, lovely. You may go now. If I require further attendance,' and she paused to offer Arenfall a heavy-lidded glance, 'I'm sure the High Fist will provide.'

'Of course,' Arenfall said. 'It would be my pleasure.'

As soon as the handmaid was gone from the chamber, Shamalle suddenly leaned forward. 'Va'Shaik has this day spoken to me. In my head! Her voice, coming with sudden intrusion, startling me so that I nearly choked on a chicken bone, can you imagine? And the subject of such revelatory interruption of my poor mundane existence? Why, sir, to deliver a message to you, High Fist Arenfall.' Her eyes widened, expression evincing disbelief. 'Shamalle, be a good girl and deliver a message! Can you even comprehend how humbling – if not humiliating – this was?'

Arenfall tilted his head. 'I would think,' he said, 'given such rarity as that kind of direct visitation must be, you were left neither humiliated nor humbled, High Priestess.'

Leaning back, Shamalle waved one plump hand. 'True enough. The point is, I should have been humbled and humiliated, don't you think?

Never mind. Let's move past my intercessionary self and proceed to the gist of the message then. To whit.' She paused, lifting the same hand and pointing her index finger upward. 'A nefarious band of mercenaries have descended upon a poor village to steal children. To what end? Likely deviant sexual exploits, followed by the recruitment of however many worthies survive that. Do you know,' and she leaned forward again, 'is there anything more depressing than to be reminded of the very worst examples of humanity, when so effectively off the leash of civilized imposition? Is it any wonder I invite apocalypse? Is it—'

'Forgive me, High Priestess, for interrupting. But where is this happening and how is it of such importance to your goddess?'

'Ah well, you see, it's complicated. Following her reawakening in the First Holy Temple, Va'Shaik dispatched a new Inquisitor to journey out into the lands, delivering, among other things, a call to Synod. But this Inquisitor, why, he's a most noble man, but also an intractable one. He now camps at the very edge of the village, and, in his mind, he has no choice but to attempt to intervene, to indeed liberate these children and see the deviants soundly punished for being such fuckwits. Alas, his party cannot hope to defeat the poltroons. Accordingly, my goddess wishes you Malazans to, uhm, do your job, in haste.'

'To spare the life of her Inquisitor?'

Shamalle's eyes thinned to slits. 'The children and their fate, surely, High Fist Arenfall.'

'Can she not act through this Inquisitor, bringing her full manifestation of power to bear upon the bandits?'

The upright finger waved from side to side. 'Curiously, I asked the very same question. But it seems such manifestation, being fraught in every direction, must be held in reserve for a more propitious, and relevant, intervention. You see,' she added, 'this Inquisitor is on his way here.'

Inkaras snorted – he couldn't help himself, despite his vow to remain silent throughout. The sudden subject of both their attention, he shrugged and said, 'Then why save the fool at all? If he is to be the catalyst to a damned uprising? An absurd rebellion in the disguise of a religious war? Aye, the children – that's bad news indeed, and would that we could crush such things everywhere, but we do the best we can—'

'Rubbish,' she snapped. Dismissing him with her eyes, she looked again to Arenfall. 'A path through warrens shall be provided—'

'No need,' Arenfall responded. 'Just give me the location.'

'Now that is the problem. So inconsequential this village, you'll not find its name on any map. To compound matters, even my goddess has no reach there. But she can find her Inquisitor. Indeed, he has begged her assistance, knowing full well that he and his party cannot hope to defeat the sorry excuses for humanity, being too numerous and well-armed. Thus, the path through warren leads directly to him, and this you cannot do without her holy assistance.'

'How many bandits are we talking about?'

'Less than twenty. At least one powerful mage among them. Will you do it?'

*   *   *

The city detachment stockade held two rows of cells facing each other, with a corridor between them. That corridor, being slightly too narrow, was called the Gauntlet. This night, however, Sergeant Jangler seemed at ease as he led the Adjunct and Arenfall into the passageway. Only a few lanterns lit the area, which in itself seemed odd.

It appeared to Inkaras that Arenfall had a particular squad of marines in mind for this mission. What did not make sense was this peculiar side trip to the company stockade.

As it turned out, only one side of cells was occupied, figures rising and shuffling in the gloom as Jangler, carrying his own lantern, led Inkaras and Arenfall to the one at the very end. Through the bars of this cell the Adjunct could see a short, slight figure with a snarl of reddish hair above a narrow face.

Halting opposite this man, Arenfall spoke. 'Captain.'

'High Fist.'

Arenfall glanced back down along the row of cells. 'All here then?'

'Yes, sir. The sappers were chased out from the Under Quarter.'

'Well,' Arenfall sighed, 'you can tell me about that some other time. In the meantime, until there's a cure for boredom, I suppose this serves.'

'Aye, sir. So it's time?'

The High Fist's attention swung back to the captain. 'Not quite.'

The captain's shoulders slumped. He reached up and tried running fingers through his hair, but the knots defeated him.

'Still,' Arenfall continued after a moment, 'we have need of you and the Twelfth Squad.'

'Very well. I think they're all awake, sir.'

'I can see that, yes.'

Jangler produced keys, paused to touch his forehead and then both shoulders and finally a single tap of his right index finger over his heart, lips moving in a silent prayer throughout, whereupon he inserted the key into the lock and opened the door.

The captain stepped out and collected the keys from Jangler. 'I can take it from here, Sergeant,' he said gently.

Inkaras watched the sergeant of the guard make a quick exit.

Arenfall turned to Inkaras. 'Adjunct Inkaras Sollit, may I present to you Captain Hung of the Fourteenth Company of Marines.'

'Ah,' said Inkaras, nodding. 'Your reputation is known to me.'

Captain Hung frowned. 'I think you may be confusing us with Captain Dunsparrow and the Fifth and Sixth Squads, sir. We're not much insofar as marines go.'

A soft grunt from Arenfall, who then said, 'Until handed a mission. Which is what I am doing now. Let out the squaddies, Captain.'

'At once, High Fist.'

There was something both magical and alarming in the emergence of the soldiers of the Twelfth Squad. None spoke; they remained mostly expressionless, and lined up with their backs to the cells they had occupied. They were dishevelled, the men among them unshaven, divested of all armour or issued kit. At the Adjunct's own request, the captain introduced them one by one.

Lieutenant Ormo Foamy, likely from Kartool, was tall, thin, and pale as bleached paper. He glanced once at Inkaras only to studiously ignore him thereafter – a common response among mages, to be sure, so the Adjunct took no offence. Next was Sergeant Breech, who might have been Genabari, with perhaps some Rhivi blood in him as well. Bandy-legged like a horseman, he had the look of a man who wrestled cave bears for fun, with the scars to prove it.

Corporal Scrapes was a Falari woman who'd taken plain to a fine art, a detail applied with such perfection that Inkaras was reminded of the legendary Bridgeburner named Blend. The rest of the squad consisted of a Seti healer named Gains, two heavies named Flutter and Scatter, both big men from one of the southern Dal Hon tribes, and finally – a true oddity – two sappers who were women, named Fedilap and Pulcrude. Both held guilty expressions, suggesting that their sojourn beneath Bastran Hill had been a mess.

The captain ordered the squad to gear up and the soldiers filed out. He then turned to the High Fist and said, 'Details, sir?'

'Another journey through warren. We have some mercenaries conducting illegal recruitment of children in an obscure village. Mages in play.'

'Numbers, sir?'

'Less than twenty, I'm told.'

'This warren, sir, will that be Corporal Hasten again?'

'Not this time, Captain. I will be your guide. That said, the warren will be Va'Shaik's own.'

Though Inkaras was studying Hung with acuity as this detail was revealed, nothing in the man's expression changed. He simply nodded.

'Any other details for me, sir?'

'Some bystanders were intending to act against these mercenaries. We need to meet with them and talk them out of participating.'

'Reason, sir?'

'For their own safety.'

'Of course, sir.'

Arenfall glanced at Inkaras. 'Adjunct, if you and Hadalin intend to accompany us, you will have to divest yourselves of your otataral weapons.'

'Hadalin will remain here,' Inkaras snapped. 'But I have no compunction leaving my sword behind. Any blade will suffice.'

Arenfall's gaze held steady on him. 'You wish to fight with the Twelfth?'

'Won't you, High Fist?'

'No, I don't expect to be needed.'

'Was there not mention of mages among the mercenaries?'

Captain Hung spoke. 'We can handle mages, Adjunct. Perhaps not as easily as you with an otataral sword, but we'll manage.' He then surprised Inkaras with a faint smile. 'We're modern marines, sir.'

In other words, all of you are mages as well. 'I am aware of that, Captain. My concern was the possibility of the enemy mages cancelling you out in that regard.'

'Sounds interesting,' Hung said.

*   *   *

The temple of Va'Shaik in G'danisban held a courtyard crowded with fruit trees. A spring-fed stream wound through the lush undergrowth with an incessant chuckle that Inkaras was finding irritating while they waited for the High Priestess to appear. Shamalle's handmaiden stood close to one of the entranceways, as motionless as a statue. Invigil Ban Ryk was also present, glaring at the Malazans, in particular the marines.

Arenfall seemed to be studying the man. At last, he spoke. 'Invigil, is there reason for your presence?'

'None that invite explanation, High Fist. This night, the power of my goddess fills this chosen temple. We are to witness the miracle of her manifestation.'

'Through High Priestess Shamalle, yes,' said Arenfall, possibly amused, although in the heavy shadows it was impossible to make out his expression.

'Our beloved High Priestess indeed,' Ban Ryk replied in a flat tone. 'But such glory descends upon all Va'Shaik's faithful. This is an auspicious night, barring you and your thugs.' After a moment, the Invigil's gaze shifted to fix on Inkaras. 'Sometimes,' he said, 'the Emperor reaches too far.'

Inkaras shrugged. 'It's been known to happen, yes.'

'Here you stand, a plain sword at your hip. Was that wise?'

'We are here at the request of your goddess, Invigil, in case you have forgotten that detail. It would seem that the higher realms dispense with the parochial provincialism of ours, in itself a lesson worth considering.'

'Do not presume to deliver lessons to me, puppet!'

Inkaras glanced at Arenfall, but the High Fist shook his head.

Serendipitously, Shamalle arrived, in a flowing stream of multihued silks and slightly out of breath. 'Dear me, so many steps! My legs tremble beneath me. My heart pounds with fierce urgency somewhere beneath this—' and she set hand to her left breast - 'but no, slightly to the right, in fact. Why, I'd always believed my heart to live in this tit, or under it, like a mouse burrowed beneath a melon. A titmouse, in fact. My entire worldview has been knocked askew! Invigil, what are you doing here? Don't you ever sleep? Your diligence will be the death of you, dear.' She turned to regard the marines of the Twelfth Squad and its captain. 'So few? So thin? Good High Fist Arenfall, did I not say near twenty dullwhips including at least one powerful mage? Surely two, even three squads!'

'This will do,' Arenfall replied.

'Truly?'

'My word on it, High Priestess.'

'I wonder, does my dismay and alarm belong to me, or to my goddess?

For she is within me, all aquiver. Oh, I may be the quivering one, never mind. She's here, and the urgency I feel is surely hers – why are you all dawdling? Gather close – the warren's portal is a dreadful tear in the fabric of everything. Oh, explaining magery is such a bore—'

'High Priestess,' cut in Arenfall, 'no explanations are required.'

'Hmm, very well. Perhaps, at some later time, and in proper luxuriance, you can explain it all to me, then. Now, cease distracting me with your handsome self – a detail upon which both me and my goddess agree, by the way. Now – oh dear, must let go of you-know-what – both hands required, you see!' Raising her hands, she closed her eyes and mumbled something under her breath.

The portal opened behind her.

Inkaras saw Shamalle pause, one eye slightly opening for a peek. Then both eyes snapped wide open. 'Oh! Where did it go?'

'Behind you,' Arenfall said.

'What? Ah, there it is! Who turned me around? Well, go on, then! Shoo! Shoo!'

Arenfall gestured and Captain Hung led his marines through without pause. One by one they vanished into a shimmering, swirling, vertical veil of something like quicksilver. The rustle of weapons and armour vanished the moment each soldier passed through. Bowing to the High Priestess, the High Fist said, 'Goddess, blessings upon your chosen vessel this night.' Then he too strode through the portal.

Inkaras hesitated, fighting the urge to fling a knife into the Invigil's throat.

Shamalle waggled a finger. 'Now now, all in good time, Adjunct.'

Startled, Inkaras wondered which of the two – priestess or goddess – gave voice to the admonishment. Then he half-smiled and nodded. 'As you wish.'

'Shoo!'

He walked into the portal.

The veil was without substance, yet delivering a sudden, momentary iciness that rippled through Inkaras as he stepped clear, boots crunching on something like gravel. Blinking against blazing sunlight, he paused to take his bearings.

The squad had fanned out into a semicircle around Arenfall and the captain. Hands were on crossbows, bolts nested and the weapons cocked.

They stood on a battleground, but unlike one Inkaras had ever seen before. The bodies strewn about – for as far as the eye could see in every direction – were all fully armoured, with not a single patch of skin visible. Even the faces were hidden behind some kind of smoky, smooth obsidian. Dwarfing the multitude of the dead were huge war-wagons of some kind, torn and smoke-blackened, their iron hides peeled back or punched through. Pieces of strange mechanisms were scattered about these broken, lifeless behemoths. The air stank of pitch.

High overhead wheeled huge birds of some sort. Squinting, Inkaras frowned. They all appeared to be headless, as if the wings alone rode the thermals, like kites.

'I did not think on the aspect,' Arenfall said into the heavy silence. He turned to Inkaras, his face ashen. 'Visions of apocalypse. This is what she desires? Madness.'

Lieutenant Foamy glanced back at the captain and said, 'Someone coming, sirs. Directly ahead.'

Inkaras followed Arenfall and the captain forward, passing through the defensive ring of marines to halt a few paces beyond. A figure was indeed approaching, clanking, rocking as if walking on stilts. Though human in form, armour covered it from head to foot. The only indication that something organic was within it was the long, ragged grey hair drifting out beneath the helmet's neck rim.

The Adjunct thought it to be a woman, but in truth there was no way of being sure. Not yet, in any case.

Walking towards them with awkward strides, the figure slowly revealed itself to be taller than a human, taller even than a Jhag of the Odhan. And impossibly thin, both at waist and neck. Its arms were too long, its dented, scorched breastplate peaked like a ship's prow. A complicated, ornate club of some kind was slung by a leather strap on one shoulder.

It halted five paces before them, was silent for a long moment, then a woman's voice emerged from beneath the polished, opaque face-guard. 'Forgive me.'

'Goddess?'

'She whose body I now occupy was dead, but not too broken. I was witness to her last visions, the moment of her death. A death she ran to like a child to its mother.'

'The myriad end to all things can be no blessing, Va'Shaik,' Arenfall said.

'We are misunderstood.'

'How so?'

'Only one thing persists in every mortal world, High Fist Arenfall, and that is corruption. Sweet cooperation, the gifts of community, the moments of perfect accordance, there hides even in these things a seed within each of us, a promise of discord. Apocalypse is always deserved. Always.' One mechanism-like gauntleted hand lifted and gestured. 'See how they killed each other? See their machines of destruction? But look more closely, High Fist. We stand upon ploughed earth of old, but no plants can grow in this poisoned, lifeless soil. Did war kill the land? No. Humans did. Farming exhausted the soil. Chemicals washed it clean of life. Before the farm there was forest here. Cut down, the roots dragged from the ground. They deemed this progress.'

'Enough!' said Arenfall. 'Your thoughts are a vortex of despair, goddess.'

'Corruption is eternal.'

'As is renewal. You describe a cycle as natural as any other.'

'But do we not deserve better?'

'Better than this wasteland? Aye.'

'Then do something about it.'

Those words reverberated through Inkaras. A challenge that left him trembling, such was the power of this goddess here in her warren. The others too had received the words like blows to the chest, fists against the heart.

Slowly crossing his arms, Arenfall said, 'The Malazan Empire, from its very inception, vowed to never interfere in matters of faith. No imagined immortal hand to guide policy or dictate to its citizens. Mortals claiming to speak with the voice and will of their god invariably do so without the blessing of that god – and we both know it, Va'Shaik. Unless and until that god manifests in the mortal realm, its followers are free to do as they damned well please, all in that god's name. What greater crime of hubris and presumption is possible?'

'None, Arenfall. Upon this we are agreed. Yet, here stands your empire, upon the brink of yet another civil war.'

'In *your* name!'

'Indeed.' There was a long pause. 'Perhaps there is a solution. Perhaps not.' The hand gestured again. 'Come. We have corruption that needs answering.'

*   *   *

The sun was long gone, the moon yet to rise. Starlight painted the ruins dull silver. Bornu Blatt sat contemplating the misery of cursed places, wondering what ancient crime could set so deep a stain upon this site. History itself could haunt a land, and often did.

Upon another level, he could sense the approach of Va'Shaik, or at least her partially manifested power. This whisper of magic crawled along his skin, shivered awake the hairs of his forearms and the back of his neck. He knew himself to be an unpleasant sack of meat and bones, but rarely did he feel so inconsequential besides. His spirit felt to be on shaky ground, as if he was becoming aware of being frightened of himself, when for all his life that capacity seemed foreign.

Some nights, death seemed the easiest invitation to peace. Weathering these sentiments was a challenge. Before the charge set upon him by the goddess, the great tasks of his life had felt simple, unambiguous. His future, laid out before him, was mostly level ground. Ugliness bestowed a solitude he had grown used to. All was well.

He longed for those days.

The others, seated nearby or wrapped up in cloaks and blankets, were mostly silent, possibly dozing, their heads dipped, faces hidden in shadow. Amidst his companions as he was, Bornu felt utterly alone.

The portal opened with the sound of tearing canvas near the gap in the stone wall. A vertical slit bleeding foreign sunlight. Figures appeared, blocking much of that light, boots crunching as they strode into view.

Bornu rose to his feet.

In all, eleven Malazans emerged from the portal. For a brief instant, Bornu thought he saw a twelfth figure, tall and thin, but it drifted back, swallowed by the light. The portal then snapped shut.

The sound of boots and rustling armour and weapons had stirred awake the others. Both Gracer and Gilakas straightened quickly, weapons drawn. Stult backed off a few steps, holding his staff defensively.

The power of the goddess drifted away, emptying the night.

One of the soldiers muttered something like a curse in a language unknown to Bornu, and then in Malazan he added, 'Takes a necromancer, I guess.'

'For what?' another soldier asked him.

'Hearing the clattering bones, Flutter, that's all. Captain, let's not stay in this camp any longer than we have to.'

241

'Very well, Sergeant,' replied a short, thin man, evidently the captain of this troop. He gestured to the gap. 'Close them up over there.'

'Aye, sir.'

Six soldiers followed the sergeant through the break in the wall.

Bowing to the captain, Bornu Blatt said, 'Welcome, Captain. Perhaps my goddess was unclear. The mercenaries are a full troop, in your parlance.' He glanced over at Gilakas and Gracer, then back. 'We will of course throw in ourselves, but that still leaves us at half a troop.'

It was not the captain who replied, however, but the man standing to his right. 'Troops refer to wings of cavalry, sir. Captain Hung here commands marines. In this instance, the Twelfth Squad.' He paused, and then added, 'I believe, with the addition of myself and Adjunct Inkaras here, there is no need for you or your companions to participate. After all,' he said with a faint smile, 'the legal responsibility is ours, not yours.'

Bornu heard a sword slide down into a scabbard and he turned to see Gilakas, now relaxed and nodding, slowly stepping back. Meeting Bornu's gaze, Gilakas said, 'He's right, Inquisitor, we won't be needed.'

The man who'd spoken a moment earlier now said, 'Ah, then you are Va'Shaik's charge.'

'Bornu Blatt, sir, and you are?'

'High Fist Jalan Arenfall.'

From Gracer came a hiss of breath, and then, 'And the Emperor's Adjunct? What in the Limper's name are you two doing here? They're just mercenaries, not a dog-headed army of fanatics!'

The captain of the marines spoke. 'I understand there are mages among them?'

'A few,' Gracer allowed, 'but it's only one you need to look out for. Arat.' Then she shrugged. 'The Adjunct can take care of her, I guess.'

'Alas, I am without my otataral sword,' said Inkaras.

Clearly confused, Gracer fell silent, but she did follow Gilakas in sheathing weapons.

'She does have a point,' said Bornu Blatt to the High Fist. 'Your presence is unexpected, particularly in that my prayer was to my goddess—'

The Adjunct said, 'And she in turn called upon her High Priestess in G'danisban, who called upon us. Given that this is a matter of enforcing imperial laws, why, here we are.'

242

'I was unaware of such levels of cooperation,' Bornu said, bewildered.

'As we totter on the edge of a new religious war,' said the High Fist, 'yes, I can understand why this arrangement surprises you.' He paused, and then said, 'It certainly surprises us. But then, what mortal can fathom the mind of a goddess?'

But Bornu was not yet ready to let go. 'Yet you bring a single squad—'

Behind him, Gilakas said, 'Of marines, Inquisitor.'

Turning to him, Bornu lifted his brows. 'Yes, and?'

'It will do.'

Captain Hung addressed the one man who'd yet to speak, 'Lieutenant, some scouting is required. See to it, please.'

'Yes, sir. Do you want quiet scouting or loud scouting?'

'Hmm, good point. Pick out for both.'

'Aye, sir.' The lieutenant set off to join the others outside the compound.

The High Fist said, 'Adjunct, do you still wish to assist the marines in this matter?'

'I do.'

'Then by all means, join them now.'

But the Adjunct hesitated. 'What of you, High Fist?'

'Here I will remain,' Arenfall replied. 'I believe that the Inquisitor and I are due a conversation.' He then faced the captain. 'You have leave to begin.'

'Thank you, sir.'

The Adjunct followed the captain.

Gilakas had collected up his blankets and was moving off to his bed-roll, although Bornu suspected that sleep was unlikely for any of them, not this night at least. A few paces away, Gracer now huddled with Stult, conducting some whispered exchange with many glances towards the marines.

Facing the High Fist again, Bornu shrugged. 'I am forever startled by the human capacity to adjust to unexpected circumstances. If only I shared the talent.'

'Your goddess said little for most of the journey through her warren,' Arenfall said, folding his arms - perhaps against the chill. 'But it is clear that she values you, Inquisitor. Sufficient to set this unexpected precedent.'

'In collusion?'

'Cooperation, surely.'

'I am a child of Seven Cities, High Fist. How you likely see the history we have shared is not how I do.'

'An assumption that, this time, proves utterly invalid. I, too, am a child of Seven Cities.'

Bornu Blatt frowned. 'Korbolo Dom was a renegade Malazan. Until his manumission. My assumption was that his officers were the same, including your father. Indeed, at least one imperial historian has posited that, had the Whirlwind succeeded, Korbolo would have struck for Unta itself, to depose the Empress and proclaim himself Emperor.'

'The truth is less clear than that,' Arenfall said. 'In any case, it was not Korbolo Dom's ambition that held any relevance; rather, that of Mallick Rel. In that context,' and he met Bornu's eyes, 'it seems at least one scheme reached fruition.'

Bornu grunted. 'In that light, I see your point.'

'I am told that G'danisban is your destination, Inquisitor.'

'The possibility was mentioned. But in truth, it was news to me, High Fist.'

That admission startled Arenfall, and a moment later he laughed. 'Well, perhaps all of this was to make certain of where your journey would end.'

'It ends where it began, High Fist. As far as I know. I am tasked with announcing the synod, to be held at Hanar Ara. It is to there that I shall return.'

'And G'danisban was not among your intended temple visits?'

'Initially, I admit that I hadn't planned on travelling that far.'

Arenfall laughed a second time. 'Then it may be that High Priestess Shamalle will be disappointed. Your shared goddess, too.'

Bornu Blatt sighed. 'No, I think not. I hear the message clearly enough. G'danisban it shall be, then.'

'Her warren will hasten the journey, Inquisitor.'

'But I'm not yet – oh, she concludes that I am. Very well. If I have done enough in her eyes, so be it.' He considered for a moment, and then asked, 'High Fist, is there something special about G'danisban? I would have thought Y'ghatan.'

Arenfall's attention seemed to have wavered, as he was now watching Gracer and Stult. 'Hmm? No, Y'ghatan's of no interest. As for G'danisban, why, modest I may be, but I am also not foolish enough to discount the strategic significance of where I am headquartered, or that of my person, and now, additionally, the presence of Adjunct Inkaras.'

'If you travelled with a legion or two, High Fist, you'd be a much more difficult target, don't you think?'

Arenfall looked back at him. 'But I've done such a fine job painting that target, Inquisitor.'

Bornu Blatt blinked.

*   *   *

Pulcrude squinted at Inkaras. 'You sure you want to come with us?' she asked. 'We're the noisy scouts.'

The Adjunct glanced at Sergeant Breech and Gains, who were off to one side strapping down and tying off their weapons and anything that might make noise on their persons. 'So, they're the stealthy ones?'

Pulcrude's teeth flashed in a quick smile. 'It's all relative, sir.'

The other sapper, Fedilap, had just nested a quarrel in her crossbow, a quarrel to which a sharper was attached. 'It's complicated, sir,' she explained. 'The priest's party was trailed out here and there are eyes on us even now. One set of eyes, but impatient ones, meaning maybe a few more are on their way, plannin' t'pay the party a visit.' She straightened, leaning the cocked crossbow across one shoulder. 'But we should get going.'

Pulcrude edged closer to Inkaras. Some kind of spicy perfume reached him. She said, 'We're slipping into a warren, sir. You okay with that? Sometimes, all that otataral in your blood messes things up. I mean, we ain't goddesses, right? You might pop out at, uh, the wrong time. And that sort of stuff.'

'I've managed traversing warrens thus far without mishap, Sapper.'

'Good. No surprises then.'

Fedilap snorted, but added nothing.

The other two marines now set off, back towards the village. 'If those are the quiet ones,' he observed, 'our hidden watcher's already marked them.'

'Aye,' said Pulcrude, 'that's the idea.'

The remaining marines, along with their captain, were hunkered down on the ground outside the gap in the wall. The two heavies seemed to be dozing.

Inkaras said, 'I admit to not having paid much attention to the imperial military. Marines, regulars, cavalry, all just uniforms to me.'

245

'Just soldiers doing the soldiering, right, sir?'

'I suppose. But I have to know – why were you all in cells?'

'We get restless, sir. Safer that way. Now, Fedilap here's going to open her warren. Get ready to run, Adjunct, on account of it not being welcoming. With the Lady's pull, though, we won't be in there long. Fed? Wake 'er up!'

The rent that the sapper opened tore with a wet sound, decidedly unpleasant.

'I'll lead,' Fedilap said, pulling her crossbow down. 'Adjunct – if you hear this weapon knock, hit the dirt. Don't even think, just straight down among the worms, right?'

Inkaras nodded. He drew his sword.

Fedilap plunged into the portal, vanishing from sight.

Following a bare two steps behind, Inkaras found himself suddenly traversing a mist-laden bog. The wintry, damp air was a shock. Thin plates of ice crunched underfoot, the peat crackling as it sank down beneath his boots. The light belonged to late afternoon, dull under a lowering sky. A distant stand of skeletal trees a hundred or so paces to their left was crowded with crows, all of them taking flight, their caws echoing as if within a cave.

'Shit,' said Pulcrude behind Inkaras.

He shot her a look over a shoulder. 'What?'

'They're worse than a signal flag,' she said, nodding towards the wheeling murder of crows, which seemed to be drifting ever closer. 'And even worse, you see their spiralling? Widdershins, sir. Fucking widdershins.'

'What warren is this?' he demanded.

'Fucked if I know, sir.'

'But she's your—'

'She ain't nothing. Fedilap's insane. Maybe I am, too, but my insanity's under control. That hag in front of you? No such luck.'

At that, Fedilap glanced back at them, a taut grin fixed on her face, her eyes wide and wild. 'Time t'sprint!'

The shattering of ice erupted on all sides. Figures were climbing out of the peat, the sinkholes and puddles, the root-matted black mud – an entire army was rising into view, dragging free rotted swords. Slick, puffy faces, cured betel-brown, were turning towards the three Malazans, eyes like dried dates fixing upon them – eyes that to Inkaras seemed both dead and alive.

'Big tree up ahead!' Fedilap shouted, swerving to run directly towards it.

The tree looked as lifeless as everything else in this wasteland, but its girth was massive, the bole's bark like peeling skin, its skeletal branches spreading out wide. The roots made a mound – the only high ground in sight.

Inkaras fended off a sword-stroke, the attacker's sword so rotten it did not shatter, just folded over in a rain of rusty flakes.

Twenty paces from the tree, Fedilap fired her crossbow. 'Down!'

The command was madness itself, but Inkaras threw himself onto the frozen muck.

A skull-thumping concussion. Then branches and twigs were raining down around them. Lifting his head, Inkaras saw a blackened, shattered gouge in the tree-trunk, gaping bright red.

'That's the door!' Fedilap shouted, once more on her feet. 'Run!'

The army was converging on them, but the mud dragged at limbs, sinks opening up beneath figures to make them reel, legs snapping, arms flailing.

'Don't mind them!' Pulcrude gasped as they staggered towards the tree. 'They don't hate us or anything. They just want to come with us, and can you blame them? This place stinks!'

Ahead, Fedilap threw herself into the wound. It swallowed her whole.

Another portal, but the ugliest one I've ever seen.

He reached the mound, scrambled up the root-bound, treacherous slope, and then plunged into the rent.

'Oh shit!' Fedilap, just up ahead, staggered to a halt.

They should have returned to their world, to the village or at least its outskirts. Instead, they were surrounded by the scorched, blackened stumps of trees, spreading out as far as they could see. The sky was the colour of ash. A moment later, insects descended on all three of them.

'What the fuck is this, Fed?' demanded Pulcrude.

'That nasty mage set warren-traps!' She paused to hawk and then spit. 'Bugs! I hate bugs! They're biting me!'

'They're biting all of us, idiot! Get us out of here!'

'I can't! Unless you want us jumping back into an army of undead swamp stickers! Use *your* warren, Pulcrude!'

'Oh sure, let's go to the bottom of a lake! That'll help!'

Inkaras turned to study Pulcrude. 'Nerruse?'

She shrugged. 'I prefer puddles to oceans.'

'Meaning?'

'Meaning I keep it small,' she answered, then scowled at his expression. 'You'd be amazed how much I can do with a puddle! Vicious, horrible things, with just a puddle! Below Bastran Hill – uh, never mind.'

Between cursing and slapping at insects, Fedilap was reloading her crossbow. This time, the quarrel had four sharpers attached to its head. 'Range is an issue,' she muttered, possibly to herself. 'Maybe no time to duck. Just shoot and throw yourself flat. Flatter than a flatworm. Flatter than a wet piece of kelp. Fuck! Biter! Die, you little shit. Die!'

'I once drowned three men in a puddle, Adjunct. And then, another time I–'

'That's fine,' Inkaras cut in. 'What's Fedilap planning with those munitions?'

'Huh? Fed, what are you planning with those munitions? Adjunct's asking. Me? What do I care? This is a world of hungry insects and we're the only food in sight. I'm being drained of blood faster than a nicked artery here. Blowing us up will be quicker for sure and I'm fine with that.'

'Shut up, Pulcrude,' Fedilap snapped. 'We're going back to the Land of the Tannin-soaked Undead Frog Warriors.' She hefted her crossbow. 'Need to clear a path. Just maybe six steps or so, so I can get a breath in before cracking open another portal. Ideally, back to where we started.' Then she smiled and added, 'So crowd close to the rent on this side, right? But, you know, lying flat. Real flat. I shoot through and the other side goes boom and bits of frog-people fly everywhere – assuming they're lingering and of course they're lingering. It's not every day they get a call to arms, right? Then up we jump and through and keep running. I'll open a new hole in front of us and then we're through again, got it?'

'Four sharpers?' Pulcrude's eyes were wide. 'Forget lying flat – I'm standing way over here.'

'But I'm not holding this portal open. At all. You've got maybe three heartbeats to dive through.'

'I'll make it. How about you, Adjunct? It's an important question, since I'm taking up the rear and all, on account of us being responsible for keeping you alive.'

Fedilap turned at that. 'I missed that bit. I mean, this guy volunteered, didn't he?'

'He's still the Adjunct.'

'Not my problem. Who made it yours, Pulcrude?'

Busy crushing huge mosquitoes on his forearms and the back of his neck, Inkaras paused and said, 'I'll be right behind you, Fedilap. Just get going, will you?'

'Ooh, those bites are swelling you up real bad, sir. Must be allergic or something.'

'Get on with it!'

Grinning, apparently bubbling with excitement, Fedilap gestured with one hand and the portal split open. Lifting the crossbow, she cried, 'Flat, sir! Flat flat flat!' Then she fired.

The explosion on the other side of the portal did more than send a gout of raging fire back into this already scorched realm. It also ripped the rent open, to more than twice its original size. As the swirling flame dissipated, amidst the brief flaring sparks of roasted insects, black water began seeping in around Inkaras where he still lay flat, his ears ringing like a tower-bell. A hand clutched the back of his collar and lifted him upright.

Disoriented, fumbling, Inkaras was not prepared for the hard shove that sent him into the gaping portal.

On the other side, Fedilap was crouched in a crater of mud and red splinters of wood, the hole fast filling with ink-like water. Just beyond the crater, undead soldiers were slowly picking themselves up, while overhead the crows were shrieking their outrage.

Until the clouds of insects arrived, at least.

Squinting at Inkaras, and then at Pulcrude, Fedilap said, 'That hole might be permanent.' Then she brightened. 'Just think! Two worlds connected! Undead Frog Warriors with only burnt tree-stumps to fight and starving insects with nobody worth biting at all!' She stabbed a muddy finger at Pulcrude. 'And you say the universe makes no sense? Hah!'

'Next portal, you miserable witch!'

'Stop complaining,' said Fedilap, opening the next rent. 'We're alive, ain't we?'

Inkaras wanted to kill them both.

*　　　*　　　*

Arenfall was lingering near the captain and his squad, when he was startled by the sudden return of the sappers and the Adjunct, looking much worse for wear. He stepped forward. 'Adjunct? Are those hives?'

The poor man's face – indeed, every area of exposed skin on his body – was lumpy and red.

'Mosquitoes,' was the reply.

Captain Hung joined them. 'Pulcrude?'

But it was the other sapper, Fedilap, who answered, 'She warren-trapped us, sir. No way in the sneaky way. And it was good work, nearly did us in, in fact, but didn't on account of my fast thinking and—'

'Sharpers,' Pulcrude finished. 'Lots of sharpers.'

'I could open a warren high over the village, sir,' Fedilap said. 'Then we just lob cussers and stuff through, flatten everything, right?'

'Too indiscriminate,' Hung said. 'There are imprisoned children in the enemy camp, Fedilap.'

'Well, they're lower to the ground then, ain't they? Less likely to get their heads blown off by the concussion and flying bricks and whatnot.'

Captain Hung turned away. 'Lieutenant Foamy.'

'Sir?'

'Wake 'em up. We're going in.'

'Straight up? Aye, sir.'

Sighing, Arenfall turned to the captain. 'Your Sergeant Breech and Gains are heading into an ambush.'

Hung glanced over. 'As it turns out.'

'They were ready for us.'

'Yes, sir, it seems that they were.'

After a moment of silence, Arenfall said, 'I will endeavour to extract them, assuming they're still alive. You, Captain, take your squad in.'

'Oh, they're alive, sir. Those two can take a lot of punishment. But, very well, I will leave their fate to you, sir. Foamy, it's time! Sappers, you're with us, but flanking wide if you please. Adjunct Inkaras?'

'If only to distract me from this infernal itching, count me in, Captain.'

Arenfall left them to it. Moving off to one side, he quickly removed his heavier gear: webbings, cloak, and armour. A mage who set warren-traps was both powerful and clever. That said, he was mildly surprised that the sappers had found a way back. Use of munitions? Innovative, he supposed. But warren-traps were intended as mazes without any way out, simply a continual plunge into ever more obscure realms. All it took was emerging in one inimical to life to finish things.

So, as with the marines, Arenfall would have to proceed above-ground, making stealth difficult indeed. Not that Hung and his squad were being subtle. That alone would provide sufficient distraction for Arenfall to slide into the settlement unseen.

He hoped.

A whispered incantation blurred his form. Knives in his hands, he set out overland.

The magic he employed was not intended to thoroughly hide him; rather, it would simply make him a more difficult target to skewer with an arrow or bolt, since the blurring effect randomly shifted sideways, or lagged, or then jumped ahead.

In any case, moving at a quickened pace, he reached the first of the settlement's buildings without mishap. Off to his left, Hung's squad, with Inkaras trailing, were double-timing it on the main track. Crossbows were out on the flanks, with the sappers moving crab-like, darting like addled squirrels.

Arenfall shook his head. Marines were a mystery to be sure, but sappers were something else. Well, they were moments from hard contact, he was certain.

As for where the sergeant and the healer were holed up . . . Arenfall paused in a deep shadow cast down by an outer wall, listening for sounds of battle. Sounds of anything, in truth.

But silence still held the village in its embrace.

Frustrated, Arenfall looked upward, gauging his chances at scaling the smooth, almost featureless wall. While he stared upward, he saw the silhouette of a head and then the shoulders of a figure now looking down at him. A moment later, knotted rope uncoiled down to slap the dusty ground at his feet.

Arenfall quickly climbed to the roof, joining Sergeant Breech and, a few paces to one side, the healer, Gains.

'Saw you coming, sir. Figured you was looking for us.'

'I was. You didn't get far, did you?'

'Oh, we been there and back, sir. Scouting, right?'

'You weren't seen?'

'Aye, we were. They seen us, we seen them. They set up an ambush. We ambushed their ambush. Those ones are dead. Only now the bodies have been found so everybody's all stirred up. And now the captain's leading a punch-in-the-nose, meaning that mage on the other side is damned good.'

'As the sappers discovered, yes. Warren-traps.'

The sergeant nodded. 'Lucky they got out then.'

'Agreed.'

'Those two are lucky a lot. Under Bastran Hill they— Well, sir, shall we travel the roofs? In case the captain gets stalled by something?'

'Lead on, Sergeant.'

*   *   *

The mercenaries were positioned directly ahead, blocking the main street, fully armed and ready for a fight. A tall, thin man in grey and black leathers was standing in front of the line, his arms crossed.

Inkaras moved up alongside Captain Hung as they approached. 'I think he wants a conversation.'

'Aye, sir,' said Hung.

'You are of a mind to have one?'

The captain glanced across at him. 'Wasn't planning on it, sir.'

'I see. Well, shall I?'

'If you like. Thing is, sir, you're not looking too good.'

'That bad?'

'Like you've been bitten by a hundred bloodflies, sir. Let's hope they're not bloodflies that bit you.'

'They weren't, Captain. Just mosquitoes the size of locusts.'

'Point is, Adjunct, he may have trouble taking you seriously.'

Inkaras sighed. 'If there is a chance to negotiate regarding the children they're holding—'

'They're holding children, sir. There's nothing to negotiate.'

'Very well.' Inkaras shrugged. 'Just consider me an auxiliary then, Captain.'

Nodding, Hung drew out his short-sword and brought his shield around. These two gestures alone sufficed for the marines behind him, as weapons flashed into moonlight. Inkaras fell back a step as Foamy, Flutter and Scatter closed up, Corporal Scrapes nearby and the sappers drifting in on either side.

With twenty paces between the two groups, the black-clad man unfolded his arms and lifted them palms-up. 'Really? There's no point in you dying tonight, is there? Wouldn't you rather—'

His speech ended then as two crossbows made sharp wooden *knocks!* and, an instant later, the quarrels struck high up the buildings to either side of the mercenaries, where the sharpers exploded. The sudden rain of shrapnel and shattered brick struck the gathered fighters, flinching them in towards the centre, where, amidst screams of pain and anger, all order broke down as weapons fouled, wounded figures staggering, dust still descending and billowing around them.

Inkaras saw Corporal Scrapes move to the right, while Captain Hung slipped to the left even as the wedge of Lieutenant Ormo Foamy at the centre with a heavy on each side rushed forward to slam into the line.

The black-clad man had leapt to one side, evading the onrushing marines, only to find himself facing Captain Hung.

This was when the sorcery started, when something hit Lieutenant Ormo Foamy and tore him apart.

*   *   *

'Shit!' cursed Sergeant Breech. 'Scan the nearby rooftops!'

Arenfall edged off to one side, unveiling his warren and questing outward. The scrap below intensified. He sensed that another sorcerous attack was imminent, since the marines were cutting down mercenaries on all sides.

He saw the flare of magic on the rooftop opposite, in the same instant that a deafening concussion hammered both Breech and Gains not ten paces from where Arenfall crouched. Both soldiers were left lying stunned on a roof that was now slowly sagging.

Ears ringing, Arenfall slipped down over the edge and dropped to the ground. Moving quickly, he skirted the battle, enwreathed in magic that deceived, misled, made his form slippery, barely seen. Moments later he reached the ragged ruin of the building's corner, where a sharper had done damage. The wreckage made broken steps leading straight to the roof, which Arenfall scaled without mishap.

She was waiting for him.

Like a giant fist, the ethereal force of her attack pounded into him. He felt its frantic desire to dismember him, clawing from all sides. He ignited his own magic, making it pulse bright a moment before slipping away from it. The glowing energy, vaguely matching his own form, lingered for barely a heartbeat, but sufficient to draw to it the attacking sorcery. It was torn apart in a blinding flash, even as Arenfall moved forward.

He saw the startled look in her eyes.

An instant before he closed, she stepped back, vanishing into a warren. Growling under his breath, Arenfall shook his head. 'Not so easy, lady.' A gesture made the fast-closing portal seem to hesitate, edges skittering, wavering.

Arenfall pushed through, on her heels.

A heavy blade flashed at him, seeking the side of his neck. Twisting, ducking, he managed to evade it, even as his knife shot forward in a straight-thrust.

The point struck her dead centre, jamming in her sternum.

In her act of spinning away from him, Arenfall felt his knife's blade bend, so he released the weapon, leaving it projecting from her chest. She staggered, cursing, and he saw the shock of the blow weaken her knees. A second knife appeared in his hand, now driving up under her left arm, incapacitating her shoulder.

The sword fell from her grip as she sagged and fell.

Letting go of that knife as well, Arenfall drew a third one and dropped onto her, knees pinning her arms down, setting the blade against her throat. 'Don't even blink,' he said as her warren collapsed around them.

She was breathing hard, in pain, fresh beads of sweat now on her brow and face, even as all colour slowly drained away. Despite this, she managed a faint smile. 'That slippery stuff . . . impressive.'

Scrabbling, clattering sounds – Sergeant Breech and Gains had appeared on the rooftop, both advancing with short-swords in their hands, both looking half-dead.

'We'll finish her, sir,' said Breech.

'No,' Arenfall said.

'She killed Foamy,' the sergeant said, teeth bared, eyes flat. 'Nearly done us, too.'

'We fell through to the floor below,' Gains said. 'That hurt like fuck.'

'In my custody now, marines.' Arenfall looked back down. Her gaze was fixed on his, expression still pinched with pain, shock well on its way. 'You will yield, yes?'

She nodded.

The sounds of fighting had ended from the street below. Arenfall glanced at Breech. 'Who's standing below, Sergeant? Us or them?'

'Us, sir.'

'Lose any more other than the lieutenant?'

'Some wounds, sir. About to send Gains down.' Then he hesitated.

'Out with it,' said Arenfall.

'The Adjunct, sir. Bad hurt, and you know the problems with magical healing, otataral and all.'

Arenfall returned his attention to the woman pinned beneath him. 'You'll get healing, just not right away.'

'Of course.'

Arenfall pulled the knife from her armpit. She passed out. He then worked free the knife in her sternum. He climbed to his feet. 'Bind these wounds, Sergeant. Then we'll carry her down to the street. Best send your healer to the others.'

Breech was scowling, but he waved Gains away. 'I'd rather be bandaging up my own people, sir.'

'I know.'

*   *   *

It was, Adjunct Inkaras admitted, difficult not to laugh. Some nameless mercenary with rotten teeth, taking a sideswipe with a sword in passing, had laid open his left side, just above the hip, and deep enough to reach to his intestines. Inkaras had been busy engaged with the woman in front of him; indeed, had just delivered a likely fatal wound to her.

So they fell together, tangling into something like an embrace.

Not even a man to hold while dying.

A woman. Gods above, I like not your sense of humour. Laughter, yes, but bitter, so very bitter.

The captain now crouched over him, expressionless, but gauging. 'We can sew it up, sir. But if your guts have a nick or any kind of hole, it's going to be bad. Painful, I mean. A painful death.' He paused. 'Gains is good, but you'll resist him, and he's not High Denul.'

'Understood, Captain,' Inkaras said, trying to ignore the maddening itch of the mosquito bites. 'Was my error anyway. I could have held back. You were all more than adequate. My damned pride.'

'Well, lie still, sir. Gains is now here.'

'And Arenfall?'

'Him too,' the captain replied. 'He's got us another prisoner. That mage. Arat is her name, I believe.'

'I would speak with the High Fist, while I can.'

Nodding, Captain Hung straightened and moved away.

A short time later, during which Inkaras felt his body leaking in unnatural ways, with itching so fierce it threatened to overpower his wounds, while he lay still half wrapped up in the hug of a dead woman with sweetly perfumed hair, Arenfall appeared.

'Adjunct. I have summoned the Inquisitor and his party. It's my thought to see the goddess intervene on your behalf. I will insist that Bornu Blatt call upon her.'

'Va'Shaik to heal the Adjunct to the Emperor? You cannot be serious.'

Arenfall grimaced. 'When you put it that way . . .' Then he shrugged. 'I still mean to try.'

There was pain, like acid eating through the flesh surrounding his gut, but it felt strangely distant compared to the bites. Inkaras sighed. 'Turns out, Arenfall, I don't fear death as much as I thought I did. This has been an unhappy travail. When you see too clearly, the idea of justice becomes a curse.'

'How so, Adjunct?'

'An ideal never reached, but forever reached for. Our most fervent desires are the first ones to be mocked. And should we win one – even one – we are shown its illusion. I tire of the game, Arenfall. Tell Hadalin, it was never his fault. Not any of it. Love who he will – tell him to never set aside the moment for a future promise. That promise may never come. To lose the present for a false future, it's . . . wrong.'

'Let us at least extricate you—'

'No, leave her be. Leave me be as well, Arenfall. I took her life, after all. Now she can take mine. One last thing. I was meant to kill you.'

'I know.'

'The Claw in G'danisban will attempt the same.'

'I know.'

Inkaras managed a sigh. 'No wonder the Emperor fears you.'

As the High Fist rose, Inkaras faded away.

*   *   *

The street was a slaughterhouse to Bornu Blatt's eyes. Only two among the mercenaries, Arat and Futhar, remained alive. Rubble amidst the corpses and scattered weapons, pools of black mud where spilled blood settled, a stench of bile, shit and piss. He could sense echoes lingering in the night air, of shock and hurt, of fear and pain in waves. Bemused spirits swirled and milled in confusion, hovering over bodies once their own. Loss and bemusement, ends and beginnings, a strange, haunting wonder.

Two marines had gone into the camp, discovering that the ones guarding the children had fled into the night, so now the children were each, one by one, pulled into the arms of parents, as the entire settlement was awake and out from their homes. Wailing filled the air, as many of the fathers and mothers came to understand the damage already done, revealed in hidden wounds, torn flesh and bruising, and in the dulled eyes set so incongruously in innocent faces.

It was a struggle to keep from weeping.

No one had accompanied him down from their place outside of the settlement. Bornu had taken this particular walk alone, and this hesitation – and then refusal – among his party left him feeling abandoned, in a peculiar, almost hurtful way. Emotions he could make little sense of.

By the time he arrived, Adjunct Inkaras was already dead. Lord Arenfall's upset was clearly evident, and yet Bornu found himself struggling to commiserate, another failing of his purportedly empathetic nature. Instead, he found himself standing before the mercenary leader, Futhar, who sat, trussed up at wrists and ankles, the right half of his face a swollen mass of bruising that still bore the imprints and blots mapping a fist. One eye bloodshot inside a slit of puffiness, the other flitting, uneasy.

'Gracer's tales of you,' said Bornu, 'leave me regretting that you still live.'

'I've nothing to say to you,' Futhar replied, words slurred and blunted.

'You are indeed free to say nothing to me,' Bornu replied. 'But you are not free in any other way, are you? The Malazan Empire has outlawed your kind. You knew that, yet took the risk, and now you will pay for it. I'm wondering, was it worth it?'

Futhar glanced away. 'There's not a person in the world who'd answer "yes" to that, Inquisitor.'

'No, I expect not. Of course, you never bothered asking yourself that question, did you? Not until it was too late. Is that a common way to live, do you think?'

Futhar looked back up at Bornu. 'You want to jaw about this? Questions of philosophy? Listen, I don't give a shit. People like me, we just don't, and that's something you can't understand, is it? You with all those blanks inside, and people like me, with no blanks inside at all. We've got no time for you. So, the Malazans will now kill me, and that'll be that.'

'I don't think they will. Kill you, I mean. Not right away, in any case. Otherwise, you'd be dead right now, like all the others.'

'They'll send me to the mines? I hope they do.'

Bornu looked around. The marines were dragging bodies into rows, ignoring the locals who came up to spit on lifeless faces. Inkaras, however, left lying in a dead woman's embrace, was skirted round as if the configuration had somehow become sacred. Arenfall stood nearby, speaking in low tones with the captain, whose left hand looked to be broken. A last group, of silent locals, stood in a half-circle, all staring at Futhar.

'Ah,' said Bornu, 'now I see.'

'See what?' Futhar demanded.

'Justice will come from these villagers, Futhar.'

That silenced the man, taking the flush from half his face.

*   *   *

'We're taking the sorceress into our custody,' said Captain Hung, 'assuming you're fine with that.'

Arenfall frowned. 'That depends.'

'Oh, we're upset enough about Foamy. But a fight's a fight, sir. Soldiers die. Anyway, we won't be torturing her, or killing her, or anything like that.'

'So, what will you do with her?'

Hung said nothing, casually looking away. 'You ready to hand Futhar over, sir? I see one local the others keep pushing forward, to talk with us. But they're nervous.'

'You plan on recruiting her,' Arenfall said.

Hung looked back, eyes flat. Then he shrugged. 'She's very good, sir.'

'And possibly a rapist.'

'Ah, no, she's not that. Crimes like that we can sniff out, sir. Surprised you can't.'

'Not my particular talent, Captain.'

'It clings to a person, the blood of innocents.'

'I imagine it does. Even so, Captain, she was complicit.'

'We're not decided, sir. It's in the air. Sergeant Breech and Gains agree with you.'

Arenfall's frown deepened. 'We may return to this subject, Captain.'

'Of course, sir.'

Turning, Arenfall walked over to where Futhar was sitting. Wordlessly, he reached down and grasped the man by his sword-harness. He dragged him over to the crowd of locals, dropped him at the feet of the man who seemed to be the leader, however reluctant that role.

Arenfall walked away, rejoining the captain. 'Gather your squad, Captain. Inquisitor Bornu Blatt, we will have need of your goddess again.'

'We should return to my camp then, High Fist.'

'Very well.'

A sound like a dog's whimper came from Futhar, followed by the mingled noises of the man being dragged off to the nearest family house, but Arenfall did not turn to watch. Instead, his gaze fell to Inkaras. 'The rest of you go on – I will meet you at the camp.'

They set off a short time later, with Bornu Blatt among them, leaving Arenfall alone with the two bodies entwined on the ground. A pocket warren would have to do for now, he decided. Then, in time, a proper tomb. As far as interments went, he reflected, future generations, if ever stumbling upon their bodies, would surely mistake them for lovers, this man, this woman. And in their minds they would nurture soft sentiments of love and loyalty, two souls bound as one, and this would ease their day, and every day they returned to the imagined scene would add another comforting caress.

Between the truth and the lie, Arenfall knew which he would choose, were he able.

So it was that one could envy the ignorant, for all the right reasons.

*   *   *

Death without peace felt unjust. From the formless grey transition, this drifting slippage away from broken flesh and bone, details of the village and its cold, lifeless street dissolving into nothing, Inkaras Sollit found himself, eventually, standing upon the shore of a silver sea. What passed for water barely mustered waves, so that its rhythmic edging up and back along the black-sand beach washed through him like the beating of a vast heart. But there was no matching calm within his soul. Instead, he sensed a growing rage.

An instant later he felt a presence close by on his right, and, turning, he saw Va'Shaik, or at least the body the goddess had occupied when escorting them through her warren. 'If you removed the helm,' said Inkaras, 'you might encourage closer . . . kinship.'

The black, shiny face-mask shifted towards him. Then she said, 'There is nothing inside this helm, Adjunct Inkaras Sollit. Nothing of flesh and bone, that is.'

For some reason, her answer did not surprise him. 'Why am I here? Why are _you_ here?'

'There may be a need for you. I but followed a compulsion to inter-vene in your passage from one world to the next.'

'A compulsion?'

She made no reply.

Inkaras said, 'You require precisely what from me, Goddess? I am dead. Nothing of the world I just left means anything to me, not any more. It simply fades away.'

'Then why are you so angry?'

'*I want some answers!*'

'Ah,' was her only reply.

He returned his attention to the sea. Not water at all, something thicker, a quicksilver ocean. Rising slow, settling like a chest emptying of all breath, rising yet again. Watching this calmed his inner storm, quelled his burning frustration. 'What place is this, Goddess?'

'You may see this sea as the wellspring of Apocalypse.'

'Terrific,' he muttered.

'Have you ever pondered the nature of otataral, Adjunct?'

'No.'

'I don't believe you.'

'I will say this,' Inkaras said. 'This place stinks of it.'

'Linger here, Adjunct. Walk the shore. Explore. If able, I will return for you.'

'I'd rather you didn't.'

'Do as I ask, and you will be granted the answers you seek.'

'By you?'

'No.'

'Then from whom, Goddess?'

'Why, the one with the answers, Adjunct.'

A few choice words came to mind as he turned to leave her, all of which he managed to bite back. Instead, he did as she had suggested, walking along the strand, the crunching black sand taking the weight of a body he felt but could not even see. A ghost in truth, then.

Restless, haunted, weighted and invisibly savage.

CHAPTER TEN

In this furrow whence all things began
Sown seeds heave up great cities
All the fingers entwined in the great game
Propping high the elite over the multitude
Silos bulging with grain to ease winter's pangs
The labours of commonfolk garland the dais
And here now comes war unfolding
Captives in lines chained and bowed
Beheading by blade yields nothing of worth
Exile sends vengeance into the future
Better to shackle and fold into the commerce
Of labour, surplus, wealth and excess
See now the rise of slavery to reward
The crown's subjects with ease and indolence
Into the fields and quarries no longer
And thus chain breeds chain out from the furrow
Whence all things began

Civilization Born
Kulliss

Nub is King of the Bhokarala. *See Nub's power! See Nub's glorious pro-file stamped on coins of clay, plop-plop-plopping into the waters of the flooded city beneath the hill. Dissolving in blooms and were they ever coins at all? Of course not. Bhokarala have no need for currency, unlike their benighted skinny-limbed subjects with silly hair atop their heads. But the regal profile remains, floating upon the slick oily surfaces, in every stream and pool Nub looks down upon – well, not in profile when looking down upon, except by* tortured side-slant of one eye, which is not easy, but is it not true that every liquid surface bears the visage of Nub and none other than Nub? Certainly, every liquid surface he deigns to look down upon!

Proof, then, of Nub's eminence, his ubiquity – why Nub is everywhere!

He had no words for all of this, of course. Words were silly and confusing besides. Instead, he had the truth of his eyes and the truth of his big fists pounding down on the shiny coconut-heads of his subjects, his rightfully cowering indolents. What more was needed?

But he was far from his tree-throne looming high above Bastran Hill. Compulsion plagued him, stirred him into agitated confusion. Who dared force King Nub into this inexplicable servitude?

Shadows. Shadows, from which whispering voices emerged, like claws on the ends of long fingers, sinking deep into his brain to drag him hither and thither, worse than one of those snag-haired lapdogs some humans carried about or stood leashed to (good eating though, those lapdogs).

Deep into the Under Quarter for King Nub, to find a second royal perch upon which to squat with knuckled brow and glimmering glower, motionless witness at Shadow's behest, but for what? Nub knew not.

The ignominy of it all!

So here he perched like a gargoyle atop a moss-bedecked gate-post, in the deepest-sunk of the myriad depressions of the buried, half-crushed city, where water surrounded the tilted edifice at his back. The flanking gate-post bore its own gargoyle, this one of stone but no less belligerent of expression and disposition. It didn't look anything like Nub. Not at all, not even close. The confused genuflections of his subjects in the swirling waters directly in front of the carved ugliness was clearly deliberate in its insult. Nub looked nothing like that thing!

Anger swirled in every reflected visage of King Nub. Rage, even, only moments from becoming explosive, terrifying, devastating. If not for Shadow's firm clutch upon the nape of his thick neck. Outrage!

But what could he do? Why, nothing.

The unfairness of the world was bitter, so very, very bitter. He would take it out on something, shortly. A fist to the top of a head, perhaps.

*   *   *

'But are they truly gone?' King Sug asked, fidgeting on his throne, the sound of dripping water so confoundedly incessant he feared it would drive him mad.

Grimacing, Stipple said, 'As good as. The marines went out on a mission.'

262

'And when they return?'

She shrugged. 'They'll be busy elsewhere, soon enough.'

'You seem unduly confident, Stipple. For all I know, you're a Malazan Claw.'

Stipple snorted. 'Listen, Sug—'

'King Sug.'

'You do know your title is temporary, don't you?'

Beside Stipple, Hench cleared his throat. 'We been with you from the start of this, Sug. We did what was needed to take over all the other neighbourhoods. You rule, that you do, but without us it would never have happened. And, hate it all you want, those two sappers marching through the Under Quarter like a two-headed dragon spitting sharpers, why, they finished all opposition. Permanently.'

'They nearly collapsed my entire kingdom!'

'It survived,' Hench replied. 'Anyway, now they've left.'

'I exiled them!'

'Right. They left, on account of running out of sharpers. Oh, and criminals to kill. Water's still pink in some places, you know. Even now. Still pink.'

'It shall be a permanent exile,' Sug said, leaning back. 'Kill on sight. Put out that command to all my guards and patrols.'

Hench and Stipple exchanged glances.

Sug scowled. 'What now?'

'I guess we were wondering,' ventured Hench.

'About what? Out with it!'

'The apparent lack of, uh, irony.' He squinted up at Sug. 'I mean, is it an act?'

'What are you talking about?'

Hench shrugged. 'Like Stipple said, the title's temporary. Not on account of, you know, usurpation or anything. But on account of all the rest.'

'What "all the rest"?'

'Might be a metaphor in action,' Stipple suggested to Hench.

He grunted in reply. 'Could be. Still, at some point, you gotta laugh, right? Right?'

Sug thumped one arm of the throne. 'What are you two going on about?'

Hench sighed. 'Oh, Sug on High, Glorious Eminence, Supreme Ruler of Under Quarter, your kingdom is about to drown.'

At that instant, from one of the rooms behind the throne, and as if to punctuate the observation, a large piece of plaster fell from a soaked wall with a sloshy splash. Moments later, ripples exited the doorway and spread out across the flooded floor of the throne room.

Stipple made a snorting sound, then covered her mouth and coughed.

Fuming, Sug struggled to slow his breathing. He needed calm thoughts. 'Yes, of course. Ironic title, whatever. Very well, we obviously require a new throne room, one higher, drier, with no dripping water. Didn't the marines say they'd stop the flooding?'

'No.'

Sug frowned. 'I'm sure they did, Stipple!'

'Well, sure,' Stipple said. 'Using cussers to collapse everything down, and that would be, you know, *everything*.'

'And even then,' added Hench, 'it would've been a temporary solution, on behalf of G'danisban, not the Under Quarter.'

'Because,' resumed Stipple, 'the Under Quarter would have ceased to exist. That was their solution.'

Sug sighed. 'No wonder I exiled them.'

*   *   *

The acolytes, agents of Invigil Ban Ryk, spread out through the city. Some were true believers, many were not. They simply delighted in the delivery of suffering upon the lives of others, and to witness the misery of their victims was to sip of the sweetest nectar. Among the truly faithful, only certain details differed. Chaos and anarchy was the goal in every instance, lurking behind whatever personal motivation inspired these adherents to the Apocalyptic. The new world would be announced in screams, smoke, and blood.

Such was holy war, wherein zeal wore a thousand masks.

Ban Ryk was not so naive as to believe in some kind of universal purity among his flock. In the countryside, after all, they had already made use of bandits, thugs and mercenaries. But these weapons were soon to be discarded, if not utterly broken. If that was by the hand of Malazan marines, or in the wake of liberty, it made little difference to the Invigil.

. He could envisage that liberation in a multitude of imagined details. It would begin with a raucous celebration following the ousting of the Mezla oppressors, a bursting of shackles, the goddess's blessing of freedom for all Seven Cities. How many days and nights of this? Unknown.

Until exhaustion drained away the last of the euphoria, he imagined.

In the wake of that would come reorganization within the temples of the goddess. The fate of rival temples and deviant cults would involve more than just crucifixions. Such dens would be scourged and, not to be too coy about it, systematically looted, to assist in financing the exigencies of the one faith. Unfortunate but necessary.

And then?

In his mind's eye, he saw the future open out, edges crumbling, a pit black and depthless and growing larger with each passing moment. Civilization would know its death-throes, but faith held on to would answer the embrace of oblivion, whispering of inevitability. And was not that very inevitability the gift of peace, of struggle's end?

The death of the unbelievers was a preface of sorts, clearing the path. The death of the faithful who remained was a different kind of death, a peaceful, accepting kind. This, Ban Ryk knew, was at the core of the Apocalyptic. Death was indeed inevitable, inescapable. The only gift to accompany that moment was found in acceptance, because only through acceptance could the world beyond death be transformed into an eternal paradise.

For the faithful. The unbelievers, the first sacrifices that preceded the final apocalypse, would not find the world beyond to be a paradise. No, instead, they would find themselves as lowly slaves, bound to eternal service. This fateful dividing line was precise.

A scuffling of feet interrupted his pleasant musing on the times ahead, and he looked up to see Pash standing in the doorway. 'What is it, Pash?'

A dip of the head, bird-nest hair bobbing, and then she said, 'The High Priestess has been made aware of the return of the Malazans.'

'Made aware? How?'

'The goddess.'

Ban Ryk rose from behind his desk. 'I have sensed nothing of her holy presence.'

Pash made no response to that.

'Are they bloodied?'

'Invigil?'

'The Malazans. Did they not fight bandits? Were there losses? Does the High Fist still live?'

'The High Priestess didn't say,' Pash replied.

'Where is she now?'

265

'In the garden.'

'Indeed? How unusual.'

Again, Pash said nothing.

Ban Ryk scowled. 'You are growing lax in your reporting to me. Why has she left her rooms? What possible reason would she have to be in the garden? She hates the garden.'

'She prepares a garland by her own hand.'

'A garland?'

'To make it a gift to the High Fist Arenfall, for his sacrifice.'

Ban Ryk stared steadily at Pash, seeking some hint as to her disposition, but that face was a blank wall, the eyes so flat they might as well be painted on stone. Then he said, 'A sacrifice implies there were losses. That's good. Excellent. Very well, lead me to her.'

'Invigil, she extended no invitation.'

'Nor do I need one! I will speak with her. Lead me to her or get out of my way.'

Ducking her head again, Pash stepped back.

The small, wiry woman strode a few paces ahead, her bare feet silent on the tiles, her tunic shapeless around a shapeless body, her neck thin as a tent-peg. Her very presence averted attention. For all that, something about her made him uneasy. Was she worth keeping around? He knew doubts, and not for the first time.

Shamalle's carelessness was to blame. Imagine, lifting up a lowly orphan servant from the filth and dust whence she came. Was this not the breaking of a universal law? A child born to a station belonged there for the rest of its days, from birth to old age and everything between. Instead, here Pash was, guiding the Invigil himself into the presence of the High Priestess. There would surely be a price to pay for this unnatural elevation. Ban Ryk himself might have to deliver it.

But all things in good time.

Ahead, luminous light bathed the courtyard and its overgrown garden, the sun's glow almost blinding where it reflected off the high lime-painted walls. The vines and creepers climbing those walls showed blooms of red and purple, the colours so vibrant as to seem almost obscene. Hummingbirds cavorted around each blossom.

Shamalle sat on a stone bench near the fountain, her plump feet surrounded by discarded cuttings and crushed flowers. When she looked up to Pash, her eyes were red-rimmed and puffy.

'Sweet ruby, thank the false gods you're here – oh, you're here, too, Ban Ryk? Well, I doubt you can help me. Then again, who knows what hidden talents you possess.' She held up a misshapen ring of bruised leaves and wilted blossoms. 'See what a sorry thing I've made of this! Nothing like the vision in my mind's eye at all, in which I saw a garland of impossible beauty, a thing worthy of one of his songs! Where did that perfect creation go? Not into the real world, that's for sure. Pash, I needed your hands, not mine. Oh dear, I am despondent!'

Ban Ryk could not help but curl his lip. 'You want to woo High Fist Arenfall. Have you lost your mind, High Priestess? Unless you seek to inveigle your way into his confidence, for the purpose of betrayal, indeed, assassination. Is this your plan, Holy One?'

Shamalle let the garland drop to the ground.

Pash moved to collect it up, then sat cross-legged to begin working on it, making use of the heaped blossoms and cuttings close to the bench.

'Poor Ban Ryk,' Shamalle sighed. 'I grieve for the paucity of your inner world, I truly do. Devoid of softer things, of heart's longing, of things worthy of desire and indeed, worthy of heartbreak. Have I lost my mind? No, only my heart. My pained, labouring heart. Such sentiments, I see by your visage, simply rebound from the impervious indifference of your cold carapace.'

'Carapace? You liken me to an insect?'

'Dear me, no. More . . . crustacean, perhaps. A thing of mundane hues only enlivened to lurid excitation by being, well, boiled alive.'

'You are more palatable when drunk,' he observed.

'No finer insobriety than love's liquor, Invigil. Why, I find myself palled by the very thought of insipid wine. The fumes have all rushed from my skull, stripping the veil before my eyes. I am filled unto bursting with the love of life, as befits a soul's loneliness brought to a sudden, astonishing end. Now, why, even in the midst of all this sunlight, the stars dance before me, my vision of the world itself gilt with gold and silver. Is not the world and all within it wonderful? Barring crusty crabs, of course.'

Ban Ryk sighed. 'You truly begin to weary me,' he said. 'I wish more details of the return of the Malazans.'

She waved a hand. 'We all wish for things, don't we? You, the heady poppy seeds of gossip, snapping upon the pan of your scalding brain. Me, the luxurious physical perfection of Arenfall's body wrapped tight by my limbs and whatnot. And what of Pash, here? What does she wish for? Pash?'

'I have all I need, Holy One,' Pash replied, still working on the garland.

'Bless you, darling ruby, for your simple self. How can any of us not envy such equanimity? Hmm, Invigil? Imagine it for yourself if you dare. An end to the acidic gnawing in your ample gut, the cessation of your ceaselessly darting eyes, all the jumping, twisting thoughts, fears and agitations bouncing around inside that not-quite-round-enough skull of yours, chitin though it may be. Think of peace within and without, Invigil!'

'At the moment of the Apocalyptic, so shall it be, Holy One, for all true believers.'

'And are you a true believer, Invigil?'

'Of course I am!'

'Thus destined for peace at the moment of the Apocalyptic?'

'Yes!'

Shamalle stood, smoothing down her silks. 'Then what point all this present discombobulation?'

Ban Ryk blinked, and then scowled. 'Preparations are necessary, of course.'

'Why? You are a true believer. There's nothing to prepare.'

'The world beyond—'

'Invigil! Such an excess of presumption! Such delusions of grandeur! See what comes of unending discord within your laboured mind? You have been driven mad, sir, to imagine yourself the arbiter of the entire world.'

'I am not entirely alone,' he hissed, trembling with rage and utterly incapable of hiding it.

'A quorum of idiots, what a relief.'

'The Apocalyptic is—'

'In flux,' she replied. 'How could it be otherwise? The goddess walks among us.'

'Her will—'

'Is not for you to determine, I should think. And the moment may be drawing near, good sir, when she tells you just that, in no uncertain terms.'

'I welcome it!'

'Do you? How curious.'

'Will you tell me nothing more of the Malazans?'

'If the goddess did not see fit to inform you, who am I to challenge that determination?'

'I am done with you!' Ban Ryk said. 'The time is soon when this temple will be truly cleansed. Think on that!'

'While you're at it,' Shamalle said, 'clean this up, too,' and she waved at all the cuttings and blossoms scattered across the tiles.

Ban Ryk stormed from the garden.

*　　　*　　　*

Hadalin's face was desolate. Alas, there was little that Arenfall could do, or say, to enliven once more the man's landscape of grief. Only time awaited him now, the season's turning, new shoots of green to rise from the colourless, flattened ground. Only time, which had now slowed to a crawl.

He remained seated on the settee, Hadalin standing before him. There was birdsong outside the shuttered window, slats of mote-filled sunlight stretching across the tiled floor of the chamber. Arenfall's fingers itched for the taut caress of strings, plucking to life a haunting tune. The instrument lay within reach and he longed to take it up, to let his voice roll out in accompaniment to whatever solemn melody he might fashion.

But these were not gestures of a High Fist of the Empire. Not with the broken man standing before him. 'It pains me,' he said into the silence that followed the news of the Adjunct's death, 'but we must confirm your elevation to the rank of Adjunct.'

'The Emperor has been informed?' Hadalin asked in a rasping voice.

'Of the death of Inkaras Sollit? Yes.'

'By his command, then, I am to be invested as the new Adjunct?'

Arenfall frowned. 'Not yet, officially. He still hasn't replied. I have, however, made the recommendation.'

After a long moment, Hadalin snorted. 'Then he will choose someone else, High Fist.'

'Ah, I see. I appear to have fallen far in the Emperor's esteem, then.'

Hadalin seemed about to speak, but didn't.

Sighing, Arenfall rubbed his eyes, then sat back. 'At the very least, you will have to take command of the hands of Claw in the city. One must also assume that you will also stand in place of Inkaras regarding my future.'

Hadalin blinked. Then he said, 'Nothing was decided on that matter, High Fist.'

'Having lost my legion,' Arenfall resumed, 'the threat I appear to represent to the Emperor is surely diminished.'

'Are you pleading for your life, High Fist?'

'It was an observation,' Arenfall said slowly. It was clear that this man was quickly finding his feet. Perhaps the grief had not been as deeply rooted as Arenfall had believed. In any case, Hadalin's prod – seeking an angry response, no doubt– had just stripped all warmth from the room. 'It may be that the Emperor's hesitation in replying to the news has nothing to do with the situation here in Seven Cities. It's a big empire, after all.'

Shrugging, Hadalin said, 'Or he hesitates because he has no faith in me at all.'

'You now command the Claw in the city.'

'Do I? Perhaps. In any case, this was a clever blow.'

'By whom?'

'Why, Va'Shaik, of course.'

'Va'Shaik had no hand in the death of the Adjunct, Hadalin. He engaged the enemy in melee.'

'And you, High Fist? Where were you?'

'On a rooftop, incapacitating a mage. The Adjunct elected to join the marines in their attack. It was not for me to dissuade him.'

'You made no effort?'

'He was the Adjunct. That said, if you truly need to blame anyone, then by all means blame me. I permitted his presence in the meeting with the High Priestess in the Temple of Va'Shaik. I could have gone to that meeting alone. In which case, it would only have been me and the marines to undertake the mission.'

'True, you could have done that. Limper knows, you keep enough other matters secret, after all.'

'Just so.'

After a moment, Hadalin glanced away and something in his posture sagged slightly. 'But no. Inkaras was determined to stick close to you, to be your very shadow, in fact.'

'The shadow from which his knife would find my back.'

'Just so,' Hadalin echoed. 'That is why I do not understand why he did not accompany you to that rooftop, against the mage.'

'He left behind his otataral sword.'

Hadalin's eyes widened briefly, and then narrowed. 'The warren.'

'Va'Shaik's holy path, yes.'

'So, perhaps her intent all along. But not just the Adjunct's death, but also yours, and the squad of marines as well.'

'The mercenaries were tough, but not that tough. A plan such as that would have used a much bigger trap, Hadalin. One with a more certain outcome.'

'At the same time, a slow whittling away of opposition has its own value. Leaving us scrambling to reorganize. Not to mention renewed discord in our position.'

'There has been plenty of that already,' Arenfall pointed out, 'of which she would have known nothing. Indeed, simple patience might well better serve her in the long run, assuming you're still intending to kill me here.'

'You appear unconcerned, High Fist.'

'Your otataral sword prevents my use of magic, it's true, but I have other skills.'

'Our first meeting on the rooftop and the speed with which you acted, High Fist, was without doubt impressive. I was simply too far away to respond in time.'

'You closed the distance quickly enough.'

'If I choose to kill you here, High Fist, you would not be able to prevent me.'

'Then act,' said Arenfall. 'I weary of your indecision.'

'I do not think I wish to serve Va'Shaik's interests.'

'Unless, in agreeing to the goddess's request for assistance, I am now compromised.'

'Are you?'

'I don't think so,' Arenfall said. 'We have a master assassin loose in the city. I've lost a half-dozen agents in the past month, beginning with my best one, who happened to be the first woman you slept with upon your arrival.'

'No end to your secrets,' Hadalin muttered in obvious disgust.

'You were careless. You needed protecting. Not of late, it turns out. We can deem that progress.'

'High Fist, what have you done with his body?'

'It resides in a safe place. You have a wish to pay your respects? You will need to leave your sword behind.'

Hadalin's answering smile was tight. 'I don't think so.'

Shrugging, Arenfall rose to his feet. 'For the time being, I will consider you to be acting as Adjunct, until I am informed otherwise. There are other matters I must attend to.'

With a faint nod, Hadalin turned about and left the chamber.

As the door closed, Arenfall drew a deep breath, trying to calm himself. Thrice in the conversation just completed, he'd considered killing the man. This was a flaw among Adjuncts. They held too much faith in otataral, but also their skills with the sword. Here, in this room, a sheathed weapon was useless. Between one breath and the next, or between one word spoken and the other begun, Arenfall could have buried his knife up behind the man's chin, the point driving deep into his brain.

But Arenfall had seen the fragility of the man's arrogance, a shield raised up in lieu of anguish, and this had taken the sting from the threats. Hadalin's posturing answered a need, the renewed sense of physical prowess, which in turn was a promise to himself, that someone would answer for his lover's death, and that he was the man to deliver that answer.

He could picture Hadalin now, walking down the corridors to his room, every step taken dull with emotional exhaustion. Wrapped in a fog of dislocation, numbness, the distant echo of terrible screaming coming from some dark corner of his mind.

Arenfall was of the intention to now speak with Captain Hung, seeking the whereabouts of Corporal Hasten and news of the other mission which was so critical to what was coming here in G'danisban. But that could wait.

He had music to compose, and a poem to write. In that respect, he concluded that he was probably not a very good High Fist.

*   *   *

'None of it's settled,' Captain Veroosh said. 'I can't sleep until it is, dammit. And look at you. More miserable than normal. Bad luck about Foamy. I'm emptying the jug, you don't mind, right? We can order another if you like. Obly the Boy's in the back. Probably. Personally, I don't think anything's back there. At all. A closet, maybe. The boy lives in a closet. He's standing in there right now, staring at pegs and hooks. It's amazing how some people live, isn't it? How's your cell, by the way? Heard you had flying ants. Just a hatch of queens, you know. Most of the time they stay in the walls.'

272

'Hasten hasn't returned?' Captain Hung asked.

'No. But you did. Well, you know that, obviously. Surprised your sappers didn't get you all killed. Been hearing rumours about their work in the Under Quarter. They're insane, you know.'

'It's not settled down there?'

'Oh, it's settled all right. Apart from all the streets with bodies floating in them. Now tell me about this new mage of yours. Arat, right? Who murdered Foamy. That's awkward, or am I overstating it? I might be. I mean, every squad's different. Maybe nobody liked Foamy anyway. Did they hate him? That could make it easier. Is she nice?'

Hung stared at his fellow captain for a long moment, and then he said, 'I like you better when it's all settled.'

*   *   *

Stipple positioned herself in front of Pulcrude's cell. 'We need you,' she said.

Lying on the cot, Pulcrude opened one eye to squint at the woman. 'Oh, it's you. You don't want me. Go ask Fedilap.'

Stipple looked to the cell beside Pulcrude's. 'She's sleeping.'

'She's faking. Aren't you, Fed? She won't answer, of course. She's like that.'

'We need both of you.'

'We're low on sharpers,' Pulcrude pointed out. 'Well, we're not, but we're hoarding right now. Besides, we're planning on how to kill our new recruit.'

From Fedilap's cell came a muffled voice, 'It'll be an accident, of course. Now stop talking about it, Pulcrude. It's supposed to be a secret.'

From the cell behind Stipple there came a soft scuffling sound, then the creak of the front bars. Turning, Stipple saw a woman with a heavily scarred face now leaning against the grilled door. 'I think I'm supposed to be afraid,' she said in a south-tribal accent. 'Thing is, I can kill everyone in here,' she continued, 'without even leaving this cell.'

Stipple turned back to Pulcrude. 'Who's that?'

'The recruit,' Pulcrude replied, closing the eye that had been open.

'I didn't ask for any of this,' resumed the recruit. 'The High Fist should've killed me. Captain Hung should've killed me. The goddess should've killed me.'

'Listen to her,' said Pulcrude. 'She never shuts up about how everybody should've killed her. But me and Fedilap talking about killing her? Oh, she doesn't like that. Some people are never satisfied.'

The recruit snorted. 'You'd have done it by now.'

'We like to stretch out our vengeance. Make you suffer.'

'I hate this,' Stipple said in a mumble, then she raised her voice. 'We need you two sappers. A new problem's shown up. Sort of.'

'You want us to blow it up?'

'No. It's engineering work.'

'Drainage? No point, we told you that. You're all taking a bath. Not long now.'

'We know. Still.'

Fedilap suddenly sat up. 'Let's do it, Pulcrude. That way, we can make our plans in more privacy. You know, the plan to kill her in an accidental way.'

'Please,' the recruit said wearily, 'do it now, I'm begging you.'

Grunting, Pulcrude got to her feet and looked across at Arat. 'This is our vengeance, you see. We can stretch it out for years. You not knowing when. Or where. Years, Arat, years. Anyway. Stipple? It's Stipple, isn't it? Right, the cells are locked on account of them being, uh, cells. Go find the jailer and get us out. It'll be good to stretch our legs and all that.'

'You'll need to bring your digging tools,' Stipple said as she turned to find the jailer.

'Spikes, sharpers and crackers,' said Fedilap, now also standing. 'Oh, and a trowel.'

'Proper digging tools,' said Stipple from the end of the corridor.

'Can we change our minds?' Pulcrude asked.

But it was too late.

*　　　*　　　*

Invigil Ban Ryk studied the three figures standing before him. Each commanded a team of ten adherents. Together, they comprised the core of the temple's operations in G'danisban. Orotol was the eldest, a veteran of the Whirlwind. Tall, thin, with a narrow, lined face and deceptively bland eyes, he had a dozen notable murders behind him; rival high priests included. A most venerable follower of the faith, was Orotol.

To his left was Baek, ten years younger, hot-headed and inclined to excess, but useful nonetheless. A foundling raised in the temple, his eyes blazed with religious fervour.

The last of them was Wrest. She remained something of a mystery, although Ban Ryk did not question her loyalty, given her active knives and the corpses left strewn in her wake. A particular hatred for rival cults, especially those of the Feather and Crow. Indeed, anything even remotely related to the Wickan Demon, Coltaine, was her favoured target.

Ban Ryk was satisfied with them. Clearing his throat, he now said, 'The Under Quarter we can leave alone, since it will not be long before the rising waters drive everyone out of there. Any cults in their midst can be expunged once they're on the streets, out in the sunlight, with nowhere to hide. I leave their fates to you and your team, Wrest.'

'They'll not live long,' she promised.

'Baek, you and your team can remain on the fringes. We need eyes on every track and road and every gate. There will come a point when we seal the city, when we turn away everyone seeking to enter it. On the day of the revolution. Remember, Malazan marines are known to infiltrate disguised as merchants.'

'Marines are already in the city,' Baek pointed out. 'They don't need to sneak in.'

'If they're to be reinforced, they might.'

'Easy enough to sniff them out, Invigil,' Baek said with a shrug. 'They display an arrogance they can't hide.'

'Be vigilant.'

'We shall.'

Shifting attention to Orotol, Ban Ryk said, 'Speaking of the marines in the city.'

'We are positioned to pounce,' Orotol replied. 'They'll not leave Blue Sky alive, not one of them.'

Baek looked to the man. 'Why not fire the gaol? They're locked in the cells, after all. Think of their screams as they burn.'

'They have magic,' Orotol pointed out. 'Fire won't do. And there are wards around the compound. No, we'll strike when they emerge from the colonnade.'

'And when they retaliate with their magic?'

'We'll take losses, yes. But since we'll have surrounded the plaza, our attacks can be relentless. Enough quarrels and arrows, and soldiers will fall. Baek, I have done this before. I have killed Malazan marines. Stick to your own task and leave me mine.'

Ban Ryk spoke. 'I have confidence in you all. Attend to your teams. Our waiting is almost at an end.'

*   *   *

King Sug stood with crossed arms. The only detail affecting his imposing, regal pose was the water seeping in through his leather boots. He had been seeking to catch the attention of the sappers, or, failing that, Stipple or even Hench. But none of them were paying him any heed at all. He could, of course, clear his throat, but that would make a thin sound. His timbre was nowhere near stentorian enough. He couldn't manage a low, threatening throat-growl at all. Frustrating.

Finally, he voiced a hissing sigh and said, 'Excuse me, but here I stand. My instructions were far from complicated.' He pointed a finger at the swirling water they all stood in. 'Dig a drain. Install a culvert. I need this new palace to be high and dry.'

One of the sappers – Pulcrude – eyed him sidelong, then leaned against the stone pillar of the gateway flanking the winding path into the brooding building, directly beneath a leering gargoyle perched atop the post. 'This palace of yours . . . looks high and dry enough.'

'Though it shouldn't,' Fedilap added, scowling, her hands on her hips as she studied the squat building with its weirdly bulging sides. 'Is that steam rising from around the foundations? Am I seeing steam, Pulcrude?'

'I know very well it's dry over there,' King Sug snapped. 'It's the approach that's flooded.'

'Well,' Stipple pointed out, 'so is the street behind us, oh King of Greatness.'

'Your new titles for my august self are gratifying. You challenge my natural modesty. In any case, I too am aware that the street behind us is also flooded, as are all the surrounding buildings – or what's left of them. But that's precisely my point. We're in a lower section, which is why everything is soaked through, crumbling and rotting, and why the water is so deep. But then there is this building—' and he pointed. 'Utterly dry. This shall be my new palace, as it's clearly unoccupied.'

Fedilap grunted. 'Yes. Why is that?'

Sug frowned. 'What do you mean? This quarter's flooded. Once I occupy my new palace, it can be considered a kind of moat, do you see?

Look, if you can't drain the yard, then at least build me a bridge, a walk-way to the front steps.'

'Any mason can do that,' Fedilap said. 'You don't need us.'

Stipple said, 'About that. Nobody wants the job.'

'Why not?'

'They're just being superstitious,' King Sug said. 'It's well known that stone-carvers have primitive minds. Almost childlike, in fact. And stub-born? You have no idea. No, we have need of you and your engineering skills, Sapper Fedilap. And Sapper Pulcrude, too, of course. You, uh, sappers.'

Hench now said, 'I can bring a few people down here to pile blocks of stone. Not too close, but close enough. That should help.'

'Not masons,' said King Sug.

'No,' Hench replied. 'Even stupider people, of course.'

'Of course. Excellent. Well,' he added, 'we have plenty of *them* down here, don't we?' And he laughed. Not a booming laugh, alas, but thin and a bit high-pitched.

Pulcrude pushed off from the post and moved to stand between the pillars, on the threshold. Squatting, she reached one hand down into the black water within the yard. Rummaged for a time, and then slowly lifted a handful of mud. She sniffed it. Then, as water continued to drain from the soil in her hand, she dipped her head and lapped some mud with her tongue, then worked it in her mouth. A moment later, she flung the mud away and straightened, turning to Fedilap. Her eyes were bright in the lantern's yellow glow. 'We were right, Fed. There *was* one down here. And this is it. Look at us. We're standing here, just like Kellanved and Dancer, all those years ago.'

Fedilap licked her lips. 'Limper's wonky knee,' she whispered.

Turning to Stipple, Pulcrude spoke. 'This building got a name?'

'Sug's Palace,' said King Sug.

But Stipple was shaking her head. 'Hench, you any idea?'

Hench scratched in his beard for a time, and then said, 'Don't quote me or anything. But I'm thinking, maybe, "Underhouse"?'

With an exasperated hiss, Sug rolled his eyes and said, 'Yes yes, that's what it *used* to be called. But now it's Sug's Palace.'

'Underhouse,' Pulcrude repeated, as if tasting the word along with whatever mud was still left in her mouth. 'Utterly nonsensical.'

'And yet perfect,' finished Fedilap. 'We need to report this, you think?'

'Report? Who? Captain Hung?'

'High Fist Arenfall?'

'Corporal-Not-Corporal Hasten Thenu!'

'Shit,' muttered Fedilap. 'But he ain't here, is he?'

'No. We'll have to wait. Keep it to ourselves for now, I mean. Hung's not good. Not even Arenfall.'

'You're right. It's got to be Hasten. The bastard.'

'But why? I mean, it was my suggestion, but now I think on it, I don't know why I made it.'

'Why? Because we don't know why, that's why. Hasten is all about *why* without anyone knowing why at all. That's Hasten, isn't it?'

'Exactly. Clever me.'

'What are you two even talking about?' King Sug demanded. 'I just want you to build a bridge! A little one. Nothing too fancy. Just solid, you know? You marines are good at that stuff, right? Solid but not fancy. I'll even pay you!'

Stipple pushed close to Pulcrude. Though she whispered, Sug could hear her anyway. Everyone could. 'What's going on, Sapper? Out with it.'

'Nothing. We got nothing to report, or for you to, uh, report. If you had to, you know, make a report. We've got nothing.'

'Only,' Fedilap interjected, 'Sug needs to find a different palace.'

'What?' King Sug shouted, reedily, 'No! I want this one! I want the Underhouse!'

Baring her teeth, Fedilap asked, 'But does it want you? That's the question.' She gestured. 'You been in yet? Tried the door yet?'

'Well, I was waiting for a bridge, of course. The water there might be deep. Might be potholes and sinks. Might be quicksand.'

'Might be all of that,' Fedilap said, nodding. 'But go on, give it a try.'

*   *   *

King Nub could not recall the last time he laughed, and he wasn't about to now. Though it would have been perfect. And oh how he'd been tempted, when that red-haired woman leaned against the pillar he was perched upon. Tempted to just reach down, or even swing a big, knobby fist, right there on top of her head. But he didn't. That would have spoiled the entertainment, as they chattered and chattered, and then chattered some more.

Stupidity was a human trait. Disastrous for them. But fun for King Nub.

Why, when his thinned eyes tracked the one named King Sug (such presumption!

Only one king in the below-world, and that was Nub!), who, after much fluttering and flapping, set off into the black inky waters surrounding the Underhouse, boots splashing as he searched for the paving stones of the path to the raised door – why, even when with a yelp the great false king reeled, tottered, plunged with a vast sludgy explosion of brown water – and even when roots snaked up as if from nowhere to wrap tight about his thrashing limbs, and even when the man vanished in churning reddish foam – leaving the others standing just beyond the threshold, mouths agape—

Even then, Nub made no sound. No chortle, no squeal, no chuckle, no braying belly howl.

This was what it meant to be regal, to be of proper comportment for the royal self.

Dignity personified, on his throne of mossy stone.

Positively statuesque.

King Nub!

BOOK FOUR

NO LIFE FORSAKEN

Stone into pond –
some proof of passage
would be nice
to make me
to make you
bound by tumult
and ripple –
not this swallowing all

In a Time of Despond
Kullys

CHAPTER ELEVEN

The Synod took some time to assemble, as vast distances had to be crossed by the most outlying, remote temples. It is curious, then, that all the necessary hard work was achieved long before the first delegates even arrived.

Excerpt from
The Last Holy City
Bornu Blatt

It was late afternoon and, at long last, they were upon an imperial road, broad and level with drainage ditches flanking it. This latter detail amused Bornu Blatt, even as it delivered a sobering reminder of the hidden spine of the Malazan Empire. In a land with almost no rain, what need these ditches and culverts? But the armies that had built these roads adhered to a system of construction that was applied without deviation. There was a single-mindedness to this that was worth thinking about.

Then again, what empire existed anywhere that did not depend upon order? The scaffolding of power was built on solid, measured foundations, after all. Mobility of armies was central to that. Hence these well-engineered roads. And once order was established, then trade could follow, as well as a reliable and relatively swift organization of messengers, in effect diminishing the distance between centres of control, weaving the tapestry of imperial rule and domination.

It behooved local settlements, towns and the like to fall into this new order, since, even as news travelled, so too did wealth.

Roads were the veins and arteries in this sprawling body that was the Malazan Empire. That Bornu and his party were now part of this pulsing flow was ironic, he reflected. Assuming rebellion was at the very end of this journey. That said, he was beginning to have his doubts about that.

They were not alone on this road, of course. Riders passed them on occasion, patrols and messengers and others less identifiable. At other times, they overtook wagons, or drovers with their flocks of goats, or lone traders pulling two-wheeled carts or leading burdened donkeys or mules. And as they neared and then entered settlements, they passed customs houses and the occasional fort on a hill. And, of course, temples. Many, many temples.

Gilakas rode at Bornu's side. Immediately behind them were Gracer and Stult and the pack-mules. Heat and weariness made conversation scarce. The aftermath of the battle with the mercenaries still swirled and bubbled beneath the surface. So much had been revealed. So much more had been left unanswered.

One thing was certain, at least in the mind of Bornu Blatt. The goddess walked in his shadow, witness to all that he witnessed, a silent presence in every conversation he conducted. What was less certain was the extent of her reach into his mind, into the realm of his thoughts. And that was unsettling.

The town they'd just entered had a name, but none in the party knew it. That was not unusual. The journey had been long, the scrublands with their decrepit islands of humanity seemingly endless. The imperial road that ran through this town was crowded on its flanks, with numerous stone bridges crossing the ditch, beyond which dusty walkways of weathered boards ran along the building fronts. The wood visible in this construction looked old, and most of the more recent buildings employed quarried stone and fired bricks. A forest had died making this town, but that was in a time long before the Malazan conquest.

'Hostel ahead,' Gilakas said, loud enough to be heard over the myriad sounds of the crowded street and walkways, along with the raucous calls of flycatchers and rhizan flying overhead, the latter voicing a keening hiss along with the leathery flap of their wings. Gilakas continued, 'The one with the railings on the upper floor.'

Bornu nodded and said, 'I saw it.' But his attention had been drawn to a temple dominating the intersection on this side of the hostel. A colonnade of thin pillars surrounded the entire building, but they held up no roof. Instead, surmounting each pillar was a stone-carved dog- or wolf-head. Or so he had initially surmised, but as they rode closer, those snarling heads began looking less and less canine.

A soft curse from Gilakas told Bornu that the Malazan had finally taken note of the temple. 'Again? Whence this obsession with a damned Toblakai?'

From the squat, rectangular temple itself hung rusty chains from roof's edge to the ground. Set in each link of chain was a caltrop, forming a star of sharp spikes. The unadorned stone facade of the walls behind the chain curtain was barely visible, as there were hundreds of such chains, the draping row broken only by the temple's main entrance, a single bronze-banded, tarred wooden door inset above three shallow stone steps. On the outer sides of each step was a low clay bowl from which drifted black smoke. This smoke was heavy enough to stain the stone of the steps, and all the downwind chains themselves, including the stone heads.

'What a ghastly place,' Gilakas said. 'Spare my nerves, Inquisitor, and tell me we're avoiding it.'

Smiling, Bornu Blatt shrugged. 'As you like . . . for now. Let us see if there's room at the hostel.'

'I see stables attached to it,' Gilakas added. 'Good sign.'

Twisting round, Bornu caught the attention of Gracer and Stult. He gestured towards the hostel and both riders nodded. It had been a long day.

At that moment, as they approached the intersection, the door to the temple on their right opened with a squeal of hinges. Glancing over at the sound, Bornu squinted, and then reined in.

Gilakas rode on for a few steps and then, seeing that he was alone, turned his head, scowled, and halted his own mount.

The figure standing in the temple's doorway was still hidden in shadows, but its bulk filled the entire space.

Bornu Blatt sensed its attention. He sighed, and then dismounted.

He had never imagined his life as worthy of such notice, beyond the macabre fascination some held with his ugliness. But now, wrapped as he was in the presence of a goddess, it seemed that he blazed bright as a beacon – at least to some people. High priests of rival cults to be sure. Turning to the others, he said, 'Proceed to the hostel. I will find you there shortly.'

Gracer sniffed, evincing her irritation. 'If Gilakas won't guard you, then I will.'

'No need for anyone to guard me,' Bornu replied, 'beyond that provided by the goddess herself.'

'So it's like that again, is it?' Gilakas muttered in a grumble. To the others he said, 'Let's go and leave him to it. I've had my fill of earthquakes, volcanoes, catching fire and hoary undead in bad moods.'

'I don't take orders from you,' Gracer snapped.

'Fine, you two can sleep in the ditch.'

The three continued on towards the hostel, with Stult adding the reins of Bornu's horse to his train of beasts.

All these days in the saddle had settled a deep ache in Bornu's lower back. Worse, he even smelled like a horse. Pushing down his general irritation, he strode towards the temple and its huge, brooding resident.

Reaching the spindly columns with their snarling trophy-heads of stone, Bornu halted. He could see more of the figure now, including the shattered-glass tattoo on the broad, scarred visage. Raising his voice, he asked, 'An affectation of the cult, or truly once an escaped slave?'

The figure made no reply. After a moment, one gauntleted hand gestured in invitation, and then the figure stepped back into the alcove or atrium beyond, retreating into shadows.

Bornu Blatt followed the man inside.

The temple was newly built. Beyond the unlit apse a chamber opened out, the murals on its walls brightly coloured and devoid of chips or scars. Oil-lamp bowls set on the floor beneath the paintings cast upward rich golden light, bathing the chamber with a warmth that surprised Bornu, especially given the mostly fanciful, blood- and gore-spattered depictions of the god Toblakai amidst his myriad triumphs and conquests. By measure of the illustrations, the newly raised god had left in his wake enough destruction and death to shame an army. The past was a fertile field for even the most unlikely harvests of glory, he reflected.

Standing just within the entrance, Bornu watched as the lone occupant strode towards the far wall, where a knee-high, rectangular, solid stone altar dominated that end of the room. Upon this altar were the leavings of supper: a single pewter plate crowded with picked chicken bones, a plain tin goblet with a clay jug of wine standing beside it, and half a head of lettuce that had seen large bites taken out of it. Off to one side, tucked in a corner, was a cooking brazier with faint, dying coals in its bed.

The occupant in question was almost half again as tall as Bornu, the

Toblakai contribution to his ancestry undeniable. The ceiling above his head was close enough to touch his bound-back mane of hair, and as he walked, each brief contact made him duck. Reaching the altar, he straddled it and sat down, collecting up the jug. Before refilling the goblet before him, he paused and glanced over at Bornu. 'Join me,' he said in a rumbling voice. 'The wine is passing fair, but the more it breathes, the more it edges to a vinegar aftertaste.' He seemed to consider his own words for a moment, and then continued, 'Not that I mind, too much. There is much to be said for the health benefits of vinegar. More than of wine, to be sure. Come, Inquisitor, be not shy. I mean you no harm.'

Bornu walked to join the man.

Reaching down behind the altar, the half-blood produced another goblet, this one dusty and dented. He used the sleeve of his linen shirt to wipe it clean. 'Apologies. Guests are few. To be more precise, you are the first.' He hesitated again as Bornu reached the altar, and then said, 'The plate and cups came from a burial I inadvertently opened when digging out the cornerstone pits. The bones, alas, were already crumbled to dust. From this I conclude that the grave was very old. A plate and two goblets, all plain and cheaply made, constitute a paltry assemblage of grave goods, don't you think? Seat yourself, please.'

'Upon the sanctified altar of a rival god?'

The man snorted. 'The god is not witness to everything, Inquisitor.'

'But here, surely, he must be.'

'I suppose so, but I doubt he cares. He denies his ascendancy, after all. Where he should be standing in the pantheon there is naught but empty space. No matter how insistent his followers, he remains unmoved.'

After a moment, Bornu sat, not in the straddling fashion of his host, but perched at an angle, a position his spine did not enjoy at all. 'Then why do any of you bother?'

The man's broad, flattish face creased slightly, and when he spoke, some iron had come to his tone. 'Slaves and ex-slaves deserve a god.'

'Is it to be just them?' Bornu asked. 'Forgive me, the cult of the Toblakai remains somewhat mysterious.'

'An aspect, without question. Slaves and ex-slaves. What does it take to make someone kneel? Name me the weapons threatening that person?'

'Life and death seems sufficient threat.'

'And is life a thing one must bargain to win?'

'Perhaps we all do that, every day of our lives.'

287

'Between us and the natural world, aye. Between you and me, however? The master voicing the threat presumes much.'

'While clearly able to enforce it.'

'For a time, yes. Tell me, Inquisitor, the revolution your goddess seeks, will it return us to an age of enslavement? If so, I shall modify my prayers to Toblakai, in ways unlikely to please Va'Shaik. Did you know, they knew one another?'

'So it is said.'

'In the fiery cauldron of the Whirlwind, in the very heart of Raraku. It was Toblakai who killed her tormentor. You will see the scene upon the wall to your right.'

Bornu did not turn to examine the image. 'In truth, sir, I cannot even say that my goddess seeks any sort of revolution or rebellion. You are a half-blood. By your manner of speech, I believe you have Fenn in your ancestry.'

A shrug. 'It is of no relevance. Wine?'

'Very well. Thank you.'

His host poured wine into the dented cup and passed it across to Bornu, who took it, sniffed its bouquet, then looked up at the man with raised brows. 'More than passing, sir.'

'I have cultured tastes, but this is no boast. Here in this town, it proves to be something of a curse. My previous master was to blame. A wealthy merchant with few constraints, yet possessing sufficient refined taste to be selective.'

'From whom you fled more than once,' Bornu noted, eyes on the shattered tattoo of the man's face. 'My name is Bornu Blatt—'

'Yes indeed. The great scholar of Hanar Ara.'

'I was unaware of my infamy.'

'We usually are. I am Aravath. As a bastard child I was not blessed with a second name. Even the name by which I know myself – this one I have just given you – came from my master.'

'You wish a new one?'

'If so, I've yet to earn it.'

Bornu sipped the wine. He sensed nothing of vinegar in the aftertaste. 'You built this temple. Are you now its High Priest?'

'Among the cult of Toblakai, a high priest is known as First Witness.'

'Ah, then some formal organization has taken place. Is there also a First Temple?'

'Undecided. Perhaps this one.'

'Truly?'

'I doubt it. Cullar is a small town. Besides, I have no flock.'

'And how long have you been here?'

'Almost two years.'

'The drapery of spiked chains is hardly inviting, First Witness.'

'Please, call me Aravath.'

'If you dispense with "Inquisitor". Or "Scholar", or "Librarian".'

'Well, that's a relief. The spiked chains, yes, to keep out the flying lizards. I hate flying lizards.' He paused, and then added, 'A bit overdone, I suppose.'

'And then there are the Deragoth heads.'

'Ah, you have correctly identified them. Excellent. The locals think them big dogs, or even Hounds of Shadow. Toblakai killed two Deragoth, took their heads and dragged them into his wake at the end of chains, as you'll see on the wall behind you.'

'I doubt they lasted long.'

'The heads? True, they would have eventually fallen apart. Though no account of that is given.'

'Is there anything else you wish of me, Aravath? Beyond your query on the intentions of my goddess?'

'I was compelled to make this acquaintance.'

Bornu leaned back slightly, studying Aravath's face. 'The presence of your reluctant god?'

'Perhaps. How can you tell?'

'You sense Va'Shaik within me?'

'Is she? She is certainly here, yes. Is she also *within* you, Bornu Blatt? A foreign entity in your mind, present yet closed off from you? A thing of eternal regard, too silent to be a conscience, too vigilant to be a blessing?'

A sudden lungful of breath escaped from Bornu. 'You describe it precisely, Aravath.'

'Then we have something in common.'

'So it seems. And now that you followed the impulse and here we are, what next? Do you feel any further compulsion?'

'Yes. I believe I am to convey an apology. To Va'Shaik.'

'From Toblakai?'

'If indeed it is Toblakai who compels me.'

'But you're not certain.'

289

'No, I am not.'

'Then, an apology from an unknown source.'

'Given who I am and where we sit, Toblakai more likely than any other, don't you think?'

Bornu nodded. 'There is that. I cannot tell if my goddess is satisfied.'

Aravath shrugged. 'We've done what we could. Is this our purpose, then, to be the mortal vessels of immortal intentions, desires, even discourse such as we are having here? If so, I am discontented.'

Eyes narrowing, Bornu finished the wine in his goblet, then held it out for a refill, which arrived swiftly enough. 'Your reason, Aravath?'

'Flawed as we mortals are, we are bound to disappoint.'

'I can't argue with that.'

'In fact, with the vagueness of said expectations, failure is pretty much guaranteed. As pieces in a game with unknown rules, I hear the rattle of chains I cannot see.'

'Perhaps,' Bornu ventured, 'this is precisely why Toblakai resists the call to godhood.'

Aravath seemed to rock back slightly. 'Master and slave, he recognizes the inherent truth of all worship! By the Severed Heads, Bornu Blatt, you may be on to something. If indeed this is the source of his reluctance, well, can I blame him? Yet, how can one avoid the contradiction? If he is to be the god of slaves and ex-slaves, is he not then their master?'

'It may follow that to become an ex-slave is also to win free of worship.'

Nodding, Aravath said, 'The god seeks the *divestment* of his worshippers, as symbolized among mortals by their escape from slavery. His blessing therefore becomes freedom itself. Scholar, you astound me with your insight.'

Bornu grunted. 'Well, it makes a kind of sense. In a typically Toblakai way.'

*   *   *

'He looks drunk,' Gracer said, watching the Inquisitor amble up the dusty street towards them. She stood with arms crossed, leaning against the wall beside the hostel's entrance. Stult was seated on the second step above the walkway, while Gilakas was inside, in the tavern section, doing whatever he was doing. Probably eating. Gracer had decided to wait for Bornu Blatt before taking a meal. Stult despised the Malazan spy and so he remained in her company.

'He is that. Unusual.'

Gracer grunted. 'It's pointless trying to figure out that man. Or his goddess. Imagine, calling on Malazan marines. What are we to make of that?'

'Saved our skins, though,' Stult pointed out. 'The Inquisitor would've gotten us killed by Futhar's band. Well, you and me anyway. No doubt his goddess would've spared *him*.'

All of that was probably true, but Gracer felt no need to say anything. Even in conversation, Stult took too much from the thinnest gruel, no matter how plain she'd made her disinterest in what he wanted from her. He seemed oblivious to the message. What else could she do to cut him away from her life, her future? Worse than a stray pup, was Stult. Still, in spite of all of that, she often knew comfort in his company. So, she wondered, how would it feel with him gone? *The loneliness of liberation can make freedom taste bitter.* That thought wasn't hers, but she'd obviously heard it somewhere, somewhen. Now, at least, she understood it. Not that it had happened yet.

Bornu finally reached them, offering up a brief nod before passing them both and entering the hostel.

Snorting, Stult stood. 'That's it? We awaited him for that?'

'Needs a belly full of food, I wager,' Gracer said. 'Go join him, Stult. I'll be in shortly.'

'If you're staying out here—'

'I'm staying out here *alone*, Stult.'

Grumbling, Stult went past her and inside.

Gracer sighed. It wasn't the best of situations, was it? Love made a mess of things, assuming it was love. Could just be infatuation, the one pearl destined to be for ever outside his reach, making its lustre all the more enticing. Or maybe he was just one of those men who, when finding what he couldn't have, promptly threw his heart down at its feet, knowing full well it was due for a stomping. A kind of deliberate self-wounding made into a life's habit. Some endless ledger of disappointment to wear in the guise of hard-won wisdom. But there was no wisdom won in making the same mistakes over and over again, was there?

She'd taken Futhar's measure and done what she'd had to do, which was flee, get as far away from that sick bastard as she could. Running into him a second time had been damned unfortunate. Only to have it all turn out well, anyway. She'd heard enough details when the marines trudged back to the camp to know that Futhar had been handed over to the villagers, and what had followed hadn't been pretty.

Good. Just what the man deserved.

But Arat as a prisoner, that was disturbing. Mage-talent was a commodity for sure. Could buy a person their life, and that was unfair to everyone else, wasn't it? Typical Malazan thinking, though. Find something useful, make it your own. Failing that, crush it utterly. Clearly, Futhar himself had been beyond redemption, suggesting that even the empire had standards.

The foot traffic on the street before her kept the dust in the air, but she remained where she was, since the sunlight was lingering. It had been some time since she'd last felt relaxed enough to just settle back and watch people pass by. No tension gripped her neck and shoulders. Her gaze didn't flick nervously from one stranger to the next, riding the jagged edge of fear. What made all of that sour was where this comfort came from.

The damned Malazan Empire. Its mailed fist of law, order and peace.

So what is it we're railing against, anyway?

But she well knew the answer to that. No one liked being told what to do.

Hearing chanting from the left, she shifted her gaze. A procession was coming up the main street. Black-feather cloaks swathed a half-dozen figures at the centre. In the forefront walked four children, bent beneath the weight of leather sacks. With each solemn stride, the children dipped their white-dusted hands into the sacks, pulling out fistfuls of crushed, burnt fragments of bone, that they scattered onto the path before them.

At the very least, Gracer observed, they were on the street, not the raised walkway. No wonder it was so dusty, if this kind of thing was going on every few days. From the muted reaction of others in the street, it clearly wasn't an uncommon sight.

Taking up the tail of the procession walked two more acolytes, these ones carrying banners made of long tribal spears or lances, the shafts intricately carved. In place of spear-heads were two crow-wings bound to a wooden cruciform, spread wide.

If the cult of Va'Shaik had a true rival, it was this one. Everything surrounding the Fall, all the Coltaine nonsense, the Knowing Sacrifice and the Immortal Arrow, there was something formidable hidden in there, somewhere. How many witnessed that death? As far as these cultists were concerned, every damned one of them. The truth? Hardly anyone, she suspected.

Strange that a defeat could lead to a resurrection, that failure could become a virtue. Then again, who didn't know loss in their lives? Who didn't lift tear-stained eyes to the heavens in search of hope, a better future? *Some reason for all of it, somewhere at the end. Something, anything.*

Sudden shouts to her right and she turned to see a new procession, more a mob, actually, marching fast to intersect the Crow cultists. Telabas dyed the hue of rust, or red sand, the gauzy veils of desert-dwellers fluttering like spider's webs in front of every face. *Va'Shaikists.*

The sudden tension among onlookers told Gracer that this was new, unexpected.

The children with their heavy sacks were suddenly backing away, shrinking into the clutch of cloaked priests. One boy stumbled and fell, pulled over and to one side by his heavy bag of bones. In that moment, the newcomers rushed forward, collided with the procession.

Fists flew. Knives flashed. Someone screamed.

The fallen child had been battered into the ground, small limbs flopping amidst dust and ashes.

Cursing under her breath, Gracer drew her long-knife and moved down into the press.

'Back away! You're killing the boy! Back off!'

But none paid her any heed.

Then a man lunged into her path, thrusting a dagger towards her gut. The blade's point bit into her hauberk's chain-links even as she twisted to one side, snapping the weapon out of the man's hand. As he reached up with his other hand to grip her throat, Gracer's patience ended. The long-knife's edge whispered across her attacker's throat, under his beard. It slid deeper, at an angle, and was only slowed - briefly - when it cut through a vertebra, slicing the bone in half. As the long, narrow blade emerged on the other side, the man's head fell onto his right shoulder, the bulging eyes blank, emptied of life. An instant later, blood shot upward from the stump of the neck. Head and body sank from sight.

Cursing again, Gracer pushed ahead, reaching down to close one hand around a thin, dirty arm, lifting the boy into view.

His head lolled, limbs limp, his small round face swollen, bruised and smeared in grime.

Hard to tell if he still lived.

Backing from the still heaving press, she raised her weapon, daring anyone to challenge her retreat.

Someone finally noticed the severed head jostled about underfoot.

'She killed Nazra! She cut his head clean off!'

Three Va'Shaikists swung to face Gracer. Two with clubs, the middle one gripping a short-handled axe.

'Don't die for this,' Gracer said in a growl. 'He tried to kill me. I'm saving a child, damn you!'

'Fucking Crow imp,' the original speaker – the man with the axe – now snarled. 'Lookin' pretty dead t'me, woman. You wasted your time – and killed a good man!'

'Your good man tried to disembowel me.'

'And you deserved it for interfering, bird-fucker!'

The man on the left attacked, but managed to pull back before Gracer skewered him, although he then lost his balance and dropped to one knee.

Taking advantage of that, she kicked under his chin. The way his head snapped back, and the sound that made, told them all that his life had just ended.

With a roar, the man with the axe charged her.

Still gripping the dangling body of the child, held slightly behind her to keep it away from the weapon now coming at her, Gracer brought her long-knife up, intersecting with the hand swinging the axe. The point punched deep into the heel of the man's palm. His fingers spasmed open, but the axe continued its path, the head burying itself in her right forearm.

Now that's bad luck.

Her own weapon fell with a clatter as the shock of the wound ripped through her.

The third man, clutching a two-handed cudgel of some sort, now closed, swinging for her head.

A spear-shaft parried it, the shaft sliding over the cudgel then pulling back horizontally to slam into the man's face, across the bridge of his nose—

Barely comprehending, Gracer stumbled back another step.

The spear had been one of the banners, though its double-winged head had been broken off. Its wielder had just moved up behind her attacker, and now the shaft dipped beneath the shattered nose to close up across the throat. That second impact collapsed the trachea. Gracer stared at her attacker's dying face, the purpling flush of asphyxiation, the bursting eyes, the confusion and disbelief, and finally, the going away into the place no one alive could follow.

Eyes lifting, she looked up into the face of the priest who still held the spear. But his attention was on the child.

As the body between them fell, the priest stepped over it and readied the spear again. 'Drop him or die.'

'You blind fool,' Gracer said in a rasp, fighting to stay conscious as the shock of the axe-blade driven between the bones of her wrist began its inexorable spread through her body. 'I tried to save him.'

'Put him down.'

Shaking her head, she let the body settle onto the boards, then released the tiny arm.

A moment later, Stult was at her side, his features twisted, and Gilakas was speaking from somewhere off to the left, but everything was crowding everything else, even as daylight shrank down, then winked out.

There it is, Stult, into the place where you can't follow. Finally.

*   *   *

Something cold, almost icy, flooded through Bornu Blatt, delivering a sudden sobriety he did not find welcome. He stood on the landing in front of the hostel, struggling to make sense of the chaos before him. To his left, Gilakas had a knife, half-raised, in each hand, hesitating between attacking or defending, as a few bedraggled, dust-smeared Crow cultists faced him, all of them shouting, adding their incomprehensible voices to the screams, cries and shrieks of pain coming from the wounded and dying figures lying in the street. Amidst that scattering of bodies were more than a few that did not move, nor make any sound. And off to one side was a severed head, patchy with dust and blood, the eyes already fly-clumped and swarming, the gaping mouth a dark cave.

At the foot of the steps, almost directly in front of Bornu, Stult knelt beside Gracer, her head in his lap, her eyes closed as if asleep. The woman's right wrist was split open, with an axe wedged between the bones. The blood that had gushed down from that made a puddle of black mud where the street met the wooden steps.

There were two flavours of horror within Bornu Blatt, seemingly at war. His own and that of the goddess. One of them raged with fury. The other wanted to weep. It was impossible to tell which was which. After a

295

moment that seemed eternal, he managed to step down, and step again, until he could crouch above Gracer.

'Does she live?'

Stult lifted his gaze, his expression ravaged, desolate. He sought to speak, then failed, his attention collapsing back down. He began stroking Gracer's face.

A garrison detachment had made an appearance from further up the main street, and that was enough to scatter the cultists, only a few bothering to help their wounded comrades. The living ones left lying wept and pleaded, and were ignored.

Gilakas appeared at Bornu's side. 'That's foul luck,' he said in a growl. 'She bled out fast, and you can see why.'

A strange crooning sound came from Stult, and he began rocking back and forth, one hand struggling to keep the hair from Gracer's face, but a wind was now blowing, hot and fetid. Telabas and cloaks began flapping among the otherwise motionless bodies lying in the street. The sound reminded Bornu of wet laundry being shaken out before it was hung to dry. A snapping thud, a sound both eager and punctuated, over and over again as the wind pulled and tugged like an old woman battling a sheet. Or was it more like a flag above an army? But this battle had come and gone, and there was nothing left worth claiming.

'Took a man's head clean off,' Gilakas continued. 'That's her long-knife, there on the street. Impressive cut, but she kept it sharp, didn't she? I didn't not like her, you know.'

Three town guards arrived. One, a Mezla and a sergeant by the sigil on his half-cape, positioned himself in front of Bornu, who had straightened and ascended the steps to the walkway. Thumbs tucked into his belt, the sergeant stared up at the Inquisitor. His two companions moved out to examine the bodies in the street.

'You happy now?' the sergeant asked.

Bornu frowned. 'Your question confuses me.'

'I trust you're just passing through,' the sergeant continued. 'On your way to G'danisban, where, with luck, the High Fist's prepared you a warm welcome.'

'I don't think—'

'So, one night's stay here in Cullar. Just the one, and no lingering tomorrow morning, either. We'll have an escort waiting here a bell after dawn, t'see you on your way.'

Someone screamed in the street. Bornu's attention shifted in time to see one of the guards straightening from a body, her short-sword lifting into view above threads of blood that the wind stretched out briefly before taking away.

'I did not summon the followers of Va'Shaik,' Bornu Blatt told the sergeant. 'I was unaware of them at all, having just arrived.'

'Oh, they've been eagerly awaiting your arrival, Inquisitor. And wanted to put on a performance, it seems. They're holed up in the temple now, I'd wager.' He paused, and then said, 'Not sure why they think we hold to laws of sanctuary. We don't. Never did. Must be a local thing, that idea. As if your chosen god's happy to see you scuttle under an arm when you've gone and done horrible things.'

'All dead,' one of the guards reported, coming up with her companion to once more flank the sergeant. 'We think only two or three Crows survived.'

'And the orphans?'

'Three dead, one missing.'

The sergeant sighed. 'That's it, then. No more handing orphans into the care of *any* temple.'

'We'd be better off taking them into our ranks,' the guard said.

The sergeant turned to her. 'Who? Us?'

'Legion ranks, I meant.'

'Legion's leaving, Mult.'

'I know,' the guard named Mult replied.

Bornu spoke, 'Excuse me, Sergeant. Did you say the Va'Shaik cultists have fled to their temple?'

'I did. Why, you want to join them? You can, you know. That'll make things cleaner.'

'Cleaner?'

'We're about to go there and kill 'em all. We find you in there, why, we'll be doing the empire a favour. Or doing the High Fist a favour, anyway. As if G'danisban needs you.'

'I see,' said Bornu. 'Very well, hear me now, Sergeant. The Goddess Va'Shaik is with me. She insists that we now go to her temple here in Cullar.'

The sergeant turned his head and spat into the dust, then, with bared teeth, he said, 'Like I said, we ain't stopping you.'

Gilakas then spoke up. 'Sergeant, you would do well to heed this warning.'

'It's a warning, is it?'

Bornu said, 'Va'Shaik will deal with this herself.'

'Will she, now?'

Descending a few steps, Gilakas positioned himself between Bornu and the sergeant. The flanking guards both readied their short-swords. 'Ignore the temple, Sergeant,' said Gilakas. 'At least until we leave tomorrow. This evening belongs to the goddess. I say this as an agent of the empire.'

'An agent, huh?'

'Claw,' muttered Mult. 'But you never know with them, right? I say we skewer him, just in case he is. Or isn't.'

Grunting, the sergeant tilted his head. 'And what's an agent of the empire doing in the company of Va'Shaik's Inquisitor?'

'Keeping people like you out of the way, Sergeant. Until G'danisban.'

'The goddess needs an escort?'

Gilakas shrugged. 'Whose empire is this?'

'Now that's a question, all right. Listen, there's been other Inquisitors, here and there, making all kinds of mess, especially in the countryside. Murdering pilgrims and worse. Now, us garrisons, we've just about lost our patience, and with the Legion leaving, well, who d'you think's left to make things tidy again? You "agents of the empire"? I doubt it.'

'Assault the temple in the morning, Sergeant.'

'I'd like to. I really would. Thing is, a whole bunch of people just died here, and that irritates me, since I live here – for now at least – and I take my job seriously. Waiting until the morning is a bad precedent. Goddess or no goddess.'

*　　　*　　　*

Disincarnate, Va'Shaik slowly realized that physical constraint delivered no impediment to her emotions; that limitations to her rage simply did not exist. This, perhaps, was the secret power to the Whirlwind, as it once had been, and indeed to the Apocalyptic itself.

The obstinacy of these garrison guards, while annoying, was also admirable. She had no desire to impose her will upon them. Indeed, she'd rather spare their lives.

For this reason, and this reason alone, she elected to make plain her command of the situation.

Alas, the power of will rarely heeded any question of right or wrong, and too long removed from mortal considerations, the goddess thought nothing beyond her need, and its purpose. Another kind of carelessness.

Flowing into the broken, cooling body of the woman once known as Gracer, the goddess repaired what damage needed repairing, and then took hold of bone and flesh, life and breath, and, pushing away the man known as Stult, she climbed to her feet. The axe that had been buried in her right wrist fell to the ground with a thump. She raised her hand and flexed the fingers, pleased that everything seemed to be functioning in a proper manner.

Ignoring Stult's horrified cries, she swung her attention to the sergeant of the guard, and then spoke. 'I go now to my flock. Do not impede me. I will find the flavour of their rage. If it is found wanting, their lives will end.'

The sergeant's gaze did not waver. 'And if it tastes good?' he asked. 'That rage?'

She realized that she had no answer for him. 'I am their goddess,' she said. 'I will answer their prayers.'

*   *   *

Bornu and Gilakas had been on the second level of the hostel, the proprietor showing them the rooms they had been given, when the clash erupted in the street below. A mundane, marginally helpful moment on the landing above the dining area, yet it was enough to end Gracer's life. With that life having fled, no healing was possible.

Could the goddess have intervened? Reached out into the ether to drag back the woman's soul? Bornu had no idea, and before the thought even arrived in his still wine-muddled mind, Va'Shaik had, with entirely different motives, pounced.

And surely this was indeed a pounce, into the vacated vessel that was Gracer's body. What of the metal-clad golem she had occupied before? Of that apparition, no sign. No, instead, here she stood before him, wearing a face that had been at peace, and that face was not Va'Shaik's, and the peace that remained in those death-composed features, now promised horror.

Flat, dusty eyes regarded him for a long moment, then the goddess spoke. 'Inquisitor, the world grows dull.'

'It's almost dusk.'

'Ah, an explanation. Very well. Now, accompany me to the temple.'

'Why?' he asked.

It was a few moments before the goddess said, 'You wish not to? Why? Do you disapprove?'

'Disapprove? Oh, yes, I certainly do.'

'Please explain.'

'I barely know where to start. The temple's priests and acolytes, all your followers, they have done nothing wrong. As far as they are concerned, that is. Do you understand that, Goddess?'

Again there was a protracted silence from Va'Shaik. Standing nearby and with faltering patience, the Mezla sergeant was studying the undead Gracer with little expression, while behind him his squad had doubled its ranks and looked eager to go.

Noting this, Bornu said, 'Goddess, perhaps we should indeed leave this to the guards.'

'That would be untimely,' Va'Shaik replied. 'Malazan justice here could set spark to the tinder. Such things are beyond the control of anyone, even that of a goddess. We must be seen to deal with our own.'

Bornu glanced at the sergeant. 'That makes sense, doesn't it?'

Shrugging, the sergeant said, 'Starts here or starts somewhere else, does it even matter? Whatever sets it off, the details don't mean shit, Inquisitor. It's coming, and we all know it.'

Va'Shaik spoke again. 'My followers seek to begin the Apocalypse, with violence and chaos. They consider it their sacred calling, their duty.'

Nodding, Bornu said, 'Just so, Goddess, and that was my point.'

'That is not an obstacle, Inquisitor. Do you think me obtuse?'

'Obtuse? No, Goddess. I would say, indifferent to nuance.'

'How so?'

Sighing, Bornu crossed his arms. 'My second point of disapproval, Goddess. You have just possessed the body of a friend, a woman who has travelled with us for weeks now. A companion in every sense of the word. Your disregard, not only for *her* sanctity, but also for myself, Stult and Gilakas – for the life we shared with her – brief in your eyes it might seem – but to us, and given the breadth of our adventures, most worthy of respect. You leave us no opportunity to honour any of that.'

As if mocking, Va'Shaik tilted her head – Gracer's head – and then said, 'I have wandered far from my mortal memories. Those of a life lived. This was indeed careless.'

'As careless as the animation you lend the lifeless face of our friend.'

'And yet, if I leave her now, how shall I journey to the temple? I must be seen as the goddess. It must be understood by all who witness.'

'What of the golem you possessed before?'

'The golem? Ah. That was a disquieting occupation, Inquisitor.'

'Disquieting?'

'Many were the echoes of her past existence, which cannot, I believe, be called a life. To dwell within was . . . haunting.'

From one side, Gilakas snorted. 'The one who haunts is in turn haunted. Listen, Bornu Blatt, leave her the use of that body. For now. For this night. We can mourn tomorrow.'

At that, Stult suddenly pushed forward, his visage twisted with hate. 'Mezla bastard, what do you know of mourning? What do you know of—'

Gilakas had stepped close to Stult, and the sudden end to the man's rant came from the dagger blade pressing against Stult's throat. Grinning, Gilakas said, 'You at least won't be worth mourning, no matter what.'

'Put the knife away,' interjected the sergeant. 'Agent of the empire or not, this is my town. You want to commit murder right in front of me? Fine. I'll hang you.'

Gilakas twisted round to glare at the man. 'In the Emperor's name I can do as I damned well please!'

Grunting, the sergeant said, 'So can I.' Even as he said these words, his fist flew out, crunching hard into Gilakas's face. As the Claw's head snapped back – his eyes wide in shock – another hand appeared to grasp the wrist above the hand holding the dagger, this one from the guard, Mult, who had somehow appeared directly behind Gilakas. Twisting that wrist, she forced the knife to fall from senseless fingers. Then, dragging the stunned man around, she kneed him in the groin.

Gilakas collapsed, curling around his agony.

Frowning, Bornu Blatt stepped back, his eyes narrowing on the sergeant, and then on Mult, and then, at last, on the rest of the squad. 'You're not town guards,' he said.

'We are,' the sergeant replied. 'That is, we're also Legion, this squad, anyway. Temporarily stationed to bolster the local garrison.'

Mult cackled. 'Three years' temporarily stationed!'

'Posting's ending,' the sergeant pointed out in a tone suggesting he'd had this discussion with Mult more than once of late. 'But until it does, this town's mine to police, and that's that.' Stepping forward, he looked down at Gilakas. 'What's a Claw really doing with an Inquisitor, anyway?'

'Keeping an eye on me, I expect,' Bornu answered.

'And you're fine with that? No, don't answer. I don't care. Mult, take this Claw and slap some otataral shackles on him, then drag him to the gaol. He can sleep on our coin tonight, on almost-clean straw. Inquisitor, your goddess is making a bit of a spectacle, but I get her point about being seen. So tell me you're off to the damned temple with her and I'll hold back, for now.'

Va'Shaik then spoke. 'It is already too late.'

'Goddess?' Bornu asked, frowning. 'What do you mean?'

'A more precise apology is being made,' she replied.

*   *   *

Perhaps the voice in his head belonged to his god. Perhaps it was nothing more than his conscience, all tangled up with the madness that came from a lifetime of degradation and suffering. To see the wise speaker set to one side, and to hear it murmuring of sympathy, even compassion, while all else within the head did what needed doing.

Aravath confessed to no real understanding of this. His very role as First Witness was suspect, although it seemed that the assertion alone was sufficient to convince others of its veracity. But no true investment had taken place. No order had conveyed the sacraments. Even the holy tattoo obscuring his face had been earned in the traditional fashion; namely, escape and subsequent recapture. And as for the final winning of freedom, well, that had been a legal manumission, bowing to the will of his late master.

No explosive unleashing of liberation in the spraying of blood, then. Rather, simply a meek departure from an estate still locked in its gloomy state of mourning. And while many a slave did weep over that passing, what meaning could be taken from that? *The child still loves the abusive parent.* Accordingly, how could any of this be a surprise?

He'd wanted his anger to be righteous, a thing to wield in a clash of violence against all oppressors, both real and imagined. That particular kind of madness had its appeal. Or was that being too honest? This laying out a justification that justified nothing at all, but simply stood in place of reason?

Va'Shaik had been a child once. Named, named and renamed. As Felisin Younger, she had known abuse and abandonment. Then abduction. Then possession, and the goddess that possessed her was a dissolute creature, yielding no regard for physical well-being. In this respect, the legacy of abuse had never ended, and the indifference to whatever mortal vessel the goddess commandeered was a poor substitute to reconciling the damage done to it.

Aravath wasn't entirely behind this apology. In fact, Toblakai did not strike him as an apologetic god, unless simple acknowledgement could serve as apology, and this would be, it seemed, at least an acknowledgement. Of some sort. If the old tales were true, then Toblakai had indeed punished Felisin Younger's abuser. It was just the timing that was unfortunate.

Then again, what orphan did not know suffering? To be severed from mother and father was not a thing to be disregarded, nor its difficult legacy so deftly dismissed.

Bornu Blatt had spoken of Aravath's *Fenn* heritage. But such traits as he had inherited from the Fenn was all he knew of his parentage. And so, as with Felisin Younger herself, he too was an orphan. This limited a person's past in curious ways, though he could not yet make sense of how. Was the eternal dislocation within him part of that? This disconnected voice that might or might not be a god? This whispering possibility of madness?

The Temple of the Apocalyptic was one of the oldest constructions in Cullar. Raised early in the history of the Whirlwind Cult, it had weathered well the Malazan conquest and the First Rebellion, and then the rebellion's collapse and the end of the Whirlwind itself. Some edifices had a way of outliving their history, wearing them like layers of paint, like new murals over old murals, turning their very age into armour.

Trails of blood dotted the dusty street leading up to the temple entrance. A retreat of the wounded laid out in sacrificial spatters. And why not, he told himself, when blood too was a kind of paint?

His approach had been noted – perhaps via one of the murder-holes flanking the entranceway – and three figures emerged to block his path. Short-handled axes seemed to be the weapon of choice, and all three axes on display had seen recent use.

'You were next, one way or the other,' the woman in the middle said. 'Cullar belongs to Va'Shaik.'

One of the others then spoke. 'We watched you build your temple. One man alone, we did not think you would finish it. Then we awaited your followers, but they never came. So, we will make you an offer.'

'What can you offer me?' Aravath asked.

'Coin, to buy your temple. To use as an annexe. De-sanctified, of course. You built well, no denying that.'

The third acolyte barked a laugh. 'But we'll do without the chains and the dog-heads.'

'I have never known wealth,' Aravath admitted. 'Accordingly, I should long for it. But I do not. In any case, my master left me with a stipend following his death. It was his thought that I purchase a farm, land to work, grapes to grow.'

'You fail to convince,' said the woman. 'Your shattered face announces your criminal past.'

'Until my final master, I did indeed seek to escape, many times. From other masters. But in the end, I was legally freed.'

'Doesn't matter,' the woman said, shrugging. 'You can lie all you want. The choice is simple. You can have coin. Or we can kill you and just take your temple. Hurug here has a generous heart. Says he respects the law and proper ways of doing things. He's never been cheated, you see. Or betrayed. That makes him a fool, since we all know what's coming his way sooner or later.'

'Besides,' added the third acolyte, 'you don't even have any armour. And I can't see a weapon. So a fight's not what you're here for, is it? That was smart of you, since our blood's up. Take the coin and leave. We're about to head off to finish the last of the Crows. Show him the bag of coins, Hurug. It's almost a fair price.'

Aravath sighed. 'Under normal circumstances, I would happily accept your offer, as it seems no followers will find me – or my temple – here in Cullar.'

'True enough.'

'Alas, I am not here entirely of my own accord. I am afraid something is approaching, in my wake. Which, if you know anything of Toblakai, is most apt.'

Behind the wind, there had been a certain sound coming from farther down the street, frenzied, chaotic, many-voiced, slowly rising as it drew closer, and above it was a dust cloud, lifting ever higher and dragged into wild swirls with every gust, spinning round and rolling in its advance above the main street. If other sounds accompanied all of this, such as shouts or even screams, the wind and whatever approached swallowed them up.

304

The three Va'Shaikists were finally looking alarmed. The double doors behind them opened and a half-dozen more acolytes emerged, their telabas whipping in the wind, axes or clubs in their hands.

'What comes?' the woman demanded. 'What have you summoned?'

Aravath shrugged. He had to raise his voice when he replied. 'Not me. That is, I don't think it is mine. Is my god here? I believe he may be. I believe he has his own answer to the Whirlwind of old. In any case, violence and abuse in the name of *any* deity offends Toblakai.' He paused. 'I surmise.'

And now the source of the chattering, seething, shivering noise lunged into view. Filling the entire street, wrapped in spinning dust and writhing like frenzied serpents, were all the chains that had previously girdled the Temple of Toblakai. The apparition heaved forward, as if the spiked chains wrapped round an invisible behemoth, with every chain in ceaseless motion, the links rasping, the caltrops clicking and snapping, all of this making a sound that was horror incarnate.

Like a hundred wolves feeding on a battlefield, if such wolves had fangs of iron. But even this evocation failed as far as Aravath was concerned. There was also the spinning wind, the sleeting sand and dust. And above all, there was the *will* behind the manifestation.

Moving to one side, Aravath watched the churning, flailing chains tumble and roll towards the temple.

Wisely, the acolytes broke and ran.

Two drew too close in their flight, and chains whipped out, caught them, dragged them shrieking into the centre of the glittering mass. In an instant the suspended dust and grit turned red, the convulsing white clouds shifting into shades of pink, and a sticky rain fell.

Reaching the steps, the apparition that Aravath had elected to call the 'Wake of Toblakai' began tearing the temple apart.

He moved well back then, to avoid the flying pieces of stone.

It was, Aravath concluded, a most peculiar apology.

*   *   *

Va'Shaik, still clothed in the cold flesh of Gracer, stood facing what little remained of her temple in Cullar. Standing beside her in the street, Bornu Blatt reached up and rubbed the back of his neck. A headache was building in the wake of the wine he had drunk earlier. His throat was parched with all the drifting clouds of chalky dust.

He saw First Witness Aravath seated on a stone trough opposite the scoured floor of cracked and gouged tiles that, along with four corner stones, marked where the temple had once stood. Heaped around him and filling half of the street was a mound of heavy chains – it was a few moments before Bornu recognized them as having last been seen on the Toblakai Temple.

How had they come to be here? He turned to his goddess. 'What has happened? Do you comprehend this, Va'Shaik?'

Hearing a scuffling behind them, Bornu turned to see Stult standing a few paces back, like a dog uncertain of its welcome. His gaze was fixed upon Gracer, of course, but Bornu could not make sense of the expression on the man's hairless, round face.

'We must blame Icarium,' Va'Shaik said, her voice cracking, as if emerging from a throat gone dry. 'This is the flux of his new Warrens, a deep and wide river of magic, in which you will find many swirling pockets of madness.'

'But where have your followers gone?'

'Those who could flee did so,' she replied. 'The Malazans will hunt them down, at least the ones who have not departed the settlement. Those who sheltered within the temple are no more.' She turned away from the scene and looked upon Aravath. 'My interest in engaging Toblakai is at an end.'

Bornu squinted at the huge figure. 'He was ever a reluctant participant.'

'The mortal or his god?'

'Both, probably. You do not wonder what he plans next?'

'No.'

'Well, I do.' He set out across the street. Reaching the edge of the heaped chains, he saw that the caltrops driven between every link were brightly polished but mostly blunted, as if heavily worn down. A few were bent, claw-like, their points ragged. Bits of dirty meat gummed the chain-links.

'The spikes will heal,' Aravath said from where he sat. 'I would not advise you come closer, my friend. Quiescent is not the same as lifeless.'

'They were somehow animated? I wish I had seen that.'

'Be glad you didn't. Those who did appear to have been driven mad. I may be the only exception to that. All others fled. The Wake of Toblakai, when fully unleashed, becomes a whirlwind of iron, Bornu Blatt. Even stone walls cannot stand before it.' He paused, and then said, 'But I do not think that is its purpose. Something else awaits it.'

'Sounds ominous, Aravath. Do you lead it, or are you led?'

'I am led, I believe.'

'Then these chains are destined to . . . move again.'

'Yes. My discontent deepens.'

'Why?'

'I spent weeks painting those murals. Never mind building the temple. No, it's the murals, Bornu Blatt. All that effort. All the minerals I ground into paint, all the binders and oils. The compositions, the sketches. When I was done, it felt like my life's work.'

Bornu considered the man's despondent words. 'I doubt your temple will be immediately occupied by anyone else, First Witness. When I arrive in G'danisban, I will find your followers and inform them of your temple here. They will send a mission. I am certain of that.'

'Before or after the rebellion ignites all of Seven Cities?'

'I will do my best,' Bornu promised.

After a moment, Aravath sighed, and then stood. 'If I lock it up, leave the tooth-claws with the garrison—'

'Tooth-claws?'

'The locks are elaborate. So too the keys. So much so that I struggle to call them keys.'

'Tooth-claws.'

'Just so. In any case, I will do what I can, then, to keep the temple secure. Thank you, Inquisitor, for your offer. I will go now and assemble my gear, should the journey be long. And you, sir? When do you depart for G'danisban?'

'Tomorrow morning, I suspect. It's been a difficult day.'

'In your company, Bornu Blatt, dying is risky.'

Bornu turned to see Va'Shaik watching them both. But it was Gracer that he saw, of course. Rather, the mask of who she had once been, and was no longer. 'Does her soul linger, do you think?'

Aravath frowned. 'The cult of Toblakai has an understanding of the binding of souls, Bornu Blatt.' His attention dropped to the glittering heap of chains. 'A few are already bound to this thing.'

Frowning, Bornu then shook his head. 'Such a thing seems anathema to the ethos of your cult, or have I misunderstood the aversion to slavery?'

'You haven't,' Aravath admitted. 'I do not understand the purpose of the Wake. We must see it as a weapon, I think, one eager to invest itself with the souls of its victims. There is precedent to this, yes?'

'Probably, if certain poets wrote of things that were real.'

'Well, they often do.'

Bornu nodded.

On the other side of the street, Gracer had turned and was now walking away, returning, perhaps, to the hostel. Stult followed.

Aravath now asked, 'Do you await the Malazans?'

'Here? Ah. No, I think that won't be necessary. The temple's fate, after all, is self-evident. And no doubt any surviving witnesses to the destruction itself will be able to fill in the details. That said, Aravath, I don't think they will welcome your restless chains. This thing you call the Wake.'

'I can see your point. Well, I am off, then.' He paused, shifting his attention to the chains. He pointed and said, 'Stay.'

Bornu Blatt blinked. A moment later, he set out after his goddess. For now, at least, he was not inclined to intercede on Gilakas's behalf. He'd collect up the man in the morning. A night in a cell might do wonders for his humility.

And why not? It may be that Icarium is not yet out of miracles.

CHAPTER TWELVE

'I decry the virtue of suffering,'
said the man on his knees.
'I have seen sacks upon the shoulder
making a burden of peace and silence,
these things we carry
from place to place.
But now you speak to me
of value found in the distinction
between these pendulous bags
and upon the stony ground,
my knees' bloody kiss.
So tell me a hidden truth
to wet my parched throat
and bring ease to this most
dreadful virtue.'

Ninth Beseeching
Awaiting Answer
at Toblakai's feet
Darujhistan in the
Days before the Awakening

'*Their voices were incessant in the deep, chambered wombs of the sunken city. To human ears, perhaps childlike in their ceaseless murmuring, the chuckle and trickle and measured drip, the chattering swirl and spinning spiral, the gulps and swallows, the hitches and watery sighs, but there was nothing childlike in their essence. The spirits of water were old, old beyond measure. They were the blood of life's first rising, godlings of current and flow,* rise and fall to the moon's contrary whims. They spoke, endlessly, of beginnings, and when they could speak no longer, when the world brought sun and heat, and pools dwindled and mud hardened to stone, they died. Only to be reborn beneath the weeping skies.

'These spirits, godlings still, had slept for millennia in the sands of Raraku, but now the waters had returned, rebirth a fulmination of potential and growth, and in rising, the waters gentled the sun's fierce glare above that vast stretch of sand, and elsewhere, the waters flowed beneath rock and hills of layered stone sediment. Unheard the cacophony of voices, far beneath the feet of surface-dwellers, until such time that the godlings seeped into the ruins beneath G'danisban, and into other submerged places well inland from the shores of the Raraku Sea, to fashion an unseen girdle of rivers, streams, chutes and flows, all one, interconnected, bound in veins and arteries of restless life.

'A great heart resided under Bastran Hill. Its beat was too slow for mortal senses, but its heat was palpable, and where water touched its stony sides, steam rose. The water swirled round it in a sodden moat, and above it, where collapsed buildings made a domed ceiling of crushed layers of brick, rubble, mortar and sand, rain descended in steady deluge.

'The heart's carved lines and angles were softened now, after a near decade of this rain. But none of this weakened the life-force within it. Nor were the godlings of water eager in their assault upon its foundations, for within the thick, black sediments surrounding the massive edifice waited a host of the imprisoned.

'Not all manifestations of the Azath belonged to the land. Indeed, the majority of the Azath Houses' first generation were children of the sea's dark, unlit depths, born in the time when water was life's only realm.

'Who could say what manner of beings walked – if walked they did – upon the sea-bottom in this ancient time, each step raising a bloom of sediments even as it thundered and shook the bedrock? But of vast, terrible powers existing there could be no doubt.

'The Azath will rise to meet the need. To take within it and beneath its soils all those who would break the world. Yet even this impulse to mitigate, to preserve a balance, is but part of a greater necessity.

'To live there must be a heart, the muscled pump to regulate the rhythm of purpose that is life itself.

'And, so it follows, to be the guardian of such a heart is the highest calling imaginable.

'Unfortunate, then, that such guardians were, almost without exception, reluctant residents.'

The seated figure hunched over the table paused, quill hovering above the parchment. Then, setting down the quill, one elongated, spindly hand closed about the sheet and crumpled it. 'Oh, what's the point?'

The voice was feminine, curiously dry in this humid, steamy chamber where she sat, and even as the words were uttered, the closeness of the air swallowed each one, leaving no chance of echo or resonance. Nor was there a companion to hear her complaint, or give answer. She was alone.

'And what of it? To indulge in the wonder and majesty of language is to offend those for whom language is a mere scatter of leavings in a cavernous vault, of such penurious state as to invite despair; yet those will in turn unleash no end of disdain in their condemnation of anyone for whom language is magic. Yet magic is to be celebrated, is it not? Ah, but not when it exposes the reader's own paucity in said condition, oh no, not then. Never then. Purple indeed.'

Distant drips and trickles were her only replies, the godling chuckles and cackles exploiting a thousand throats, a thousand tongues, yet never once managing a true word, a clear meaning, a whispering revelation.

Guardianship, alas, was boring.

There, the pronouncement was uttered, if not out loud, then within the internal sanctum of wild, unconstrained narrative that was the mind's ceaseless chatter. It had been her thought to set down upon parchment one such blathering stream, to spew it out and so leave behind an empty wake, scoured of notion, as blank and vacuous as a vacated skull.

But even this failed in its essential intent. It was a demonstrable fact that if one held up a skull, a human skull – sure, why not? – and shouted into the nasal passage, there would come a reply from the cavernous space behind, something like a moan wrapped round an echo, managing little more than a mangled repetition of that original shout. The same for what amounted to an ear-hole, or even an eye-socket.

Accordingly, skulls, in and of themselves, had nothing to say. Nothing original, anyway.

She picked up the crumpled parchment on the desktop before her and threw it to the floor, to join myriad others amidst the piled skulls, then rose to her feet. There was activity outside, irritating activity, truth be told. Even more bemusing, the Azath's flooded yard had fed recently. Years since that had last happened. Were changes afoot?

The godlings thought so. Speaking so excitedly of the coming flood.

'Is it hot in here? It feels hot in here.'

She paused to adjust her gown, though 'gown' was perhaps somewhat excessively bold by way of description. The rags she slept in, awoke in, wore all day, and never bothered changing out of, then. But there was a curtness to 'gown', an elegant brevity, in fact. It slipped in easily and slipped out just as easily. It embraced and encompassed, enwrapped and enwreathed, and it flowed at least a little as she walked across the chamber to the door, like a ragged sigh made visible.

Down the hall, her bare feet almost soundless on the warm stones, and then down the stairs, one, two, three and so on, until the eleventh step was reached and revealed to be the floor itself, which spread out before her in a faintly glowing expanse of paving-stone-sized tiles.

Within the heart that was the Azath House awaited a near infinity of possibilities. No doubt the tiles represented that, in some arcane fashion beyond her comprehension. Being long-lived, after all, did not necessitate a confluence of interests in sorcery, or even worse, metaphysics. No, she had little interest in magic – at least, not this kind of magic. The other magic, the one touched on in her discarded treatise, was another matter entirely. It was, in fact, her obsession.

The universe was a mess of layers. Only a few were available to the senses at any one time. There was waking reality, such as surrounded her here in this chamber, and extended beyond (one assumed) to the yard and the ruins and crooked makeshift streets and alleys with their low roofs, and further still, eventually out into the sunlight and all the beings scurrying about on the world's surface. That reality, then. Another might be said to exist in dreams, or rather in the state of dreaming. It was, in the midst of its conjuration, no less real than the waking reality. Though its rules were fundamentally different.

Were there still others? Of course there were. Leave it to the truncated mind inside whatever skull housed it to delude itself otherwise. Akin to ignoring a flood as the water rose and rose, and rose some more, causing all manner of grief on account of that water being invisible. 'Unseen forces,' she muttered, eyes on the tiles with their swimming, ever-changing images, 'are always at work.' She paused, and then her tone hardened. 'Aren't they?'

From one tile, a man's figure grew into being, squat, wide-shouldered, scarred and sluicing streams of water down his muscled form. Though he rose to stand in open air now, still water appeared, as if from nowhere, to

312

run down his skin, his limbs, the pool beneath his feet growing. Lifting a gaze to her, he sighed and said, 'Things are a bit out of hand.'

She snorted. 'You think so? The bhokarala have gone mad. They deliver me skulls. Skulls, skulls and more skulls. The rooms are filling up. Every step kicks one aside. What is all of this about, Mael?'

'Skulls?' The Elder God frowned. 'I have no idea about that. Look to Shadowthrone for answers.'

'Shadowthrone? Lord Wisp himself? He passed through here once, long ago. Him and his assassin. Already half-insubstantial, like ghosts. And like all ghosts, miserable company.'

'I doubt he bore his godly name back then,' Mael observed.

She shrugged. 'The tiles tell their tales. I pay attention. Sometimes. Other times, of course, I forget about the outside world for years and years. Decades, even. But not,' she added, 'lately. So, out with it. What's going on?'

'I was manipulated. I hate being manipulated.'

'By Shadowthrone?'

'Not directly. No, a mortal in his service. Mortals! A mere handful constitute worthwhile company. But most? Azath take me, I'm tempted a dozen times a day.'

'To do what?'

He gestured, a wave of one water-shedding hand that sprayed droplets everywhere, but added no words to that gesture, since its meaning was clear.

'Flood!' she cried delightedly, clapping her hands.

'Let's call it a global bath, shall we? A cleansing long overdue.'

'Well, you're drowning this buried city. That's a start.'

'Manipulated. And it gets worse.'

'Tell me. I hang on your every word.'

He eyed her. 'What was your Forkrul name?'

She scowled, hesitating, and then sighed. 'Paucity.' She paused, added, 'I had few friends.'

'And why is that?'

'Matters of law bored me.'

He barked a half-choked laugh. 'You poor woman.'

'But now I am Guardian.'

He shook his head. 'You and who knows how many others, each once ensconced in an Azath House. You'd think there'd be some variation.

313

But no, you all choose the name of your purpose and leave it at that. I'd rather call you Paucity.'

'Why? Do you converse regularly with Guardians?'

'No. Given the choice, I avoid it.'

'And yet here you are.'

'I was in the neighbourhood.'

'Manipulated.'

'Just so.'

'Does that manipulation extend to you visiting me?'

Mael blinked, frowned, then cursed under his breath.

Paucity shifted her attention from the Elder God while he fumed and muttered, and resumed scanning the shimmering floor of the chamber. After a time, she said, 'It turns out it wasn't you who drew me down here. You were not the source of the heat and pressure. In fact, the tile you rose from wasn't of any interest to me at all. You may indeed have been lured here, to witness another arrival.'

'Well that's just great. Who is it?'

'I don't know. The more salient query would be, why here and why now?'

'Queries, not query.'

'Oh do shut up, Mael. Pedantry is my forte, not yours. Indeed, you have no idea how often I wished I had been named thus. "Friends, meet Pedantry, she hangs on your every word."'

His grunt might have been a laugh.

They stood waiting. Whatever was coming was having a difficult time of it. The air in the chamber, already hot, grew hotter still. Before long, the water streaming from Mael's bald pate and scarred body turned into steam, while all that continued streaming pathways down his skin became oily sweat. He fidgeted. 'There's nothing easy about this one, is there?'

'Clearly not a god, and certainly not an Elder God,' Paucity said, nodding. 'It – or they – travel an unfamiliar universe, one that resists passage.'

'Mortal?'

'Possibly. Mortals.'

'It gets worse.'

'Yes, it does.'

Still they waited. After a time, Paucity said, 'I have in my study a mound of crumpled pages. Hundreds of them. They constitute a book.'

'Oh joy, you can argue literary styles with Gothos.'

'No, thanks. Still, you are welcome to read it.'

'In its present form? Shall I select pages at random?'

'Since its content is a disjointed mess anyway, I don't see why not.'

'Hmm, your intended audience? I ask only because I am intimate with a Royal Library, its patron ever eager to add to the collection, and I have on occasion rescued works.'

'Oh, and does my book need rescuing?'

'Sounds like it. Of course, you may not want anyone to read it, ever. You may refuse the very notion of audience. You may disguise your fear of approbation, if not judgement, in florid terms of self-indulgent therapy—'

'That's enough, thank you. I withdraw my offer.'

'Not that I'd gainsay the value of therapy—'

'Be quiet.'

'There was one library I saved from burning—'

'Honestly, Mael, please stop. My book's audience consists of a few thousand skulls looted from the burials in the hill above us. When the air-flow is just right, they moan in a chorus of critical dismay.'

'The living are known to do the same on occasion.'

'Who is this library patron to you, anyway?'

'A king. I advise him. He advises me.'

'Why bother?'

'Well, he's utterly bonkers. But in an amusing way. He has made life so fair and equitable for his subjects that their hate for him has no limits.'

'So he's doomed. You're just hanging around to witness the inglorious, blood-soaked demise of a decent man.'

'No, he's not doomed. They are. Justice, after all, isn't really about people who are smart; it's about people who are stupid.'

Paucity's gaze sharpened on the Elder God. 'You dare speak of justice to a Forkrul Assail?'

'Why not? It's not like your kind ever understood it.'

'Point taken, and as I noted earlier, it's not my area of interest anyway. The point is, do you want my book for this library or not?'

'In its present form – a pile of crumpled pages, was it? – I would have to say, only as a work of art. Perhaps on a raised dais just inside the grand entrance. Preserved, yet at the same time unread.'

'Oh, that's genius. Will your patron agree to something like that?'

'He'll insist, as will his wife. The written word is not the only art form after all, is it?'

'Well then, it's yours.'

'Thank you, not a wasted visit after all.'

Ten or so paces behind Mael, a tile audibly cracked, then erupted upward in shards. The Elder God turned to observe.

Paucity narrowed her gaze. A huge double-bladed axe rose into view, followed a few moments later by the arm gripping its handle, then the rest of the figure, clambering upward from the gaping hole where the tile had once been. A Toblakai, or perhaps Tartheno or Thelomen or Thel Akai – she could never tell them apart. He seemed to be covered in ash and grit, as if he'd been rolling in a funeral pyre, and indeed, small fragments of white, burnt bone shed from him as he slowly straightened.

Seeing Mael, the giant bared his teeth. 'Azathanai. I hate Azathanai. Tell me, where is K'rul? Skillen Droe?'

Shrugging, Mael said, 'There's no point in hunting them down, you know. Pretty much un-killable. In fact, the less attention given them, the weaker they get. Or, rather, they become less relevant. You'd have a better chance at vengeance by ignoring them to death. Of course, this doesn't apply to just gods or Elder Gods, or Azathanai, but then, my advice is rarely heeded. Do as you will. I don't know where they are.'

The Toblakai's attention now shifted to Paucity. 'Forkrul Assail? Still not wiped out and consigned to oblivion? It seems I have work to do in this new world.'

'Ha ha,' Paucity replied. 'You are in an Azath House, and I am its guardian. Your bluster is pointless. Your threats are pointless. And being a Toblakai, you are pointless. Clearly, you've come from the realm of the dead, though how you managed that is a mystery – no, don't tell me, I'm not interested. But you're here now, and I am happy to escort you, uh, from the grounds. Safely, that is. Now, accept my invitation or go back where you came from.'

His expression twisted. 'They fed me to an Azath House.'

'Who did?'

'People. Humans.'

'But you escaped.'

'I had help.' The Toblakai then stepped out from the hole and positioned himself to one side, eyes narrow as he looked around. 'Not this Azath House, though.'

'They wander in the manner of minds wandering,' Paucity explained. 'The power of intention and desire is most formidable. Azath Houses appear in answer to mortals beseeching the universe.'

Mael cocked his head. 'Beseeching what?'

'Fairness, of course.'

'You believe this?'

She shrugged. 'It's a theory. In my long life, I yielded the obsession with justice for the simpler – if more hazy – notion that is fairness.'

'If only your kin had done the same.'

'I am late to these notions, Mael. Besides, had I argued such long ago, when I lived among my own, they would have flattened me under a rock.'

Mael grunted. 'Didn't know you did that to each other. I thought it was only everyone else eager to flatten your kind under rocks.'

'We set the precedent. One of our myriad gifts to the world.'

Now another figure was clambering into view. Slighter, human in scale, a woman. Once she rolled free, in her own cloud of white dust, she lay on her back, coughing, gasping. 'That bastard with the mask,' she said after a time.

The Toblakai replied, 'I enjoyed our beating each other senseless. In the living world, they are known as Seguleh. No one likes them.'

She turned her head to him. 'It's not even your world. How could you know all that, Grey Shore?'

'We conversed while fighting. It was most civilized. In any case, our battle permitted you to slip past, Satala, did it not? And once he decided he could not hold me in the realm of the dead, why, he stepped away. Do you know, we bowed to one another? Then discarded our wounds like dust? It was miraculous.'

Mael spoke to the woman as she slowly sat up, '*You* at least were dead, I surmise.'

She glanced across at him. 'What's it to you?'

'It's said that Iskar Jarak rarely yields what comes to his realm. Unlike Hood. The borders are most assiduously patrolled these days.'

'Soldier ghosts,' she muttered, 'what a terrible combination.' Standing, she wiped herself down. 'Where are we, and who is that horrible-looking demon?'

'Already I miss the interminable silence of the past century's delicious if maddening solitude,' Paucity said. 'I am the Guardian of the Azath House you have found yourself in. You were not invited, by the way.'

'Fine, and where is this House?'

'Beneath the city known as G'danisban.'

'Yes!' Satala hissed. 'It's where I wanted to get back to, where I died the first time around, and where that skinny mongoose of a woman is probably still prowling the rooftops. Oh, I will have her scrawny neck in my hands soon enough!'

Smiling at Mael, Paucity nodded and said, 'Intention is everything, as I told you, Mael.'

The Toblakai, whose name was apparently Grey Shore, now pointed at Mael. 'This, Satala, is Mael, the Elder God of the Seas. He was ugly when I first set eyes upon him, and ugly he remains. I've never had much luck consorting with Azathanai. I doubt this time will prove any better.'

Satala said, 'You're remembering more of your past, aren't you?'

'I am, to my regret.'

'Your name?'

'His name,' cut in Mael, 'is Kanyn Thrall. Victim of an unfortunate encounter with K'rul, Skillen Droe, and Ardata. And the Gate of Starvald Demelain. Best let bygones be bygones, Kanyn. That was long ago.'

'Not long to my mind at all!'

'Really? How about half a million years, you idiot.'

The Toblakai's jaw sagged.

'Really?' Paucity echoed.

'Give or take,' Mael replied. 'Though the truth is, time got messed up back then, in the Sundering of the Realms.'

'That sounds like a thing,' Paucity observed, '"The Sundering of the Realms".'

'Histories vanish more often than they survive,' the Elder God replied.

Satala now spoke. 'Guardian, I want out of here. We're not your prisoners or anything, are we? That would cause problems. Grey Shore has a thing about imprisonment. Is there a way to the surface? You said we're beneath the— Oh, are we in the Under Quarter? We are, aren't we? Good, I can get out easily enough.'

'You will have little choice,' Mael said. 'I'm flooding this entire rat's nest even as we speak.'

Satala turned to him. 'You've been making the waters rise? What's your problem? Stop it!'

Turning to Paucity, Mael grimaced and said, 'Stupid mortals, right?' To Satala, he then said, 'You misunderstand. I don't mean to just flood your Under Quarter. I mean to flood the entire world. Or, rather, most of it. A few islands here and there. Libraries on the hill and the like, a palace or two. But for the rest, a cleansing is long overdue.' He paused in the silence that followed his pronouncement, and then added, 'I don't like being manipulated, and I mean to show the full consequences of the abuse.'

Satala drew her knife. 'Grey Shore – or Kanyn whatever – can Elder Gods be killed?'

'No. If it had been possible, believe me I would have marched back and forth across the world back then and murdered every damned one of them.'

'I've often wondered,' ventured Paucity, 'if the Elder Gods guide the forces of nature, or just hide behind them, taking credit for things they never did.'

'A bit of both, to be honest,' Mael replied. 'It's all down to working with what you have. And what we have here, why, is ground-water. Lots and lots of ground-water. My involvement relates to denying the arrival of stasis for as long as possible. Let it rise.'

'The Jaghut will resist you,' Kanyn Thrall said in a growl. 'They'll freeze half the world to stop you.'

'Maybe. They're so irritating that way. But the truth is, Kanyn, the Jaghut have relinquished Omtose Phellack. Everywhere in this world, the ice melts, vanishes, flows down to join my realm, thus making me ever more powerful. Once they discover their error, it will be too late, for the most part. Besides, they are too few in number these days to be of any real concern.'

'Flooded world or not,' Paucity said, 'it's of no difference to me. Besides, I tire of your company – yes, all of you. Toblakai warrior and pet human, follow me. I'll lead you out. Mael, don't be here when I get back.'

'And your book?'

'Take it, as I said. For that library on the hill.'

*   *   *

The sun had fled the sky, and the deepening cerulean hue of approaching night was filled with insect clouds, bats and rhizan. High Fist Arenfall stood on the rooftop of the tower, his gaze scanning the crowded clutter of roofs spread out before him. Torches were visible here and there, wavering fistfuls of starlight moving in alleys and streets. Clothes and dyed cloths, hung to dry, were draped like shrouds from countless lines now that all wind had died away. There was the smell of smoke in the air.

He turned to Captain Hung who stood a few paces back. 'The Underhouse is best avoided.'

'The sappers agree,' Hung replied. 'Once that idiot king got swallowed up in the mud, all ambitions to claim the place more or less ended, sir. Apparently, the place was crawling with bhokarala in any case. Throwing bones.'

Arenfall's brows lifted. 'Throwing bones?'

'At passers-by. Mostly human bones, it seems.' Hung paused, and then added, 'Probably from the graves on the hill.'

'The bhokarala are looting graves?'

'Gains pointed out that not all the bones were human, and neither were all the graves. He holds the unlikely conviction that the squall-apes once buried their own.'

'Unlikely indeed.' Arenfall considered for a moment, and then said, 'Now then, it's heating up. Are your squads ready to respond?'

'Aye, High Fist. It would've helped if Captain Dunsparrow had returned with hers, especially with all her new recruits. And Corporal Hasten as well.'

Arenfall nodded. 'I can see that. Unfortunately, not likely. They have their hands full.'

'You've received a report, sir?'

'The uprising is somewhat coordinated,' Arenfall said. 'In any case, I'm ordering Veroosh and his squad out beyond the city walls. Do pass that on, please.'

'Why out there, if I may ask?'

'As escort.'

Hung was silent.

With a half-smile, Arenfall said, 'I know. No escort is likely needed. Even so, a squad present means we have witnesses to what follows, and if we need to respond, or act, well, we'll have the opportunity.'

'Sir, you are relying on Captain Veroosh's judgement for that, uh, response?'

'I'm making do. You, I'll need closer to hand.'

'I see.'

Frowning, Arenfall studied the captain in the fading light. 'Surely, at

320

least one soldier under his command has some measure of discrimination? Assessment?'

'They take their lead from their captain.'

'Oh dear.'

'All the misfits ended up in that one squad, sir. Intentionally. Assuming, I suppose, they'd trigger some disaster and end up wiped out before too long. Alas, that didn't happen.'

'No, it didn't.'

'So, considering all of that,' Hung resumed, 'your idea of getting them outside the city walls is starting to sound like genius.'

'I thought so. But it seemed you did not approve.'

Hung snorted. 'I just needed to think about it, sir. If they do that escorting, well, that'll take them back into the city anyway.'

'But any preliminary mayhem will have been avoided.'

'Exactly, and I happen to know that Veroosh's sappers are loaded up.'

'To what extent?'

'To an excessive extent, sir.'

'Gods below, you marines grow increasingly unwieldy, if not outright alarming.'

Hung made no reply.

After a few moments, Arenfall said, 'Very well, dismissed. Have the aide below direct the Adjunct to join me up here, will you?'

'Of course, sir.'

*　　　*　　　*

The title of Adjunct seemed thin, flimsy, to Hadalin. He wore it like a shroud. Following the awaited summons to that infernal rooftop, he departed his chamber, adjusting the sword-belt on his hips as he trailed a few steps behind the aide.

His otataral sword was now his constant companion, and was it not ironic that he feared Arenfall more than he did agents of Va'Shaik? Yet here he was, about to cross words with the man yet again. This time, however, he was more than prepared.

The empire was a beast in the best of times. A thousand limbs reached out from it, each with its own purpose, bearing weapons or a crushing grip, and often even the will of the mind at the centre of this vast creature was known to strain, to struggle to control each wilful, wayward limb. As the right hand of the Emperor, the Adjunct was but one of these, and

321

yet Hadalin wondered at his own command of the situation. Perhaps it was nothing more than a delusion.

Was it possible that the Emperor himself felt the same? That this beast was in truth headless, each limb acting entirely on its own? That was a disturbing thought.

Yet here, now, he would act. He believed that he had no choice. There was – he had no other way to describe it – too much of Arenfall. Inkaras Sollit had known it, had struggled with the necessities such an individual demanded. It was not that mediocrity was welcomed; rather, it was competence that, if deemed too capable, was feared.

How curious that the human mind, within its sprawling tapestry of culture, society and civilization, would so cleave to the familiar and the conservative, ready to recoil at every challenge to the status quo, whether real or imagined – and in truth, the distinction wasn't relevant most of the time. A single mind, too perspicacious, too unblinking in its regard of naked truths, too capable of challenge, could so stir awake the vast beast.

To reach out, unfurling its deadly claws.

Was Arenfall the man to crush this rebellion? Given the High Fist's discourse with this goddess, Va'Shaik herself, Hadalin was no longer so sure. Of course, it was more than that. The High Fist's reluctance to detach the marines, to send them to rejoin the Legion where it assembled on the far eastern coast, was as close to a defiance of orders as one could get.

The High Fist's reasoning was timing, and the timing – this new religious uprising – was, according to Arenfall, imminent.

Perhaps.

Perhaps not. His Claw agents in the city had reported nothing more than a minor cult-war on the streets, in the alleys and on the rooftops. Fanatics killing fanatics. Was there anything new in that? Too many believed they possessed the right to make others believe as they did, and failing that, the right to kill in the name of their faith.

Was madness inherent to that faith? To make such a call upon its believers? Well. The Apocalyptic saw its own destruction as its crowning achievement. But also insisted on taking everyone else down with it.

Of course people would resist, and why was that a surprise? Most people just wanted to get on with their lives, with those shining knots of family, loves and all the labours for sustenance and shelter. Gods take the rest.

Hadalin could see no true uprising. More a wave of senseless violence, and in answer to senseless violence, the Malazan Empire did what was necessary. That suppression was High Fist Arenfall's responsibility. No more and no less.

Leave this to me, then. And after tonight, the Claw at my disposal. We'll cut the heart out in mid-beat. Ban Ryk, Shamalle, and then this new Inquisitor on his way to the city.

The aide stepped aside at the ladder leading to the roof, and Hadalin climbed alone.

Emerging through the trapdoor, he clambered onto the rooftop. The sun was finally down, darkness claiming the world. Overhead, the stars seemed to swirl behind waves of heat, but the desert's chill was creeping in from all sides, despite the stillness of the air. Straightening and facing Arenfall, who stood in his usual place overlooking the city, Hadalin approached to within five or so paces, then halted. 'High Fist.'

Arenfall half turned. 'Adjunct. It begins tonight, I believe.'

'I see. Are your agents in place, then?'

'My agents?'

'Such as you had following me.'

'Ah. Well, I've lost more than a few to this unknown master assassin.'

Hadalin frowned. 'I am unconvinced this assassin of yours even exists, High Fist. Yes, you've lost people, but so has the other side. It's been a long, drawn-out war, after all.'

'There is an element of sorcery to this hidden assassin, Adjunct.'

'Nothing I need fear, then.'

Arenfall now faced him fully. 'Not that kind of sorcery. This is more . . . elemental. Tell me, how familiar are you with the Runts?'

'Just another variation on the Deck of Dragons,' Hadalin replied. 'Are there new warrens in play? Certainly. But twenty years ago, we saw the same, in the rise of Shadow, and then the House of Chains. The Warrens forever evolve, do they not?'

'There was a structure back then,' Arenfall said, seeming to be musing rather than engaging in an argument. 'But these Runts, these are not the same at all. No discernible structure, as if a single mind were somehow carved up, divided into disparate parts, all natural connection between the pieces lost.'

'Is this what you wished to discuss, High Fist? If so, I am not the best choice of audience, much less participant. I chose otataral to dispense with the complexities of magic. Sorcery lacks predictability, resists control.'

'More now than ever before, I should think,' Arenfall replied. 'But no, I requested your presence to inform you that tonight is when you can unleash your Claw.'

'The target? The Temple of Va'Shaik, I assume.'

'No. Take to the rooftops. Provide overwatch.'

'Overwatch for whom?'

'My marines.'

Hadalin looked away, to hide and then suppress the sneer that threatened to twist his features. He trusted to the darkness to hide his reaction to Arenfall's words. 'Given their legendary prowess, I'm surprised you feel they need it.'

'I don't mind redundancy.'

'I have other purposes in mind for my Claw,' Hadalin said.

'And they are?'

'Well, it begins here.'

The proximity Hadalin maintained with the High Fist – five paces – was enough to dampen the man's access to sorcery. But beyond this deadening sphere of otataral, nothing constrained magic at all.

The Claw struck from all sides.

The first attack came from the air opposite the rooftop's low wall, upon the city side. Suspended, Aliksos and Formult burst from warrens flashing open in the darkness, their knives barely seen darts crossing the distance between them and the High Fist.

Arenfall lived up to his reputation, in spinning away in a blur, though one knife without doubt struck home, and even as he spun, he countered with one flung knife that caught Aliksos in one shoulder. The two airborne Claws vanished back into their warrens an instant later.

Almost simultaneously with that attack, and Arenfall's sideways evasion, Ibinish, Lalt and Bulk appeared in shimmering flashes on the rooftop, rushing towards the High Fist, the first two on the man's left, the third on his right. Thrown weapons made streaking glimmers beneath the starlight.

Hadalin saw Lalt stumble, clutching at her throat, where a handle and pommel projected out from beneath her chin. Mouth spraying blood, she collapsed.

At least two more knives struck Arenfall, and before Hadalin – his otataral sword now out – could close, the High Fist pivoted on one foot and fell from the roof edge. A flash of magic from below, and when Hadalin reached the edge to look down, he saw no body on the cobbles beneath.

Bulk was half crouched above Lalt's body. 'She's dead,' he pronounced. 'But I saw four knives in the bastard.'

'Yet even so he used a warren to escape us,' Hadalin said.

'Once he dropped past your influence, Adjunct, aye. Still, he went somewhere to die and that's that. Our blades were tralb-stained.'

Aliksos and Formult reappeared, now above the rooftop. They dropped to the surface, landing in a crouch, weapons out as they scanned the area. Aliksos had withdrawn the knife from her shoulder and was breathing hard, expression knotted in pain.

Stepping towards her, Hadalin asked, 'How bad, Aliksos?'

'Could've been worse,' she replied. 'I need some salves, and sewing.'

'Arenfall predicted the uprising would begin this very night,' Hadalin said. 'Though I'm unconvinced, best stay at my side, Aliksos. Even healed, you've lost too much blood to be dancing on the rooftops tonight. The rest of you, go out and wander, but not before I've firmed up my command. As I said, I'm not convinced anything will happen this night, but better to be cautious and watchful.' He sheathed his sword. 'We will now go below and assert my authority. By morning, the marines will be on their way to the coast and gods be with them, with my blessing.'

Bulk said, 'Could use a squad to bust its way in to the temple. A dozen or so sharpers would save us the bother.'

'I don't entirely trust them,' Hadalin replied, 'especially now. No, we'll assault the temple just before dawn. So, stay alive in the meantime. With Aliksos out, I'll need the rest of you fit for killing come then. Now, let's be off.'

Unruly though the beast might be, the empire was nothing if not efficient. At least, when the blades finally came out.

*   *   *

The body that had once been Gracer, now home to the goddess, had begun to bloat. Though the sun had set, they remained on the road to G'danisban, and it seemed the dead woman, so cruelly animated by Va'Shaik, was determined to continue on to that faint glow beyond the line of hills to the west.

Tiring of Gilakas's unending curses – about everything – Bornu Blatt had edged his weary horse up close to where Gracer's body still walked – as close as the beast would allow, in any case.

'This claiming of Gracer, Goddess, is not working.'

The head swivelled slightly, the pale, lifeless face coming into Bornu's view. 'I am careless in my attentions, Inquisitor. Will this body last much longer?'

'You don't know?'

'It grows . . . loose.'

'You'll be a horror arriving, to be certain,' Bornu said. 'They might well seek to bar the gate.'

'If I become discorporate again,' Va'Shaik said, 'my presence will not be announced at all.'

'Can you not repair her?'

'I am uncertain.'

'It's the gases that are the problem, Goddess. That and your inability to sweat. Decay has begun within the flesh. The blood is breaking down.'

'I shall ponder the matter, Inquisitor.'

Subsiding, Bornu relaxed the reins and the horse fell back – away from the walking corpse – of its own accord. Accompanied only by the clopping of hoofs on the road's polished cobbles, Bornu allowed his thoughts to drift.

Ahead, beneath a faint dome of reflected lantern-light, waited G'danisban, the presumptive end of this journey. Thinking back on its beginning, he wondered at how the path had become so twisted. It was one thing to stand before the Queen of Dreams in her idyllic realm, exchanging what passed for pleasantries, but the myriad other distractions, each one fierce in its own way, left him floundering.

As an unbeliever, a denier of all worship, he had clearly been ill chosen for this task. Nowhere within him could be found the power of the goddess, barring her occasional voyeurism. And as for the Apocalyptic, as prophecy or promise, he could not but be dismissive, perhaps even contemptuous. What value such destruction, where even the survivors would have little but ashes to wander through when all was said and done?

This journey had scoured him clean, left him hollowed out. His faith in humanity itself had never been robust to begin with. But now he saw, behind him – and, perhaps, just ahead – bodies on the ground, motionless, lifeless. And would any answers come of that? Surely, he knew, they hadn't yet.

Abruptly, Gracer fell to the ground and lay unmoving.

Hearing a startled cry from Stult behind him, Bornu reined in and dismounted. He strode to the body and crouched down. But already his senses were telling him that the goddess was gone. Was it failure of the corpse, or Va'Shaik finding another way?

Gilakas joined him. 'Just as well,' he muttered. 'We would never have been admitted to the city, led by a rotting corpse.'

Straightening, Bornu said nothing.

'Now what?' Gilakas persisted. 'Do we simply return to our original purpose? What awaits us in G'danisban?'

'I have no idea.'

A moment later, Stult arrived, edging past Bornu and then crouching, taking up Gracer's body by the shoulders. 'Someone at the feet, please,' he said in a dull voice.

With a soft curse, Gilakas took hold of the body's cold, dusty ankles.

Together, Stult limping badly, they carried Gracer's body to the road-side, down into the ditch, and up onto the other side; a broken plain of stones and scrub stretched out for a distance, where they set her down. Looking back at Bornu, Stult said, 'I would see her buried now, Inquisitor.'

Nodding, Bornu joined the two men. 'Rest your limbs, Stult,' he said. 'Gilakas and I will collect the rocks for the cairn.'

The stars were sharp and cutting in the black sky above by the time Bornu laid down the last stone. Wiping sweat from his brow, he turned at the sound of boots on the road behind them, where the horses and mules still waited.

Eight figures stood there, arrayed in a rough circle looking outward. Bornu saw crossbows cradled in the arms of more than half of them. The glint of helms, the soft glitter of chain. One face was turned to them.

'Evening,' the man said. 'It's almost settled, officially.'

'Marines,' Gilakas said under his breath. Then he crossed the ditch and scrambled up onto the road, halting a couple of paces from the soldier who'd spoken. 'You were looking for us . . . Captain, is it?'

'Veroosh, aye, and aye, we were.'

'Well, you've now found us. What next? Assuming this is the High Fist at work, that is.'

'You're the Claw?' The captain glanced to another soldier. 'See, Hazy Drip? Told you. They're worse than vermin.'

'I assure you,' Gilakas drawled, 'the contempt is mutual. That said, your arrival is well timed, since I assume the city gate's all locked up for the night.'

'We're to escort you to your temple.'

Bornu, now alongside Gilakas, asked, 'Why would an escort be necessary, Captain Veroosh?'

'City's restless tonight. You're the Inquisitor? Had one of those in the city a while back. He was a prick.'

'Easy to shine in comparison, then,' Bornu replied.

To that, the captain grunted, then turned to his squad. 'Sergeant Buckpug, take Torbo with you on point. Corporal Hackles, you and Strip Ankles on the right flank. Hazy Drip and Gripcocker on the left. Puler's got the rear.' Facing Bornu, he said, 'You all in the middle, if that's all right with you.'

'As you like. But I have a question.'

'Oh, what's that?'

'The soldier's names . . .'

'What about 'em?'

'Not ones they were born with, I presume.'

'With some of 'em there's no telling, Inquisitor. Puler? You born with your name?'

'Probably.'

Sergeant Veroosh returned his attention to Bornu. 'Well,' he said, 'that answers that. Let's get going, it's dark and scary out here.'

*　　*　　*

A brief flicker as a warren was prised open, then closed, leaving a figure standing on a flat plain surrounded by squat mausoleums. Brushing dust from his clothes, the man looked around, then upward. Empty and almost colourless, more like stone than sky. He returned his attention to the ground, and saw there a blood-trail leading to the nearest sepulchre. It began only a half-dozen paces away from the tomb's gaping entranceway. No footprints were visible on the clay ground, just the scraped path of a man wounded near death.

Corporal Hasten Thenu sighed. 'Gone for a little while and this?' The motionless, cool air swallowed his complaint. After a moment, he strode to the crypt, peered into its dark maw.

He could just make out a pair of boots, the soles facing him.

Hasten walked inside, came upon the lone body lying just within the threshold, and crouched down. Awakening a few warrens, he studied the motionless form of High Fist Arenfall. Knives jutted from the man. Three, no four. Maybe more under the facedown body. Claw weapons, which meant poison-smeared blades. Probably tralb or paralt. None were buried deep, their impacts weakened by the thin mail beneath the cloak. Likely not fatal in themselves. If any had been, Arenfall would not have made it this far.

'And so here you lie, sir. Fatally poisoned.' He paused. 'But not dead.'

It was a characteristic of Arenfall's pocket warrens, this suspension of time. Once solely the purview of Azath Houses, but since the dispersal of Icarium, no longer. Many practical advantages to this new manifestation of magic, he mused. Storing food for a journey, for example, since it would not spoil. He needed a conversation with . . . people. Plenty of potential, beyond keeping oneself alive – or somewhere between alive and dead – and storing the bodies of fallen comrades, since Hasten doubted the other tombs were empty.

Yes indeed, this whole messing with time had possibilities.

'Now, sir, let's see what we can do about all that poison, shall we?'

*   *   *

Trailed by eight hooded killers, Baek approached the east gate. Only one guard stood near the closed portal, a clay pipe clenched between his teeth as he leaned against the closer of the two flanking mud-brick gate-posts. Hearing the footfalls, the man swivelled his head to study the group.

'Letting you lot out's no problem,' he said when they arrived. 'Letting you back in before dawn is. High Fist's curfew and all that.'

Baek held up a small leather pouch. 'Find a tavern, friend. This gate's ours tonight.' He tossed the pouch over.

But the guard simply watched it fall at his feet in a puff of dust, then looked back up. 'Tip for my service? Mighty kind of you.'

'Just be off with you.'

'Everybody saying the constabulary's in someone's purse, anyone's in fact, if enough coins are involved. Thing is,' the guard said, 'it just ain't true.'

'It's the only option you have,' Baek said, 'that has you seeing the dawn.'

The guard reached up to the heavy rope dangling down the gate-post. 'And if I ring the alarm?'

'Messy. But either way, you still won't live to see the dawn.'

'Well now, that's a problem, or maybe it isn't. You see, since I have the first half of the night-watch, I sleep through every dawn anyway.'

Baek bared his teeth. 'Listen, you shit. Get lost or die.'

'See, was that so hard?' The guard released the rope, bent down and collected up the small bag of coins. He opened it and peered within, then looked up. 'Cheap bastard, too. Modern-day bribery has gone downhill, is all I'm saying.' Then, shrugging, he set off.

Prapp moved up beside Baek. 'We should've just killed him and saved the coin.'

Baek shot him a glare. 'You even cheaper than me, Prapp? It doesn't matter. If the man's smart, he'll stay in whatever tavern he's about to enter. Otherwise, he's likely to end up dead anyway. Now, four of you outside to watch the road. The rest of us will flank the gate here and remember, nobody leaves the city.'

'Once it all starts up, Baek, we'll get mobbed by people trying to get out.'

'We've got our people in the streets, Prapp. And at least three teams have this gate as a rendezvous, so we'll be getting regular reinforcements. Besides, most will hide in their homes, cowering under tables or in closets.'

'Street's wet,' another acolyte observed.

Baek grunted. 'Ban Ryk's timed it right, then.'

*　　　*　　　*

'High Fist Arenfall has been removed from command,' Adjunct Hadalin said. He stood leaning against the desk, his arms crossed. Two men Stipple had never seen before flanked the Adjunct, who she guessed were Claw. Definitely a dangerous pair, their blank, fixed expressions more than a little chilling.

Sighing, Stipple turned to Hench. 'What do you think?'

Hench scratched at his stubbled beard. He'd tried shaving it all off earlier that day, probably in the morning during whatever minimal ablutions he engaged in, and as far as Stipple was concerned, 'minimal' was being generous. In any case, he'd done a terrible job, leaving whiskery patches everywhere, and already stubble was growing back to fill in the gaps.

'Don't know,' Hench replied. 'We're here to deliver our report, only the man we were supposed to deliver it to isn't here any more. It's a conundrum.'

The Adjunct spoke. 'No, it isn't. Give me your report. But first, what was it the High Fist had you doing? I don't recall having seen you two before.'

'We're slippery,' Stipple said. 'Comes with the job. Anyway, it's about the Under Quarter.'

'Well, only partly,' Hench corrected. 'It's really about the Underhouse, Stipple.'

'And what,' asked Hadalin, 'is the Underhouse?'

'Oh,' said Stipple. 'It's our resident Azath House. Probably inaccessible by now, on account of the flooding.'

'You think the biggun boko drowned, then?' Hench asked her.

'What? The giant bhokaral on top of the gate-post? Well, it was squealing like it was doomed, so yeah, probably drowned by now.'

'I don't,' said Hench. 'Bhokarala can swim, you know.'

'But can they hold their breath?'

Straightening, Hadalin took a step to loom directly in front of Stipple. 'There is an Azath House in G'danisban? I sincerely doubt that. The empire has mapped every Azath House in its territories.'

'It's not in G'danisban though, is it, sir?' Hench said, his heavy brow beetling. 'It's *under* G'danisban.'

'And was High Fist Arenfall aware of this?'

'Of course,' Stipple replied. 'That's why he sent us down there.'

'Partly,' Hench corrected. 'The other stuff was all that criminal rubbish.'

'It only turned to rubbish,' Stipple countered, 'because of the flooding.'

'More like the sappers.'

'The flooding doomed the whole enterprise.'

'But we were supposed to hold it together to control the exodus, keep it from turning into a panicked mob, little children and old women drowning and all that. Instead, the sappers blew everything up.'

'No they didn't,' Stipple objected. 'I'm telling you, Hench, the flooding did us in.'

'King Sug drowning in the Underhouse yard did us in.'

'Okay, that didn't help—'

'Both of you, be quiet,' Hadalin snapped. 'Stipple, is it? Stipple, have you anything else to report?'

'Not really,' she admitted. 'Except for the fact that the water all around the Underhouse is, uh, boiling.'

'So the exodus has already begun,' added Hench. 'That steam's scalding, you know. And the water down there everywhere else is starting to heat up, too.'

'And the upsurge,' Stipple threw in. 'So, Adjunct, expect a few thousand bedraggled under-dwellers bubbling up from the drains tonight.'

'And bedraggled bhokarala, too,' Hench said.

'That ends the report,' Stipple said. 'Sir.'

The new Adjunct stared at them both. No one spoke for a few moments, then Hadalin nodded. 'Very well. Go to the city garrison and inform them of the impending exodus. We'll need constables in the streets to manage the crowd. The refugees can be directed to Blue Sky.'

'Blue Sky won't hold them all,' Hench said. 'Uh, by way of post-report appendix.'

'Leave the details to the garrison commander. Now go.'

Stipple looked at Hench, who shrugged but said nothing. A moment later, they left the office.

Out in the corridor, Stipple glanced at the third Claw, posted beside the office door, then, taking Hench by the crook of one beefy arm, quickly guided him away. They reached the far end and began descending the stairs.

'What's your hurry, woman?'

'My skin was crawling.'

'Is Arenfall dead?'

'Probably. Those fucking Claw. Only three of them, not a full hand. I'd wager the High Fist took a couple down with him.'

'Or the other two were hiding in the Imperial Warren, in case we decided to try them on.'

She glanced at him as they approached the building's front doors. 'You were thinking about it?'

'Weren't you?'

'He's the Adjunct, you know.'

'And Arenfall was our High Fist.'

'Adjunct's closer to the Emperor. And that's my point. He could've taken over at any time, and kept the High Fist doing what he was doing, but he didn't, did he?'

'Well, this Hadalin didn't. Word was, the other one was getting along fine with the High Fist.'

'Inkaras Sollit. Who died when accompanying the High Fist on a mission. Maybe Hadalin figured that was no accident.'

'So he struck back.'

'Maybe. Who knows what goes on at the higher levels, right?'

They stepped outside and paused.

Hench suddenly said, 'Look at the fog on Bastran Hill.'

Following his gaze Stipple frowned. 'That's not fog, idiot. It's steam.'

'Oh. Of course it is. I knew that.'

And now they could hear a vague noise in the night air, murmuring, or perhaps a susurration. Or some strange energy, sizzling, hissing. Along with something like groaning bricks and stone. It was, in fact, a bit noisy.

'They're going to be pouring up and out any moment now,' Hench predicted. 'Weren't we supposed to go to the city barracks?'

A bell was now sounding from that direction.

'Too late to say anything they haven't already figured out, Hench.'

'I suppose you're right. What should we do?'

She thought about it. 'I've got it.'

'Yes?'

'Nothing.'

'What?'

'We do nothing. That's my answer. You have a problem with it?'

Hench scratched at his beard-thing. 'Let me think. No, I don't. I don't have a problem with it, I mean. It's a good plan.'

'Let's get a drink at the Petals.'

'Does that count as nothing?'

'With that watered-down shit they serve, yes, it does.'

'I could do with a pint or two of nothing.'

'Same here.'

The two set out, boots splashing in the thin slick of black water covering the cobbles.

*   *   *

Arenfall opened his eyes. A vague yellow light filled the sepulchre. Corporal Hasten Thenu was crouched directly above him, looking down with a gauging eye.

333

'Glad you found me,' Arenfall said, not yet ready to move. 'I'd hoped . . . tell me, how much time has passed?'

'Since your removal by the Adjunct? Not long at all. Same night, in fact. But, as we predicted, it's all about to light up back in G'danisban.'

Arenfall studied the strange man, and he truly was strange. His smooth face seemed ageless, the circlet broken-chain tattoo the only line on his smooth forehead. His eyes were calm pools. 'How was it you managed to respond so quickly, Corporal?'

Straightening, Hasten said, 'Well, I came back to G'danisban since we knew that Inquisitor was likely to arrive tonight. And the goddess would be in his shadow every step of the way. Then, when I couldn't find you, I wandered around in the headquarters and watched the turn-over of command.'

'No one accosted you?'

'Oh, they couldn't see me. Anyway, there are four Claw assassins with the Adjunct, no longer hiding. One is wounded. Shoulder, I think. Rough Denul healing – it clearly still aches. Your work, High Fist?'

Nodding, Arenfall slowly sat up. His garments were stiff with dried blood and bearing knife-slits. Broken chain-links from his mail shirt trickled down his torso, sharp against his skin. He'd have to shake them out, once he was standing. 'It was a very good ambush.'

'Otataral.'

'Yes, half-sheathed to keep its influence close. The Claw attacked from outside that influence.'

'That's how they take down better mages,' Hasten replied. 'High success rate.'

'Then it was just thrown knives.'

'Poisoned blades.'

'Almost an entire Hand, plus the Adjunct. I'd been assuming his arrogance meant he would try me personally, otataral sword against my mundane skills. Instead, he followed protocol, as you say. I killed one for certain.' Slowly, Arenfall climbed to his feet. He pulled the skirt of the mail from under his belt, then shook slightly. Broken links clinked on the pave-stones. That shiver brought pain from all of his knife-wounds. 'Rough Denul,' he muttered.

'Unguents. Good stuff, mind you,' Hasten added. 'I sewed up the wounds.' He paused, tilting his head slightly. 'Surprised you managed to stand.'

'You're not a healer?'

'Not really. Negating poison, though, that I can do. Especially this close to Poliel's Temple. It's a ruin now, of course, but the goddess died there, so her residue lingers. After all, there were two sides to the Mistress of Pestilence. People sometimes forget.'

Grunting, Arenfall said, 'Plagues will do that.'

'The real problem started when they split her in half. Just as with Oponn, Poliel and Soliel were originally twin goddesses, two sides of the same coin.' He said nothing for a moment, and then shrugged. 'Never did find out why the priests did that.'

'No one wanted to pray to a leper,' Arenfall suggested.

'She never was, not by choice, anyway. The *statues* made her into a leper, or pustule-ridden, or whatever other disfigurement they could think of. Anyway, so much of disease is just growth in the wrong direction. But poison, that just kills, and that's what offended Poliel and Soliel both, since they were the Ladies of Suffering and Healing.'

'I seem to have thrown all my knives,' Arenfall said.

'Not sure you're ready to take on the Adjunct and his Claw tonight, sir. Best you wait, rest, and stay here for a while.'

'And you? Will you take down the Adjunct?'

'Me? You burning with the need for vengeance, sir?'

Arenfall thought about it, and then sighed and said, 'No. I'm a veteran of political expedience. Still, the Adjunct isn't prepared for what is coming, is he?'

'Probably not.'

'But I am. At least, as a master assassin.'

'If not all cut up first, then aye, sir. You were, but you aren't now.'

'Has the Adjunct delivered new orders to the marines?'

Hasten nodded. 'He has. Of course, only Captain Hung's squad is in the city at the moment.'

'Ah, and will Hung sit tight if so ordered?'

'They weren't that kind of orders, sir. Just a more general "prepare to rejoin the Legion" kind of orders.'

'Of course. Corporal, are *you* prepared to act on my behalf in the city tonight?'

Hasten suddenly looked uncomfortable. 'Well, that might give things away, sir. I need to stay . . . unnoticed.'

'Why?'

Hasten blinked. 'To avoid convergence, sir.'

Convergence. Arenfall stared at the corporal. Just how powerful was he? More to the point, as far as Arenfall knew – and as far as written accounts contained mention of this soldier when sporting his previous name – he'd been useful but hardly devastating. Not even a High Mage of the old empire days was enough to unleash the wild confluence of powers known as convergence.

'Or,' Hasten resumed, 'rather, this convergence doesn't need another player involved. That would be bad.'

'Corporal, are you saying G'danisban is the site of a *convergence* right now?'

'Uh, yes? But, sir, it's a protracted one. Geographically spread out, I mean. Not just here, and not even just in Seven Cities. Though maybe it's starting here. It won't end on this continent, I don't think.' His thoughtful expression suddenly brightened. 'Luckily and by happy coincidence, we have marines stationed at both relevant places here in Seven Cities, ready to do their work.'

'And the link between them is . . . you.'

Hasten frowned. 'Well. The thing about convergences, sir, is all the stuff that happens pretty much beneath notice of the major players. It's there that mortals can mitigate things, keeping the damage down. That said, I think this one's turning into a handful.'

'But you think you need to keep your head down,' Arenfall said.

'Exactly.'

'I see. So what should we do, Corporal?'

A sudden smile. 'As we are. In other words, relax, sir, we're doing it.'

'Who is "we" in this instance?'

The smile fell away. 'Uh, right. Captain Hung and his squad. *They're* doing it.'

'Doing what, precisely?'

'That would be, kicking it off with our response to the religious uprising?'

'Corporal, at some point you're going to have to explain yourself.'

'Oh? I thought I had, sir.'

Arenfall studied the man yet again. 'That broken-chain tattoo on your brow, what does it signify?'

'This little sketch? Nothing much.'

'Corporal.'

Hasten glanced away, and then back. He offered a half-shrug. 'Sometimes, we end up doing things that are . . . never seen. But they still count for something, sir. You know how it is.' He made a faint gesture with one hand. 'Like these tombs, or should I say, repositories. Dead comrades, dying comrades, dying enemies, too, I'm sure. All frozen in time for reasons only you know. We do stuff for ourselves, right? Nobody else has to know about it, because it's none of their business anyway.'

Arenfall moved to a wall and gingerly sat down on the floor, setting his aching back against the cold stone. He drew up his legs and rested his forearms on his knees, hands dangling. 'I believe it was in Pan'potsun, about five, six years ago. I was playing in a tavern, to a small crowd. At least, it started small. With my eyes mostly on the strings while I worked some elaborate fretwork, I didn't notice that someone had come to a table close by, and with her sitting there, why, the place started filling up. Had they followed her? They must have. But when I looked up and continued the ballad's instrumental, I watched the room get packed. For me? I didn't realize it at the time, but no. For her.' He paused, remembering the scene, feeling it come alive once more in his mind.

'Beautiful, was she?'

'I suppose. Pardu tribe, I think. Late thirties, even early forties. But there was a grace to her. It was undeniable, almost a glow. Anyway, she seemed to know the song, and knew as well the very long section without any singing. It's what preceded the final stanza, and often I'd stretch it out if the audience was fully engaged—'

'What was the song, if I may ask?'

'Fisher's "He Who Fell Shall Rise".'

Hasten seemed to start. A moment later he too moved to a wall, this one opposite Arenfall, and leaned his back against it, arms folded under his chest. 'Go on,' he invited, his gaze hooded.

'As I extended the interlude, she rose to her feet and stepped into the space before the stage. Once there—'

'She began a dance.'

Arenfall's gaze narrowed on the corporal. 'She did. Now, understand me, Corporal. Fisher's song – the poem I put to music – I took to refer to . . . well, could've been anyone. Coltaine. Sergeant Whiskeyjack of the Bridgeburners, or even the Bridgeburners themselves. Or, perhaps,

Anomander Rake. Personally, I believed it to be about Coltaine, and the Fall.'

'It's not about any of them,' Hasten said in a low voice.

'No,' Arenfall replied. 'I saw as much that night. I saw it in her dance. The truth of it. Fisher's poem was about the Crippled God.'

'Yes.'

'And, since that was the case, then the god's vanishing from the world wasn't a death at all, as most people believe. He was returned to his own world. The few lines of the poem that never quite fit Coltaine or the others, but were vague enough to not bother me, were, I realized, perfect fits for the Crippled God. *But only if he didn't die.* But then I was confused all over again. I had thought the poem to be a promise, a pronouncement of faith in some future moment. But it wasn't, was it? It was a recounting of something that had already happened.'

'In that poem, the Crippled God was returned to his world, yes,' said Hasten. 'Of course, it's just a poem, with plenty of artistic licence.'

'I have heard rumours of a great tome, something called the Book of the Fallen.'

'I doubt it exists,' Hasten said, reprising that half-shrug. 'That god's release was never recorded, by anyone. No account to be found anywhere.'

'Unwitnessed.'

'Just so, sir.'

'That woman, who danced, bore the very same tattoo as do you, Corporal. The only time I have ever seen it before, on anyone. And, fool me, I never learned her name. Her dance – my music – it broke the entire room. It broke me as well. When I was of enough mind to look up, to seek her out, she was already gone.'

'Was it a good dance, sir?'

'It was . . . transcendent.'

After a few moments while they regarded one another, Hasten broke his gaze and pushed off from the wall he'd been leaning against. 'A good memory to have, then. Now, sir, I'd better check on Captain Hung. While I'd strongly advise you to stay until I return, I know you probably won't. In any case and as you can probably tell, time's at work here in your little warren, for now. You can lock it up again later, but I needed normal time to negate the poisons and deal with the wounds. And you need it that way to heal up.'

'Understood.'

'Be careful, sir.'

'I'll do my best.'

Hasten left the sepulchre.

*   *   *

A half-dozen paces from the tomb, Hasten Thenu paused, moments before opening a warren and returning to G'danisban. Under his breath, he said, 'Her name was Lostara Yil, sir. And just like me, she wasn't even there.'

*   *   *

The great Nub, King of the Bhokarala, clambered half-drowned out of the muddy hole. Fangs bared, he snarled at nothing, or maybe it was everything. All around him on the pocked surface of Bastran Hill, his subjects were pouring out of crevices, cracks and holes, hacking and gasping and coughing in sharp little barks and spats.

Before long, the humans would follow. Because that was all they were good for: following. At least there was some small measure of wisdom in that, when survival was at stake. Still, it would make for a most dyspeptic scene in the city's streets and alleys.

Nub growled. Fangs still flashing, he scrambled towards his tree and moments later was climbing, all four limbs propelling him upward to his glorious throne, that being the well-worn saddle-shaped crotch between trunk and branch loftily high above the inglorious tumult.

The waters had arrived, black and deadly. Or, if not personally deadly, then generally so. And for those for whom it wasn't deadly at all, it was certainly inconvenient.

Already fading in his mind were the chaotic moments at the Underhouse. Why, could any argue against his perfect place atop the pillar flanking that dread path of soupy mud? And did not the cursed building remain enclosed within a pocket of hot, steamy air, even as the waters continued to rise everywhere else?

And was this not Nub's infernal compulsion, to witness the arrival of an Elder God?

Not Nub's fault the ancient fool then lost his temper!

But that wretched shadow from which emerged endless – and endlessly irritating – whispers, why, so suddenly, ominously, falling silent! What help from there? None! Abandoned, poor Nub! Abandoned! And very nearly drowned, too. Drowned and boiled in fact!

339

Thus the foul mood, the glowering regard upon the bedraggled minions scurrying about in the gloom below. And now alarm bells sonorously shivering the night air. What happened to a peaceful evening, one in which the great king was free to doze and lounge, scratching the occasional itch, yawning wide to warn off any challengers via the immensity of his canines, leaning back to expose his magnificent belly to the stars, so that they might quake in awe.

His bhokarala were scrambling, seeking high places and now avoiding the armed mobs appearing as if from nowhere to descend upon the sodden humans clambering up and out of every known passageway between the surface and the drowning world beneath. Violence! Shrieks and screams and rolling waves of fear, eddies of carnage, bodies making bulwarks against the currents as water now gushed, flowed in dark crooked streams from Bastran Hill's slopes, while elsewhere, in the sunken dips and rounds of G'danisban, more water pooled, already ankle-deep and warm as blood.

Such a miserable night, well suited to the great king's mood. Why, even he wanted to kill something.

CHAPTER THIRTEEN

It was better back then, you say.
Indulging, as you will, the romance
of delusional nostalgia
this sense of yours so bound up
in some dream state of childhood
smudged, smoothed, and all of a blur
to make a landscape that never was
and portraits of perfect faces
foremost your own
and woe to the world of now
its jagged edges and cutting truths
so flee you will, back into that past
to be a child again, glowering
and spiteful, aiming every arrow of hate
into the present so indifferent and unmindful
of your blessed, blissful, oh so precious
memories.
As if I care one whit for your memories.

You Say, I Say
Galvas of One-Eye Cat

'Darling ruby, is it raining outside?'
    'No, Holy One.'
        'But I hear water.'
'Yes, Holy One.'
'Isn't that odd. Never mind. Have the Invigil attend me.'
Pash hesitated. 'And if he refuses, Holy One?'

341

Shamalle blinked. 'Would he? How extraordinary! Should I be offended? Even by the mere possibility? Well, let's see, shall we? Refusal or obedience, laggardly or with alacrity, bright-eyed or stone-visaged, purr or snarl, why, think of the myriad options awaiting us! What say you – oh, she's already left. To do my bidding. How sweet of her, though in her absence and in the absence of anyone else, why, I make the discovery – most perturbing – of talking to myself. And even more alarming, remaining perfectly entertained, if not enthralled. By my own voice, no less. And let's face it, it's a sultry voice, isn't it? None of that nasal squeeze as is the habit of Ban Ryk and others of his ilk. Like croaking frogs, ugh!

'And what ilk might that be, I ask me? And here I give myself a sly wink. See? Most sly. And we share a smirk, which, in truth, is but one smirk. Though I have, on occasion, been so drunk as to see double, not once in such circumstances did one of the doubles speak independently of the other, or show a singular expression. As far as I can recall, anyway. Still, it's but a lone smirk, sweetly shared between me and my audience, said audience being me as well and that of course makes it the best audience ever.

'Let's muse, shall I? She informed me that it wasn't raining, and yet I hear water, and this water comes not from the stream in the garden because I can't hear that one at all above the sound of water everywhere else, so, clearly not the stream, although its incessant trickle is likely buried in there somewhere, adding to the overall slosh.

'If not rain, if not rain, then what? My bladder? No! Thank goodness. That was a frightening option indeed, especially given my not noticing until the question was asked. Well of course I didn't notice, precisely because my bladder it wasn't! After all, there are floods and then there are floods – oh . . . of course! The city is flooding! Or, rather, the city under the city is now flooded. Hence the slosh and all the murmuring and shouts, screams and all the rest. A night of growing cacophony, it seems. Pash, where are you? How malingering his delay in answering?

'Must I actually stir from this plush repose? Actually rise to my feet, to wobble above all too narrow ankles? Even swing my rudder – that would be hips and behind – to face steps, floor and door? Just how much arduous physical labour is being demanded of me? And worse – see how expectant that audience! They want . . . they want, oh dear they want me to *move*.'

342

She thought about it. She truly did. But then her features set with stubborn resolve. 'Damn the audience! I refuse! I shall not bow, nor bend, nor even flex! Not a single finger will so much as crook. Pash is on her way, after all, either with the Invigil or without him. Yes, the world comes to me, as it should. Not because I am High Priestess, however. Oh no, not because of that. The world comes to me because I am a woman. And, as we women know, that's precisely how it should be.

'Woe the man to challenge that assertion! See my vengeful weapons arrayed before me, all within languid reach. Disdain, disgust, contempt, spite, but, deadliest of all, the perfect visible inflection that is a woman's eye-roll. Take that, you grunting, farting, hairy fools!'

Satisfied with the conversation thus far, Shamalle reached for her cup of tisane.

To soothe her quivering nerves.

Then paused and scowled. 'Oh blast, all that trickling and sloshing! I have to pee!'

*   *   *

Baek was outside the gate now, with all seven of his exceptional, deadly killers. Blooded in the streets and alleys, every one of them. He had already turned away three merchants, and few were the complaints in the face of him and his well-armed 'guards'. An impromptu caravanserai was being set up outside the wall, off to the right, and the spicy aroma of late meals drifted across, making everyone hungry, including Baek.

Discipline, he reminded himself. Through the speak-hole in the gate, his new team of inside guards had been keeping him up to date on the exodus from beneath Bastran Hill, and the streams of water now spreading through the city. Chaos, the wails of the deprived and helpless, the eruptions of violence. While on the rooftops . . . Baek smiled at the thought.

To be sure, they had full mastery of those vantages, by now.

He wondered if Orotol had struck yet. He didn't think so. That clash with the marines would surely have risen above the clamour in the streets.

'Baek,' murmured one of his killers. 'More travellers. Coming up on us.'

Shifting his attention to the road, Baek could see a party approaching. A quarter-moon was up, casting the world in a silvery sheen. 'Shit,' he muttered. 'Those two out front are marines.'

The man at his side, Gorlid, grunted, then asked, 'Your orders, Baek?'

'I see more on the flanks, too. It's a squad. Surrounding . . . ah.' He gestured. 'Relax and step away from the road,' he commanded his followers. Turning to the speak-hole he called through, 'Jukra! Unlock and open the gate. The Inquisitor has arrived!'

'You sure it's him?' Gorlid asked.

'Said to be ugly – what do you think?'

Gorlid grunted a second time. 'The ugly robed one on the horse?'

Baek snapped a glare on the man. 'Wake up whatever wits you have, Gorlid!'

'Sorry. You're right. That must be him. Sorry, Baek. I'm just hungry.'

'Well, after this, you can raid that merchant camp over there and help yourself.'

'Nice,' said Gorlid, teeth flashing in a grin. 'After that, we can maybe start killing people trying to escape the city.'

'Patience,' muttered Baek.

The locks were thrown and the gate began creaking open.

Baek swung to face the approaching marines. He held up a hand, then said, 'The city is riotous and troubled tonight, Malazans, but I have an escort to help you get through. Flooding, you see.'

The party halted. Another marine came forward between the two soldiers at the front, likely an officer. 'Unsettled, is it?' he asked in the accent of Quon Tali.

'Very,' Baek replied. 'But we should be able to get you through to the temple.'

'Oh, and how do you plan to do that?'

'As you can see, we acolytes are armed.' His lifted his gaze to fix upon the ugly man on the lead horse. 'Inquisitor, we bid you welcome.'

'With swords about to be drawn against frightened refugees? Captain Veroosh, decline their offer.'

The marine on the captain's left now said, 'They must've locked *all* the gates, Captain. Keeping people out but more keeping 'em in. If there's going to be riots in the city, we now know why.'

'The refugees are of no consequence,' Baek said. 'Heretics and criminals. No room for them in any case.'

'Then guide them out through all the gates,' suggested that same soldier.

'If any remain by morning, we shall,' Baek offered.

Captain Veroosh was smiling, somewhat vapidly. 'Sergeant Buckpug, a word if you please.'

The marine who'd been speaking now joined his captain.

Veroosh gestured at Baek. 'See this man?'

'Aye, Captain, I see him.'

The captain turned to the Inquisitor, raising his voice, 'Water in the streets right now. And killing going on. You want your path to be all red?'

'Not particularly.'

Veroosh waved at Baek and the other acolytes. 'These people yours, Inquisitor?'

'I cannot say.'

'Need a better answer than that.'

The Inquisitor guided his horse forward. 'Children of Va'Shaik, do you acknowledge my authority?'

Baek frowned. 'We have been instructed by the Invigil Ban Ryk, Inquisitor, who holds authority over the city's holy servants.'

'And how do you place the authority of an Inquisitor?'

'The last who visited did not interfere with the Invigil.'

'Passing through, that Inquisitor?'

'Yes.'

'Thereby pronouncing no Inquisition of the Temple and its family.'

Baek said nothing, his eyes narrowing.

After a moment, the Inquisitor continued, 'I, on the other hand, shall indeed announce an Inquisition. Furthermore, you will leave this gate open and make no impedance to refugees who wish to leave the flooded streets.'

After some frantic thinking, Baek shook his head. 'The Inquisition can only be announced within the Temple, as you know. Until then, I must follow the commands of the Invigil. In such obedience, surely no dereliction can be found. You do not wish us to escort you? Very well, we will remain here.'

The Inquisitor sighed. 'Captain Veroosh, lead us in.'

'In a moment,' Veroosh said. 'Buckpug.'

The short-sword appeared as if from nowhere, its blade a blurring glimmer in the night.

Baek staggered back as heat flooded down his chest. Confused, he brought up both hands, to find his throat gaping wide and gushing blood.

At the same moment, even as his vision dimmed, he saw a shimmering among the other marines. Their forms vanished, reappearing an instant later, but now in a solid row on the road, their crossbows out from under their half-cloaks and making snapping sounds that echoed in the cool night air.

The sergeant named Buckpug was moving past Baek now.

He thought to turn and watch the man pass through the gate. Instead, he fell to his knees, his limbs suddenly icy cold, weakening into lifelessness. The spilling blood had slowed to sullen spurts that struck the underside of his chin.

Baek then found himself lying on the road. The night had grown very dark. Too dark to see a thing. Too dark to even think.

*   *   *

Ignoring Stult's curses, Bornu Blatt glowered down at the captain who stood in the gateway, only now scabbarding his weapon. 'That was unnecessary.'

'We're your escort, aye,' said Veroosh. 'Now, maybe you calling your inquisition in the temple can settle things, but for a lot of folk that'll be too late. Our other job is to keep people from killing each other. At least while we're posted in the city. How we do that is our business and if you got a problem with that, take it up with High Fist Arenfall.'

'That was an impressive working of Mockra,' said Gilakas from just behind Bornu. 'I'd wondered why no one but you and your sergeant were moving much, or even looking interested. Which one of you was doing that?'

Sergeant Buckpug barked a harsh laugh. 'Hear that? The Claw wants to know which one of us won't have any trouble killing him if it comes to that.'

'I don't think we should tell him, Sergeant,' said Gripcocker.

Buckpug closed his eyes to pinch the bridge of his nose. 'Gods below,' he muttered under his breath, and then he raised his voice, 'No, Gripcocker, you're right. We really shouldn't tell him.'

Gripcocker nodded, then pointed a thick finger at Gilakas. 'We're not telling you.'

Heels tapping his mount's flanks, Bornu rode under the gate's arch and, horse edging past the quarrel-studded bodies sprawled on the cobbles, entered G'danisban—

At that instant, Va'Shaik struck.

*   *   *

The goddess grasped Bornu Blatt's soul in one hand, tore it loose, and flung it away, far from the flesh she now poured herself into, in a burst of scintillating power.

His body, twisted from birth, brought her a sudden wrench of pain – a pain she never knew he had lived with for years – and she cried out. A long, quavering scream that ended in blistering rage.

Who punished him so? This child spilled out onto the mortal earth – who bent his bones, kneaded the soft bones of his newborn face, made him so cruelly misshapen? Who chose to see him sicken to the very foods he needed to live? Made spring blossoms a torture, the dust of books a curse?

Who did this to a newly born innocent? What demon preys so eagerly upon the weak and defenceless?

You would speak to me of suffering's virtue?

And in the next breath, ease through life by one soft hand the wicked and venal?

You would speak of choices made in utter freedom, with half the knives in each choice hidden. Freedom itself a promise of blood, the wounded self, wounded others, this wretched liberty.

Who, upon seeing all this suffering, delivered of its own devising, would dare announce that it would have it no other way? But lives of pain, torments inside and out, each body so much a temple of promised glory – why, not one of you would dwell in such as your sole domain. Not for a lifetime. Not one! Not for an instant!

No. Your gentle forbearance is hypocrisy. Your every blessing has sharp teeth. For you promise that paradise waits not in the valley where a mortal life is lived out, but in the valley beyond, with life's passage but an ordeal down a dark road.

Bornu Blatt lived with the pain you gave him, but quenched his own anger. With every breath. With every beat of his heart, he pushed down his righteous rage. At this betrayal of flesh and bone, at the unseen hands who gave shape to his monstrosity. And all to give the world what? The irony of a most beautiful soul hidden within an ugly, mangled shell?

Who are you, to smile and say 'I would have it no other way'? This small morsel of your indulgence was a man! A lived life! Reluctant husband to pain, flinching at her every loving caress! How dare you!

Well.

She would be his rage. She would awaken what his gentle soul denied in itself.

I too shall have it no other way. Here, then, you unseen god of gods, is my Apocalypse.

347

The fire of her sudden awakening within the body of the man, Bornu Blatt, turned night into day.

*   *   *

Before the arrival of the new, untimely dawn, the lone squad of marines left in the city were gathered in the barracks.

'That garrison's out on the streets,' said Captain Hung, 'but the gates have been locked.'

'Whose brilliant idea was that?' demanded Fedilap. 'Get those city guards to open the damned things.'

'They're having trouble even reaching them,' Hung replied. 'That's why we're heading to Crimson Gate, since it's the biggest. We'll clear it and then move on to the next one.'

Gains spoke. 'New orders from the Adjunct, Captain?'

'No,' Hung replied. 'But it's getting messy out there. The High Fist—'

'Not to be obstructive, sir, but the High Fist's been deposed—'

'Murdered, you mean,' cut in Pulcrude. 'And as for obstructive, you're always obstructive, Gains.'

'The High Fist is actually missing,' said Hung, his voice slightly raised to quash the growing argument between Pulcrude and Gains. 'As for the new Adjunct's orders, they're yet to take effect. In the meantime, we proceed as planned.'

'Arenfall planned a flood and a riot?' Fedilap asked.

'No, just the response, Sapper, and it's neither the flood nor the riot that is our reason for heading out. That stuff's in the background. The Apocalyptic seeks to rise again. Tonight.'

'So,' said Pulcrude, after a long glance at the other soldiers in the squad, all of whom stood near the barracks doors, geared up and sweating, 'opening the gates just pulls the stopper on the crowds, leaving the fanatics alone in the city.'

'Who we then mop up,' concluded Fedilap.

Captain Hung nodded. 'Until told otherwise.'

'About these fanatics,' Gains said, 'is it just the Va'Shaik ones we take down? What about the other cultists out there?'

'Likely fighting for their lives,' observed Pulcrude. 'Not to mention the refugees who instead of being saved and taken care of, climbed out into a mad abattoir. Bad luck or what? Why, you'd think the timing was deliberate or something.'

Pulcrude and the other marines saw their captain hesitating. None spoke, only waited. Eventually, Hung's expression tightened, and then he said, 'Powers are at work here tonight, and not just a bunch of religious fanatics.'

'Oh,' said Fedilap. 'As in "high" powers, Captain?'

'There's something of that in the air, aye.'

'I feel it,' announced Fedilap.

Moments later, all the other marines chimed in as well.

So, Pulcrude concluded, it hadn't been just her, all this mounting anxiety. 'Captain, are we talking convergence?'

Hung scowled. 'Let's just see if we can cut that off at the knees.'

'But we're only one squad!' cried Flutter. The others all looked at him, saw his wild grin starting to spread, and then he laughed. Then all the marines were laughing.

Shaking his head, Captain Hung turned away, faced the doors. Over his shoulder he said, 'Shut up, all of you. Bring your shields to bear, to help us push through the crowd. Now form up.'

He opened the doors and led his marines out into the colonnade.

*   *   *

Orotol had positioned those of his agents armed with bows and crossbows upon rooftops facing the entrance to the Dryjhna Colonnade – he refused to acknowledge its new name, Coltaine Colonnade – while clustering the rest of his killers at the mouth of Crimson Road, just outside Open Gate, sixty in all.

As was the custom every night, both the North and South Gates leading into Blue Sky were locked, while Arched Gate, the mouth of Traders' Track, was firmly barred. Since most of the refugees from under the city had emerged on and around Bastran Hill on the side opposite the Malazan company headquarters, none of the gates giving access to Blue Sky were easily reached, even had they been open, and it was clear to Orotol that Wrest and her holy soldiers were wreaking havoc among the panicked crowds. The sounds of slaughter filled the air, rising from the city's southwest quarters.

The death-cries of heretics was a sweet sound indeed, and Orotol smiled.

'The barracks doors have opened,' reported Udulle, whose hawk-like stare had been fixed on the building at the far end of the colonnade. 'The marines are emerging.'

Orotol quickly shifted his attention, watching as one squad marched into view. Their shields were slung on arms but not yet held up, but even that detail annoyed Orotol. He had been hoping those shields would be still strapped to their backs, instead of readied to respond to arrows. 'Anyone fires too early and I'll cut the fool's throat myself,' he said under his breath. 'We want both squads in sight.'

But his orders were being followed, as the first squad continued on between the twin rows of columns unmolested, unsuspecting.

'I see no second squad,' said Udulle.

'Nor I. Well, we can still take down this first one, once they clear the avenue and come out on Blue Sky. That's the fall-back order, after all. Let them march too far to retreat.'

Another of his hunters on this rooftop, Lavit, now hissed, 'Orotol! Look at the well in the centre!'

Pulling his attention from the advancing squad, Orotol squinted at the well in the middle of Blue Sky. Its water was clearly boiling, billowing steam that rose in a column still climbing into the dark sky.

'What's happening?' Udulle wondered. 'Is this the work of the Apocalypse, do you think?'

'No,' muttered Orotol, 'I don't. Never mind. Ignore it. The squad's almost—'

Eager bloodlust pre-empted his command to fire, as the sharp, heavy *knocks* of crossbows sounded from the rooftops. Quarrels darted down—

And in that moment, the night simply vanished.

*   *   *

Scatter cursed, then staggered, leaning hard to one side over a failing leg that had been impaled by a quarrel. Fedilap went down with a grunt.

Sergeant Breech, sprouting three quarrels, fell over like a sack of turnips.

Other quarrels had struck the paving stones, scattering chips of limestone, and now arrows began hissing in, mostly from the north and northeastern sides of the square.

By this time, the marines still on their feet had drawn up their shields, forming a protective barrier.

Under blindingly bright light, they began backing towards the colonnade, as quarrels and arrows struck their raised shields again and again.

350

In their midst and dragging his leg was Scatter, though he too had managed to lift his shield to guard his head. Only Breech and Fedilap were left behind, both prone and motionless on the cobbles.

From Open Gate now rushed a disordered mob of armed Sha'ikers. 'Shit!'

That might have been Gains. Pulcrude – miraculously unscathed – wasn't sure, but she shared the sentiment.

'When I call it,' came Hung's command, 'break for the colonnade, and then take cover between the columns, all the way back to the barracks door, and don't dally.'

'Hold on,' countered Pulcrude, her eyes now on Fedilap's body. She couldn't see a quarrel sticking in the sapper, not anywhere. Maybe she'd fallen on it, or maybe—

Fedilap suddenly leapt to her feet. 'Wait for me!' she yelled, but as she came, she limped badly, agonizingly slow.

In the strange unwavering light, throwing sharp shadows towards the west, Fedilap was suddenly the target of every crossbow and bow.

Snorting under her breath, Pulcrude said, 'Now, Captain, now!'

They broke, retreated quickly – Scatter lagging slightly and leaving a trail of blood – towards the colonnade entranceway, or, rather, its flanks, where stood the twin rows of columns.

In the meantime, Fedilap had been skewered by at least a dozen quarrels and arrows, but somehow she remained on her feet, weaving and staggering as if blind drunk, hands held out and groping. 'I'm dying!' she cried. 'Or badly wounded! Ow, this hurts so much!'

The squad reached cover, and moments later were filing back towards the barracks between columns. Pulcrude lingered, to watch Fedilap's glorious death-scene. Then, noticing the onrushing mob of axe-wielding maniacs already moving past the well, she swore under her breath. 'Too bad, woman, no audience left – except the bad people, of course.' Turning, she sprinted between columns, joining up with a staggering Scatter just at the barracks doors.

Who scowled at her. 'Nobody helped me, Pulcrude!'

'Because nobody likes you, Scatter. Here, lean on me – gods, that was a mistake! Just . . . let's . . . drag . . . ourselves – in here! Doors!'

The doors were slammed shut behind them, then the bars dropped with twin clangs that echoed loudly in the room. A moment later, only gasps could be heard.

'What was that light?' Gains asked.

Captain Hung was spattered in blood. A quarrel had gouged a gaping trough through his left forearm, from the wrist to the elbow, right along the laces of his vambrace. Ignoring the steady drip of blood, he looked around, then frowned. 'I was expecting to find her here,' he said.

Pulcrude glanced over, watching as Gains attended to the captain's wound. 'Fedilap? Naw, she probably went the other way. Miffed. Very miffed.'

They were all startled when Scatter fell over in a clatter of armour, hitting his head hard enough on the floor to dislodge the now-dented helm.

'Someone tie up that leg,' Gains said. 'He loses much more blood and even I won't be able to save him.'

Flutter went to the other heavy and squinted down at him for a moment, then knelt beside the man, pulling free a strap from his harness. 'You all seeing this? He owes me. He owes me, in a reciprocal way, and by that I mean I'm owed and courtesy's got nothing t'do with it—'

He might have continued his sermon, but at that moment the barricaded doors shook to the sudden press of bodies on the other side, and now axes began chopping into the wood.

'I see the problem,' said the captain. 'Without Arenfall, his night-agents were left hanging, and for all we know, they might in fact be dead as well, knowing how thorough the Claw can be. We were expecting an overwatch, but in truth, we had no eyes out there, none at all.' He straightened, stepping away from Gains. 'You've done enough. Go work on Scatter.'

'You fully healed's more important than Scatter—'

'Debatable. We may need our heavies tonight. Anyone tried their warrens, barring you, Gains? Lively or dull?'

Frowning, Pulcrude said, 'Dull, and getting duller.' She was about to add something else, but then stiffened, looking around. 'That recruit! Arat! I didn't see her go down out there! Just Fed and the sergeant! Where'd she go?'

'Bailed on us,' snapped Gains, 'obviously.'

'She stepped out for sure,' said the captain. 'I didn't see it as much as felt it.'

'Should've kept her locked in her cell,' Pulcrude said. 'Never did trust that woman.'

The captain shrugged. 'Never mind. Either way, we've been mauled, and those doors aren't going to last much longer. Flutter, your warren liking that daylight out there or not liking it?'

'Not, Captain. I can barely reach it. Whatever that magic is out there, it's pushing away everything I got.'

'Not for everybody,' Gains said from Scatter's side. 'My healing's fine, but then it would be, since Poliel died here, and that spilled blood's going to shrug off pretty much anything else.'

'Fedilap wasn't bothered,' Pulcrude said.

'Unless that was really her,' suggested Flutter.

Pulcrude snorted. 'You didn't see how bad her acting was, Flutter. Nobody dies for real like that, except maybe from embarrassment, and that'll only happen after the critics have stopped laughing. No, she Mockra'd the whole thing.'

'So where'd she go?' Flutter demanded.

*   *   *

Fedilap was pretty pleased with herself. Even with a quarrel in her shoulder – its impact mostly spent in carving through bronze scales and then heavy boiled leather, but hurting like the Limper's leg on a rainy day – she'd managed to open and roll into her warren, while throwing out that collapsing body that looked like her, face serene in death. Not that anyone could have seen it, since it seemed the whole squad was taking a beating and had other business to attend to, like staying alive.

Fedilap, meanwhile, stayed in her warren – scary as it was – only long enough to scramble over muddy, metal-scattered ground, ignoring the blasted wasteland surrounding her, along with the acrid stench of rotting meat – to reappear among the columns even before the others began their retreat.

Padding quickly, into and out of the shadows under that scintillating light, she reached the last inside column, the barracks doors on her right. Another shimmer through a thin sliver of her warren and she was scrambling atop the damned column – no statues on these ones, fortunately, just lots and lots of bird-shit. Playing with all this new, unnatural light, she made herself unseen.

From there, she could still see her body lying on cobbles. So delicate, so piteous – she wiped a tear from one cheek.

Noticing the steam billowing up from the well, Fedilap frowned, then, shrugging, used the sleeve of one forearm to wipe her nose. Crazy night for sure. The squad would have to retreat. She decided to help them with the perfect distraction. The sudden, miraculous resurrection of skewered Fedilap!

And sure enough, that exquisite performance had drawn every attacker's eye. Took a whole lot to kill her, of course. Tough woman! Legendary! Eyes bulged to witness. More and more arrows whizzed out. Quarrels followed. Fedilap, the human porcupine! But she just wouldn't die!

At least, not until the squad bolted and made cover among the columns, whereupon the porcupine Fedilap threw up both hands, spun in an exquisite pirouette, then, with a final, wavering cry, collapsed in a heap. A few more arrows slammed into her. Clearly, for some, her demise had been too subtle, or something.

But her fellow marines were safe enough. She'd thought then to let them know where she was, even join them at the barracks doors. Then changed her mind, upon seeing the mob on foot barrelling in pursuit.

Fedilap smiled, drawing up her bag of well-packed (lucky no quarrel had hit that!) sharpers.

This was going to be fun. For her. Not them.

She watched the front of the mob crash into the doors and rebound, and that made a bit of a mess, as the recoil rippled back through the press – they were suddenly all so packed together weapons were cutting flesh amid yelps and cries of pain.

Too tight a press to toss in a sharper, in fact. No, she needed them a bit more spread out.

It took some time to get the axes biting into the bronze-banded doors.

Not long, then, before this bright cloudless day in the middle of the night started raining sharpers. Too bad Pulcrude couldn't see any of it!

*　　*　　*

Pash had disobeyed her beloved mistress. But nothing was right in the world this evening. The Invigil would have rejected the summons and there would have been difficult moments there that Pash was not yet ready to deal with, so she had not bothered finding the man. Instead, she slipped outside, feet slapping on the thin layer of streaming water in the alley behind the temple; then she was climbing, finding the rooftops.

Looking south, she saw steam enwreathing Bastran Hill's pocked sides, then watched as the bhokarala emerged, fleeing the rising waters – and scalding heat – while, in the sunken areas surrounding the hill, the massive chaotic low-roofed sprawl of the Hill Quarter, figures were appearing from ceiling traps, or just scrambling higher wherever they could, even as, out on the sides, refugees from the subterranean city began pouring from the passageways, out onto Cedar Squat and against High Wall of the old Dryjhna Garden, now part of the Malazan Company compound. And no doubt elsewhere, though she couldn't see those portals from her present vantage point.

She did note, however, scores of figures on surrounding roofs, many armed with crossbows or bows. The Invigil's agents, eager to set flames to the rebellion.

Temple child or no, Pash was indifferent to that. This night, her service was to her High Priestess, whose life would surely be at risk, and not just from the Malazans. But Pash was just one person, one blade. She hesitated, wondering if it would be wise to go back into the temple, to find Ban Ryk now, rather than later.

But no, he was a man obsessed with symbols and portents. For this uprising, he would want to announce it with the dawn, awash in the blood of this night's slaughter. There was time.

For now, she knew her most immediate enemy.

She set out, in the shadows.

Until, all at once, the shadows vanished in a blaze of light.

There was nothing for it, then. To the nearest edge she scrambled, slipped over then down until her feet splashed in the stream, then settled on the cobbles. Before her, at a wide passage between buildings six or so paces away, a throng of people. She darted forward. Plunging into the milling, half-panicked crowds was like coming home. A face too plain to draw any eye, her body scrawny beneath a shapeless tunic, of no imposing height, possibly a child, possibly an old woman, Pash blended into humanity's mass, one among a thousand forgettable faces, a thousand forgettable lives.

The land has known this. More times than can be counted. The oldest trees still standing have witnessed this blurred human flow again and again, until each one sank into the other, and history itself becomes a grey passing.

I am Pash, the sweet red ruby, riding the mindless currents. Pay me no heed, not even worth a glance. And if a blade rides this torrent, it but adds blood's kiss, lost in the grey.

The water was ankle-deep, already filthy, already unpleasantly warm and soupy. Moving in the human tide, she passed the old temple to the Nameless Ones, empty now and believed to be haunted, then joined the press coming down from Green Wend, and down the narrow chute that opened out alongside the barracks wall – but this was a dead end, and already the crowd was folding back on itself.

She recalled a shop selling leather hides, marking the apex of the street. It leaned against the back wall that was part of Blue Sky's enclosure, directly opposite the old Gallows Row. Even though it had already been broken into, there was nowhere to go, no exit at the back.

Slipping through the heaving mass, she came up alongside the walls of the New Market Quarter, found handholds, and quickly climbed upward, pulling herself onto an angled tile roof. To the southeast she could see the Blue Sky wall, rising more than a man's height above the roofs where she now perched.

As she paused, considering, there was a sharp eruption from the other side of Blue Sky wall, followed by agonized screams. A moment later, another, then another.

The marines.

Attacking or defending made no difference to Pash. All who threatened the High Priestess needed to be eliminated. She set out towards the high wall.

*   *   *

Stipple and Hench finally made it to the Petals Tavern. Leaning up against the doors, they paused to recover.

'I've never been mugged for a whole damned bell before,' Stipple said. 'Or was it groped? Either way, I didn't get robbed and nobody was hating us or anything, so there's that.' She paused to glare at Hench. 'But you – you made them mad, Hench. That's what nearly did us in.'

'Bodies kept getting in the way,' he replied. 'Elbows and heads – I'm bruised all over, well, from the shoulders down. And stepping on people's no fun.'

'Those would be the ones you knocked down, idiot.'

'Worked up a thirst for sure,' he said, grinning across at her.

'It's awfully bright for it being around midnight, don't you think?'

'We've been dismissed from service,' Hench pointed out.

'Sure, but from the sounds of it, Blue Sky's seeing some fighting.'

'Bit further on, I'd say.' Hench pointed. 'As in outside the barracks.'

'So a mob rushed the marines. That explains the sharpers and all that loud dying.'

'Exactly,' said Hench. 'The marines are taking care of it. Nothing to do with us and besides, not only are we outnumbered, we're barely armed, and sharpers make no distinction anyway.'

'I know all that and I wasn't suggesting we do anything about any of it. We haven't even seen any others, have we?'

'Who?'

'The rest of us. Brindala, Thread, Garas.'

'Well, if the Adjunct dismissed us, he probably dismissed them, too.'

'If Hadalin knew who we really were, he would've done more than dismiss any of us, Hench. We're Talon. We're not even supposed to exist.'

'Outlawed, too.'

'Pain of death.'

'Just my point, Stipple.'

'No it wasn't. It was my point.'

'Well, one of us made the point.'

'Which was?'

'I forget. Is this door locked? It's locked! Can you believe that?'

'Obly the Boy's hiding in there for sure,' said Stipple.

At that moment, some rubbish fell at their feet, and they looked up to see the feet of three figures now hanging from the inn's lower roof-edge. Gear was strapped to those figures. Two with crossbows and empty quivers, one with a hunting bow and another empty quiver.

The one in the middle was the first to drop, landing in a lithe crouch directly in front of Stipple.

She stabbed him in the right eye, the motion so quick the man's expression didn't even have time to change to surprise. Pulling the blade back, she kicked him in the chest, just to help him fall backward. A score of nearby faces began turning her way.

The other two dropped to the ground. As the one in front of Hench landed, the Talon stepped forward, took the man's head in his hands and snapped it around, breaking the neck.

The last one, a woman, staggered slightly when landing, flinching when someone in the packed street behind her suddenly shrieked. When she spun at the sound, she spun the wrong way, presenting her back to Stipple.

Who drove her knife into the woman's spine, severing it. Then, as the woman began to collapse, Stipple stepped up behind her, left palm pressing against the woman's forehead while she brought the knife up under the chin, driving the blade upward until it reach the brain-stem. Yanking the weapon free, Stipple let the body fall.

There was a lot more screaming now, and more than a few expressions of outrage and fear. But no one dared close. Indeed, they were all backing away from Stipple and Hench, and the three bodies lying motionless in the gap.

'If he hadn't locked the damned door,' said Hench.

'I know. Well, don't just stand there, try knocking.'

At that moment, somewhere out on the other side of Blue Sky, a cusser exploded.

*   *   *

Okay, Fedilap allowed, that cusser had been a mistake. Her regret stayed with her, internally rising to a wail in her skull – despite her being momentarily deaf – as the great column under her continued rocking amidst eerie sounds of grinding she could feel through the stone itself. So, holding on for dear life, she caught periodic glimpses of the gory mess below.

And it was bad. Horribly so. The mob was pretty much gone, blown apart and spattered all over the rocking, pitching columns, the walkway itself a jumbled mass of meat, shattered bone, clothing, weapons, and hair still clinging to pieces of scalp and skull.

The barracks doors had vanished, knocked inward and maybe killing half the squad – who knew? she didn't – and the entire front of the building was now painted red.

A column opposite gave up, began its slow topple directly across the walkway. Of course its top smashed into one of the columns on *her* side, and now the domino effect began in what seemed every direction.

Eyes wide, lying flat on her perch, Fedilap watched as cracked, battered columns began falling everywhere, shattering in explosions of broken marble, joining the carpet of slaughter. Then, eyes widening even further, she stared as the two nearest columns – the one in her row and the one in the back row behind it – suddenly pitched her way.

Rolling to the opposite side, possibly adding her own scream to the cacophony, Fedilap opened her warren and, an instant later, was bodily thrown into it by the impacting columns.

358

She skidded across gritty mud, slammed up against some foundation stones, and found herself staring at a skeletal tree on the other side of a trench. The air was thick with bitter smoke, the ground beneath her jumping to distant explosions, pools of grey water rippling and making sobbing sounds – 'Ah, my hearing's back! No permanent damage. My body amazes me!'

She heard the squelch of boots, swung her attention towards the noise and saw three helmed, cloaked figures slogging towards her. They carried strange spears, but the long, narrow blades at the business ends looked deadly. Of their faces she could see little, given the strange round-eyed masks they wore.

'I'm not supposed to be here!' she shouted at them. And, to punctuate her pronouncement, she gestured—

Alas, no warren opened.

'What? Shit! Where in the Limper's crappy knee am I?' She pulled out a sharper – oh, not a sharper, she had none of those left. This was a burner – 'Stay back or we'll all be sorry! Listen, I need a bit to recover, get my magic going again. Go kill someone else!'

The three figures had halted at her first cry, but only briefly. They halted a second time when she pulled out the burner.

Fedilap grinned at them. 'Aye, you know this ostrich-egg thing, don't you? Or something like it, anyway.' She waved with her free hand. 'Back off! Go away! I ain't in your war and you ain't in mine, so get lost!'

They raised their spears and pointed them at her.

Something popped in her head – not a thing anyone else could hear, she guessed. Her smile broadening, she sought to open her warren. And lo, it did. 'Sorry, you poor soldiers, got to go. Gods shield you all.' She rolled backward, into her warren—

—and found herself lying on marble rubble and mashed body parts.

A scuffling to her left and she turned to see Pulcrude standing in the gaping doorway of the barracks. 'Bet you thought you'd killed us all,' she said, fists on her hips. 'Figured we were idiots, didn't you? Crowding up against the doors or something. But I was counting sharpers, knowing how many you had. And I knew when you were done you'd pull out that damned cusser, and sure enough, you did. So aye, we knew when to back off, Fed. So there!'

'But I wanted a new squad!'

'Get off your ass and get in here. Captain wants to decide what to do next.'

Sitting up, Fedilap said, 'Count me out. Bag's empty but for a couple of burners and one cracker. I'm useless. Oh, and my shoulder got scraped.'

'Don't think I'm sharing, woman, because I don't like you and we don't get along.'

'I don't like you either,' Fedilap said, climbing to her feet. 'Especially since you missed my spectacular death.'

'I did. We all did. Never saw a damned thing.'

'You must've seen it start! Why else bolt when you did?'

'We heard it and that was enough. But we didn't hear all of it, either. Just enough to know you were still flopping around back there like a carp in a muddy field.'

'I saved all your lives!'

'If you say so. Get in here, the water's rising.'

Turning, Fedilap saw the truth of that. The water gushing up from the well was all foamy now, the foam somewhere between yellow and red, and it was spreading out across the cobbles. 'Good,' she said, 'place needs a wash. Hey, Pulcrude!'

'What now?'

'Why's it so bright?'

'The entire world thought you were dead and couldn't help itself.'

Fedilap got ready for a rejoinder – as soon as one dropped into her head – but saw Pulcrude retreat into the barracks. *And that's another reason for hating you, woman. You always get the last word. Oh, shoulder's starting to hurt.* 'Hey, Gains! I need healing!' She hurried into the barracks.

*   *   *

Smoke and dust still lingered over Blue Sky. Pash picked herself back up. The explosion had been brutal, throwing her flat, and then, as columns began falling up and down the colonnade, it seemed the thunder would never end. In the wake of all that was a heavy silence, at least nearby, that seemed reluctant to yield.

Back on her feet and edging towards the high wall, she began to hear distant sounds of fighting, or maybe just panic and chaos. Far off to her right, she could see figures on the rooftops facing into the open concourse surrounding the holy well. They were even now withdrawing, finding ways back down into the crazed, packed streets.

Eager to vanish, or hungry for more blood?

They would have been agents of the Invigil, battling the marines – and she could see at least one dead marine lying on the cobbles, arrow-stuck. Even as she watched, two figures ran up to that corpse and began dragging it away – off for desecration, no doubt, the body stripped naked, flensed, dismembered—

The sudden report of crossbows sounded from somewhere amidst the fallen columns, and both figures at the marine's body fell. A few moments later, marines appeared, crossbows already reloaded and held at the ready. Moving forward, sloshing through the water, now at their shins, they approached the body of their fallen comrade.

Pash watched with narrowed eyes. No chance of reaching any of them. Not yet. Besides, they too were out for blood.

She would have to return to the streets, flooded though they were. Only within that crowd – with all this blinding light – could she do her work.

* * *

The Azathanai, Mael, Elder God of the Seas, appeared near the lone tree on the summit of Bastran Hill, observing the ever-rising waters with considerable satisfaction. Steam swirled across the slopes on all sides of the hill. Somewhere overhead a gibbering bhokaral was throwing sticks down, none striking its intended target so far, that being Mael himself, who was still standing with crossed arms when another figure appeared nearby, in a muted flash of sorcery.

Mael scowled without turning, hoping the newcomer might go away. But it was not to be. Irritated, he finally fixed his gaze on the man slowly climbing towards him, and his eyes narrowed.

A strange man indeed.

Halting ten paces away, not quite on the summit but, given their differing heights, more or less at eye level, the man spent a moment adjusting his clothing.

Mael spoke. 'Nothing about you makes sense.'

The man glanced up. 'Ah, well, you're not the first to make that observation.'

'You know who I am? Or, rather, "what" I am?'

'Azathanai are a mystery none can fathom,' the man replied with a faint smile. 'Not even the Azathanai themselves. But yes, Mael, I know who and what you are.'

'Then you have me at a disadvantage.'

The man sketched a lazy salute. 'Corporal Hasten Thenu, at your service.'

'At my service?'

'A figure of speech.'

'Well then, just who *do* you serve, Corporal Hasten Thenu?'

'How about "common interests"? That being, the interests of the common.'

Mael grunted. 'Speaking for all the innocents out there, soldier? Alas, there are no innocents. None, in fact.'

'Not even children?'

'Damp slates of clay awaiting the first cut.'

'You've grown sour of disposition,' the man observed.

'I was never a kind god.'

'I've seen your more gentle repose, Mael, in sighing whispers along a strand. Or indeed, utterly becalmed beneath a motionless sky.'

'Temporary moments of exhaustion. By those means do I lure mortal fools into my realm. There is no graveyard as large as mine, soldier.'

'No, I suppose there isn't. And now, it seems, you desire to expand it.'

'I do. Now, I sense curious powers around you, mysterious ones, in fact. Which, given how long I've lived, is most unusual. But I warn you, attacking me will see you dead. Besides, I cannot be killed.'

'Thank goodness,' replied the corporal. 'At least, with you and your myriad offspring, there remains a certain logic to the realms. Without you, nothing but chaos. So yes, I'm glad you cannot be killed, Mael.'

'Nor can my will be denied here.'

'Your will? No, not a thing to challenge. But what of your mind, Elder God? Can *that* be changed?'

'Not this time.'

'What makes this time different?'

'Oh, this isn't unique, you know. I've done it before.'

'And it failed, ultimately,' Hasten Thenu pointed out. 'Begging the question: why repeat that which never works, foolishly seeking a different outcome? But of course, none of this is about outcome – it certainly isn't about justice.'

Mael's scowl deepened. 'And what would it be about? Please, enlighten me.'

'Vengeance.'

'Against whom?'

'Oh, whoever you think has been manipulating you. Then again, as a god, you must be used to being manipulated.'

'I was, once, but that was long ago. None worship me now, soldier. They worship my children, but not me.'

'Oh, a few do, I'm sure.'

'Not enough to bother me.'

'Vengeance.'

'Manipulation,' snapped Mael. 'Is this game yours?'

Thin brows lifted. 'Me? No, not at all.'

'The Magus of Shadow accosted me not long ago. A very rude man. Possibly insane.' Mael paused as a stick struck his left shoulder and then fell at his feet. He sighed. 'Do you know how he summoned me? I will tell you. He stuck a giant hook into the carcass of a horse and pushed it off a cliff into the Raraku Sea.'

'And that worked? You can't resist dead horse?'

Mael stared at the man for a few long breaths, then he said in a flat voice, 'Some levels of absurdity prove irresistible to me.'

'Ah, then he knew you well.'

'Someone knew me well.'

Hasten Thenu nodded. 'Of course. As Magus to Shadowthrone, then. An official meeting.'

Mael snorted. '"Official"? Is there some bureaucratic level needing to be achieved here, Corporal? I don't recall any involvement from your empire.'

'Oh,' Hasten murmured, rubbing at his clean-shaven jaw, 'any of *that* kind of involvement wouldn't be official in any respect.'

'Your obnoxious Emperor has done it before!' Mael snapped. 'And not even an emperor back then. A mere—'

'Any imperial benefit,' Hasten cut in, 'would be incidental. That said, I doubt Shadowthrone was interested in seeing you flood the entire world, was he? And, more to the point, why G'danisban?'

'G'danisban wasn't even mentioned,' Mael allowed. He shook his head. 'Underhouse was convenient, that's all.'

'And the rising waters?'

'Also convenient. A new sea was born in the Raraku basin – what did you think would happen?'

'Reborn, surely.'

Mael shrugged dismissively. 'Too long ago to count.'

'Even for an Elder God?'

'No, for you mortals. You all think you've got your narrative down, from beginning until now? Every age fully mapped out to make of it all some grand tale of progress with you, happily, at the pinnacle? Is this your first climb to such civilized heights? Your hubris astounds me.'

'The original Raraku Sea dried up because of Omtose Phellack,' said Hasten. 'The Jaghut unleashed ice-magic all over the world, seeking to block the T'lan Imass. Those glaciers dropped sea-levels, changed weather patterns, and in this case, took away all the rain from inland Seven Cities.' Hasten smiled. 'How is that for a narrative?'

'Who are you again?'

'I'll grant you the hubris, Elder God. Our delusions of continuity and progress. But we seem to have stepped off the path here—'

At that moment, at the east gate, the goddess manifested in a bloom of light that swept the stars from the sky.

Mael turned a glower upon the incandescence. 'She's worn so many bodies. Eres, Imass, human. But at her core? Nothing but barely self-aware chaos. Vitr in her veins. Ever restless, doomed to lash out again and again.'

'Hmm,' said Hasten, 'sounds like an Azathanai.'

Mael shifted his glare back to the corporal. 'You know too much and it's really beginning to annoy me.'

Hasten answered with his own shrug of indifference, the smile still at play in his expression. 'So, which apocalypse will it be? Hers, or yours?'

With a sudden grin, Mael said, 'I'm prepared to step back and leave her to it.'

'That's a relief. We wouldn't want a full convergence here, would we?'

'You can't stop her, you know.'

'Me personally? I wouldn't even try.'

'She'll annihilate the world.'

'What of your agreement with the Magus of Shadow?'

'Shadowthrone's mad fool? Well, it's lost relevance, wouldn't you say?'

'Maybe, but you'll hold to it anyway, won't you? I mean, you gave your word, after all.'

'Very well, as pointless as it will be.'

Hasten smiled again. 'And your word that you are stepping back? No global flood and all that?'

'Well,' Mael answered, 'I admit a few forces have been awakened already. But mostly natural. Too late to stop any of that.'

'Where, if I may ask?'

Mael ignored the question. 'She won't stop at Seven Cities.'

'Now, the water under G'danisban—'

'Entirely natural! Simple seep and aquifers. Limestone and tufa. The water was always there – are you even aware of the vast underground waterways built by past civilizations? Their only legacy, mind you. Everything else is dust.' He barked a laugh. 'Imagine Dessimbelackis's shock when he stumbled on the one linking Ehrlitan with Pan'potsun! First Empire? Now *there* was hubris!'

'But this upwelling will subside again, won't it?'

After a moment, Mael conceded the point. 'Yes, there is a blocked channel a few leagues southwest of here, but it's already about to burst. Still, the Under Quarter will stay flooded. Well, half-flooded. Useful as a sewer – with a bit of construction work – but why am I even bothering talking about it? That goddess is about ready to begin her slaughter. Of everyone.'

Hasten bowed. 'Then, sir, I take it you're leaving now?'

Eyes narrowing, Mael hesitated. A stick struck his right foot. From the branches overhead came cackling laughter. 'Why do I have this growing suspicion that I've been outwitted here?'

Hasten's thin brows lifted. 'I have no idea, Azathanai.'

'I've committed your face to my memory,' Mael said. 'That tattoo as well. I will find out who you are, eventually. You see, you made a mistake. This world and this time, I am known, if known at all, as an Elder God. But you name me Azathanai. A title that hasn't been used in thousands of years. So, this guise you're wearing, I will pierce it.'

The next stick struck him atop his head, and that one stung. Snarling, Mael waved one hand and vanished from the hilltop.

* * *

Corporal Hasten Thenu looked up. It took him a few moments to find the hairy hulk of the bhokaral. It was glowering down at him, a big broken branch in one hand.

'Don't even think it,' Hasten warned.

'Abalallahh ab yarallla ah!'

'Stop panicking. You didn't really think Mael was ever going to stop Va'Shaik, did you?'

365

'Jaraalalah yarbbalal!'

The creature then threw the branch, but, as was not uncommon among his kind, he let go at the wrong moment, sending the branch upward instead. It clattered directly above the bhokaral's head, then fell straight back down. Yelping, the creature dodged it at the last instant. The branch continued bouncing and clattering to land at the base of the tree.

'Serves you right,' Hasten said. 'Now, I've got me a soul to find. Wish me luck, oh king of kings.' Opening a warren, he stepped through.

*   *   *

Va'Shaik revelled in the anger, especially since so little of it was her own. Oh, there was plenty of that as well, on behalf of this poor man's body she now possessed, although such were the myriad flavours of anger that outrage cast its own quality of burning light, as distinct as seething fury, or cold rage. The last of such forms was the flowering into intention, and then motion: into violence, in other words. But for now, she could – and would – build all these nuances into a blinding, blistering whole.

Night's sweet gift was gone. Though no sun touched the eastern horizon, this anger made its own sun, this fiery sphere surrounding her, making her unapproachable, unstoppable. Any who dared close would be instantly incinerated.

Anger as armour, how fitting, so perfectly fitting. And here, at the very heart, I can feel these souls in their thousands. Ignoring their fear, supping only upon their anger – all the causes, all the formless furies of entire lives of wounding, of oppression, slights and abuses, insults and disappointments. And to think, I thought to bring peace to all of this? Really, what would be the point?

Taste this! Anger so sweet, the bitterness a lingering not yet discovered. No, we shall nurture it in this moment, you and I – all of you, and I. Fed unending, cradled, coaxed again and again. Let anger be your lover, as I make it mine, and watch me lead it – and you – to its inevitable conclusion: the negation of life itself.

She stood just within the gate, not yet ready to begin her glorious journey through the city. For the moment, the rage of mortals was in every street, and in the tenements and in every room where someone huddled or stalked – all this rage! It made her drunk, pulsing through her in fierce waves.

I will ride this across the land, drawing every injustice, every unreasoning righteousness, every blistering indignation, the tallies of lifetimes, all of it, into my Whirlwind.

Decry none of this! It's what each of you wants, there in the core, there in that cauldron of rage you would dance around – see how drunk it makes us! How dizzy, how wild and staggering, my whirlwind of fists to the face, boots to the ribs, the heels stomping the skull, hands to the throat, the solid push beneath the surface to see the mouth gape, eyes bulging, the drowning face – the drowning face!

The world gives you this rage. Its gift, its eternal laughter to your beleaguered sense of what's fair – it isn't fair, no, you are not fair, it's just the word you use to rationalize whatever you want, whatever you desire, and guess what? Your neighbour thinks the same!

Families, hamlets, villages, towns, cities and empires, cauldrons nested within cauldrons within cauldrons – do you not see? The shape of the smallest dictates the shape of all the others, bigger and still bigger, all now the same shape!

Ignore the interludes of peace. They never last. Let's end it, all of it!

It finally made sense to her now. She would be the repository of human anger, gathering, ever gathering, drinking deep every righteous belief, every impulse of the offended, and this would become her Whirlwind. Those who preceded her had never understood. Even Dryjhna, the Holy Book, indulged too much in the Apocalypse itself, not its bright, eternal fuel, its mortal wellspring of human anger.

This would be a Whirlwind of their own making and against it, nothing could survive. And indeed why not? *Well, because no one wants to.*

She sensed the ones around her, all pushed away as she remained reluctant to abandon this body of the man who had been Bornu Blatt. They could see it in the heart of the light, the bent, ugly man so cruelly abused by nature, and then by her own need and will. She saw the marines from the gate pull back, set out into the heaving crowds where the weapons of her followers rose and fell in a slaughter of refugees, innocents, apostates, heretics. She watched them killing the Invigil's agents with perfect, breathtaking efficiency.

Gilakas remained close, the poor Claw assassin, wondering if he could throw a knife into this sphere of light.

And Stult . . . what of him? This limping man, so knotted with stresses inside no hair would grow on his body, so grieving for the woman, Gracer, who had never loved him and whom he loved with all his unwelcome heart. What did he want? From Bornu Blatt? Nothing. From Va'Shaik?

Why, everything. For what I did to Gracer. Oh, you poor man. Your hatred of me is like nectar on my lips.

And beyond these, into all the blurry faces and roiling human currents – *ah, all you angry people! Feed me unto excess!*

She gathered more and more, almost ready to begin her fateful march, the first step on destruction's journey.

Bright as the sun. And the sun's heart was a storm without end.

*   *   *

In the absence of High Fist Arenfall, there wasn't much for it. Brindala, Thread and Garas had set out, at first, to provide overwatch for the marine squad emerging into the city, only to find themselves in a chaotic press of refugees as every building's ground level began filling with water; and before long the dwellers of the Under Quarter appeared as well, along with squalls of excited bhokarala clambering and scratching their way to rooftops. Every street and every alley was suddenly so tightly packed that even panic did little to move people along.

The three of them could have followed the wisdom of the bhokarala and taken to the roofs, and indeed were planning to do so, when weapons appeared in the press, and then people started screaming and dying.

Brindala saw Garas push his way towards the killers. Thread was a short distance away, being shoved by the throng towards an intersection where more slaughter had erupted. Twisting round, the woman locked gazes with Brindala, who raised one hand and made a rapid series of hand-signs. Nodding, Thread slipped from sight a moment later.

Off to the left, things looked even worse. It was clear to Brindala that someone had not only locked Iron Gate, but was also preventing anyone from forcing it open. A quick check of her weapons confirmed that none had been snatched or torn away, then she set out for Iron Gate.

She was almost at the walnut-tree grove occupying an island in the middle of Iron Street, the churning water pouring along the cobbles making it an island in truth, when she heard marine munitions going off, from the direction of Blue Sky. The implications tumbled through her mind as she pushed her way through the heaving humanity – their own failure to provide overwatch from the rooftops around Blue Sky, the cost in lives of whatever ambush had just occurred – and now, after a succession of what sounded like sharpers, a cusser, the sound like lightning hammering stone, followed by crashing masonry that seemed without end.

And now the crowd surged, pushing her in the opposite direction. She fought against it, helpless to even find solid purchase underfoot. Twisting, she tried working her way to the closest wall, somewhere where she could put her back against solid stone and hold herself in place.

It took some time, but eventually she did just that, and was able to watch the crowd surge past. Then, somewhere to her left, more screams erupted, and just as suddenly the surge halted, jolted into a reversal of direction.

Startled, she caught a quick glimpse of Thread, riding the current back towards Iron Gate and her gaze fixed upon Brindala. She sketched another sequence of hand-signals, saw them acknowledged.

Satisfied, she stepped into the crowd, no longer fighting against the current, but instead riding it back towards her original destination. Before long she was once again at the walnut trees, and then past.

Here, it seemed the flow slammed up against something that pushed back. More screams, now from ahead. Brindala fought once more to work through the now milling press. Until, at last, it seemed she won through, into an eddy, a momentary pocket.

Swearing under her breath, she fixed her attention on the scene at Iron Gate. Va'Shaik acolytes were holding it. Armed with spears and what looked like antique halberds, they had made a body-strewn gap between them and the mob, the ankle-deep water red in the unnatural light, victims lying face-down, their hair spread out like seaweed.

In front of this bristling barrier, more Va'Shaikers were plunging into the crowd, cutting down all before them with axes and swords.

Brindala set her gaze on the nearest of these attacking groups. It was going to take some time to reach it, as now people were flinching back, the fear rising towards panic. Three men, two with scimitars and the third one wielding a single-bladed axe. The axeman had reached out with his free hand to grasp a woman's telaba between shoulder and neck, and was forcing her down to her knees. Two children were clinging to her, both screaming.

The axe swung down, twice, and small bodies fell away. The mother's shriek was brief as he finished her as well.

Brindala reached the nearest swordsman, who had paused to watch his companion kill the woman and her children. His own curved blade was slick with blood, bodies at his feet.

She came up on his blind side.

The third attacker saw her and shouted a warning.

Too late, as Brindala's knife cut through the front half of his throat, stopping only at the vertebrae. Yanking her weapon free, she stepped around the collapsing man, her left hand rising to intercept the second swordsman's overhand chop, catching the scimitar's blade on her buckler. There had been anger behind that downward swing, and the scimitar's narrow base was where her buckler blocked it. The old weapon snapped clean off just above the hilt.

She saw his look of astonishment, the last expression of his life as she drove her knife into the man's brain through his left ear.

When she pulled her blade free, leaping back as best she could – hoping to evade the axeman's attack – she stumbled over a corpse, then fell onto her backside with a splash.

But the axeman was nowhere to be seen.

Scrambling back upright, knife readied and buckler lifted, she finally saw the axeman. Lying motionless atop the woman he'd just killed. Brindala could see no wound. Wildly, she looked round, but the crowd had pulled back, away from the fighting, and every face she saw in her scan gave her nothing but fear and despair – not one even so much as looking in her direction.

'Shit,' she muttered.

More killing not far away, from another handful wading into the press – she'd need to get rid of them before turning her attention to those holding the gate.

She set out, and for a moment it seemed the crowd parted before her.

Brindala never felt the knife enter her spine.

*   *   *

In the rush of people moving into the sudden gap left behind by the woman killing the three men and then suddenly dying, Pash let herself be carried along, flattening her knife-blade against the inside of her wrist, feeling its warm stickiness – not much, the stab had been clean, precise.

That was two of them done now in this crowd. There was a third one, busy near the walnut trees – busy killing the Invigil's beloved servants – and Pash had no issue with that. She'd no issue with this woman either, nor the other one the woman had signalled to with hand-signs. Killing them had been simply necessary – besides, she'd seen both of them before, on the rooftops, and knew them to be Malazan agents. Maybe even Claw assassins.

Pash had known the man with the axe, too. Mean, dismissive of unbelievers, a pure adherent to the Apocalypse, he'd been one of the Invigil's favourites. Killing him had settled old scores, from back when she was a young foundling in the temple. Once, he'd kicked over the bucket at her side when she'd been scrubbing the floor. Then laughed, before yelling at her to mop it all up.

Pash remembered. She remembered everything, in fact. Tonight, then, she had many scores to settle. Even while she ensured her beloved High Priestess was safe from all harm.

Riding the human currents, she let herself be carried ever closer to those acolytes holding the gate. She'd not try any of them, of course. This savage press of people was perfectly suited to her needs. No, best keep those gates barred. And every other gate as well.

The bright light wasn't so bad after all. Who paid attention to plain Pash?

No one.

Now the tide was drawing her around, and before her, at the walnut trees, there was the third Malazan, who'd just killed four from the temple and was now standing, head lifted, straining to catch sight of the other two.

She drifted towards him like a leaf in a stream, and each time his gaze swept past her, seeing nothing, she felt her inner smile broaden.

Like a leaf in the stream.

*   *   *

In the commander's bedroom in the official residence that he never used, Jalan Arenfall emerged from his warren. The room should have been dark. Instead, what seemed like daylight was coming through the shutter slats, painting bright ribbons across the furniture and floor.

Had he lost his sense of time's passage? Had not Hasten told him that most of the night still awaited him?

Wincing slightly at the tug coming from the crudely sewn wounds on his body, he moved silently to the window. No, he was not at his best, but it would have to do. He lifted the shutters and looked across to Bastran Hill.

The light came from behind it, pulsing, flaring. Stretching out across the shanty roofs were wild, bizarre shadows. The source seemed to be Seven Gates.

The goddess.

And, closer to hand, it seemed that G'danisban – at least – was in full rebellion.

Magic erupted just to the north, on this side of Blue Sky's South Gate, sharp and short, followed by screams. Arenfall waited, but it was not repeated. Even so, he sensed something pushing in his direction – towards, perhaps, Imperium House.

He wondered what the Claw were doing – likely they had decided to strike for the Va'Shaik Temple. Even the new Adjunct would have seen that quelling the chaos in the streets was not possible. No, they would seek to decapitate this uprising by taking down the High Priestess, the Invigil, and probably everyone else still on the temple grounds.

It was a struggle opening a warren, but he managed, wrapping himself in subtle magic, and moments later began moving, through the window and up onto the roof. He paused to take in the situation on surrounding rooftops. Bhokarala everywhere, many of them lined up like crows or gargoyles to look down into the heaving streets. Elsewhere, people armed with bows or crossbows were positioned overlooking intersections, loosing missiles down into crowds.

Well, one thing at a time.

Arenfall leapt across to the roof of the Imperial Guard building, then ran five paces south to jump across the gap of Empress Street, landing lightly on the low roof of a cobbler's shop. Without his sorcery, that roof would never have taken his weight. But blurring into and out of the world mitigated things just enough. Six paces to his right brought him facing the high wall of Imperium House. He eyed it.

The barred windows opposite were dimly lit, shuttered from the inside.

Below him, Empress Street made a sharp right-angled turn at the corner, heading south along the back wall of the House. It was unpatrolled and mostly still in shadow. Water flowed over the cobbles, cluttered with litter.

Drawing heavily on his warren, Arenfall threw himself across the gap, hands closing on the bars of a window, knees bent and the balls of his feet against the wall beneath the shallow sill. Pulling himself up he fashioned a rent between the wall and the room on the other side and pushed himself through.

Unoccupied, fortunately. High shelves lined all the walls, sagging beneath copper scrolls. He knew the room. The written word was born for the list-makers, of course. The tax collectors and accountants who, in order to continue their essential careers, required the rise of civilization itself. These records were part of the city's archives dating back to well before the conquest.

Behold, our legacy. We'd all be better served melting the scrolls down, or hammering them out into cups, plates and pots.

While these idle thoughts passed through his mind, he crossed the chamber and opened the door leading onto the main passage that ran the length of the building.

Again, no one in sight. Had the Adjunct panicked, sent every single guardsman to the front door below?

He came to the spiral stairs leading up to the landing just beneath the roof. Arriving at the ladder, he drew his warren close about himself, then began climbing.

*   *   *

Gilakas had lost sight of the marines. They'd carved through the Va'Shaikers on the ground until they started taking fire from the rooftops, at which point they seemed to have completely vanished.

Seven Gates had been built for defence. Passing through it was complicated. Both the south exit and the north exit debouched facing the outer wall. Perhaps randomly, they'd come through via the north one, to find themselves facing a three-storey tower, the ground floor of which was an armoury. In any case, there'd been no guard there and the bronze door was locked tight.

The manifestation of the goddess – taking Bornu Blatt in a manner that looked no different from when Va'Shaik possessed the corpse of Gracer – had occurred at the mouth of Cedar Squat, in front of the Stavro Inn. She'd only taken a few paces towards the Squat itself before halting Bornu's body, and hadn't moved since.

The mob in the Squat had briefly dispersed – somewhat – during all the killing, not to mention recoiling from the sphere of blazing light surrounding the goddess, especially after a few hapless souls had been pushed into it, where they burned to ash, the deaths so quick there'd been no time to even scream. But now, pressures from all the alleys and streets feeding into the Squat were bringing the people back. Reluctantly.

Gilakas could feel their terror. He stood with his back to the Seven Gates wall, twenty paces down along its length. The goddess remained to his right. He'd seen an arrow fired into that sphere and saw its incineration, so he now knew a thrown knife would never reach the body at the heart of the emanation. Still he hesitated, since that sphere wasn't entirely unoccupied. Somehow and for some unknown reason unharmed by the fire, Stult knelt almost directly in front of Va'Shaik. His head was bowed and he'd not moved at all.

Someone unseen moved up alongside him, and an instant later, Gilakas heard a familiar voice, 'Took your time.'

'Ibinish. Where are the others?'

'The Adjunct finally relented. We're preparing to assault the temple.'

'The rest of the Hand?'

'Lalt's dead. Aliksos was wounded bad enough to stay back with the Adjunct.'

'I saw the Adjunct die.'

'We take our orders from the *new* Adjunct. Hadalin.'

Gilakas grunted. He saw a few people nearby turning to frown at him as he spoke seemingly to no one. He offered them a rude gesture, then drew a knife, which proved sufficient to dampen their interest. 'Where's the High Fist?'

'Dead. How do you think we lost Lalt and damn near lost Aliksos?'

'So all of this is Adjunct Hadalin's doing, is it? What a Rope's tangle.'

Soft laughter, then, 'Inkaras intended the same. In any case, we've got our orders.'

'The goddess is here.'

'That's who that is?'

'Well, the body belongs to the Inquisitor I travelled with. She's possessed it.'

'Completely?'

'I'd say so.'

'So why is she just standing there?'

'No idea.'

'Gives us time, though, right? Let's go clean out the temple.'

'The others are close?'

'We were skirting the inside of the city wall – only way to move unseen. So yes, Bulk and Formult are close. It was Bulk who saw you.'

Gilakas frowned. 'Hold on, why are you having trouble moving unseen?'

'Those fucking bhokarala. They're everywhere and they can see us, or smell us, or both. Either way, they shriek and point at us.'

Sighing, Gilakas said, 'All right, let's go kill everyone in the temple.'

* * *

For her to reach the elaborate, almost delicate door to the Immanence Chamber which served as the Invigil's sanctum, four acolytes needed to die. This hadn't taken particularly long; she'd been expecting more, to be honest.

It wouldn't have mattered. Four or forty made no difference as far as she was concerned. Her necessity was plain. Into the Temple of Va'Shaik, and, if needed, every single damned room, from the lowest scullion's cell to the Holy Altar Room itself. Killing only to keep things quiet, to keep things proceeding as needed.

In fact, it amazed her just how much her cold fury felt so . . . empowering. As if, indeed, she was somehow immune to all harm, as if the righteousness of her anger was now an undeniable force, against which no mortal could stand.

Madness. Absurd. But heady even so.

Standing before the curious door with all its carved reliefs, its gilding and studded precious stones, its garish painted trim, she wondered at the nature of this Invigil. Having never seen him, all she knew was his reputation. A man whose fanaticism had nothing to do with faith or religious belief, despite the depth his own well-rehearsed pronouncements had sunk into his own soul – until, perhaps, he half-believed his own words. But only half. The rest was cynical, acquisitive, just one more mortal fool lusting for power.

A man rumoured to have poisoned the two previous High Priestesses before this most recent one.

But he wasn't her target, just perhaps the final obstacle. So, there was no choice.

Stepping back, she lifted one foot, then kicked in the door.

It splintered at the hinges and fell away. Within, the Invigil had clearly been pacing, as, standing in the centre of the room, he now whirled to face her.

375

She stepped inside, looked around. 'You're alone? How disappointing.'

'Who are you?' the man demanded. 'What has happened to my—'

That last question was answered by her lifting into view one blood-slick blade.

Ban Ryk shook his head. 'Pathetic assassin. The goddess has manifested, here in G'danisban. When I call upon her, she will defend her chosen Invigil. You cannot harm me.'

'And have you called upon her?'

'I have.'

'So, this knife here can't take your life, Invigil? That may not matter, to be honest.'

'Are you a Claw?'

'No,' Satala replied. 'I'm a Talon, and I'm looking for Pash.'

*   *   *

By the time Gilakas and his fellow Claw assassins came within sight of the Temple of Va'Shaik, all use of sorcery had been surrendered.

'Why be surprised?' Gilakas asked the others. 'She's here, after all, or almost here.'

Cursing as he wiped sweat from his face, Bulk said, 'No matter, we're close enough. I see no one at the Grand Gate. Still, we could avoid it and go over the garden wall.'

'Actually, I do see guards,' Gilakas said. 'Two of them.' Without adding more, he set out, straight across to the Grand Gate. Ibinish, Bulk and Formult followed.

The two guards were lying motionless to either side of the double gates, and the gates were partly ajar. Crouching down over one of the corpses as it rolled slightly in the water, Gilakas grunted and then said, 'Clean kill. Knife.'

'Same over here,' added Bulk.

Ibinish then said, 'There was a hint—'

'Barely that!' Formult cut in.

'Even so, a hint. The High Fist had his own agents to be sure. Skilled as this? Maybe.'

'So we may be too late,' Gilakas said. 'Let's confirm it, shall we? And if indeed one of the High Fist's agents has done our work for us, well, no reason to complain about it, is there?'

That said, he pushed open the gates. Just beyond was a cobbled

376

compound open to the sky. Ten paces opposite waited the doors to the temple proper. A huge figure that had been lounging in the shadows off to one side now straightened and stepped forward, placing himself between them and the door.

Lifting an enormous double-bladed axe in one hand, he said, 'Do you speak Satala's language? I can work with that . . . somewhat. I am afraid I cannot let you inside. Not until my companion has done her work.'

'Fenn?' Bulk asked.

'Never heard of them until recently, to be honest. But close enough.'

'We can kill you,' Bulk continued, smiling. 'Or you can be nice and let us past. We'll not hurt your companion. We just need to confirm that everyone who needs to be dead in this temple is in fact dead.'

'I'm not known for being nice. This does seems to be a night for killing. I should think my companion will be most thorough. She's very angry, after all. You will of course have to take my word for it.' He paused, and then added, 'She and I are on a great adventure. There's bound to be some killing involved both for her and for me. For me, I can start here if you like.'

Gilakas laid a hand on Bulk's arm and gently pulled him back. 'How long do you think she'll be, this friend of yours?'

'I cannot say.'

'If we return at dawn, say, and she's yet to reappear, it may be the case that she failed and is dead. That seems reasonable, wouldn't you say?'

'Dawn? Well, yes, that's too long. Adventures such as ours brook few extended stays in any one place. So, go away and come back at dawn to do your explorations. That way, I don't need to kill all of you.'

Bulk laughed. 'It doesn't matter how big you are, there's one of you and four of us, and we're very quick. Too quick for you.'

The giant nodded. 'I have heard much the same thing said to me many times before.' Then he smiled.

That's enough for me. Gilakas bowed and turned to his companions. 'Let's go.'

Bulk scowled.

'Stop getting your back up for nothing, Bulk,' Gilakas said. 'With what I've seen getting here from Hanar Ara, I've learned that avoiding a fight is always the better option.'

'For a Claw?' Bulk demanded.

'For anyone not a fool. Now, with Aliksos not here, I'm in command of this Hand. Do you want to contest that, Bulk?'

'Of course not. I just don't like his attitude, that's all.'

'In that, too, you're not the first to say such a thing,' the giant said, still smiling. 'Now, for your memoirs, I will inform you that my name was once Kanyn Thrall, but for this adventure I shall be known as The Grey Shore. Thank you. You may go.'

Gilakas waved his team back out through the gate. Then he hesitated, looked back at the giant. 'Your companion, is she good at what she does?'

'I have no idea. I think so.'

'She killed the guards outside the gate?'

'Yes.'

'Well, that's something.'

The Grey Shore shrugged. 'My appearance may have distracted them. But yes, it's something.'

'Good luck on your great adventure,' said Gilakas.

'It has been an auspicious beginning.'

CHAPTER FOURTEEN

You would unleash a soul?
Cut away from flesh and bone,
an end to the tethering
that makes small the world?
Beyond the body's skin border
by every measure unconstrained,
there is this circling
round a sense of something lost.
But that is no more than memory,
a lingering echo of emplacement.
Some will circle forever –
you can see in their ghostly faces
bemusement and confusion
while they hover in no special place,
and make even of their manifested selves
the semblance of who they once were.
But turn instead outward
to see the universe infold,
and take of your self an essence
of every truth of your being.
Then witness, as before this
and this alone,
the universe
trembles.

Paen
Fisher kel Tath

It was not in Arenfall's nature to harbour grudges. Even in considering the Adjunct's attempt on his life, it was an expedience he well understood, though to his mind there'd been little valid reason for it. Betrayal after all had been the last thing on his mind. He believed he had convinced Inkaras Sollit, but alas, that had achieved nothing with the man's untimely death. As for Hadalin, well, their first meeting had been one of humiliation for the Adjunct's bodyguard and if so, then surely that man could hold a grudge.

Complicating things, no doubt, would have been Hadalin's suspicion that Arenfall had in some way been responsible for the death of not only his Adjunct, but also his lover. In all, plenty of reasons for drawing the assassin's knife.

Could anything be salvaged?

That remained to be seen.

He had sensed the Adjunct's presence on the rooftop, a magical deadspace positioned, somewhat ironically, on the very place Arenfall himself often stood, offering the fullest view of the city laid out before him. Likely not a pretty sight at the moment.

But the effect of the scabbarded otataral sword was not enough to negate Arenfall's sorcery as he emerged above the trapdoor and stood, lingering in his warren as he fixed his gaze upon the Adjunct's back, less than ten paces away.

Killing Hadalin in this moment would not be difficult. In many respects, the man was already dead, should Arenfall decide on that path. But was it even necessary? Was it not simply a matter of differing strategies in dealing with this uprising? After all, Arenfall had already lost control of his legion. He was now but one man, no longer even a Fist. The Emperor's paranoia wasn't even relevant to the crisis now before them.

Was not Hadalin a reasonable man?

Sighing, Arenfall relinquished his warren, fully manifesting on the rooftop.

*   *   *

Waiting within her own warren, Aliksos wasted no time, appearing in a flash, both daggers driving for Arenfall's back.

Somehow, impossibly, he ducked and twisted to one side, evading both blades.

She felt a punch to her back, faint and momentary, leaving her bewildered.

She remained bewildered as she fell to her knees, and then onto her side, blinking in the strange daylight. It seemed she had no body left to feel.

A soft voice above her. 'Apologies. I have severed your spine.'

Aliksos found that she could speak. 'You couldn't have . . . I was too quick, too close.'

'A peculiarity of my warren of choice,' he replied. 'A certain delaying effect between what you might see and what is.'

'Deadly.'

'It can be. Now, I must speak with the Adjunct. Perhaps a High Denul healer can be brought here.'

'Not likely,' she said. 'Do me a favour and roll me onto my back.'

*   *   *

Straightening from the woman now lying on her back, Arenfall lifted his gaze to the man standing at the far end of the roof. The Adjunct's sword was out and its deadening effect was lapping up every trickle of magic across the entire roof.

'Unintended,' Arenfall said, gesturing down at the Claw.

'You nearly killed her the first time, and now again,' Hadalin replied. 'Tell me, Arenfall, do you expect to leave this rooftop alive?'

'You've lost control of the city.'

'The rest of the Hand is probably even now butchering everyone in that cursed temple.'

'Yet the goddess has arrived. How do you intend to deal with her?'

Smiling, Hadalin raised his sword. 'Need you even ask?'

Arenfall shook his head. 'I fear that may not be enough, Adjunct.'

'Why? Va'Shaik is not an Elder Goddess.'

'I suppose not. Very well. You might as well give it a try. I certainly have no thought of stopping you.'

'Of course you wouldn't, since she so clearly poses a threat to all Seven Cities. I would think you'd want to be at my side for this, in the empire's name.'

'Is that an invitation?'

Hadalin cocked his head. 'Perhaps. I'm undecided.'

'I see that.'

381

'Explain yourself to me, Arenfall.'

'There's little to explain, Adjunct. Plans were put into effect to stamp down this uprising before the flames could truly take hold. Unanticipated, this manifestation of the goddess herself, however. That said, we could at the very least have prevented G'danisban plunging into chaos.'

'Had you fully explained your plans—'

'You never asked, Adjunct. Inkaras, mind you, did. But he died before he could pass on to you his conclusions.'

'Which were?'

'To be honest, I have no idea.'

'So he might well have done precisely as I have done.'

'I choose to believe otherwise.'

Hadalin sheathed his sword. 'We shall do this, then. Accompany me, Arenfall. It's time to kill a goddess.'

'I am to walk at your side, Adjunct?'

'Have I your word to not attempt to kill me?'

'Have I yours?'

'Yes.'

'Then you have mine as well. Now, we should carry your Claw down to a bed at the very least—'

'It'd be lost on her though, wouldn't it?'

Aliksos spoke then. 'Leave me here on my back. I would rather study the sky than a pocked ceiling. And I should tell you, had I known you were going to shake hands, why, I'd not be lying here right now.'

To that Arenfall had nothing to say. Nor, it seemed, did the Adjunct.

*　　*　　*

Not long after the two men had left, Aliksos heard a soft scuffling off to one side, and a moment later a stranger's face was hovering over her.

'Who are you?' Aliksos demanded.

'Nobody,' the woman replied, bringing into view a knife. That weapon blurred as it passed under Aliksos's chin. Spurting sounds.

The stranger moved away, towards the trapdoor.

Aliksos continued watching the sky until it and everything else simply disappeared.

*　　*　　*

382

Fedilap reached down and began working free the quarrel from the back of the man's head. 'If this guy's skull has bent the point I'll be seriously miffed.'

'Leave it, woman,' Pulcrude said. 'There's nobody here left to object to us opening the damned gate, is there?'

'Not at the moment, no. But—'

'We've got enough quarrels! Come on, the captain needs help with the gates.'

Straightening, Fedilap looked over the strewn bodies and squinted at the rest of the squad. 'Listen,' she said to Pulcrude who remained – impatiently – at her side, 'we're probably close enough for their liking.'

'It's you they're annoyed with!'

'Fine!' Fedilap snapped. 'So go join them then! That lock's mechanism's been wrecked. Use a burner—'

Snorting, Pulcrude said, 'A cracker, surely. Bust it right open.'

'Melting it's more elegant, though. And no chance of shrapnel in the captain's forehead, either.'

'That seems a bit specific. Why the captain?'

'Well, any of them, if you like. It's your lack of subtlety, Pulcrude, that they really hate. Me, I just did what was needed. Took down that entire mob of frothing idiots and there's this point, too, the one about the Goddess of Smart.'

'The goddess of what?'

'You heard me.'

'Not that again! There is no goddess of smart!'

'There is! And she's smiling right now. My sharpers and cusser killed a whole lot of *really* dumb people!'

Captain Hung had left off examining the broken lock and was approaching.

'Not dumb,' objected Pulcrude. 'Just caught up in that fever of mind-less killing, slaughter and butchery that can hit anybody on an off day.'

'They were unarmoured, untrained and trying to take down a door between them and Malazan marines! Like I said, utter idiots! I did 'em all a favour!'

The captain gestured. 'You two are needed to open the lock.'

Fedilap glanced behind her and squinted at the milling crowd – too cowed to come any closer, but bad things were happening farther in, on what seemed every street and alley, so the mob was edging ever closer since the marines were obviously working on getting the gate open. All the corpses in the space in between was probably a slight disincentive. For now.

They set out side by side, Hung waiting then following.

'Come on, Pulcrude, here's proof of how much they like me, since I saved them all.'

'That cusser almost collapsed the entire barracks!'

'But didn't! Consistent with my calculations, in fact.'

Pulcrude sniffed. '"Calculations", hah hah.'

Hung halted a pace or two behind them as they arrived at the gate, while the rest of the squad warily looked on from one side.

Pulcrude pulled out a cracker while Fedilap found her last burner. They converged on the huge lock, heads together as they examined it.

'See? Someone jammed a knife or something into the mechanism. It's wrecked.'

'I can fit the cracker in there,' said Pulcrude.

'Only about a third of it, meaning the rest of the spike will be exposed and will kill anyone standing within five, maybe even ten paces.'

'Sure, so we all stand *eleven* paces away. Gods, you're such an idiot.'

'But with the burner all I need to do is break the glass bulb at the tip and let things heat up. Melt it to slag and that's that.'

'Right, a big lump of melted iron that will miraculously fall apart, opening the gate to a million grateful people!'

At that moment, Flutter pushed both of them away from the lock, raising into view an enormous axe.

'Hey, where'd you get that?' Fedilap demanded.

Flutter blinked, as if the question had proved to himself how stupid he was. Then he rallied and said, 'Stuck in the barracks door, of course.'

'Even after the cusser? Wow, that's some axe.'

'Some door, too,' added Pulcrude.

'Just bash it open,' the captain ordered.

It took a bit of hammering, mostly on the latch itself, during which Fedilap contemplated the vicious potential of the axe, the lock or the latch or even all three suddenly exploding in a deadly scatter of iron shards, one for Flutter's left eye, one dead centre in the captain's forehead just under the brim of the helmet, and four or five into Pulcrude's sweaty face. Disastrous indeed, horrifying and regrettable, but that's what happened when someone not a sapper went and did a sapper's job and that was the harsh lesson—

Instead, the lock fell away and the gate doors seemed to sag as the horizontal bar was pulled free. The captain gestured the three of them off to join the rest of the squad, then he opened wide both doors of Crimson Gate.

Another gesture, this time to the crowd, launched the frenzied exodus.

At which point, all those grateful people nearly trampled to death the entire squad.

*   *   *

Thinking long and hard about something presented the possibility that the decision would become moot, making such contemplation more than worthwhile; and this was certainly the case for High Priestess Shamalle, at least as far as she was concerned. The impulse to move, well, anywhere, required an extended, if not protracted, period of musing, mulling, and weighing. And yet, at least she was standing. That was something, wasn't it?

Then, happy circumstance! as the doors to the altar room swung wide to allow the entrance of Invigil Ban Ryk and, half a step behind him and with a knife held at the man's neck, a complete stranger, whose expression suggested she wasn't pleased by anything.

'Finally!' Shamalle said, or very nearly gusted, given the extent of her expulsive breath upon which the word carried. 'The city has given voice to much agitation this night, making the notion of sleep well nigh impossible. Now do tell me, Invigil, about the happenings beyond this venerable temple, and following that, perhaps an explanation regarding your companion, who has clearly become familiar enough with you to conclude that a knife to your throat is entirely reasonable.'

But it was the woman who spoke. 'Where is Pash?'

Shamalle frowned. 'Why, I have no idea. I dispatched her to convey my summons to the Invigil, but she never returned. Nor, until this moment, has the Invigil deigned to grace my presence with his illimitable self.' Her frown deepened. 'Did I say that right? I think I did, but you know how confusing some turns of phrase can be. So I cannot say—'

'She's your head assassin,' the woman cut in, most rudely. 'Don't try to convince me you don't know where she is or what she's doing right now. There are bodies all over the rooftops. It's a Limper-damned killing spree. Now, since she serves you and this man here, I'm going to begin cleaning up by killing you both.'

Shamalle's eyes began to widen, but even as they did, the woman sank her knife into the side of Ban Ryk's neck, then sliced outward until the blade flashed back into view out under the man's chin.

He crumpled straight down amidst choking followed by a splash of gushing blood that then began spreading out through the thin layer of floodwater covering the floor. One leg twitched for a few moments, then fell still.

Shamalle felt her expression change. She felt, too, the flush leaving her face. The world beneath her ample skin had gone grey and flat and cold. Her breathing slowed, and when she spoke, her voice was utterly tone-less. 'That was presumptuous. The Invigil's fate belonged to me, not you. Who sent you here, assassin? I would know the source of this offence.'

The killer's eyes never left Shamalle's as she slowly crouched over Ban Ryk's body to clean her knife-blade on his silks. 'Now I see,' she replied. 'No longer the bumbling lush, are you, High Priestess?' After a moment, she straightened once more, assuming a fighting stance. 'The only one who sent me here was Pash herself, when she stuck a knife into my chest – when she murdered me. But it seemed the Limper wasn't interested in me. I have found my way back, High Priestess.'

Shamalle considered the assassin's words. 'Unusual, but not unprec-edented. It doesn't matter, in any case. If Pash murdered you, she had reason.'

'I command the Talon in this city,' the assassin replied. 'My task was simple enough. Kill every murdering thug your Invigil sent out at night. Against rival cults. It seems you have forgotten that you are in the Malazan Empire. All faiths are allowed, barring those demanding human sacrifice. So tell me, High Priestess, how weak your religion that its adherents cannot abide anyone who believes differently?'

Gaze dropping to the motionless body lying in its thin pool of blood, Shamalle said, 'I well knew his crisis of faith, Talon. I knew, as well, the effective response the High Fist had instituted, in which you culled the Invigil's most fanatical servants of the knife. What I do not understand is your belief that my handmaiden was wandering the rooftops at night with killing on her mind.'

'You sent her out, then?'

'To spy. To witness. To inform her High Priestess.'

'She did more than that.'

'I did not know.'

The Talon shrugged. 'Your failing, not hers. Now, your goddess is in the city, but lingers at Seven Gates. Your Invigil claimed she had extended her protection to him. Clearly, he was wrong. I doubt she's much interested in you either.'

'I suspect you're right,' Shamalle replied. 'And while I understand your personal stake in Pash, I am afraid that she, too, is for me to deal with.'

The Talon attacked in a blur.

But Shamalle's wave of one hand was quicker, her power intercepting the Talon halfway to the dais, batting her to one side. Through the air she flew, across the room, slamming against the wall with a bone-cracking impact, knife spinning from one hand to land silently atop a heap of cushions. Rebounding, the woman sprawled across the wet floor, unconscious or dead.

Shamalle felt her cold, grey inner world slowly yield to this silent, peaceful aftermath, where she alone stood in the chamber, all discord dispensed with.

For now. She frowned down at the Talon. 'Oh Pash,' she murmured. 'Did you misunderstand? Or did you keep something hidden, deep inside you, that I never once sensed? It's possible. There is no end to the dark corners in which a soul can hide. Behind placid eyes. Or, in this case, eyes that rarely if ever met anyone else's.'

Well. Now it seemed that such procrastination had proved disastrous. For the Invigil, at least, not to mention this returned-from-the-dead-but-who-might-be-dead-all-over-again Talon. 'Clearly, I dither too much. Mull to excess. Give in too often to the musing impulse. Weighing this versus that, oh my, and on and on!

'The mind is such a strange thing! Alive in the eternal instant, island of now in a sea of then and soon! I think I'd better collect up my goddess, frozen as she is – and what so ails her, I wonder? I don't wonder at all. Immortal woman, you are drunk on excess! Upon the very edge of all-destroying apocalypse, you hover, totter, mull and muse, weigh and weigh again.

'I must hurry! And hope against hope that none seek to disturb you!

'To wake your anger, dear me – goddess and woman both! Aaii!'

The High Priestess looked around for a shawl. Or something. It was wet out there, after all.

Barefooted, she splashed across the floor, sending swirls through the thinned blood.

She must hurry!

Once she found a shawl, the proper shawl, and so many from which to choose! This, of course, wasn't dithering. 'No, not at all. This is *fashion*.'

*   *   *

Hadalin could make little sense of Jalan Arenfall, but he was beginning to understand Inkaras Sollit's fascination with the man. There was a reserve about him, a sense of utter self-containment, that was most alluring. But, more than that, the mystery about him was, without doubt, dangerous.

The lives we live makes that appealing, precisely because of the risk entailed. Still, I need to remind myself: his interests can never include me. And so, he hovers almost within reach, yet unattainable at the same time.

Poor Inkaras! This must have tortured you!

Gates had been opened somewhere in the city. It was late, and the crowds on the streets had thinned. But everywhere lay bodies, an unleashing of slaughter to announce the rebirth of the Apocalyptic. All so pointless.

The goddess, he assumed, was striving towards a vision, a scene where she walked alone across fields of corpses, the sky above filled with carrion birds. Mistress of the battlefields who would make a battlefield of the entire world.

They walked unaccosted, saying nothing. Upon the ledges of flanking rooftops crouched bhokarala, watching them pass. Rhizan and moths were on bodies lying motionless in the street, lapping blood. Street dogs prowled with crimson muzzles. Every now and then, Hadalin could hear weeping from some tenement window or gloom-shrouded alley. A child called for his mother, his thin voice worn raw as he went unanswered.

There were times when Hadalin could feel his Emperor's anger. At such madness, such idiocy. Or perhaps that was a weak assumption, this sense of sharing outrage. Perhaps it was dismay in which they were mired, verging on existential despair. Either would fit the moment. Two masks among many, the drama seeking endless variation, only to fall into well-worn tracks that surprised no one.

He was glad he was not the Emperor. As Adjunct he was merely a weapon, mindless as any honed blade. Hardly a role for a man who adored both women and men, was it? Trying to kill Arenfall had pushed his mood into muddy places, where his rationalization – ending a potential rival to the Emperor himself – sank beneath the roiling surface of his suspicion that Arenfall had orchestrated the murder of Inkaras. But even that was something of a lie, wasn't it? *Inkaras was obsessed with him. And me – floating free amidst a plethora of pleasures within reach – I was jealous.*

That is the truth of it. And I set a Hand of Claw to deliver my vengeance.

I doubt the Emperor would have approved.

But maybe these doubts were but forms to follow, guises to wear, to give to his unseen audience things they would recognize, and thereby nod knowingly, if unsympathetically.

So be it. We are complicated creatures, after all. Beware simple explanations. For anything involving human motivation, desire, intention. And then, to this incendiary mix, add impulse – blind, thoughtless, ridiculous impulse. Gods below, it's a wonder any of us get along at all.

'I sense a storm within you, Adjunct.'

Hadalin glanced across at Arenfall. 'If indeed you sense such things, my title is not relevant to them.'

'Ah,' he said, nodding. 'For what it is worth, I liked Inkaras Sollit. And I grieved his death.'

Hadalin grunted. 'Forgive me, but it's worth little.'

They were approaching the sphere of light. It seemed to have swallowed most of Seven Gates, as well as the open plaza called Cedar Squat. The trees that gave it its name were limned in gold light, as if in the path of a fast-approaching wildfire.

They turned from High Wall Street onto Choke Street, then slowed their steps, as the narrow passage ahead was filled with bodies.

'Have we another route?' Hadalin asked.

Glancing over, Arenfall tilted his head. 'Were you not born here?'

'The area, and yes, I knew – know – the city, but only in its wealthier quarters. The east side never interested me.'

'Noble blood?'

'Not after the conquest. We kept most of our wealth, though. It was our family's clout, its power, that was taken from us.'

'I'm not averse to climbing over the bodies, Adjunct.'

'Very well. Lead on, then.'

Arenfall did so. Falling in behind him, Hadalin said, 'You must be wondering.'

'Adjunct?'

'Why I would ever join the Malazan military, given what the conquest did to my family.'

'Actually, I wasn't,' Arenfall replied. 'You simply switched your path to power, Adjunct. Patriotism is an expensive indulgence the wealthy rarely choose, especially if it gets in the way of power and influence. Besides, look at my own bloodline.'

Hadalin found himself glaring at the man's broad back.

They emerged onto Cedar Squat. Here, amidst more bodies, the water on the ground was steaming.

Four figures suddenly emerged from beneath one of the trees and Hadalin smiled as he saw his Claw assassins. Holding up a hand, he said, 'We have reached an agreement, me and Arenfall.'

Bulk shifted his gaze to Arenfall. 'No hard feelings, High Fist.'

'Generous of you,' the man replied drily.

Bulk suddenly smiled. 'Unless you'd rather have it otherwise.'

'That's enough,' said Hadalin. 'Lead me to this damned goddess.'

'You can't get close,' said Ibinish.

'Perhaps otataral can,' Hadalin retorted, watching as Arenfall moved off to one side, attention fixed on the Claw. It had been startling – and pleasing – to see Gilakas among them, and Gilakas now addressed Arenfall.

'High Fist, could we have anticipated this when last we met, we could have cut down Bornu Blatt and his miserable troop right then and there.'

'The goddess was present then as well,' Arenfall replied. 'I doubt she would have permitted such a thing.'

Gilakas shrugged. 'Had you given the signal, I would have tried.'

'Inkaras Sollit was your commander, not me,' Arenfall said. 'But it seemed he mostly ignored you, didn't he?'

'He likely expected an opportunity to exchange a few last words,' Gilakas replied. 'Alas, he never returned alive from that debacle. Damned convenient.'

With a sudden chill rippling through him, Hadalin now fixed his gaze on Gilakas. 'Yes, you'd know more about that, wouldn't you? I was informed by the High Fist that Inkaras was killed in the attack on the bandits. Is that accurate?'

Gilakas shrugged. 'I never saw any of it,' he said. 'My charge was staying close to the Inquisitor. I don't know why Inkaras elected to accompany them into the village. I have an idea, of course.'

'You do?'

'He planned on killing Arenfall there. Out of sight of anyone else to be sure. Instead, maybe Arenfall got to him first.'

Hadalin slowly drew his sword, not yet turning to Arenfall. 'Gilakas, are you certain Inkaras wanted the High Fist dead?'

'Wasn't that the plan all along?'

No words were needed then, as Hadalin whirled to close on Arenfall, while at precisely the same time, Gilakas, Ibinish, Formult and Bulk drew knives and rushed the man.

None of them reached him.

Hadalin felt himself punched hard in the side, just under his left arm. The impact was hard enough to make him stumble, and as his left arm came down as he sought to regain his balance, it struck something that sent agony into his back, just inside his shoulder-blade, but for some reason he was unable to find out what it was, as that arm had stopped working. Drawing breath hurt, but his lungs felt clear. Slowly straightening amidst waves of pain, he looked towards Arenfall.

Four bodies lay on the soaked cobbles in front of Arenfall, who had not moved.

Confused, Hadalin stared at the man. 'No one's that fast,' he said.

'You're right,' Arenfall replied. 'But while you had your Claw, I had a squad of marines.' He paused. 'No contest.'

And now those marines were closing in from all sides, crossbows out and cocked, pointed vaguely towards the Adjunct.

'Everything almost settled then, High Fist?' one asked.

'Not quite, Captain,' Arenfall replied, eyeing Hadalin. 'Adjunct, do you still want to try killing the goddess?'

'I have a fucking knife or quarrel in me.'

'Quarrel. But no punctured lung. Puler can get it out and sew up the wound, but all that otataral in your veins won't let you get magically healed. Still, it's not like the goddess is going to swing a sword at you, is it?'

'So I walk up to her and stab?'

'Wasn't that your intention, Adjunct?'

'It was, when I felt healthier.'

'And now?'

Turning with difficulty, he looked across to where he could just make out a vague form at the centre of the glowing sphere – and someone kneeling before it as well. 'I am . . . undecided.'

'Gilakas had it wrong, by the way,' Arenfall said. 'Inkaras was part of the squad's rush. I was coming in on a flank. If he'd wanted to kill me, he'd have joined me at the start. I didn't even see him fall, but I saw the aftermath. He killed the bandit who killed him, I think. They died in each other's arms, or that's how it looked.' He paused, and then added, 'He could have killed me well before the fight, I suppose. Even without his otataral sword. I would not have been expecting it at all.'

Hadalin bared his teeth. 'Because he lusted after you.'

A pause, and then Arenfall nodded.

After a long, ragged sigh, Hadalin sheathed his sword and moved to sit himself down on the edge of a stone horse-trough. The effort left him gasping, close to passing out. An instant later, Arenfall was crouching beside him.

'Adjunct, can Puler attend to you?'

'Why not? I've been outplayed at every turn.'

'And the goddess?'

'She wants the world destroyed, she's welcome to it.'

*   *   *

In her favourite shawl – on this night at least – Shamalle stepped outside and found herself looking at the massive back of a massive warrior, standing blocking the outer gates. He held loosely in one hand a massive axe – 'Yes indeed, isn't it all utterly *massive?*'

At her voice, he turned to face her. A frown clenched his brow. 'Most unfortunate. Is my companion dead, then?'

Shamalle sniffed. 'I suspect most end up that way. But to whom do you refer, Fenn?'

'Fenn? Toblakai? Tartheno? Thel Akai? Is there any end to this list of names? I refer to Satala, knife-wielder, vengeance-seeker—'

'Not dead, just unconscious, as it turns out.'

'Are you the one known as Pash?'

'I am High Priestess Shamalle.' She gestured behind her. 'I own this house.' Seeing his frown deepen, she added, 'In a matter of speaking. I mean, it's a temple, not a house. And I don't own it in the sense of property title.'

'Then you don't own it at all!'

'Fine, if quibble we must! How could I have imagined my droll insouciance to be so lost on you?'

'Your what?' After a moment, the huge warrior raised his axe. 'I think you are the one who rendered Satala unconscious.'

'I think you're right. Of course, she was trying to kill me.'

'Which you no doubt deserved.'

'Probably, but not for her to decide. Except, perhaps, as an agent of the Malazan Empire. But then, I never personally offended High Fist Arenfall, barring my perhaps excessive mooning over his official role as a glorious man, resulting in my sending him many gifts, some of which were not quite decent. But I most certainly have done nothing to earn the ire of the empire! So, no, not for her to decide. Unless it was. Oh, now I feel bad!'

Growling under his breath – *a most rumbling growl* – he took a step towards her.

When she magically batted him aside, he went through the wall and into the garden, bricks flying everywhere, followed by a hovering cloud of mortar dust and who knew what else.

Shamalle walked to the gaping hole in the wall and peered into the garden. 'Now, are those wooden legs, or just legs covered in roots? How curious! I see no movement. Thus, dead or unconscious. Shall I determine one or the other? I think not. Not this time. I am on a mission, after all.'

Stepping back and then walking to the outer gates, which hung open, she paused again. 'Mission? Oh, I can't remember the mission!' Looking around, she fixed her attention on a narrow alley between two minor temples almost opposite. 'Ah, Temple Narrow. I think I'll go down there and perhaps, having chosen a direction, everything will come back to me in a flash. Or a flicker. I'll take flicker, or even a spark. Dear me, I'll take anything right now!'

*   *   *

He would have fled had such a thing been possible. Was not the soul free to do as it pleased, once divested of its physical prison? The body he had known all of his life, his personal empire enclosed by skin and little else, had been, it was true, an unruly one. Often clenched with discomfort, knotted with aches and twinges, general senses of being troubled, not quite right. And, surrounding all of that, like a sickly atmosphere, there had been his recognition of his own brokenness, the truth of his flaws, the basic ugliness he could never escape.

Such a reluctant ruler of his realm, was Bornu Blatt. Dismayed at his condition, an emperor who'd rather hide than expose his bent self to others.

But now freed, dethroned, light as air, so insubstantial he could not even hold up a drifting mote of dust, nor guide a seed to its place on the earth. The world passed through him, passed through his thoughts, his notions of self, passed through all that he was. Blind to his presence, or simply indifferent, his disincarnate soul no longer had reason to be here.

Yet he had found himself in a maze of shadows.

As the goddess filled the body he'd once owned, casting incandescent light that coruscated with rage, every shadow had grown impossibly precise, the borders as sharply defined as the edge of a knife-blade. And within this mangled web he was trapped, and somehow the darkness beyond them both – the true darkness of a night almost passing, in that hovering stillness that deepened just before the eastern sky sent up its first silvery sheen – that, too, remained denied to him.

How he longed for it, dancing off into the night, hungry to chase it into the west, ever westward, and in his swift freedom, why, he could ride that darkness for ever, lost in the absence of light, just one more ghost among countless others.

And did he not deserve it? Empire's cage, misshapen and misaligned, mapped out in knuckles of pain where things did not quite fit, or move in proper fashion, where his recognition of his own ugliness – and the offence his very existence delivered upon the eyes of others – had all been left behind, discarded. Nothing he could claim any more, were he fool enough to want to.

Freedom, and then, inexplicably, freedom denied. Shadows he raced along, the web-tracks he could not escape, what manner of curse was this? Had he not paid enough? Where was his reward?

Where is my reward?

The shadows slowly resolved around him, as if taking physical form. So too his insubstantial soul, his formless self, now found itself walking. Lightly, unbent, absent all aches and tiny stabs of pain. A man walking, a man perfect in form, a man as he was supposed to have been.

Where did it go wrong? In the womb? Or even before then? Did the twisting punishment wrap itself around the act of procreation itself? A cruel husband? An indifferent wife? Are they to blame, in that instant of sharing life's spark, to make of the unpleasant act a matching simulacrum in bones and flesh?

394

Or was it my soul, rushing into this newborn form in a woman's womb, that so deformed the gift it now occupied?

Is that my nature? Am I the ugliness itself, doomed to twist and bend whatever body it chooses to occupy? And if this is so, what escape awaits me?

None.

No escape.

The man walking, now on his knees.

And then a stranger's voice spoke. 'None of this is so.'

He could feel a hand on one shoulder – a smooth, proper shoulder at that, the deluded correction of an imagined body, as if he could maintain it for ever – but no, already it began to fade—

'No, friend, stay with me. Let shadow hold on to your form. Ride this body.'

Why? Why bother? It's all an illusion.

He felt amusement from the stranger when he spoke, but not the harsh kind. 'You think you are alone in this illusion? Unique in the making of your self? My friend, we are all the same, each in our own world. Tell me, why do you think the Mason appears in almost every House in the Deck of Dragons? We are builders of our own realms, each and every one of us. It's what we're given to build with over which we have no choice.'

She can keep it.

'Keep what?'

My body. My ugly empire.

'She can. Of course. And even now, she's feeding on it.'

Bornu Blatt frowned. *Feeding? Feeding on what?*

'Well. The essential injustice of what you were born with, and what you had to contend with every day of your life in that body. And that's valid, isn't it? After all, there's really no end to the injustice in this thing we call living. The impossibility of perfection – that's what haunts every soul. You, me, everyone. And the worst thing about it is, we each have a sense of that perfection. Some aspects of it we can strive towards, in how we shape our lives. But other aspects, the physical maladies, what we're born with or what comes to us as we age, why, we can't do a damned thing about any of that, can we? And that, my friend, is unfair.'

Unfair. Yes. And this is why we howl. We howl!

'She's about to, yes. Feeding on your imperfect body, but more, feeding on the price you paid when you dwelt within it.'

Bornu felt a flash of fury. *She knows nothing of that price!*

'You're right. And it gets worse. She's now reaching out, pulling in all the anger – from every soul within reach, and that reach is expanding. Eventually, she will have an entire world's worth of anger. With which she will unleash the Apocalypse. Are you getting it yet? The secret of the Apocalyptic? It's no outside force of nature. It's us. It's the rage within us. Not just rage, of course. Also indignation. Humiliation. It's all the shame we work so hard to avoid even acknowledging in ourselves. It's us and the truth of imperfection, and how perfection offers us a promise *we can never reach.*'

Unfair, he whispered.

'Gods yes. Unfairness. Given enough despair – and she's discovering plenty of it – the only perfection possible is utter negation, annihilation, the complete levelling of the entire plain of existence.

'So, she's taking who and what you were and converting it into her outrage. And, having learned how to do that, she's now doing the same with everyone.'

She has no right.

'Doesn't she? How are you now, Bornu Blatt? Your sense of bone and flesh? Your shadow-self here in the Shadow Realm. Do you remain – how did you judge it? Ugly?'

The answer was, of course, *no.*

But the choice is mine.

'Well, yes. It should be. But I have a secret for you. Will you hear it?'

Who are you?

'Oh, many things. Many names, but Hasten will do for now. I was once a priest of Shadow. In fact, I've worn the holy robes of more gods in more temples than I care to count. Though I admit a singular fond-ness for Shadow – and not because of Shadowthrone or the Rope – but because of its essence, which I'll get to in a moment. Or not.'

This is the Shadow Realm? Why am I here? Why can't I escape?

'Sorry. My fault. I can't let you go. Not yet, anyway. But if you decide, in the end, to let her do what she will do, well, I won't stop you from leaving. But where was I? Right, the secret. Will you hear it, Bornu Blatt?'

Would it matter, his hearing this secret? He was already decided. He would indeed leave her to it. Why not? *Tell me, then.*

'It's just an observation, but the import of that observation is where you will find the choice. The absolute, undeniable freedom to choose, which as I said I will leave entirely to you. All right, are you ready?'

Get on with it.

'The Shadow Realm, by its very nature, is doing its best. But ultimately, it can't. By that, I mean, it can't fully dampen the very nature of your soul, Bornu Blatt. Now, you can't sense any of that, since you are inside the phenomenon—'

What are you talking about?

'Your soul, Bornu Blatt. It blazes. With indescribable beauty. You have no idea of that, though, do you? Let me try this way, then. There is a woman, back in the First Holy City, in your beloved library – what is her name again?'

Salabi.

'Yes, her. She saw you well enough. So she gave her heart to you, Bornu Blatt. Completely, unassailably. For years, in fact. Were you aware of that? And now, in your absence, she weeps nightly, wishing with all her might that she could magically turn back time, to speak with you. Just a few words before you left. To wring from you a promise. To return. To return to her.'

No words came to Bornu Blatt. His mind was blank, still, frozen in place. This stranger's words seemed impossible. Absurd.

'You didn't know? Never guessed? Well, going back in time, that's not . . . I won't say not possible, rather, not desirable. Too many linked events, it'd be a mess. But I'll make you a promise. Assuming you want to do this. Go to her, I mean. Do you, Bornu Blatt? Do you want to go – oh, let's call it for what it is – do you want to go *home*?'

He found himself on his feet, poised in that perfect balance he'd never known. The sharp edge of shadow was directly before him. Beyond it blazed the rage of the goddess.

A world-encompassing indulgence.

'The Apocalyptic, yes, it's surely that. The most cowardly answer to unfairness imaginable. That's the point with unfairness – that it's unfair for everyone. Everyone. But at some point we stop being children about it. Don't we? But remember, Felisin Younger never had a childhood, not a true one. She has no idea that her present state is that childhood. It is what follows rebirth. And now, we are moments from her tantrum that will end pretty much everything, everywhere.'

What is your promise?

'Oh, yes. Only that I'll get a message to Salabi.'

How?

'I was thinking a particularly vivid dream, from which, when she awakens, she will feel no doubt, no uncertainty at all. The dream's veracity will be absolute. Or as near as I can get it.'

A dream of what?

'That you're on your way to her, of course. Assuming you want that, Bornu Blatt.'

He studied the line between shadow and light. *As a ghost?*

'What? No, that would be pointless for her and torture for you. No, with you back in your body, Bornu Blatt. Your imperfect, aching, bent body. I imagine that doesn't sound like an appealing prospect, does it? The thing is, it's only in your body that you can prevent breaking Salabi's heart. You back into your body. That's what answering her love is going to cost you.'

He sensed a shrug from his invisible companion, who then continued, 'If that's too much, I'll release you. Chase the night for all eternity, Bornu Blatt, here in your perfect shadow-body. It's a reasonable choice, I'd be the first to admit. You've paid enough. Nor did you choose to leave your body. The goddess didn't ask, did she? You are exculpable in every sense.'

Bornu Blatt continued staring down at the dividing line. His shadow-self on this side, and upon the other . . . *Tell me, friend, my true body. How do I get it back?*

*   *   *

What mortal did not dream of this? Va'Shaik could take within two cupped hands all anger, could shape this fierce impulse to deliver destruction, harm and vengeance – oh yes, vengeance was what it was all about, once all the other stuff had been stripped away. Vengeance in answer to the unfairness of things.

Vengeance against the more successful, the more talented, the prettier, the more youthful. Vengeance against every measure of success, earned or inherited, with no regard or weight given to whatever discipline and diligence was demanded to achieve it. No, none of that mattered. In the absence of such virtues – especially the sheer investment of time to win competence, recognition, even mere acknowledgement – resentment and envy were transformed into weapons of victimhood. And such weapons!

Giving such power to the wounded, oh, was this not the most fervent wish of every mortal to have ever walked the earth?

The goddess would be their instrument; hers would be the hands to tear everything down. Was it any wonder they worshipped her?

And now, at last, she was ready to unleash the end to everything.

At that moment, into her vision, there came a soul.

Va'Shaik smiled. 'You are transformed, Bornu Blatt, made perfect of form, and I see now that, given the chance, you would have been a hand-some man, a desirable man.'

'What you see, Goddess, is my shadow-self.'

She scowled. 'Shadow! Tell me, what shadows will be left once I reduce everything to dust? That realm's power will vanish, and with it, that ghostly body. And you, who do not believe, are you not pleased? An end to ugliness, to imperfection, inequality, all of it, done with!'

'What shadow is cast – what you see before you – is not that of my body, but my soul.'

'Delusion, Bornu Blatt. I have felt the pain you lived with, the anguish, the eternal embarrassment and shame. Your desire to not inflict yourself on anyone else, which you deemed an act of mercy. Now you would show me a blazing soul? Shadow has deceived you.'

She saw how her words weakened him, broke apart whatever resolve had brought him back to her. 'I will devour you, Bornu Blatt,' she said. 'You will know the peace of oblivion, and never again will you have to inflict yourself upon another person. You deserve that much.' She smiled. 'You obsessed me for a time. Did you know that? Your refusal to kneel proved so . . . enticing. But it did not last. A momentary thing. Now I am fully awakened to my purpose.'

'I want my body back.'

'Now that I've mended it, of course you do.'

'No, how it was. As it has always been.'

She shook her head. 'The Crippled God is gone. There is no god who will embrace the broken and destitute. Not one who celebrates flaws and all the pain that comes with them. Be glad for it. That was naught but an abomination.'

'Give me my body back.'

'Even if there was any point to that, I cannot. To manifest directly upon this earth risks too much. Even my fondness for you is insufficient reason to take that risk. Gods have died at mortal hands. I mean to give no one that opportunity.'

'When you returned to us,' Bornu Blatt said, 'you denounced the excesses that had left you immobile, near insensate.'

'I did.'

'Yet here you stand, indulging the deadliest excess of all.'

She scowled. 'To bring it all to an end. Do you not see? This is the inevitable conclusion to the argument, Bornu Blatt. For you, scholar, it is the thesis itself, brought to its most logical finality. I would have thought you would be pleased.'

She watched as he began to fade.

*　　*　　*

'Silly goddess,' said a voice to Bornu's left. Struggling against the brutal logic of Va'Shaik's assertions, and with them his own imminent dissolution, he turned to see a woman at his side, wearing a silk shawl bearing colours so clashing they almost hurt his eyes. Her lower body was disproportionate to her upper body, as if she were the halves of two women fused together just above the hips. Sliding her regard to Bornu, she offered him a bright smile. 'You must be the Inquisitor Bornu Blatt. Well, his soul, at least, clothed so handsomely in shadow. Tell me, how fares your Inquisition?'

'Poorly,' he replied.

'Hmm. The root of your title is to *inquire*. Nowhere in there will you find *drawing conclusions*. Mere questions, Bornu Blatt, and yet, as is so often forgotten, sometimes mere questions can bring a world to its knees. Answers are so overrated, don't you think?'

'You are the High Priestess?'

'I am. Shamalle. High Priestess Shamalle, born to two bemused parents thirty-three years ago in this very city. And so here we are, standing before our goddess.'

'You called her silly.'

'Did I? Goodness me, that was careless.' She returned her attention to Va'Shaik. 'I must admit, Goddess, I am disappointed.'

The sphere of light seethed, pulsed before them. Va'Shaik was silent, perhaps shocked, then she snarled and said, 'I have no interest in you. Begone.'

'At the very least,' Shamalle continued as if she'd not heard the dismissal, 'I would have expected you to display for all to see the courage of your convictions. Instead, here you hide, inside a mortal man's body. You wish to awaken the Apocalyptic? Then step forth and do so. As your High Priestess, I insist.'

'Your role, even your faith, is no longer relevant,' Va'Shaik said.

'Well, not quite.'

'What nonsensical argument have you prepared for me, High Priestess?'

'Your return to mobility was rather recent. Before then, you could barely move. Drugs poured into you until you barely drew breath. There were years of that, Goddess.'

'No longer the case. The present is all that matters.'

'Again, not quite.' Shamalle turned to Bornu again and spoke in quiet tones, '*Ready yourself.*' Facing the goddess again, the High Priestess said, 'Va'Shaik, in that corpulent state, you leaked power. You leaked it everywhere. Without constraint, given how little consciousness remained awake within you. This empowered your mortal followers in unimaginable ways.' She lifted one plump hand and made a dismissive gesture. 'Mostly wasted by those who fed on it, of course. Secular corruption being what it is. But for one or two of us, why, it became a repository, a well in reserve, if you like.'

The goddess laughed. 'You would challenge me? Your power against mine, when both in fact belong to me?'

'You, Va'Shaik, are abusing the suffering of your believers. That is unacceptable.' Another quick glance at Bornu and a whisper, '*Whilst she is distracted, Inquisitor.*'

The power that erupted outward from the High Priestess sleeted through Bornu Blatt like a firestorm, tearing away his shadow-body until his soul was left with nothing to hold on to. He spun in a vortex as Shamalle stepped forward, into the goddess's sphere of light.

It was as if two suns collided.

Va'Shaik's scream was as much pain as outrage.

When Shamalle began speaking, Bornu heard every word as if whispered in his ear. '*Va'Shaik, child of Dryjhna, your High Priestess summons you. Come forth, into the mortal realm. I command it.*'

The goddess howled, and then began laughing. 'That will not avail you. Pathetic bitch, useless mortal. You challenged my courage? But I assure you, I am most ready to step into your world, with or without your infernal command. And I will deliver upon it the Apocalypse you all secretly hunger for – I will give you all the power behind an entire world's anger – and against that, *nothing will survive.*'

In that moment, the goddess stepped forward, out from Bornu Blatt's body.

'*Now!*' hissed Shamalle.

His soul found a sudden path between twisting currents, a fissure amidst the raging flame of two warring wills. Fast as thought, he flung himself forward.

Mortal flesh awakened around him, and with it, a lifetime's worth of pain. He cried out, stumbling to one side, his bent bones feeling as if on fire.

Va'Shaik, the goddess now truly manifest upon the mortal plane, stood before Shamalle. A single gesture sent the High Priestess flying back. She struck the corner-wall of a building, was spun around by the impact, then landed face-down on the flooded cobbles.

Lying on his side, Bornu Blatt felt the pressure of Va'Shaik's presence pushing him, scraping, sliding, tumbling over the cobbles, until he came up against a stone wall. But even then, the pressure did not relent. He groaned, feeling his bones compressing. The pain flared, consumed him. Ribs cracked.

Then all pressure vanished.

Sudden silence descended like a shroud.

The growing whirlwind fell away, the coruscating fire dwindling, flickering, dying on all sides. The unnatural daylight faded to nothing, gloom drawing close.

Blinking, Bornu Blatt shifted to look back at the goddess.

She stood in the body of Felisin Younger, her head dipped, staring directly down. The hide-wrapped handle of a flint knife was visible, pushed to its hilt into her body, just beneath her ribcage on the left side. Blood was riding the length of the handle and making an almost continuous stream down from the pommel.

A figure stood before her, misaligned, hairless, his broad, smooth cheeks wet with tears as he stared up at the goddess.

Life draining from her round face, she fell then to the cobbles in front of the man. Lying on her side, face directly opposite Bornu Blatt, she stared with unseeing eyes.

Chest aching, Bornu struggled to his feet.

A burst of coughing from his right made him turn to see the High Priestess slowly rising to her hands and knees, spitting filthy water and wheezing. 'Well!' she gasped. 'That didn't work precisely as planned! Oh, I hurt!'

Feeling battered everywhere, Bornu Blatt slowly approached the figure now standing above the body of Va'Shaik. 'Stult,' he said, 'you've lost your staff.'

Stult turned his head, his expression utterly blank. But only for an instant, then anguish took hold. 'She should never have done that!'

'No, you're right,' Bornu replied. 'She shouldn't have.'

'I loved Gracer.'

'I know.'

'I would have died in her place.'

'She'd rather you didn't, Stult. You knew her well, so you know I am right.'

He seemed to shudder, then he turned away.

Bornu Blatt watched Stult move in his hitching limp towards the city gate. He thought to call him back, to guide him to a place where he could rest, gather himself. Instead, he simply watched a man who had nowhere to go limp slowly out of sight.

Dawn's arrival was painting copper the rooftops.

Hearing the soft clank of armour and weapons, Bornu shifted his attention to where a number of Malazan marines were gathered round the High Priestess Shamalle, who was back on her feet, her fine clothing sodden and filthy. She was leaning, rather heavily, on a tall, solid man at her side that Bornu was slow to recognize. *High Fist Arenfall.*

From Choke Street a second squad of marines was approaching, parting like a prow the few dozen gathering denizens.

A marine was suddenly beside Bornu Blatt, eyes fixed on the body of Va'Shaik. 'She dead then?'

'The goddess? Yes.'

'Done for good?'

Bornu Blatt sighed, though the sigh made him wince. 'I believe so, yes.'

'So it's all officially settled,' the marine replied. 'Good. Puler! Get over here, this man needs healing!'

*   *   *

With the sun's rise, the streets filled once more with people, refugees from flooded ground-floor homes, refugees from the Under Quarter, and refugees from a night of terror and indiscriminate killing. It was as if a fever had broken, leaving the survivors weak, exhausted. And they wandered the streets, not yet capable of resuming their lives. This aftermath of shock lingered on as the day awakened.

Arenfall remained close to the High Priestess Shamalle – though not as close as she clearly desired, which invoked a certain amused wariness

403

in him – watching the Inquisitor, Bornu Blatt, who, upon finding the body of Gilakas, had carried it into the shade and now knelt before it. Such evident grief surprised Arenfall and, eluding yet another murmured invitation from the High Priestess, he approached.

'Inquisitor.'

The man looked up. 'High Fist.'

'Did you not understand? Gilakas was at your side for a reason.'

'A Claw to take my life before I could cause too much trouble. Yes, High Fist, I understood. Still, we travelled together. There is much to be said for that, though I admit, at the moment I am too tired to try explaining it.'

'No need,' Arenfall replied. 'Who we share with is not always our first choice, but they serve.'

Bornu Blatt nodded. 'They serve, yes.'

'Possession is a dreadful thing. Can we help you, Inquisitor?'

A wan smile. 'This morning, in the wake of the death of my goddess?'

'Was she your goddess?'

'Not really. I yield no power to the empowered. Still, if granted such presumption, I would grieve the death of Felisin Younger, a young woman who also had no choice when it came to possession.'

Arenfall frowned, shifting to look over at the body of the goddess. 'Felisin Younger.' He paused, and then said, 'That name is familiar, but from long ago and in another place—'

'When Raraku was a holy desert, and Sha'ik Reborn gathered about her many orphans, one of whom she named Felisin Younger.' Bornu Blatt paused, and then tilted his head. 'A curious name, that. None know its story, however. Presumably, Sha'ik Reborn had her reasons.' Then his eyes narrowed on the High Fist. 'Unless, you know more than you're prepared to reveal.'

Arenfall continued studying the cloth-covered body of the dead goddess. The High Priestess had surrendered her shawl to this act of consideration. All the other bodies, of Claw assassins and nameless citizens, had been moved against a shaded wall by the marines, and now people were filling Cedar Squat, making a procession of sorts to stand before the fallen goddess just in front of the north-side gate. 'Well,' he said after a long moment, 'that was the name.' He faced the Inquisitor again. 'Felisin Younger, who became Va'Shaik.'

Slowly, Bornu said, 'The circumstances are vague, but yes, I choose to believe that she was once named Felisin Younger, adopted daughter of Sha'ik in the time of the Whirlwind.'

Arenfall sighed. 'I wonder . . . is this as tangled as I begin to think? No, that would be too . . . cruel.' He drew a breath that became a shudder.

'You have a thought, High Fist?' Bornu Blatt asked.

'What? No, it's no matter.' He shook his head and then regarded the Inquisitor again. 'Do you require more healing from Puler?'

'No, and please, do thank him again.'

Arenfall fixed his attention now on the two squads of marines, who were gathered to one side, their backs to the high wall of the Seven Gates' blockhouse. Two stood over the unconscious form of the Adjunct. The quarrel had been extracted, but Hadalin remained in a bad way.

He met Captain Hung's eyes and saw the marine take a step forward, then halt.

'Excuse me, Inquisitor. One of my captains wishes to speak with me.'

'Of course.'

Arenfall set out, through the slow-moving crowd.

*   *   *

Just another faceless, forgettable denizen of bruised, unhappy G'danisban, unseen by even the most mindful of gazes, Pash slipped along among shuffling bodies scented and sweaty, rank and fragrant, all these people who made so much in their lives of standing out, some succeeding, others failing, but even the desire was peculiar, unfamiliar to Pash, who rode the uneven flow in the slow dance of flotsam on a wide river, beneath notice, plain, so very plain.

One could take note of a forest, see its vast dusty green canopy, all the stark boles, and few of those trees would possess anything unusual, anything worthy of notice. It was the forest that impinged on the senses. A forest made up of countless mundane trees, each so similar to the others as to make even the notion of distinction meaningless.

She was such a tree, her forest a seething clump of humanity. So the eye saw nothing but the forest, never the tree, and step by step, step by step, she drew closer to the tall man now threading through the press on his way to his soldiers.

Daylight was no obstacle. Nor the proximity of the marines. And here, at last, could her beloved High Priestess finally witness the fullest expression of Pash's devotion to her, this modest ruby. *And its lovely red gleam.*

405

The silly wreaths, the pathetic gifts sent to that man. Clearly, Shamalle had stumbled from the proper path, dew-eyed and distracted. But all was moments from correction.

The handmaid had many responsibilities. Few even understood that. They saw only the obvious acts, the swift attention to whims and desires. But so much was done unseen by anyone, the leaf-scatter on every garden path swept away before her mistress ever set foot upon the threshold, the cobwebs cleared from the winding staircase upward, downward. Ashes emptied from bowls, goblets and cups polished, all clothing brushed, scarves and shawls properly folded or laid out – so much of the secret tasks that none ever saw!

Well, this morning, not so. This morning, the handmaid's sweeping away of distractions would be witnessed by everyone.

Closer, step by step.

Heat, human smells. Sweat, breaths, the brush of clothing. The knife slipping down from beneath the loose sleeve, the grip settling into the palm, held point-down, out of anyone's sight.

And closer still.

She could see him, his face in profile. He was handsome, too much so. Pash still carried the tile he gave her. Today, she would return it to him. His crimes were many, but the deepest crime of them all had been his noticing her that night. Not just noticing her, but speaking with her, giving her the tile – none of that was permitted.

Such men were never supposed to notice people like her. It was a rule, a law of nature, a universal truth. She needed it that way.

Step by step.

And now—

*   *   *

Fedilap watched Hazy Drip join her and Pulcrude where they stood in the shade. Expressionless, she nodded at the man. 'Sapper.'

Hazy Drip nodded back, eyes flicking between the two women. 'Sappers.'

From off to their left, Gripcocker snorted. 'Witness, if you will, as the three creatures converge to re-establish their status in the face of mutual wariness and the potential for sudden, catastrophic violence.'

'Shut up,' Pulcrude said. 'You don't—'

'*Oh fuck!*' Fedilap's casual scan of the crowd had caught on a familiar face. Drawing her sword, she hissed, '*She's coming up behind the High Fist! That backstabbing bitch!*' Then she was surging forward, drawing breath to scream a warning—

*   *   *

A loud snap of magic, and suddenly the crowd pressing in around Arenfall was stumbling away, flinching back with shouts and screams. He whirled to see a figure crouched above the body of what seemed to be a child, lifting into view a blood-wet knife the blade of which flickered with sorcery.

It was a moment before recognition registered in Arenfall. 'Arat?'

Both squads of marines, led by Fedilap, were now around him, pushing everyone else away. Fedilap had her short-sword pointed directly at Arat. 'Damn, you sneaky witch, take one step closer and you're dead!'

'That would be a mistake, Sapper.'

Pulcrude said, 'You have no idea how lucky you are right now, Arat. Fedilap makes mistakes all the time! So, what in the Rope's name are you doing, killing tiny defenceless people?'

During this exchange, the other marines had formed a protective cordon around Arenfall, crossbows out and cocked. The crowd surrounding them was quickly withdrawing.

Ignoring most of this, Arenfall stepped closer to the ex-bandit.

Pulcrude pushed between them, pointing a finger at Arat. 'You deserted us, soldier! And now you show up stabbing citizens? That's done for you for sure, hah!'

Arenfall reached out and gently pulled the marine to one side.

'Oops,' the marine said after a quick glance over a shoulder at Arenfall. 'Sorry, High Fist. But she bailed on us like we knew she would. It's like I always say, you can't recruit ex-bandit sorceress assassin witches and expect 'em to behave at all!'

Arenfall continued pushing the marine to one side, until he was facing Arat with no one between them. 'Why have you killed a child, Arat?'

Sheathing her knife, she crouched, grasping a handful of wiry hair on her victim's head and lifting the face into view. 'Not a child.' With her other hand she reached down to take the dead woman's wrist, twisting it to reveal the knife nestled in it. 'Eyes on you alone, High Fist.'

'Ah,' said Arenfall, looking down on his would-be assassin. 'I recall her. The handmaiden of the High Priestess.' He shifted his attention back to Arat. 'Have you been shadowing me all along?'

Arat nodded. 'Not easy. You have a habit of disappearing, sir.'

'I see. Now I can't help but wonder, why save me at all?'

'You could've cut my throat—'

'I would've,' commented Pulcrude.

'—but you didn't. Now we're even, High Fist.'

Arenfall turned to search the plaza. He saw the High Priestess and the Inquisitor standing before the body of their goddess. He strode towards them. The marines formed a protective cordon around him as he did so, but he barely noticed.

*   *   *

King Nub looked down upon his great realm, bemused at all the efforts to collect bodies and clean things up, as if such gestures of order were anything but temporary interludes between manic chaos, violence, slaughter and death.

His human subjects were such fools.

But the dawn had broken clear and surprisingly cool, harbinger to the new seasons the great sea to the west now delivered upon his demesne. Rhizan were flitting about along with swallows and martins, and even the water on the streets was draining back into the stony, rubble-filled underworld.

He stretched on his perch in the tree atop Bastran Hill. Then he opened his mouth as wide as he could manage, to show the world – to all who dared raise eyes to look – his enormous white, gleaming fangs.

Take that!

EPILOGUE

'The death of our god is but a minor inconvenience.'

Gamlod
High Priest

Bornu Blatt watched the High Priestess slump on the broad, deep sofa on the dais, feebly lifting one hand to settle on her brow as she leaned back, eyes closing. 'What a night and what a morning! And now, what hope have I in attending upon you all the hospitality you deserve, Inquisitor? Everyone has fled the temple, and if this is not upsetting enough, I must confess to you that I am sorely shaken by the modest viper in my midst, upon whom I bestowed all manner of trust, warmth and indeed, love. Ah, Pash, you have broken my heart.'

'I require nothing, High Priestess,' Bornu Blatt replied.

'Not even wine?'

'Not even wine.'

'But aren't you thirsty? Grieving? In dire need? Nerves shaken, or otherwise discombobulated?'

Looking around, Bornu Blatt saw, upon a stone ledge along the wall to his right, a row of clay amphorae in their hoop-stands, as well as a half-dozen goblets. He strode over and poured one goblet full, which he then brought to the High Priestess.

Withdrawing her hand from her forehead at hearing his approach, her eyelids fluttered as she watched him. 'For me? Oh, how did you guess? What a wonderful man you are, Inquisitor!'

'I would divest myself of that title,' Bornu Blatt said.

'Oh? Well, you do have a point. One that, oh dear, applies to me and mine as well. Very well, sir, how do you wish to be now? Just Bornu Blatt?'

'Librarian might suit, since to that profession I will return.'

'In the First Holy City?'

He nodded.

'Now that raises another point.' She paused to drink down half the wine in the goblet, following that with a loud, moist sigh. Looking around, she frowned. 'Both gone, I see.'

'High Priestess?'

'Oh, two guests I left here. One here in this very room, lying upon the floor with a most blissful expression upon her temporarily inanimate face. The other, having gone through the garden wall – whose rude passage the effects of which you no doubt saw on our way in – also curiously missing, despite he too being of somnolent repose. Mind you, neither were invited in the first place.' She finished her wine and held out the goblet.

Collecting it, Bornu Blatt made his way back to the ledge.

She continued speaking behind him. 'Now there is a synod pending back in the First Holy City, one for which all reasons have utterly changed, to put it mildly. Tell me, Librarian, how see you the future of our faith?'

'Unchanged,' he replied as he filled the goblet once more.

She watched him return to her. 'Look how I impose upon you, and with such an imperious gesture, too!'

'It is your temple, High Priestess.'

'Still, indolence engenders the most pernicious habits. Do forgive me my prodigious thirst, not to mention my rudeness. Tell me, Librarian, will you escort me to the synod? There is much work to be done, if we are to salvage our religion.'

Handing her the goblet again, Bornu Blatt cocked his head. 'You wish to salvage this?'

'No, but I see the necessity nonetheless.'

'Why?'

'It was as you have just pointed out. Nothing changes, goddess living or goddess dead. After all, how many faiths in truth circle an unanswering void at their core? Hmm, best not answer me there. But the point holds, does it not?'

Bornu Blatt considered for a few moments, and then he said, 'I would be happy to escort you back to the First Holy City, High Priestess. And as Librarian, I can assist in finding all relevant precedents, if the continuation and new formalization of our faith is what you seek.'

'I see no choice,' Shamalle replied, eyes suddenly level and fixed on his. 'Belief is not a thing to be instantly extirpated, is it?'

'Rebellion postponed indefinitely.'

She made a face. 'That nonsense is the first thing we'll expunge – assuming I have my way, that is.'

'I believe you will,' he replied. 'After all, you were the last High Priestess who stood before the goddess manifest.'

Her eyes narrowed. 'And the nature of that meeting?'

He shrugged. 'Whatever we decide, I should imagine. Either way, I am your witness.'

'You would twist the nature of my fateful clash with Va'Shaik?'

'I see little need for that,' he said. 'The relationship between a god and its mortal adherents is anything but clear, to anyone. While I suspect there will be some who will object to you having saved the world, we can probably assume that such objections are but posturing, intended to disguise secular ambitions.'

'You are a clever man, Librarian.'

'If I am, I am in good company, High Priestess.'

'Don't be absurd, I'm clearly witless, vain and shallow. But we are agreed, then! Upon you I shall depend, not only in our journey, but in the synod's proceedings as well. Do your best, Librarian, in hiding my feeble intelligence and whatnot, I beg you.'

He smiled, then bowed his head. 'To the best of my ability, High Priestess.'

'Excellent! Now, I need to pack – oh, and when you gather our necessary victuals, be modest, as I intend to whisk us to your home via Warren. Roads and dust and insects and scratchy bedding? Not for me! Never!'

He bowed a second time.

'Besides,' she added, 'can you imagine how horrifying we'd look as we crossed half the width of the continent? You with your hunched back and me navigating narrow trails with the stern of a trireme?'

Bornu Blatt laughed. He could not help it. 'High Priestess,' he said, 'you are a wonder.'

She blinked with heavy lids, then purred, 'We make do.'

Bornu Blatt decided that one goblet of wine would suit him now after all, so he walked over to the ledge. He paused.

Home.

Salabi.

Behind him, Shamalle said, 'We'll take those amphorae with us, of course.'

*   *   *

Arenfall looked up from his desk as Captain Hung entered. In the marine's arms was a soldier's kit, including the shoulder-fixed bronze sigils denoting the rank of corporal.

'Sir.'

'What is it, Captain, and why are you carrying that gear?'

'Necessity.'

'Explain.'

'First, sir, may I ask, how fares the Adjunct?'

'He will live, I think. But still unconscious.'

'He is attended to by the resident staff?'

Arenfall frowned. 'Well, of course.'

Hung nodded. 'Then, sir, the situation remains ideal.'

'For what?'

'For your disappearance. It turns out that I've lost both a corporal and a sergeant in my squad. The marines have been summoned to the east coast, to rejoin the Legion. As a soldier within the ranks of the marines, you can remain anonymous.'

Arenfall studied the officer standing before him. 'I see.'

'I'm glad you do, sir.'

'You believe my life is at risk.'

'I know it. Regardless of the Adjunct's disposition, once he returns to duty. An entire Claw Hand was cut down here, in your city. That will not go unanswered, now that you've returned to rank as High Fist.'

Rising, Arenfall walked around the desk and took the gear into his arms. He stared down at it. 'I'd be a fool to refuse you.'

'Yes, sir, you would.'

He looked up. 'Have you heard from Corporal Hasten lately?'

'No, sir. But Pulcrude thinks she saw him last night, in the crowd.' He paused, then added, 'People say that a lot.'

'Fleeting glimpses of the corporal?'

'Yes, sir.'

'I would know the fate of Dunsparrow and her squad.'

'We all would. But in the meantime, we're getting ready to march.'

'Very well. I am to be under your command?'

412

'Yes, sir.'

'As a corporal, not a sergeant.'

'Take your pick, then, sir.'

'Corporal will do.'

'Very good.'

'I'll need a new name.'

'Aye, sir, you will.'

'Let's give that some thought. In the meantime, your orders, Captain?'

*　　*　　*

Satala awoke to a damp cloth patting her brow. Eyes opening, she found herself looking up at the enormous face of Kanyn Thrall, The Grey Shore.

His expression brightened. 'Ah, finally! Will you live?'

'Where are we?'

He looked around. 'To be honest, I have no idea. It's been four days since G'danisban. I've encountered only two merchant trains, and both of those two days past. Neither seemed happy to see us, alas. As they fled.'

She slowly sat up. 'That High Priestess knocked me aside like a gnat.'

'You are not alone in that experience. I thought to take umbrage with her, and indeed considered dismantling her entire temple. But then, my concern for you encouraged me to adopt discretion regarding the whole affair.'

'I still need to kill Pash.'

'Ah, no need. She is dead.'

'How do you know that?'

'A ghost told me.'

Satala ceased her examination of the scrubland surrounding them and fixed her attention on the giant once more. 'A year ago and I would think you mad.'

'No longer?'

She shook her head, then climbed to her feet. 'My head hurts.'

'Mine too. But let us not let that despoil the moment before us.' He too stood and began looking about. Then he smiled down upon her. 'Satala, are you ready to resume our great adventure?'

'Sure, why not?'

'Where to?'

Shrugging, she pointed. 'How about that way?'

ABOUT THE AUTHOR

Archaeologist and anthropologist **Steven Erikson** is the bestselling author of the genre-defining The Malazan Book of the Fallen, a multi-volume fantasy that's been hailed 'a masterwork of the imagination' and one of the top ten fantasy series of all time. The first novel in the sequence, *Gardens of the Moon*, was shortlisted for a World Fantasy Award. He has written several novellas set in the same world. *Forge of Darkness* was the first Kharkanas novel, taking readers back to the origins of what would become the Malazan Empire; *Fall of Light* continued this momentous tale.

A lifelong science fiction reader, he's written a trilogy that affectionately parodies a long-running television series as well as *Rejoice!*, a story of first contact.

Set in the world of the Malazan Empire, ten years after the events recounted in *The Crippled God*, *The God is Not Willing* heralded the start of a thrilling new series – The Tales of Witness. *No Life Forsaken* is the second Tale in this epic adventure.

Steven Erikson lives in Victoria, Canada. To find out more, look for him on Facebook: Steven Erikson – Author